# ALASKA FREEDOM BRIGADE

## WILLIAM L. CASSELMAN

ALASKADREAMS
PUBLISHING
eBook Available
www.alaskadp.com

**ALASKA FREEDOM BRIGADE**
©2020 By William Casselman

Production design by Robert Jacobson
Cover Art Copyright 2020 by Alaska Dreams Publishing

Published by Alaska Dreams Publishing
www.alaskadp.com
1st Paperback Print Edition October 2020
PAPERBACK PRINT ISBN-13: 978-1-7359713-0-8
1st Hardcover Print Edition April 2021
HARDCOVER PRINT ISBN-13: 978-1-7359713-3-9
E-Book version available.
Please visit http://www.alaskadp.com for links.

*Part one of this book was previously published as "Homeland Security."*

# DEDICATION

*To my beautiful wife, Mona, who has spent the last 40-years at my side.*
*To the men and women carrying the badge and who continue to maintain*
*integrity, courage, and honor in service to the public.*
*To the members of the numerous legal militia forces across our great nation, who*
*stand ready in to support the National Guard against foreign and domestic*
*enemies and aid during natural disasters.*
*To the men and women of our active duty armed forces, as well as the veterans of*
*the armed forces. Let them never be forgotten.*
*To both of my grandfathers who served in the Navy during World War II, my*
*father served in the Army in Korea, and my mother, who worked as a "Rosy the*
*Riveter" in WWII.*
*My war was Vietnam, and now my children have served in Afghanistan and Iraq*
*and the drug wars of North Africa. To them also, this book is dedicated.*

# CONTENTS

# ACKNOWLEDGMENTS

I would like to thank for their online services, the Alaskan Independence Party, the United States Air Force, and Eielson Air Force Base Office of Information. From these sources, I obtained the information I needed to complete this story.

I would acknowledge my publisher, Robert Jacobson of Alaska Dreams Publishing Company, Susan Smith, and Mona Casselman, my Editors. Patrick and Canaan Miller, my grandkids, who worked hard to ensure I was taken good care of while working on my various manuscripts.

My children, who served as law enforcement officers and in the military, who have helped me in the writing of my stories, including this one.

Lastly, I wish to thank the Father, my Lord Jesus Christ, and the Holy Spirit for being such a large part of my life.

# PART I

# THE WHITE FIST

*The White Fist Militia Training Camp*
*Blue Ridge Mountains of Tennessee*
*1:14 A.M. 13 September*

H e hated bugs! Anything that crawled, bit, stung or slimed, spun a web, or siphoned his cherished blood.

From gigantic camel spiders of the Middle East to the mosquitoes of Tennessee, US Army Captain Clay B. Jefferson maintained a strong dislike for the world's insect population and did his part to reduce their numbers at every opportunity. He had spent the last six years on various black ops duty assignments between the Middle East and North Africa deserts and forced to deal with spiders of all sizes and colors, sand fleas, and kissing bugs that landed on his lips while he slept and left his mouth numb. There were scorpions that could do all sorts of nasty things to him, and the black fly that grew big enough to resemble a black bean with wings. A soldier had to be careful when he consumed his government rations because there were lots of beans in GI chow. Yes, Clay really hated bugs!

He had left the desert and his time with the Delta Force and was now on loan to the FBI as an undercover operative. Previously, he had dealt with militant Muslim insurgents and their fanatical clerics. His new assignment forced him to deal with a different sort of insect; to endure the neo-Nazi and KKK racists inside the USA.

He glanced at his watch. The fluorescent dial showed he'd been on duty for exactly three hours and fourteen minutes. His post was along a rocky ridgeline, and the insects were plentiful. His Grandpa used to tell him that if a naked man was left out on the tundra in Alaska, he'd be drained of blood overnight and the rest consumed by other critters. Nothing was wasted in the Alaskan bush, where Clay was born and raised.

Tonight's assignment, along with two other guards, was a one-half mile of a well-worn ridge-top trail. The trail surrounded a 24-acre training camp, hidden in thick woods. His post included two currently dry stream beds. Clay hadn't seen any rain since he came here, and the thick forest was dry and ripe for a major fire. There was a stationary two-man guard post at the east end of his route and a second post at the main gate at the west end of his position. The remaining perimeter was covered by the two others.

The former YMCA Summer Camp was filled with deer and black bear. Pesky bears often caused a problem with the camp's trash pile, a quarter-mile downhill from the camp. The streams and a medium-sized lake in the valley were of fresh clean water, non-polluted by city industry, and Clay had caught and cooked up a dozen bass since he arrived over a month earlier.

As a long time Louis L'amour fan, Clay understood these hills were the very same Tennessee' mountains the author used for the legendary Sackett Family. He knew L'amour had walked these hills as he wrote his famous stories and wondered if he had been through this same valley and fished these same waters.

Standing in the darkness and listening to the sounds of camp and the wildlife around him, he thought how much he really regretted accepting this assignment. Working with a bunch of skinheads and members of the Ku Klux Klan, he had to pretend to be one of them. His head shaved, he was clothed in a well-worn set of BDUs. The same type he had worn while with the Green Beret. Wearing them here brought on a strong desire to throw them on the ground and set fire to them. He also came to the camp in a pair of well-worn desert tan combat boots.

He carried his Remington shotgun slung over his left shoulder, with the barrel pointed down. From his combat experience, he saw this as a quick way to bring the weapon to the ready position. This also kept the rain out of the barrel, at least when there was any rain. A semi-new Glock, .45 caliber pistol with some of the bluing rubbed off, was now strapped to his right leg in a black tactical holster and loaded with one round in the chamber. Four black ammo pouches carried extra magazines for his Glock, and a black 20-round cartridge belt pouch of OO buckshot for his shotgun was on his belt. To add to his weapons, he carried a 6-inch Buck sheath knife strapped with black cloth tape to the left side of his combat suspenders. He would've preferred a K-Bar, but the camp's supply dude didn't have one.

Most of the sentries who pulled these 8-hour duties preferred to carry the older M-16 or the newer M-4 automatic rifle over the cumbersome shotgun. Clay preferred to have a shotgun in his hands in the event he happened to stumble upon one of Tennessee's temperamental black bears. An angry bear could cover a lot of space with half-a-dozen .223 caliber rounds in it; the bear's heartbeat at such a slow rate. But a single round of OO buckshot carried a lot of stopping power, and his second round was a one-ounce slug to ensure his success. He knew from past experience, the simple firing of a shotgun in the air could cause a bear to scamper off into the woods.

He came on duty at 10 p.m., and his primary responsibility as a guard was to patrol the perimeter, watch for any movement on the hillsides below and alert the nearest post of any intruders. The camp officers were concerned with local and/or federal law enforcement officers who might attempt to sneak into the camp. The officials would either be a raiding party or a smaller unit ordered to conduct surveillance and gather intelligence on the militia's operation.

The guard post to his west was nothing more than a shack of aged gray wood, which had been cannibalized from a well-used camp storage shed. There were three glassless windows and a doorway, now covered in mosquito screening to keep the flying beasties out and allow just enough room for two guards to sit on wooden stools.

Clay was fortunate tonight because this post was manned by Jimmy

Albright, a 19-year-old freckled-faced red-haired kid from the nowhere part of East Georgia. He loved to talk to anyone who would listen about his big plans to head north in a few months and join up with some big-time neo-Nazi organization. He'd have to obtain permission from the White Fist Militia, and Clay thought Jimmy would probably be used up as cannon fodder before then. The poor kid had fallen in love with the Nazi's German high leather black boots and freshly pressed tan uniforms, and their military organization of the 1940s. He'd watched Jimmy for over a week and saw the joy on his face as the White Fist formed up after dark in their black utilities for drill time. Because of the possibility of satellite observation during the day, they had no crisp and shiny uniforms to wear under the sunlight for the feds to see. During the day, everyone was wearing blue jeans, t-shirts, and occasionally gym shorts. Daytime sentry duties were carried out by personnel decked out to resemble backwoods hunters, double-barreled shotguns slung over their arms. The posts were still equipped with concealed automatic weapons; M-16s, a few M-4s, and half-a-dozen AK-47s in case of trouble.

Clay saw the dreams of glory in Jimmy's eyes, to carry out the duties where they were always under observation by the Feds. Such tasks included street pamphlet hand-outs, to create disturbances for news, and march in parades where violent clashes were hoped for. These young kids were also used for often suicidal assignments, where they bombed black churches and Jewish synagogues.

The other guard who sat in the shack was of a different type, a slacker by the name of Greg Layers. A muscular brute with no neck, heavily tattooed with anti-Semitism artwork, a 26-year old skinhead loaned to the White Fist by the Aryan Brotherhood in Kansas City, Missouri. A real blowhard who liked to rattle on about how he and his family were considered "poor white trash" by the Kansas City cops. In Layers' opinion, the Black cops were out to kill all the whites. As an 18-year old with a thick juvenile file for violence and theft, he finally spent 2 years in an Atlanta jail as an adult for beating up a 16-year old Afro-American paperboy. While locked up, he had joined the Aryan Brotherhood and bragged around the camp of his many offenses against the Black Muslims in prison and once outside, against the Black and Jewish communities.

These two outstanding US citizens were both armed with at least 10-year old Colt M-16 automatic rifles, illegally purchased through the underground arms trade. Most of their illegal automatic weapons were purchased through the black market, stolen from arms shipments returning from various war zones or military contractors who worked in Iraq and Afghanistan. U.S. Servicemen and women who worked in supply and had similar feelings toward the various races other than white went out of their way to lose a box of rifles and a crate of ammo now and then. Whenever possible, Clay recorded serial numbers for his report. Sometimes the bullets fired from captured firearms would lead to a weapon used in a shooting, even the identity of the shooter if he was captured with the subject weapon in his hands. Murderers of federal, state, and local law enforcement officers had been solved by the rifle they were using at the time of their arrest.

Six years in the desert country still made these heavy humid Tennessee nights miserable.

He stopped along the trail to take a drink from his canteen. As he drank, he looked up and marveled at the millions of stars and only the barest sliver of a new moon in the heavens, and then put his canteen away and turned his attention back to the lights of the camp below. The three wooden sided, tin-roofed barracks buildings held a total of 94 militia troops, all duly sworn members of the Tennessee and Georgia Ku Klux Klan. Only recently, they'd taken a second oath to the fanatical and militant cause of the militant White Fist Militia, which Clay considered to be the white man's version of the Taliban. He was surprised his oath with them had not been required by a signature in his own blood.

The camp personnel, outside key officers, had to be all single men and women. Non-staff strength consisted of 17-female and 77-male, and of those, a total of 12 were on sentry duty. All of these members were between the ages of 18 and 37, and though many of them were former soldiers with less than an Honorable Discharge, they were truly committed to the KKK and now the White Fist cause. Basically, they all wanted to kill all the Blacks, Muslims, and Jews they could and anyone who held a contrary opinion to the KKK/Aryan Brotherhood or the New Christian Order Church.

Until recently, Clay had never heard of this New Christian Order Church. He wondered how they could call themselves Christian after reading some of their handouts. They spoke on how God agreed with slavery and that Blacks, Muslims, and other religions were to be slaves to the Christians or destroyed. No, Clay knew these people were deceived, and it concerned him how much confusion they had already caused. Since his arrival, some of the new people in the camp had become members of this church, and it sickened him.

The camp staff was 11-men, 7 with wives, and 9-children of various ages. The married couples lived in white canvas camp tents, and the other staff lived in the headquarters building in two-man rooms.

The camp had a separate chow hall, with a walk-in freezer powered by its own diesel generator. The fuel truck came to camp once a week to refuel the various tanks. There were three classroom buildings, a head-quarters building, and a second generator shed with a 1,000-gallon diesel tank. This second generator powered the other buildings in the camp. Freshwater came from two different springs, filtered and stored in a 25-foot tall water tower, which held 1500 gallons. For toilet needs, the camp used a row of 8-outhouses. A secondary fuel tank was filled with gasoline and used for most of the vehicles. Three of the newer trucks ran on diesel, and one was equipped with a mounted 50-caliber machine-gun.

So far, besides the fifty, the largest heavy weapons Clay had seen were a case of LAW rockets and three M-60's, set-up in machine-gun positions around the camp. Clay dearly hoped the feds never tried to enter this camp; he knew several agents would lose their lives in the process.

When this former YMCA summer camp for boys had come on sale, the KKK had purchased it through one of their wealthier supporters. His firm carried it as a non-profit religious retreat. Now the camp had three new firing ranges and an armory, plus a large refrigerator, and Clay knew this was where the C-4 and newer Semtex explosive were stored. Blasting caps for the explosives were stored in a large floor safe in the commander's office. There was a new obstacle course through the woods for the members to use daily, an area for hand-to-hand combat training, which used to be the old volleyball court and an open area by their 35-foot flag pole, used for morning and evening formations, and also PT. A staff member who resembled a Spartan warrior led the exercise PT and also a daily 3-mile run. Clay knew he could've finished first in everything here and possibly even go the distance with the physical instructor, but he didn't want to look too good. So, he finished the exercises but usually finished the run in the top 10. After all, his body did look pretty fit after all the Special Forces training he'd been through.

It had better. I've been through every survival school the military has to offer and lived off that dang desert for weeks at a time. I really hate this dude!

Before arriving here, Clay knew the camp set up from satellite photographs. As of yet, he hadn't learned who were the key men behind this new White Fist faction. He hadn't yet learned who telephoned the commander every day over the satellite phone. He'd seen the commander called away from a briefing for important phone calls. But so far, he'd been unable to learn anything about how the White Fist came to be and who the real players were.

In his briefings at the Federal Bureau of Investigation's well-known building in Washington DC, he had learned that the government was clearly very uneasy about this new White Fist. Several different under-cover operatives were used to gather information, but Clay was the first attempt at having an operative actually join their ranks.

Under the alias of Willy J. Olson of South San Antonio, Texas, and former US Army Sergeant First Class, he had come to Atlanta to locate an old friend and find work. The FBI had used the background of a soldier from Atlanta very recently killed in Afghanistan. They had studied Clay's background, saw he was homeschooled in Minto, Alaska, and had earned a GED with sky-high scores. He entered the University of Alaska-Fairbanks and the ROTC Program, where he excelled. Following Officer Candidate School, he went to the 82nd Airborne, and with his language and outdoor skills, he had quickly worked his way into the Green Beret. He obtained his Master Jump Wings, HALO Wings, Master Diver rating, Combat Infantry Badge with three stars, a Distinguished Service Cross, a Silver Star, two Bronze Stars for Valor, and four Purple Hearts. He also had qual-ifications to wear the jump wings from five different countries. By the time he had pinned his captain bars on, he'd been selected to join the highly regarded Delta Force. His ethnic background didn't hurt him either. Being half Athabascan Indian, his dark coloring allowed him to fit in where a white man would make people suspicious. While in Libya and Egypt with Delta Forces, he had developed a major distrust of the CIA and their operatives he worked with.

Clay had just wrapped up an assignment 100 miles south of Kabul, Afghanistan, when he was given orders to report to FBI Headquarters for another special assignment with the Feds. 33-years old, half white on his father's Germanic side and half Athabascan from his mother, Clay was raised in the Alaskan Interior. Both his dad and mom were killed one night driving home from Fairbanks when a drunk driver T-boned them. He was only two years old and had survived the crash with only minor injuries. He was raised by his maternal grandfather in the small Indian township of Minto, Alaska, located 90-miles east of Fairbanks and reached by a single-lane gravel road.

As part of his assignment with the Feds, he was to pick up some odd jobs and hang around in the Veterans of Foreign Wars and American Legion Clubs in Atlanta, in hopes the KKK would take notice of him. The Intelligence Branch of the FBI knew how the KKK often recruited from such service clubs. They looked for men and women with combat training who shared in their views for an all-white Christian America.

In downtown Atlanta, he eventually started to talk up some racist gab and even punched out a former Black Marine outside an American Legion, who was actually an undercover Federal Officer. Clay held back, but both men knew they had to make it look good, and the Marine was left feigning unconsciousness, while Clay was taken inside the Legion to hoist a few beers with those who agreed with him. The American Legion wouldn't allow such activity inside the bar. While they did call for the police or an ambulance, if requested, they still had a liquor license to protect. A lot of vets came home with darker complexions after serving a couple tours of duty in the sandbox, and his Athabascan bloodline only helped in his new identity as Willy Olson, a half-Mexican out of Texas.

Though of a stout, muscular build, a broad chest, and massive arms from pumping weights for years, Clay only stood all of 5'9". He had large hands and carried the scars on his body from one stabbing, an AK-47 bullet to his left side, and two separate shrapnel wounds across his chest and back of his legs.

Before long and a couple hundred beers later, Clay was eventually approached by a KKK front man. Afterward, a recruiter approached. He had to really watch himself because he had a problem with booze. Most of the other service guys actually understood his problem. A lot of troops came home had a hard time dealing with either booze or dope. The initial contact was only made after they had conducted their own background investigation of him, and that was with their own informants inside the Department of Veterans Affairs and both the Texas and Georgia Department of Motor Vehicles. But with the help of the FBI, all they found for a former SFC Olson were the very documents planted by the Special Operatives Branch of the FBI. The FBI office in San Antonio had all the resources they needed to create a false family and some low-life lawyer's firm. One of the agents was a former lawyer, and he enjoyed playing the snobbish role. The ex-wife was played by a young female agent who was forced to live in a rented trailer in south San Antonio. Afterward, Clay heard of how she really hated the assignment and hanging around the trailer parks. She took a week's leave to spend time at a spa to wash off all the dirt and grime. Such was the life of undercover work; for every operative who worked the field, there were a lot of supporting personnel in the background to keep his or her tale alive. But in her case, it turns out, some of her office buddies went out of their way to find the foulest trailer possible in the worst trailer park in town. Though they always had her under observation, it took roses on her desk for two-weeks to finally get them back in her good graces, but they knew she still planned some form of revenge when it was their turn.

Based on his combat experience and fabricated record, the KKK interviewed Clay several times. Twice, the interviews were accomplished by active-duty soldiers. Rangers themselves, they were to verify Clay was who he said he was and not some federal or state cop. Each time he was checked for monitoring equipment, but the FBI was using the more sophisticated microwave stuff, and everything was being recorded from a mile away. This was also to protect Clay. They couldn't afford to have someone follow him for protection and being spotted. At one point, they used a borrowed drone to keep Clay under observation when the meeting point was made in the middle of the woods of nowhere. The FBI felt this operation was that important, and a lot of Homeland Security funds went into it.

Eventually, Clay passed all the tests and interviews, but his own schooling was what did it. He knew the same instructors, the same eateries off post for Fort Brag, and everything there was to know about Jump School. After that last meeting, he was sent to the White Fist training camp as a training officer and met with the senior staff there. He already knew where the spot was but was, in fact, surprised when no one bothered to blindfold him. It was a nice easy drive, with a stop at a nice roadside eatery for lunch along the way. This all told him how needful the White Fist was for well-trained non-commissioned officers to assist them in preparing their crew for whatever their targets were. But what he found in camp amazed him – far too many coach potato civilians, with former military service, who wanted to relive their glory days with action against the Jewish and Muslim loving anti-white United States government. This meant one thing to him; the White Fist members were all-expendable.

Every morning and every evening, the camp's loud and overzealous political officer would rant on about the growing problems inside the USA. Of how Islam, the Jewish and other minority loving so-called religions were spreading across the country, driving good white Christian families out of their neighborhoods. He burst out with diatribe of how the Billionaire Jews, who had all the money to bribe the country's legislative parties, were the ones actually behind all these big-make-peace movements and financially supported Israel, Libya, Egypt, and Iran. Their lobbying and bribes was all for the oil and with no concern with the people living in those lands.

Clay would've loved to have dragged this foul-mouthed man down off his podium and stuff his megaphone down his throat to show him how weak the US government was. It especially offended him when he had to render a straight-armed Nazi salute to the US flag at the close of every speech. A lot of his friends had died or been wounded for this beautiful flag, and it sickened him to see such slimy people, as this little blowhard, to be using the American flag as a tool for such hateful purposes.

Through mail to his fictional girlfriend in San Antonio, which was heavily censored by the camp's executive officer, Clay maintained weekly contact with his control officers in the San Antonio FBI office. A special code system was being used that the KKK couldn't break, and Clay always remembered to grin when he received one of his special love letters from his lady friend. Only he knew the woman writing him was a married fifty-seven-year-old grandmother and senior FBI agent/analyst. But from long experience, the FBI knew such letters needed to have a woman's flare as to not raise suspicions. Clay even laughed hardily when she had even remembered to send him a box of chocolate chip cookies last week, and he learned Grandma was a pretty good cook too.

Though the flag pole positioned in the center of the camp flew the American flag, inside the buildings were various sized KKK flags and self-made White Fist posters tacked to the walls. There were even a couple of Nazi swastikas, and Clay had to bite his lip whenever he walked by one of them. The camp couldn't have anything outside that a satellite, plane, or ground observer might see and dispel the religious retreat theme. But it was way too late. Within days of the sale of the property, a passing satellite assigned to Homeland Security had started observing the camp and its daily activities.

A flag had popped up in the FBI's computer system when this financial sponsor, already a suspected KKK supporter, spent a large amount of funds for this property. After that, undercover operatives on the street began to pick up a word here and a whisper thereof this new White Fist organization inside the KKK. The FBI opened a full investigation into the purpose behind this camp, and once they had footage of the shooting ranges and explosive training, the FBI now needed to know the planned targets. This was why Clay was brought out of the desert and loaned out to the FBI, which didn't make Clay a happy man. Having been burned badly by the CIA, he wasn't looking forward to working with another federal agency, and he was sincerely looking forward to a 30-day leave.

This whole assignment from day one inside the camp had depressed Clay, and he was more than happy in knowing this was his last night of being a part of this racist and dangerous organization. He knew all too well that putting automatic weapons in the hands of idiots could only lead to mayhem and butchery, especially after having seen too much of it in Egypt.

Clay had set through various intelligence meetings in camp and learned how this new faction, a fanatical limb to the KKK, had planned an attack of seven targets next Saturday. Teams were set up to bomb four synagogues throughout the two-state region, a large mosque in Atlanta, and two neighborhood civil rights legal centers in downtown Atlanta. Using his code, he'd gotten the word out to his control and had finally gotten a reply.

An early morning raid would take place today, and to help things along, he needed to find a way to be on guard duty tonight in order to allow the team's easy access into the camp.

Though he wasn't scheduled for it, the man sincerely appreciated the offer by Clay to take over the duty. Former Marine Lance Corporal Matt Winfro was smack in the middle of a poker game, and the luck seemed to be running his way tonight. He was already up by $232.00 and really didn't want to leave the table for something as boring as guard duty. Clay had explained between hands of how he had the duty coming up on tomorrow night and wanted to see his lady friend if the camp commander allowed for him to head into town for a night out, or at least a few hours for dinner with her.

"Look, man, mah babe is a-comin' into town by bus and ah need to have a couple hours with her. I'm in a bad need, man... if yuh know what ah mean, dude." Clay hated speaking like an idiot, but it fit in with his alias, and the crowd he was talking to thought this was how street Mex sounded, which was all a farce. He knew a lot of Mexican-Americans in the service whose English skills were better than most of the people inside this camp.

"Not a problem, Willy," Matt replied enthusiastically. "I'll do your night, now jus' you leave us alone, so I can fleece these boys real good now."

Having expected the FBI to have already arrived by now, Clay began to grow antsy when he suddenly froze and fought down the urge not to turn. He knew from training that it was the barrel of a rifle that jabbed him in the back, just over his left kidney. He only hoped it was who he expected and not that his cover had been blown somehow.

"Don't turn around," a man's deep voice whispered from only a foot away. "Captain, give me your name, full social security, and your wife's maiden name... and quickly!"

Clay didn't recognize the voice, and he knew the two guys in the guard shack were still there. The last time he was by there, they were both sound asleep, so he took a chance, sucked in a breath, and let it out slowly. They seemed to know his rank, so he whispered his real name, added his rank and social security number, and then added at the end, "Never been married, fella. So you're out of luck on that one."

The pressure of the weapon against his back disappeared, and he slowly turned to find a group of 6-men knelt down below him on the brushy hillside. In this darkness, he had never spotted them as he walked by. They were all dressed in black from head to toe, with Kevlar helmets and body armor, wearing night-vision goggles over their eyes, black face paint, and were heavily armed. *It's all this bug dope, really messes with my senses.*

"Guess you must be Clay, then," The closest man said, though he kept his rifle still at the ready.

In a whisper, Clay replied, "I'm sure glad you guys finally showed up. I was beginning to wonder if I had my dates wrong."

"Well, we're here now. Took us longer than we thought to get everything organized and make it to the camp without being detected. Oh, we got this for you too, but you need to hurry getting it on. Bosses didn't want you getting shot by mistake." The body armor and helmets all had small dots on them, only detectable by the infrared goggles so the good guys wouldn't accidentally shoot a friendly troop.

While Clay put on the matching Kevlar body armor, chest plating, elbow and knee pads, helmet, and goggles, the unidentified leader continued to brief him in a whispering voice. "We've searched two sides of this place until we found you and had to take out the sentries and silence one guard post with stun-guns. Thankfully we brought along enough duct tape to wrap them all up nice and tidy like. Just hope the bears don't find them. When they wake up, they're going to have some serious headaches." He then handed Clay a belt radio with a head microphone and earpiece.

"Your call sign is India-One. The SAC down below said you'd get a kick out of that."

Clay knew they were amused by his Athabascan heritage, but he wasn't sure who the Supervising Agent was for this operation. "You've got another two guys about 150 yards down that way, "Clay pointed to the northeast and where the two guards were sleeping. "You'll pick up their snores within 20-feet, but be careful of the big guy- he's got a lot of muscle."

"Thanks." The squad leader sent four of his men in that direction and listened briefly as they moved silently through the wooded area. He then turned and waited as Clay put on his tactical armor.

"How long you been with this group," the leader asked.

Keeping his voice low, Clay replied, "Feels like a year, but it's been going on two months." Only then did Clay realize the man he was talking with wasn't wearing black face paint but that he was, in fact, an Afro-American. He suddenly wondered how this man might feel about dealing with these white supremacists below.

"Are there any females or kids down there?"

"Didn't you get my information?" Clay asked.

"That's a good twenty-four hours old. I'm interested in now."

"As of midnight, we have seventeen females of assorted ages and nine school-aged kids. The children belong to camp officers. I think they have them around to fool the satellites or anyone stumbling across the camp. They also use the kids to carry racist pamphlets into their schools or shopping centers in the valley. But the women... the ones in the bunkhouses, there are some real tough fighters down there and all of them former military. Most of them were MPs in either Iraq or Afghanistan. One of the ladies is a Third Degree Black Belt, so watch out for her. She's a tall blonde with long legs, and she doesn't like men much."

"We were told to expect a well-armed group... automatic weapons and possibly grenades. Is there anything heavier... any machine-gun emplacements, LAWS, or Claymore minefields? " The leader went silent when he heard one of his men approach from the guard post.

"We found them both snoozing away like little kids. Had the both of them secured in handcuffs and gagged before they even woke up. I decided to leave two men there and one man to keep a watch on the perimeter in the event they have someone checking these posts."

"Good," the supervisor said. He then notified the Command Center and briefed them that Captain Jefferson was located, is safe and his squads now have the northern, western, and eastern perimeter positions secured. "We're ready to move in upon your command.

"Standby," an unidentified voice said over the radio.

"Hurry up and wait," Clay whispered and then added, "Just like the Army."

"Yeah, but you guys have some pretty lax security here. No need to hurry. Those clowns are lucky we just don't slit their throats for sleeping on guard."

Then Clay asked, "Like I told San Antonio, a bunch of couch potatoes… but very dangerous ones with all this weaponry in their hands." Clay was all set to move out, and then he asked out of curiosity, "Are you guys with the FBI Hostage Rescue Team?"

"Captain, just like you Delta Force boys, we don't even exist… got it?"

"Not a problem," Clay replied. He was used to all the secrecy in working special ops but thought he'd ask anyway. Ever since leaving the Green Beret to become a member of Delta Force, he hadn't realized how many top-secret special action teams existed in the federal system and military service. He had worked with three separate Seals Teams, various federal teams, and even some secret organizations from other countries. But going undercover with a racist militia organization in his own country was something real new for him, and he hoped he would never have to take on a similar assignment again. There were times he wondered if it was even legal, using military personnel for domestic operations. He recalled something called the Posse Comitatus Act in the Constitution. But he obeyed orders and left the legal matters to the big heads above his pay grade and hoped for the best.

When the order to move finally came in seven minutes later, a three-man team took out the guard shack at the main gate without firing a shot. Once those two guards were down, six five-man action teams silently moved into the camp. Four separate sniper teams had taken up positions on the hillsides to cover the teams' approach. One sniper team was now installed atop the water tower. The powers that be had originally planned to use sleep gas on the barracks but realized it wouldn't have worked all that well because there was no glass in the windows, only screens to keep the flying bugs out. So, it was decided to go in with good old fashioned flash-bang grenades, to light up the rooms and cause mass confusion with the non-lethal explosives. Another four-man action team moved in to secure the headquarters building, while four-two man teams were assigned the officer's tents. In the meantime, another six-man team was sent up to secure the guard post and roving patrol along the southern perimeter. Here they reported finding all three men playing poker and greatly shocked to find a lot of weapons pointed in their faces.

The highly trained teams moved in utter silence, using their infrared goggles to help them see and detect any human movements, which included their teammates. One team member was startled when a deer suddenly jumped into his path, but he had enough fire control training and experience not to shoot the defenseless creature.

So, without an actual shot being fired and a couple dozen flash-bang grenades being used, the highly confused White Fist faction of the KKK was taken into custody without any major injury to good or bad guys. Even the leggy blonde with the martial arts skills was taken down before she could even get a move into play. There were some hurt egos, a lot of profanity, and verbal threats about knowing this senator or that judge, which was all recorded. In no time at all, the men and women were safely herded aboard special jail buses in whatever they were wearing. The buses had moved in as soon as the camp was secure, and the prisoners were driven back down the mountain for a prolonged stay at the government's expense.

FBI and Homeland Security Intelligence Teams were allowed to take the headquarters building and barracks apart, which lasted into the morning hours. They quickly found the money to be used by the White Fist to take out their assigned targets; fifty-five thousand in twenty-dollar bills. Once all the belongings, weapons, and anything else vital to the investigation were removed, the camp was photographed in great detail, and then by order from Washington, it was to be burned to the ground. A Forrest Service Firefighting Crew of men and women wearing yellow helmets and matching protective gear was on hand in the morning to conduct the destruction and prevent the fire from spreading into the woods.

Clay was now sleepy by the time the Forrest Service Crews arrived, and he hoped someone had cooked up some strong black coffee. He stood by a typical FBI Chevrolet Suburban, his helmet still on and his face mostly covered to protect his identity by a black baklava. He'd see these people soon enough when he had to testify in their trials, but he wanted to remain faceless for now. He had quickly learned the KKK hotline was spread throughout the country, and he wanted to keep his face and identity unknown for as long as possible.

With a gloved right hand, Clay wiped the sweat from his eyes and looked up to see a senior FBI agent approach with two large paper coffee cups in his hands. The man wasn't wearing a tactical uniform or the typical FBI all-weather jacket, but Clay knew he was a Federal Agent. He stood well over 6 feet tall, had wide shoulders, and wore the famous Fed's extremely dark glasses. He also knew who Clay was, which told him the man was FBI. When the older man reached Clay, he handed him a black coffee and apologized, "Sorry, no sugar or creamer. We got the coffee from the fire crew." The older man looked about the camp for a moment and watched all the activity and the amount of evidence being secured for transport, and then, after removing his dark glasses, he offered his right hand to Clay.

In a sincere tone, he said, "Captain Jefferson, I'm Special Agent in Charge Watson. I wanted to say that you've done one heck of a job here. There's no telling how many people may have died if these nuts had been able to carry out their attacks. With some of the evidence they've already found, we'll be knocking on a lot of doors, arresting a good many KKK members and other white supremacists."

"Thank you, sir, and thanks for the coffee," Clay replied. "I'm sorry to say, they're a few good, but misguided kids in that group, poisoned by the hardliners and radicals. They've come from broken homes and fed all this racist crap. I only wish we could save some of them."

"I'd like to ease your mind by saying it's possible, but unfortunately, Captain, I doubt it will happen for these people here... except for the younger children. Most likely, they'll end up in foster homes, while the others are all headed for federal prison. Once inside, they'll have to join a white racist group to survive their time, or end up knifed some night by a Black gang." The agent pointed to the last bus going by, "By the time they come out, even these nice kids, as you used the term, will be hardline Klansmen or neo-Nazi's."

Clay could only nod his weary head in response. He'd been on the run all night to help with the various intelligence teams. He then asked, "How much C-4 or Semtex did you locate in the armory?" He knew they still had some because he was training some of the older men in the proper usage of it. A certain amount was set aside for the assigned missions, but the teams needed to know how to use their equipment to be effective.

"I haven't gotten the totals yet, but one of your Army EOD people said there's at least enough explosive charges in that one building to blow up the Capitol Dome. He believes the Semtex is all from Mexico, too, wrapped the way the Mexican military packages it. This means they probably have a connection with one of the better-equipped drug cartels... something we've been worried about for some time."

"Well, I haven't seen any Mexicans here since I arrived, but that doesn't mean the cartels haven't moved the stuff across the border and into the hands of the KKK."

"This was one serious group of loonies," SAC Watson said as he cleaned his sunglasses and put them back on.

"Sir... I am in dire need of a shower, a good meal, and hopefully, a week off to sleep and catch up on some football." Clay turned around to hand his shotgun over to an FBI evidence technician. "It's empty, and here are the rounds."

"Thank you, sir." Being a good technician, the woman verified the weapon was, in fact, cleared and then walked away to record the weapon's brand and serial number with the rest of her evidence. An extensive search will be made with all the serial numbers to determine where the weapons were purchased, possibly giving the FBI new locations to put under observation or even provide enough probable cause to raid some places for the sale of automatic weapons, grenades, or other illegal firearms. The used Glock he purchased second hand and wasn't about to let the Feds have their hands on it, and he did like his new Buck knife and saw nothing illegal about it.

The older agent laid his right hand on Clay's shoulder and said, "Captain, the shower and meal I can grant you, but that week off you want is out of the question for now. You've been ordered to Washington ASAP, and I've got a special plane waiting for you on the tarmac in Atlanta for a quick flight north. An FBI agent will be waiting for you in DC to drive you directly to FBI Headquarters..." Watson stopped as his cell phone rang. He listened to the caller for a moment and then hung up without saying anything. He then turned back to Clay, "Sorry, Captain, the shower is going to have to wait too. People in DC are in flashing red, it seems."

"Aw, man, don't tell me they've already picked another job out for me!" Clay shook his head in resignation. He'd been going from one assignment to another since he left the 82nd Airborne to join the Green Beret. Though he'd been in Iraq once, Afghanistan twice, and served black ops assignments in North Africa, he still hadn't been home on leave in 6 years. Not that it really mattered all that much. His maternal grandfather had died while he was in Iraq, leaving him without any relatives in Alaska, other than some cousins he never got along with for being part white. His father's family never wanted anything to do with him either for being part Indian. His grandfather had written his father's parents after the accident, and the only reply stated they thought he should stay with his "Indian family." Clay often thought he'd look those relatives up someday to simply spit in their faces, but never did. Clay's dad was with the US Army Infantry and on assignment to Fort Wainwright when he met his soon to be wife at a downtown Disco club. She had left the Indian way of life of Minto for the big city lights of Fairbanks. According to his grandfather, his daughter had only known Clay's father for a short time before they were married in a civil ceremony, and they had lived on Post. The Minto family only met Clay's father once in the two years before the accident, and that was for his grandmother's funeral in Minto.

So Clay was raised according to his grandfather's Athabascan ways. He learned to fish by pole, dip netting, and the usage of fish wheels, the proper ways to clean and dry fish, how to trap, and to hunt. He had bagged his first bull moose when he was twelve years old and shot his first Grizzly when he was thirteen. He respected his grandfather's traditional religious beliefs, but while attending college at the University of Alaska-Fairbanks, he had given his life over to the Lord Jesus Christ at Door of Hope Church. His grandfather was not offended, for he knew his grandson must walk his own path, and it was while attending college, Clay also made the decision to enter the ROTC program. Along with his BS Degree in Animal Husbandry and a minor in Geology, he earned his 2nd lieutenant's gold bar and a seven-year hitch in the U.S. Army.

His college was paid for with the insurance money from his parent's accident. His grandfather had placed it all into a credit union savings account in Fairbanks, having no need of the funds himself for the raising of the boy. With interest, the money grew to quite an amount and paid his entire four years of schooling, along with a new dark blue Ford F-250 4x4 and a little extra besides Clay kept in savings for the day he decided to buy a house and wanted a sizable down payment. But he ended up selling the new truck two weeks before leaving for his second deployment to the sandbox. He added this money to his savings account and dreamed of the day he met the right girl and settled down on a cushy 20-year retirement as a Major or Lt. Colonel. But as of yet, he hadn't met her, and for now, he easily lived off his captain's pay. Especially with all the extra allowances he received for being on Delta Force, jump pay, combat pay, TDY pay when assigned to the Feds, overseas pay, and couple other special payments from foreign governments for services rendered and the US government allowed him to keep. His bonus money never came to too much, but it helped cover the costs of his undercover work- especially those charges he couldn't turn in receipts for; paying off informants and buying contraband to keep his various covers up. An AK-47 didn't come cheap, even on the back alleys of Libya.

The last of the prison buses left the compound, escorted by joint FBI and Tennessee State Police vehicles. As of yet, the news services had not received any word about this raid, but once prisoner processing began, word would get out, and the FBI would have to have their briefing officers ready to handle an army of pushy news people shoving their microphones into everyone's faces. Expensive KKK and Aryan Brotherhood lawyers would be on the steps of the courthouses citing civil rights violations, while minority leaders would be for once commending the efforts of the federal officers for raiding this foul camp of would-be killers.

Clay turned his body armor over to FBI personnel, slipped his pistol behind his back and pulled his sweaty t-shirt down over it, and rode down the hill with the senior agent and two other FBI agents. "Look...Sir, I stink! I really need to wash up before I go aboard any aircraft, much less see anyone in DC." Clay began to wonder if they all bought their sunglasses at the same store or if the FBI bought them in lot and issued them. For himself, he wore the same sunglasses he carried with him through North Africa, scratches and all.

"Sorry, Captain. The order was ASAP, and it came from upstairs, and in my case, that meant pretty high up. But don't you worry; the aircraft comes with a lavatory." The supervisor then ordered the driver to turn the air conditioning up. Clay hadn't realized he dropped off to sleep until he opened his eyes and saw he was at a small private airport, and a government Leer Jet was awaiting him. He thanked the senior agent, climbed out of the vehicle wearing the same clothes he'd worn all night, and walked aboard the plane, where he was promptly asked to identify himself by a very pleasant, but official mannered, government flight attendant. She was wearing a blue two-piece pantsuit, white shirt, and her blonde hair was worn in a longish ponytail. Clay also noticed her eyes were a cobalt blue, and he suddenly wished this was a longer flight. He then noticed she was armed with a small automatic pistol on her right hip and began wondering where that lavatory was. He had too much coffee last night and early this morning and hadn't had a chance to use the restroom.

Identified and processed, he was handed a black leather fold-over suitcase containing some of his own clothes- which he was told also held a newly purchased dark blue sport coat, black pants, a light blue long-sleeved dress shirt still in the wrapper, and a navy blue tie. Thankfully, the FBI had checked his shoe size and provided a pair of simple dress black shoes and new dress black socks. He was directed to the back of the plane, where a restroom offered him enough space to change clothes and take a sponge bath. Not quite the shower he was promised, but it provided him with a traveler's kit, including a razor, two white washcloths, and a very large shower towel. He felt amazingly better afterward. Once he was dressed and seated, the plane began taxing down the tarmac. Within moments the aircraft was flying at thirty-thousand feet and on its way north. By the time Clay had enjoyed a micro-waved roast beef sandwich, a bag of chips, and an ice-cold soda, the aircraft was preparing to land outside the nation's capital. He thought about asking his hostess for her phone number but decided against it. This next assignment could be sending him anywhere on the planet, and he didn't have time to begin a relationship.

Once the plane was parked, the door was opened, and Clay found another 2016 Black Suburban waiting for him. Making him wonder, *with all these new vehicles the government buys, how could the car companies be having such money* problems?

# 2

# BACK TO ALASKA

*J. Edgar Hoover Building*
*Federal Bureau Of Investigation*
*Washington D.C.*
*8:37 P.M. 13 September*

Weary-eyed from lack of sleep, Clay finally arrived at the government's F.B.I. building and entered through one of the more photographed entryways in the US Capital. Forgetting to identify himself and show his credentials, he suddenly found himself setting off the entry's security alarm system and caused everyone nearby to freeze in place, their eyes now wide in apprehension as the federal security detail reacted. In mere seconds, he found himself shaking his head from side to side, his arms now held high above his head, of course, his face now flushed with embarrassment, for failing to advise the guards of who he was and display his credentials. His Glock Pistol had set-off the alarm system, and in his state of fatigue, he had forgotten he was still "packing" it.

Knowing he had sincerely blown it, he presented his best smile to the two uniformed federal security officers in front of him, both who had assumed a challenging two-handed shooter's stance, with their pistols now aimed at the center of his chest. He also knew that to each side of him were other security officers, also in the same stance, and they would most likely shoot him if he attempted to bring his hands down before he was advised to do so.

"I have a loaded forty-five pistol in my back. I also have my federal officer's credentials in my right back pocket. Last name is Jefferson, first name is Clay. My only excuse for being so stupid is a lack of sleep. I was ordered here at the completion of my last assignment, and again, I apologize... especially for my odor. I've been in the woods for a long time."

"Shut-up and very slowly drop to your knees. If you are a federal officer, you know how to assume the correct position. Anything else, and you may force me to shoot you and ruin the waxing job the custodians did last night. Now assume the position!"

Clay knew this was the detail's senior man speaking, and these officers took their job very seriously. Normally he was glad they did, but he also knew one of these younger officers might be applying just a little bit more pressure on their triggers than they should be. Reality and the excitement they might have bagged a real-live terrorist made for a dangerous situation. So, very slowly, he dropped to his knees while keeping his hands appear above his head; he slowly dropped forward until his palms hit the floor, followed by his forehead and then his chest.

"Keith, holster your pistol and carefully move in. First, remove his weapon from his back. You know what to do if he tries to move. And sir, just so we understand each other... if you do move, I will place two bullets into your upper backside. Do you understand me, sir?"

"I'm frozen solid, Officer.... no problems," Clay replied. He actually wanted to kick himself for causing all of this, knowing whoever he reported to was bound to go over the incident he had created and then filed a written report in his personnel file. This was not his best showing for an undercover officer to display, but it had clearly provided some entertainment for all those who had witnessed his major blunder. *Maybe they'll send me back to the Army, and then they'll retire me after spending 6-months washing dishes at the camp chow hall.*

Clay felt the pressure as his .45 was removed, and then very carefully, he heard the sound of the chambered round being removed from his pistol, followed then by the handgun's magazine. The round was then inserted back into the magazine. The magazine was then reinserted into the pistol. The officer then placed the weapon behind his back, held in place by a wide leather basket-weave police belt.

Keith then returned to remove Clay's wallet but found no police or federal credentials inside of it. "Sergeant, all I have is an I.D., and his name isn't Clay Jefferson."

"Handcuff him…slowly, I do not like the looks of this dude." The supervisor looked about and saw that people were beginning to move around again, and he shouted, "Everyone freeze! We're not finished here yet, and this man could still be carrying a bomb. So, stay where you are until I've released you!"

"Oh, Shit!" Clay's younger FBI agent and driver was stunned. He couldn't believe the man he was responsible for was laid out on the entryway floor. "What happened?" He asked.

"Do you know this guy, Agent?" The senior guard asked. He knew this man was an FBI agent but couldn't recall his name.

"Sure, he's a federal officer I just drove in from the airport. I've got to take him upstairs, but I'm betting he left his credentials in his bag. We took him right off his last assignment, he didn't even have time to grab a shower, and man, does he stink. I'm also betting he even forgot he was carrying… right?"

"Can you go get his bag and bring me his credentials. I'd like to take your word, but then I might lose my extra $2.50 an hour I draw as being the shift supervisor."

"No problem, but you might let him sit up; that position has got to be rough on the knees and forehead."

"Sure." He addressed Clay and allowed him to turn around and remain seated on his butt.

"Thanks, this feels a whole lot better… Look, this is all my fault. They flew me straight up here without time off, and I just blew it. I can't believe

I came in here without my proper I.D., especially being armed. Normally I would've turned my weapon over to the senior agent on scene, where I was working, but this is my own pistol, and I didn't want it getting lost. Over the years, I've had two pistols and a rifle go missing on me. That .45 is match-class and fitted perfectly for my hand."

"It's not a problem, sir...keeps my guys on their toes."

"Can I buy you all a beer later tonight...unless I'm going right out again?"

"You look like you could use a good night of sleep, maybe a decent steak."

Clay grinned. "I was down in the south. I think nearly half my blood was sucked out by those carnivorous insects down there, but it was worth it. I was hoping for a couple weeks of leave, but they ordered me here right away."

"Well, if you're going to be hanging around Washington, make sure you carry those federal credentials...the D.C. cops can be heavy-handed at times. They'll make you go through the system, spend twenty-four hours in lock-up before even calling your boss. They've done it to a few of us, real embarrassing."

Now with his credentials in hand and his .45 back in place, Clay shook the detail's hands and then grabbed the elevator up to the 5th floor. According to the Senior Agent, he met in Tennessee, Room # 512 was where he was to report too.

Clay was alone now; his driver was busy returning his vehicle to the motor pool, located in the basement. Walking down the hallways, checking the room numbers, he was breathing in the cool air conditioning and was so pleased to be out of those mountains and away from all those terrible people he had come to know. He now hoped 88% of them would be spending the next thirty years in some desert prison, breaking big rocks into little ones. Clay had grown so tired of listening to KKK jerks and their hate-all non-whites' lecturers, anti-Semitic literature in the latrines, and imitation Hitler monsters stomping about the camp.

Seeing the men's room up ahead, he decided to give himself another quick face and hand wash, take care of the dust he had picked off the downstairs floor. Looking into the huge wall mirror, he jumped back in time for a moment and recalled those long nights when he sat around a desert campfire, and his mind had wrestled with the problems back home in the U.S. political system and the effect it caused to his country. He liked to come up with solutions and talk them over with his team members, who often agreed with him. Of course, he usually outranked everyone, and he knew it was smart to agree with either the top kick NCO or the junior officer stuck out there with them. Most majors and above had spent their time in the sandbox and now enjoyed an air-conditioned room and steak every night at the Officer's Club.

Clay had told them of how he thought the President should be treated the same as a five-star general, a rank used up until the end of the Korean War era. He believed the man or woman would receive the same pay scale, housing, and allowances compatible with this rank, while appointed cabinet members would receive equal pay to a military's Chief of Staff. For elected Senators and Representatives, they would receive equal status to that of full colonels or one-star generals. Clay also felt that Congress could not pass a pay raise for only them, as they had done in the past, unless it was across the board for all military and civilian government workers. He'd also like to see term limits for all government elected offices and political appointees, to include the federal court judges, and elect the President for a 6-year term, so he or she isn't using half of his first term running for reelection instead of doing their job. To retire all federal judges at the age of seventy or before, if they are found to be operating within diminished mental capacity and to establish a law that prevented a politician or federal employee from going to work for any company he had any dealing with while in office for a minimum of five years, to help prevent corruption and to also abolish paid lobbyists. But, Clay was a realist; he knew that chance of these things happening was one in a million or brought about by the Second Coming of the Lord. But at least the people who held the office wouldn't be doing it for the money.

Clay then noticed there was no room number or name on the double wooden doors now in front of him, nor was there a placard tacked to the wall beside the doors to identify what was inside. But, there was another agent who stood there and the man, who wore a sullen expression, only nodded his head once to acknowledgment Clay's arrival.

"If you wish to enter, you'll have to show me an I.D., sir." The man was younger than Clay; he wore his dark brown hair short and had no facial hair. With hazel eyes, the man stood about five feet and ten inches and appeared to be in good physical shape, and Clay estimated him to be about 190lbs. Clay also saw his sports coat had a hard time concealing the holstered firearm on his right side.

"How long ago did you leave the academy, Agent?" Clay asked as he withdrew his credentials and handed them to the agent.

"Why do you ask?"

"Well, if you're guarding something real important behind those doors, you should never have allowed me to get this close to you. An expert in martial arts could have taken you down and disarmed you within fifteen-seconds, left you unconscious...or dead, and then went through these doors. So, I'd estimated you graduated less than a year ago, and you dislike this posting. You are also basing your own security on the hope the security downstairs would've already insured I was disarmed. But, I could've picked up a weapon at any point, left by a paid-off night custodian, if I was sent here to assassinate someone. But you never thought of that, did you?"

Once he had checked his credential, identifying Clay as a Federal Officer with a GS-11 rating, the agent felt much like a child being chastised by his father, and he knew he deserved it.

"Yes, sir, I graduated eight months ago, and I feel much like you just said. I hate this posting, and I've grown lax...I apologize, sir. No excuse."

"Look, the reason I said all that was to wake you up. You were apparently put here because someone sees something in you, something you've probably not seen in yourself. I know who's behind that door because I'm reporting to them, and they wouldn't want a dunce out here protecting them. So, wake up. A long time ago, I was given this same talk, and it ended up saving my life."

"Saving your life...how?"

"That's another story for another time, and we've had a couple beers. Right now, I'm late. So, knock on the door and advise the gentleman that I'm here."

"Yes, Sir." The agent had returned Clay's credentials, smiled, and said, "Thanks." He then knocked on the right-side door twice and made entry after hearing, "Come in." He left the door open, walked in, and was right back in mere seconds. "Come on in, Mr. Jefferson."

Clay was surprised to see he had entered a mid-sized conference room. A quick once over revealed three men at a conference table and a window-less room with walls and ceiling constructed of privacy sound tiles. He stood at one end of a highly expensive wooden conference table, large enough to comfortably seat ten people. There were ten very nice leather upholstered high-back chairs on chrome legs with caster-wheels. At the other end of the table set the three men, all of whom were now studying him as he had studied the agent outside.

The room, paneled in light gray cloth-like material, was brightly lit up by overhead fluorescent lighting. Behind the men, there was a large Toshiba 72-inch flat-screen TV mounted on the wall. Below the screen was a wooden table on wheels with two white ceramic urns; one marked by felt pen for coffee and the other for tea. Clay also noticed the small Bose speakers mounted in each corner of the ceiling. Always the best for the Feds! Bose yet... my tax dollars at work.

The tabletop had several yellow legal-sized writing tablets, one in front of each chair and three brown leather handle-less cups holding an assort-ment of official FBI black ink pens and brand new sharpened yellow number-two pencils spread out across the length of the table.

Of the three men who sat at the far end of the table, the one at the end was a heavyset elderly white gentleman with short curly white hair, with tufts about the ears and back of his head, but he was bald on top. Clay took notice of the older man's previous broken nose, old ear injuries, and swollen rheumatoid arthritis about his battered knuckles, all of which told Clay the man had once been a boxer, either amateur or professional in his early years. The man wore a tightly groomed white and gray mustache, had heavily bloodshot medium blue eyes, with a drooping left eyelid, with a small reddish wart planted on it. There was an ample supply of crow's feet wrinkles sprouted from the corners of both eyes and a lot of facial wrinkles that ran along the length of his cheeks. On his temples were the reddish age spots that women tried to hide with make-up, and his chin and jaw already displayed the five o'clock shadow of a man who was troubled with a heavy beard. *Bald on top, but the beard wants to come out to make you look like Santa Claus. It is so strange how that happens to so many old men.*

From this observation, Clay knew the man worked a stressful job and was clearly nearing retirement age; probably counting the days to when he could put his papers in and find a nice condo in Arizona or Florida to live out his days in and write a book about his exploits with the government. The older gentleman was the only one without a sports coat on or a military uniform blouse. He wore only a light blue button-down shirt with the sleeves rolled up to his elbows. No tie, and his collar's top button was unbuttoned to show he was wearing a white t-shirt. What troubled Clay was the presence of a half-full glass ashtray in front of the older man, for all the federal premises were now non-smoking areas. There was even a "No Smoking" sign inside this room also, but apparently, it was ignored.

The second fellow who set to the older gentleman's right was much younger by a good twenty years or more margin, and he appeared to be quite tall, well over six-foot. But, since he was sitting down, Clay was only able to make an estimation based on upper body size. He was of a thin build, with a long narrow face, hawkish nose, and long ears to correspond with the nose. His brown hair was cut short, with one-inch bangs in front, and he had a menacing mustache-goatee affair going, which told Clay he was probably not military unless he was Delta Force and Clay knew almost everyone in Delta Force. No, this gentleman was a complete stranger to him. He wore an expensive brown tailored suit with pearl-looking buttons, a multi-colored blue, gold, and yellow wool vest, and a brown tie with small yellow stripes. Clay thought it a bit too warm for the current outside temperatures. Clay then suspected the man might have come from a very hot climate; Washington weather, though warm for the locals, cooled visitors off who came from Central America to the Middle East. The gentleman also wore an official blue and white "AGENT" identification badge, which hung from a beaded chain around his neck, with a non-flattering photograph of him on it. Clay was wearing a similar identification badge on a chain, but his only said, "VISITOR."

The man's goatee caused Clay to remember how two CIA agents in Egypt had similar goatees, and their careless actions had gotten two of his team killed. He glared back at the man's deadpan expression and wondered if this man could sprout a set of devilish horns and spit fire from his mouth. From his presence here, Clay would've turned around and walked right back out through the doors right then, but he stayed because of the presence of the third man who sat at the table. This was someone he knew; an old and dear friend.

Lt. Colonel Richard Jessup set to the old man's left, and he wore a sincere smile for Clay. When he saw how uncomfortable Clay had gotten, Jessup waved him toward the chair beside him. Jessup and Clay had known each other since the first day Second Lieutenant Clay Jefferson entered John F. Kennedy Special Warfare School in hopes of becoming a Green Beret. Clay never forgot Jessup's welcoming speech. It wasn't pleasant, but in fact, it was sprinkled with dire threats and profanity, and by the look in the man's eyes, Clay believed Jessup, who was only a major back then and one of the senior training officers at the training center, was up to the task at hand to make or break the junior officers and non-commissioned officers. It was Jessup's job to make their lives a living hell, to see if they could cut the mustard and had what it took to wear the coveted Green Beret. For the officers, this meant to eventually become one of two A-Team Commanders, responsible for the enlisted men in their small unit. So, Jessup was especially rough on his young lieutenants and captains. He didn't want a man getting killed because he allowed some college boy to coast through the program, especially because this officer knew some congressmen, his daddy was filthy rich, or he was serving a high ranking officer. At the John F. Kennedy Special Warfare School, the students quickly learned rank meant little here. This became soon apparent when the enlisted men stopped saluting the student officers, and the torture began.

Today, Lt. Colonel Jessup wore his dress greens, and this allowed him to display his ribbons and qualification badges. He was built much like an NFL middle linebacker, with broad shoulders and a narrow waist. His square jaw and muscular physique made him a poster child for the Green Beret. But, his several small battle scars below the lower lip and hard piercing hazel eyes from too much time as a hunter in the bush would scare off too many mothers, who would see him and send their sons to the Air Force or the Navy. He wore his gray and white hair cut close, just enough to show the color, and he had no mustache. His uniform pants are highly creased, giving one the impression the edge could cut silk. His well broken in jump boots were highly polished, a chore he still did himself, and his pants were bloused airborne style, right at the top of his boot laces. His uniform blouse was spotlessly clean and displayed his award ribbons, two Silver Stars, two Purple Hearts, various other awards, plus an assortment of colorful "I Was There" ribbons. Above his ribbons, he wore his Combat Infantry Badge with two battle stars and Master Jump Wings. He had other awards he could wear, but these were the ones he personally held in esteem, and he didn't want to overdo it.

Lt. Colonel Jessup now found himself working under an officer who hadn't seen much combat; only the opening days of the first salvo against Bagdad and before that, he'd spent nearly fifteen years as an instructor at West Point in military history, before he finally gained the senior officer's slot as a full colonel at the John F Kennedy Special Warfare School. Normally, the officers at the Special Warfare Center had served time at the center as junior officers, but with the earlier downsizing of the Army, the military lost a lot of Green Beret officers. Majors were offered early retirement or the rank of Sergeant First Class. Less than half of the majors accepted the offer, and we're now training troops for other countries, but only those who were an ally of the United States. Clay knew some had taken jobs with U.S. Customs, the newly formed ICE department, FEMA, or state or local police departments. In any event, this would supplement their new retirement pay, which wouldn't even cover a house payment.

The Colonel was in need of a star, or he would be forced into retirement in two years, but rumors said he had a senior general in his corner. A general who hoped such a senior post like the JFK Center might get his friend his first star. Being Loyal to the Army, Jessup would do whatever it took to help the Colonel earn his star, as long as Jessup could run the school his way- tough, hard, rugged, and the students loyal to one another, the army, and their country.

Today was a day set aside for a select group of congressmen from the Armed Services Committee to visit the JFK Center, so the senior colonel decided his Executive Officer, Lt. Colonel Jessup, should be here for this conference. In this way, he would demonstrate his school to the men who would decide on his star at a later date. To help that along, Jessup agreed to be in Washington D.C. to meet with Clay. Though Clay had been with Delta Forces for over three years, most of this time, he'd been working for the CIA, and he hadn't got to know his senior officers all that well. Clay was still closer to his Rangers and Beret buddies, and this was why Jessup was in the room to ease things a bit.

Clay also noticed Lt. Colonel Jessup wore a blue and white FBI Visitors Badge draped around his neck on a beaded chain, which made Clay take notice again how the old dude wasn't wearing any kind of badge and the fact no one had bothered to give him one of those Visitor Badges when he entered the building.

With a shake of his head, Clay smiled and walked right up to Jessup to offer his old friend his right hand. As they shook hands enthusiastically, as old friends would after not seeing each other for some time, Clay took a seat beside Jessup and waited quietly to see what this was all about. He was also trying to keep from yawning. He knew that could be considered as a poor first impression, but he was sleepy and hoped these people got the ball rolling quickly before he nodded off.

"Clay, I'm only here for a few moments," Jessup said. "They've got me jumping between jobs, but the Boss asked me to be here when you showed up for this briefing... sort of to help things along. These gentlemen know what happened to you in Egypt, and they didn't want you walking right out on them before hearing their needs. They're not CIA, and I double-checked on that for you."

With a second hard look, Clay inspected the two men and waited for Jessup to continue. He was staring at Jessup's Green Beret, which was set on the conference table directly in front of the colonel. Clay missed the Beret, but in Delta Forces, they didn't wear any such identifiable headgear-except for their black Kevlar skullcap helmets they wore into combat.

"These men here are part of a larger team, mainly made up of FBI and Homeland Security personnel. The CIA has no involvement here... this is completely a domestic affair, and Delta Force believes you're the right man to handle this undercover assignment. Of course, this is strictly a volunteer assignment, but they'll not be able to begin the briefing until you accept the job and sign your life away with all their secrecy disclosure forms." Jessup pointed to Goatee man and added, "Government travels on a highway of paperwork, Clay. You've learned that by now."

"Colonel, do you know what's happening here?"

"Honestly, Clay, I know very little. But, when Delta Force or the Green Beret is called upon, we always answer with a 'can do,' and you know it."

"I was hoping for some time off, sir," Clay said. "I haven't had any real leave in over six years…Been going from one duty call to the next. Last time I had any real time off was the week I went home to bury my grandfather, and before that was my grandmother. Not exactly Disneyworld."

"Captain, if you take this assignment, I strongly believe you will appreciate the destination," the older man said, with a half-smile on his face. Then he surprised Clay by lighting up a cigarette in a no smoking building, and right then, Clay knew this man was senior enough that no one was going to tell him to put his cigarette out.

"Look, Clay, I've got to run. It took a little bit longer to get you here than we thought, and I'm out of time… you know how it is. But if you take this job, look me up when you get back, and we'll barbecue some steaks. If you decline, I'll see you at the center in a couple of days, and we'll see if you can still shoot, and we'll even make a few HALO jumps together." Lt. Col Jessup looked over at the two men and said, "Clay here was the best shot in his class… his Athabascan grandfather taught him well, and he's got over two-hundred jumps behind him that I know of." Jessup then stood up, scooped up his Beret, shook hands with both civilians, and then in a fatherly way, patted Clay on the left shoulder, smiled at him, and then walked out of the room. Clay turned to watch as the agent closed the door behind him.

"I know you just came off a rough one, Captain, but this is a priority mission, and we need an answer right now so we can begin your briefings. A lot could be at stake here, and that's the last you'll hear from me about it." The old man took another long drag on his cigarette, exhaled, and filled the immediate area around him in a bluish cloud of smoke, which, thankfully, was quickly sucked up by the room's filtering system. The man then stubbed the cigarette out and ran his tongue across his front teeth, as if to be cleaning them.

Clay wanted to walk around the room a bit to think it over but then recalled what the Colonel had said about Delta's whole 'Can Do' thing. So, he nodded his head and then, in a weary-sounding voice, said, "Let's get to signing all that paperwork, gentlemen... I'd like to catch some Z's tonight and a real long hot shower. All I got was a sponge bath on the plane."

"Thank you, Captain," the man with the goatee said. He reached down to the brown leather briefcase beside his right leg and pulled out an inch-wide blue folder. Clay had seen these folders before, remembering how many times he had signed his life away, under threat of dire consequences if he was to reveal to anyone outside his command structure his involvement in this or that assignment. There were life-long stays in Federal Prison and even threats of death under the US Treason Laws for violating his oath, but Clay wasn't considering of becoming a secret agent for some foreign power and simply signed every page he was required to. He'd read all the forms before and didn't bother to read them now. He also knew that if something happened to him and he was killed, his nearest relatives would learn that he had perished in some made-up training accident. He'd already set up his servicemen's life insurance to be paid to the Community of Minto. It was to be used as a scholarship program in his father's name to help some of the local kids attend college.

It took the better part of 45-minutes to get the paperwork taken care of and secured away back inside the brown briefcase, which was then locked by a key. Coffee had been served to all three by the older gentlemen, and some ham and cheese sandwiches were brought in by one of the building's kitchen staff.

"All right, Clay... if I may call you that?" The older man asked.

"Sure, but what do I call you two... Boris and Natasha?"

This got a polite laugh out of both of the men, which showed how tired they were, and then the older man introduced himself, "Clay, my name is Cleffinger...Thomas Cleffinger, and I am a deputy, or I should say one of the deputies to the FBI Director upstairs. Besides my other duties, I am the senior FBI liaison to Homeland Security. You can look my name up, it's real enough, and I prefer to go by Tom when you and I are working together."

"Thank you, Tom, I appreciate that." Clay then looked at the goatee man and waited.

Sorry, Clay, my mind was wandering there for a moment. I've been working for the last forty-eight hours and can use some sleep myself. Anyhow, the name is Bradley Carlson, and I am with Homeland Security. I used to be with the New Jersey State Police Organized Crime Task Force, and before that, I was a Marine lieutenant stationed in Guam and California. That was all before Desert Storm. But you can call me Brad... Bradley is what my parents use, and they toss in my middle name when I'm in trouble."

"Nice to meet you, Brad...I hope." Clay then looked to both gentlemen and waited for the shoe to drop. Working with the Feds, he knew there was always a shoe, and usually, it was a size 18 4E with sharpened baseball cleats.

"Clay, it's awful late, and we're all worn out," Tom said. "So, let me give you a quick overview now. I don't want to leave you hanging and then have trouble sleeping with guessing games as to where you're going and what you're going to be doing." Tom then directed Clay to the large flat-screen TV behind him. He then picked up a white hand control in front of him and turned the room lights down, which also automatically double-locked the exit doors and turned the TV monitor on to a bright colored screen of flashy starbursts.

Tom hit another button on the controller, and the next thing Clay saw was a black and white diagram of the State of Alaska, which took up most of the screen, and the sight of his home state confused him. He couldn't imagine why they'd be sending him to Alaska if this was what it was all about.

"Yes, you're going home, Clay, and right back to the Fairbanks area." Tom hit a button, and the screen displayed a star for the location of Fairbanks on the Alaska diagram. "Fairbanks, known as 'The Golden Heart City,'" Tom said.

Brad then took over and read a few facts from his notes. "Population approximately 88,000 people, which includes the servicemen and women of Fort Wainwright, which borders the city limits. Twenty-two-miles further east is Eielson Air Force Base and this, along with a few small communities like North Pole, Moose Creek, and Salcha, gives the western side of the Tanana Valley roughly One hundred and thirty-five thousand people in an area about the size of Oregon."

"You might have to add a bit more of the eastern side of the valley to match Oregon, but Alaskans always love to say that if you cut Alaska in half, Texas would become the third-largest state. It has a nasty effect on a Texan's ego. I've seen many a fight break out in service bars over such things," Clay said.

Brad then stood up and approached the screen, "Best of all, Clay, you're going right back into the interior as yourself, Captain Clay Jefferson. But you're going to be a former Captain of the U.S. Army and now a brand spanking new civilian. Though you'll still be on active duty, your new paperwork we're now processing will show you receiving an honorable discharge, and if anyone checked your records, which we presume someone will, it will show you were unable to obtain your major's gold leaf and with all the downsizing of the military going on, you were honor-ably discharged. The only thing missing from your records will be your actual classified assignments with the Green Beret and Delta Force... which pretty much covers everything you've done over the last 6-years. This is pretty normal since classified ops are left out of service records generally speaking."

"Now I am really confused," Clay said. He took a drink from his cold coffee, made a sour face, put it down, and poured himself a cold glass of water from a white ceramic decanter. After taking a sip, he waited for a response from one of the gentlemen.

"I'll make it brief, and then we'll call it a night," Tom said. He lit his tenth or twelfth cigarette for the evening, inhaled deeply, and then filled the room with smoke as he exhaled. Clay was glad the room filters were apparently working on overtime, or he had died of smoke inhalation.

"We're having some trouble in Alaska, Clay. As you know, Alaska has a recognized militia...the Alaska Defense Force. They've been in operation for a long time and have done quite well. Everyone who joins the ADF buys their own weapons and uniforms, and they are a lawful secondary support for the Alaska National Guard. They train their people well and have never been a problem. Well, recently, we've been picking up rumors... a word here or a whisper on the street to one of our informants in how a new radical unit... a militant faction maybe is growing inside the Alaska Defense Force. A unit is being formed and made up of men and women who are prior military and in support of the Alaska Independence Party. The word is they are preparing to act. But we don't know what that means. Now the party alone isn't a problem, it's a legal party, and they have candidates every year running for the various state and federal offices. But now we're getting word they're planning on stepping up the game, and we suspect, without evidence, with some form of domestic act of terrorism, and that does have us worried."

Brad then stepped in and said, "These people want to catch the eyes and ears of the world, and they could be planning something pretty big. But, we have to have evidence of their intent for us to act. We don't need another mess like Waco or Ruby Ridge."

"What's the issue here," Clay asked. "The Alaska Independence Party has been around since statehood in 1959, but most people consider them a bunch of nuts...especially since their founder, Joe Vogler, was murdered by some nut-ball in his own group."

"We know the party is growing by keeping track of all the internet hits on their various sites," Brad said. "We have also learned how they and or some of the native corporations plan on taking the federal government to court on several major issues around the 1959 Statehood Compact and how the voting was conducted. They may very well possibly go all the way to the US Supreme Court with their grievances."

Clay looked from Brad to Tom and then back to Brad, "What's their main gripe... other than they don't like the US Government? I mean, I'm half Indian, and we've never liked the deals made with the US Government by some of our greedy tribal leaders, but no one's ever listened to us. So, we formed the native corporations, and we have more say through the banking system than we ever had with Washington. We're not happy, but who is? I don't even understand the 1959 Statehood Compact...never even read it."

Tom smiled, knowing from his research how much money the various native corporations were bringing in every year, but not all of the natives were receiving dividends from these companies, and not all native groups had corporations. He also knew very few people knew of the Statehood

Compact, but they would once it came across the newspapers and TV news. Once people learned about how the voting was conducted, people would be offended, but he had no idea what effect it would have on current-day Alaska.

His hands shaking slightly from weariness, Tom glanced down at his notes and said to Clay, "One major issue is to show how the vote for statehood was reportedly conducted illegally and in which case, at the time, violated United Nations Laws," Tom said. He was reading from his notes. "Under United Nations Law, said territorial ballots were to offer four options to the voters, but only two options were offered to the Alaskans on the provided ballots- 'yes for statehood' or no for statehood.' Under UN Law, apparently, there should've been an option on the ballot, which allowed Alaskans to exit the US as a territory to become its own country by declaring sovereignty or to exit as US Territory to seek to join with another country…like Canada…Damn, I don't seem to have all the choices in my notes right now."

Then Brad added, "The second issue concerns money. Alaska wants to show how Congress went back on its promise to pay the state 90% of all the monies earned from the sales of Alaska's natural resources. Supposedly and I guess there is stated law, arguable of course, in how Congress promised 90% of all mineral sales from Alaska in order the new state, of such a large size and small population, to operate its government, while keeping only 10% for the US coffers. But once statehood was enacted, the US government never came forth with the 90% and 10% deal. They stated the percentage to be 33%, which is what the other states pay. But, remember all the gold and oil that comes out of Alaska. Supposedly the 10% was offered with the promise Alaska could keep the additional 23% to assist them in building their state services. But, the feds went back on this promise, once the vote was completed."

"I've never heard of any of this, and I was raised in the state," Clay said in surprise. "Except, I do know a lot of people are tired of the US Government telling Alaska what to do with its resources. When President Carter took over a million acres away from the state to make into federal land, he sure didn't make any friends up there. A lot of people were hurt in that deal, losing mining claims, access to their properties, and much more. The people were also real upset over the Arctic Wildlife Refuge being left alone when most everyone knows there's oil under there and probably a good supply of gold and silver. The tree huggers care little about the people in Alaska and their needs, and they're always butting into the fishing industries and the state's hunting regulations, but few of them live up there."

"Well, now you know why we want you up there," Tom said in a weary voice. This has become a priority operation. The last thing the government needs right now is the UN Security Council hearing about us not being able to control our domestic issues... especially after the way we've been going after Russia, Iran, and China over their own problems. It sure wouldn't help if the native corporations provide evidence that the 1959 election was done illegally. That could prove to be really embarrassing."

"Okay, that's a wrap for tonight. We'll begin our formal briefing sessions here tomorrow at 10 a.m.," Brad said. He then handed a thick manila envelope to Clay. "That's got Tom's business card and my own, plus an emergency card for FBI purposes only and a cell phone with recharger. Our emergency numbers and office numbers are programmed in it, along with the FBI Emergency Command Center...You'll give those back before returning to Alaska. It also contains a lot of cash, approximately what you'd get for cashing out upon discharge from the Army. There is a map to your hotel here in DC and your hotel key card, so don't lose it. A driver will take you to the hotel and pick you up at 9:45 a.m. outside your hotel, but you will be under surveillance twenty-four-seven, and that means even in Alaska. You'll be set up with an emergency number and some kind of hand gesture you'll use to show you're in trouble, but you'll also be on your own a lot...except for satellite surveillance. We'll be devoting special satellite service twenty-four-seven, just for this operation. It may be a drone at times or a satellite. But, you'll never be without a Big Brother watching you."

"You must've been pretty sure I'd take this assignment," Clay said with a raised right eyebrow.

"Colonel Jessup said you were one of his best, so we didn't feel you'd turn us down," Brad replied.

"Is that it then?" Clay asked. His back was getting sore, and the creaks in his neck were getting noisy, a side effect from being Airborne.

"I think so, Clay," Tom answered. "Just make sure you get a good breakfast in the morning, you've got a long day ahead of you, and your brain needs to be working."

"How many days before I leave this wonderful school, teacher?"

"Don't knock it; we could've done this at the FBI academy and had you workin' out with the recruits to make sure you were in shape." Tom glanced around the room as he figured out his response to Clay's questions and then replied, "Our bosses want you back in Alaska in five days... you still have to find a job and move into the service clubs...Veterans of Foreign Wars and American Legion...might also be an AMVETS club... but, do it all subtle like... Oh, your DD Form 214 will give you a 100-percent disability rating to cover your wounds and PTSD, and we'll have a new Military ID Card for you before you leave. This will allow you to come on to Fort Wainwright and visit Basset Hospital for doctor's visits, but you'll be visiting our doctor."

"Subtle like. And you picked me?" Clay shook his head. "Your people have to realize I'm known as a half-breed up there? My Indian brothers have little love for me and the whites... well, at least they don't spit on me anymore.

"Tom, did you know Fairbanks still had 'Indian Only' restrooms and drinking fountains in the 1960s. There were bars where the Indians or even the Eskimos were not allowed in. Civil rights were a bit slower up there, but no one in Congress seemed to have really taken notice."

"No, I didn't realize how bad it used to be, but now you're coming home a highly decorated war veteran with a college degree. We hope those citations for bravery will help make you welcome in the off-post service clubs. A lot of Alaska Defense Force recruits get picked up there, and we know the ADF is a mixture of Alaskan ethnic groups," Tom said. He lifted his briefcase and placed it on the tabletop to place some of his papers into it.

"Gentlemen, natives don't like the word 'Eskimo' anymore. This is used for the coastal native people from the north to the Southwest, and the name actually is derogatory; for most, it means 'fish eater' and not intended to be nice. Sort of like using the word 'honky' or using the 'N' word for Blacks.

"I never knew that Clay, but I'll stop using it," Tom said in a serious tone of voice.

"What about the trials for my last assignment? Won't I be needed to testify?"

"With all the evidence the FBI secured at the camp and everyone trying to burn everyone else to get a better deal, it's doubtful you'll be needed." Tom turned on the lights with the hand control, unlocked the door, and he then said to Clay, "Now get out of here and go get some sleep. I'm an old man, and I need my 8-hours too, or the wife will kill me. And if you ever happen to see me with an attractive older gray-haired lady, never mention you saw me smoking."

When Clay got back to his hotel, which was a nice Best Western located on the eastern edge of the US Capitol, he double-locked his door and braced it with a wooden chair for added security. Old habits die hard. He then got undressed quickly and spent nearly half an hour in a hot shower. Then, with a clean towel wrapped around his waist, he shaved and came out of the bathroom to lay out his clothes for tomorrow on the other bed. His watch told him it was 1:02 a.m., but his body was still feeling the excitement of the day and the thoughts of this new mission. He didn't want to watch any TV or order up any room service-especially after he looked over the hotel's menu and saw what their room service prices were; ghastly. The price for a simple roast beef sandwich started at $15.95, and gratuity was expected to be twenty-percent, which would be added automatically by the hotel. *Whatever happened 10%, and it was still an option to tip or not?*

He lifted up the phone, left a wake-up call at the front desk through their new robotic computer voice system. Clay wondered if there was a cost for this too. He slept in the raw, and as his practice, he walloped his top pillow a couple times to get it in the right shape. He slept with only the top sheet over him and turned off his nightstand light. He had already stuck his Glock 17 under his bottom pillow, and before he closed his eyes, he whispered his nightly prayers. He was asleep within minutes, but it wasn't long before the nightmares began. He was back in the streets of Cairo, and his world was about to fall apart.

At 6:45 a.m., Clay was downstairs to have breakfast in the coffee shop;

three eggs over easy, two slices of plain toast, two slices of tomato, and a thick breakfast steak cooked well done. The total price was $18.50, and he sincerely hoped the FBI picked up the costs with his per diem. The tomatoes went on his steak, and to complete his meal, he drank a large glass of low-fat milk. He also ordered a tall glass of orange juice and two glasses of ice water. As far as he could tell, there was no charge for the water, but after this, he'd be checking out the fast food joints for cheaper prices or maybe somewhere he could find a decent curry dish; hotter, the better. Clay had taken a liking to the volcanic-like Middle East spices, where a soldier needed to have a quart of water handy to cool things down or some raw vegetables to save the inner lining of the mouth. But, he really relished the initial burst of taste and, over time, had grown used to the near panic of having one's mouth on fire.

Clay was always amazed by how the small children over there in the Middle East could chow down so easily on the spiced food and not be running for the nearest water bag.

With no driver in sight yet, Clay walked about the lobby and visited the gift shop. Though he didn't have any girlfriends, a wife, or any relatives he liked well enough to send anything to, he saw no need to purchase any postcards of the memorabilia of the nation's capital. On prior visits, he had taken notice of the cutesy stuffed animals, assorted small American flags or fake flowers people were buying to be left at the base of the Vietnam Memorial, and now the newly constructed Martin Luther King Memorial. He glanced at the fake flowers and wondered who had the business of collecting all the old ones at the memorials, washing them off, and reselling them to the retailers? Had this been the Middle East or North Africa, it would be a thriving business, and the fake flowers and flags wouldn't go to waste. Then there were all the other items, such as uniforms, military rank patches, and unit patches, plus medals and an assortment of things the person leaving it had valued, and they knew the man or women who had their name on the wall would understand why it was left. Something the living and the dead had shared. Clay believed it was all of this that made the big Wall so different than the traveling Wall taken across the country to visit the cities and allow the vets and others to see who couldn't make it to Washington D.C. and see the real thing.

Having seen the Wall, Clay thought they should do the same thing for the Marine Memorial, Korean War Memorial, and possibly some of the other museum pieces. Bring them for all the Americans to see, to help the Americans be proud once again of their country.

He now wondered what kind of memorial would be left for the Iraqi and Afghanistan wars. He knew the names of the men who had fallen beside him in Libya and Egypt on Black Op assignments and how their names would never appear on any memorial wall, for their family members were told they had all died in training accidents. But, in the Special Warfare families, the parents and especially the wives knew the truth behind what had happened, and often or not, a buddy to the fallen comrade would share a bit of the truth with the family member. Black Ops or not, sometimes a wife needed to know how her husband had died and that it was for something more important than a stupid training accident.

While others stood in front of the hotel's big street-side windows to observe pedestrian and vehicle traffic, waiting for a taxi or a 'special ride,' Clay rested in an overstuffed black leather chair until he spotted his driver, with the shiny black government Suburban pull-up into the fire lane. Once inside, the driver handed Clay an official Visitors VIP pass for the FBI building. "The VIP part allows you to bypass the weapons detector and remain armed inside the building. You must carry some pretty heavy weight to get one of these."

Clay didn't reply and pulled the beaded chain over his head and stuck the plastic pass inside his sports coat. He didn't want it to be seen until he was ready to enter the FBI building. He carried his newly issued cell phone inside his coat, and knowing the Feds; he wondered if the phone had a chip in it to allow them twenty-four seven satellite location of him. Not that it mattered. He didn't have any romantic rendezvous planned for this week.

The training began in the same conference room he was in the night before, except there were no agents standing guard outside, and only Brad and a technician were present. To begin with, Clay was shown photographs of the senior staff members for the Alaska Defense Force on the 72-inch television screen, followed by known locations for the various Alaska Defense Force Units.

Brad stood up and used a yellow number-two pencil in his left hand for a pointer to show the locations on the diagram of the state, only this one had more detail and included the rail and road networks. A voice from the wall speaker then spoke, "As of right now, the ADF has its headquarters in Anchorage. But, they have training units in Juneau to handle the Southeast Alaska personnel from as far south as Ketchikan to as far north as Skagway. We estimate they have one hundred and twenty-five men and women in the Juneau unit, but they continue to actively recruit recently discharged veterans.

"The Fairbanks Unit takes in the whole Tanana Valley. We believe they have personnel from several of the villages and smaller townships, such as Glennallen, Tok, Delta Junction, Chicken, Eagle, and Copper Center. Former service personnel from Eielson and Fort Wainwright are sought after, and our records show over five hundred and fifty personnel training with them. But those numbers could be confusing as to how many show up all the time or only once in a while."

"Wow!" Clay exclaimed. "I had no idea the ADF had gotten that big. I thought it was just a bunch of wanna-be soldiers who couldn't make it in the National Guard."

"Might've been at one time, but a lot of people upset with the current government are coming out of the woodwork to join our country's various militias, and the ADF has quadrupled in size in the last two years. We have prior servicemen and women who won't join the guard because they don't want to be sent back over to Afghanistan or the next place the US Military decides it can send state guard units too. So, they'll join a militia to keep their skills in line, hang out with fellow vets, and remember the most exciting time of their life. At least this way, they don't get killed.

"Because they support the Alaska Army and Air National Guard, we're able to keep an eye on their numbers. The only thing that keeps a man or woman from joining up is a felony record or mental impairment, but the word is the ADF doesn't want a bunch of drunks, troublemakers, or drug heads either."

"Where are they getting their uniforms from?" Clay asked while he looked over the photographs of the ADF training exercises and saw how they were wearing the latest in desert and woodland camouflage. The woodland camouflage was, of course, preferred in Alaska operations, simply because the desert and urban camouflage stuck out.

The Technician, a young woman with shoulder-length blonde hair and brown eyes, answered this question, "Alaska National Guard will issue some of the uniforms, but most of the people order their uniforms from one of any number of army surplus retailers, and they can buy new uniforms from the same companies who sell to the US Government. Meantime some of the veterans will wear the uniforms they brought home with them from the Sandbox."

Clay nodded his head and then said, "I used to hear stories of how some of the Vietnam troops had to purchase their uniforms on the black market because they couldn't get their camouflaged uniforms issued." Clay stood up and walked over to the coffee cart for a white ceramic mug of hot tea.

Brad had entered at this point and picked up his own cup of coffee, "It happened."

Then Clay saw Tom coming through the door, and he replied, "My youngest brother bought his camouflage utilities from the Black Market, and then after the war ended, he got assigned to Thailand and found a warehouse stocked full of the camouflaged uniforms. A check showed that they were supposed to go to Nam more than two years earlier. He was pretty angry, and he and a couple others happened to each secure five sets of camouflage fatigues before they left the warehouse. No one said a thing, not even the sergeant in charge of the detail."

"I don't blame them," Clay said, shaking his head and stirring a spoonful of sugar into his tea.

"Okay, let's get back to the ADF... the Anchorage Unit has by far the largest unit with an estimated seven hundred and sixty troops, and we have rumors they even have a heavy weapons platoon. The Alcohol, Tobacco, and Firearms people provided us with a list of all the Class III arms dealers in Alaska, and I was actually amazed to see the number. We have a lot of legally owned automatic weapons up there... anything from World War 1 machine-guns through World War II and over a hundred M-60's from the Vietnam era. You've got your BARs, M-16's and M-4's and all fully automatic, along with dozens of AK-47's. Our paperwork copies show European and Japanese machine-guns, Russian automatic pistols, and now we have people up there with those fifty caliber sniper rifles and a truckload of suppressors or what in my day we referred to as silencers. Your Alaska now has got to be the best-armed state in the union."

"Now I can see why you people are so worried," Clay said.

"Well, to finish this part off, we have another smaller unit on the Kenai Peninsula, which takes in Kenai, Soldotna, Seward and Homer, and a few smaller communities and their personnel number less than one hundred. We have a small unit in Nome, about squad sized, and another in Kotzebue, about squad sized. I think they're the grandchildren of the old Eskimo Scouts from World War II...Sorry, I forgot what you said about the word 'Eskimo.' But, this means all together we have roughly a total of one thousand, five hundred and fifty personnel on paper and this is a mixture of women and men, most of them with previous service duty. They also have a small fleet of retired military service vehicles. At last count, we have confirmed five amphibious 706 APC's from the Nam era, a few APC 113's on tracks, four three-quarter-ton armored personnel carriers, with either fifty cals or thirty cals mounted on them. There are also assorted military jeeps and five recently purchased older model HMMWVs from Iraq."

"Brad, growing up, I heard stories of how Alaska has more Vietnam veterans per capita than any other state." Clay hesitated, thinking of a couple of his older cousins who fit into this classification and how they would never discuss the war. "They're a bunch of mostly men coming up here to hide in a state where the population still sits at less than a million people, has few roads, and most people mind their own business. They also wish to avoid the US government. Do you feel these veterans could be involved in this... suspected act of terrorism?"

"At this point, we don't even know if we have anything to seriously worry about. However, we don't want to be caught unaware like we did on 9-11 or the Oklahoma bombing, even further back to Pearl Harbor. We just need for you to go deep cover and see if there is a threat and then report to us with what you've learned. It may be nothing, and you can enjoy that 30-day leave you're owed, or...we have a problem to deal with, and you're our eyes and ears on the ground."

Clay felt edgy. He honestly didn't like the idea of going undercover against his fellow Alaskans and possibly some of his own tribal people. The whole set up felt rotten, but he also knew he was the best man for the operation. He only hoped the rumors of trouble were false. He could support his people and the other native corporations filing court challenges against the state compact decision, but domestic terrorism he was totally against, and long ago, he had sworn an oath to his country and his fellow Americans.

For the next several hours, Brad briefed Clay on the Alaska Defense Force and their mission in support of the Alaska National Guard. They then took a lengthy coffee break, and Tom took over, briefing Clay on the FBI agents in Alaska, the information they had picked up so far from their sources concerning this radical unit inside the ADF and possible targets, in the event an attack was to be made inside Alaska. One of the questions being asked is whether or not there is a kidnapping plan for the Alaskan governor or some other state officer. Possibly a military base being bombed, or bridges being taken out. They were also concerned as to possible foreign influence by China or Russia. Were the initial stages being checked out for a forthcoming invasion?

The last question Clay had that night, before breaking for dinner and meeting his driver for the ride back to the hotel, was, "Will I have anyone working with me...another undercover officer?"

Tom shook his head, placed a smoldering cigarette into a full ashtray, and said, "At this point, you're running solo. Maybe, if you pick up something, we'll put some additional people in. But, that's up to the Director."

"So, no Marshalls, no ATF, NSA, DIA, or any other acronyms you know of?"

"No." Tom shook his head and, in a fatherly voice, said to Clay, "I am fully aware how you feel about the CIA, and we have a law that prevents them from working inside our borders. But you're on your own up there... except for your surveillance team. No one will contact you unless it's to pull you out on an emergency basis, and then that team will have either Tom's or my name to give you for verification, along with a code word. They will not move in for any other reason than we order it, or if you're about to be shot... something like that."

"If it wasn't for this building here, I'd think I was being recruited by the

Russians to spy on the capabilities of the Alaska Defense Force. Sort of gives me the willies."

Tom nodded his head in understanding. "Clay, I get that way all the time. I really hate having to use that so-called Patriot Act to investigate American citizens, to see if I have any terrorists hiding out in some American neighborhood." Tom took a sip of his coffee and then let out a deep sigh.

"How'd you do in military history in your ROTC classes?" Brad asked.

"I was top in my class and ranking ROTC officer in my senior year," Clay replied and then added. "Isn't that in my records?"

"Easier to ask... You'll recall after Pearl Harbor how we locked up all the Japanese Americans and held them in camps on some of the worst lands America had to offer. But they stayed loyal to America, and their sons enlisted in the military to make up the highest decorated unit in the European Theater; the 442$^{nd}$ Division.

"Now the same thing has happened here with the fall of the towers on 9/11. Our laws have changed, and people's rights are routinely violated and mostly out of fear. Only time has a way of healing these wounds, that and the non-reoccurrences of such tragedies."

Clay gathered up his papers and gave them to Tom to secure for the night, but prior to leaving, he turned to the two men and said, "We hear a lot about what happened to the Japanese Americans being forced into those camps, but seldom do you hear a word of the Aleut People and how they were forced out of their homes by US Soldiers on the Aleutian Chain. These people were taken to Southeast Alaska to live in camps, and in climates they were unused too, to eat food, their body systems were not prepared for. Many perished from sickness, and not a word is printed in the history books of this tragedy. Only in the state do our students hear of this tragedy.

"When the Aleut People went back to their islands, their homes were stripped. All their family mementos and even the furniture was gone. Everything was stolen by US Military Personnel, and it was the officers who had lived in these homes. Their ancient handmade ceremonial masks were taken. Whale hunting seal-fur suits and carving tools over two hundred years old were stolen and all manner of scrimshaw and carved ivory were all gone!"

"You got me there, Clay. I never heard of this either. But I do recall reading of the Japanese attack on those islands, so I guess the people were evacuated for their own good."

Clay could only shake his head and then reply, "Try to remember those words when someone comes to your door and says they're taking you from your home for your own good and you can only carry one suitcase, no weapons, and no food. Imagine how you'll feel, and especially when they don't tell you where you're going, you're retired, and that gold FBI shield is gone, and your wife is scared out of her wits. Loaded into buses, you're transported to desert countryside, possibly an abandoned military base. Maybe then you'll know how those people might've felt." Clay opened the door, "Do we have a name for this operation of mine?"

"Yes, I was going to share that little tidbit with you tomorrow. The people upstairs got a little cute and recalled an old movie about Alaska… they named this Operation Ice Palace," Tom said.

"Yeah, I saw the movie with my Grandfather. We walked out about a third of the way through." Clay waved good night.

Tom stood there with a handful of classified documents in his hands and a look of disgust in his weary eyes. There were times like this; he was actually ashamed of his country and the action it had taken. He also knew what had taken place down in New Orleans, when the police went door to door and seized weapons from law-abiding citizens without warrants, and he knew some of those same weapons were never returned, and all under the covering of the Patriot Act's Emergency Powers. Operation *Ice Palace!* *I'd like to find the joker who thought that one up and knock his block off.*

# 3

# ALASKA FREEDOM BRIGADE MILITIA

*Silas Wickersham's Hunting Cabin*

E ven though it was after 7 p.m., the sun still sat above the horizon, and the night air was just now cooling off. The screens on the two-story cabin's front and back doors and several windows were covered in mosquitoes, each one fighting to find an opening and feed on one of the three humans inside. But bloodthirsty and pester-some bugs came with Alaska, just as moose, caribou, and bears did. This was one of the reasons this cabin was built right here, nearly a mile off the Chena Hot Springs Highway and alongside a large creek. The owner, his family, and friends used it for hunting spring bear and every fall for the elusive moose. There was also the occasional grizzly bear hunt, but those bears tended to have nasty tempers and could only be taken, by special permit, every three years. When not hunting, the cabin was used as a getaway spot and often loaned out to friends in need of a weekend away to help their marriage with alone time or provide some valuable family time away from the hustle and bustle of city life.

It had taken two years to build the cabin, with the help of family members and good friends. The bottom level, made with 10" and 12" thick spruce logs, provided a 10' by 12' living room, heated by a large Franklin wood stove. There was an open kitchen with a 60-year old wood cooking stove and an electric refrigerator operating off an outside generator. This huge generator also handled all the lights and the assorted plug-ins on both levels. It was only turned on when the cabin was occupied, and extra fuel was always brought out by the guests. Upstairs had three bedrooms, two smaller rooms with bunk beds, and one large master bedroom with a king-size bed. For toilet needs, one needed to walk outside 50 feet to the Birch log outhouse.

Besides a pint of blood and gallons of sweat, construction was made up of spruce and birch trees and some plywood sheets from the local lumber mill. But last year, due to the heavy snowfall, a metal roof was added to the cabin. Vehicles could be driven down a rough single land dirt road off the highway for a ¼ mile, passing other driveways to three other residences. The road then ended at a metal gateway, secured by a heavy chain and lock. Once opened, the road went for another 1/8 mile, and a parking area was provided for 5 to 6 vehicles, depending on their size. From that point, people were required to walk the rest of the way and carry whatever they needed. A wheelbarrow for no-snow days or pull-sled for snow days was usually there to assist in the hauling. There was also a large woodpile outside the cabin, and anyone using the place was requested to replenish the pile with what they used, and this included the kindling they needed to get the fire started. The forest area surrounding the cabin was full of standing dead spruce and birch, plus the cabin came with two chain saws, a splitting maul, and a minimum of three axes.

This evening, retired US Army Colonel Silas Wickersham set back in a brown leather chair of some age and wear and ran a cleaning rod down the rifle barrel of his .308 Winchester. His feet, currently nestled in a pair of handmade sheep hide and fox fur slippers, rested atop a brown leather footstool, covered in the dark pelt of a wolf. He was stripped down to an aged navy blue T-shirt with a silk-screen photo of John Wayne on it from his "Green Beret" movie, and he was also wearing camouflaged woodland pants. This was his cabin, a hunter's getaway, but his wife of 32 years, Wendy Sue, had made it her place too with various girly items; such as summertime wildflowers in all the rooms, paintings of hummingbirds scattered about and pastel-colored bedding and even colorful coasters for the coffee table. Silas wanted bears, moose, or wolf coasters, but she won, and he ended up with "Wild Birds of Alaska." Silas was at the point of agreeing to nail up hummingbird feeders outside just so he had something to shoot at when he was out here by himself.

Also in the cabin tonight were Allen Peterson and Norm Johnson, longtime friends, and his hunting partners. Both had been to this cabin a hundred times over the years, and it was moose season now. But tonight, they weren't thinking of hunting moose in the early morning, they had other things to talk about, and the first item on the agenda was dinner.

All three men were senior officers in the Alaska Defense Force Militia. In fact, Silas Wickersham was currently Second-in-Command of the statewide militia. But Silas was also the commander of another unit, the secret organization inside the militia known as the Alaska Freedom Brigade. This unit was the militant offspring of the Alaska Independent Political Party. It was this party's cause to bring sovereignty to Alaska, and the AFBM was the party's strong right arm to assist in making it possible.

Militia Colonel Silas Wickersham was 66-years old, retired from the US Army as an Airborne/Infantry Regimental Commander. Born in Seattle, he had lived in Alaska for 35 years. He had met Wendy Sue when they ran into each other at a University of Alaska-Fairbanks mixer. Silas was wrapping up his Master's Degree, and Wendy Sue was a Professor. They hit it right off and were married within 6 months. Though of a stocky build, he walked with a slight stoop, having suffered some minor spinal injury from over 100 parachute jumps. Wendy Sue referred to him as her great big bear and probably because he was only 5'10", had wide shoulders and a barrel chest. With his gray hair worn extremely short and though bloodshot, his blue eyes were always alert and his face a map of wrinkles, with a growing number of reddish age spots. Wendy Sue thought he could pass for an aged Grizzly, and when his temper flared, she thought he roared like one too.

A graduate of the ROTC Program at Texas A&M University, Silas was awarded his commission and the gold bars of a 2nd lieutenant and was on his way to Vietnam. Back then, a 2nd lieutenant's life span in combat was about 8-minutes. But serving as an assistant platoon commander, he had survived and earned himself several decorations along the way. During

Operation Desert Storm, Lt. Colonel Wickersham served as a staff member for General Powell. But Silas knew because of certain political views he held, he would never see his general's star and opted to retire. During his career, he was awarded a Silver Star, Legion of Merit, and two Bronze Stars for Valor, a Bronze Star for Merit, two Purple Hearts, his coveted Combat Infantry Badge, and Jump Wings. He'd also been awarded Jump Wings from Vietnam, Korea, and Thailand.

It was Colonel Wickersham's idea to put together the AFBM, and he personally selected the senior officers for his staff from members of the Alaska Defense Force. Men and women who were of a similar mindset; to see Alaska free of the United States of America and hopefully without the spilling of any blood. He had seen enough good men fall already, but now his cause was for the freedom of Alaska and away from political games of Washington DC.

Lying draped across an aged leather couch, Major Allen Peterson reviewed some of the paperwork the Colonel had asked him to check over. Peterson had retired for the night and was in his thick brown terry-robe, over faded gray sweatpants, bare feet, and a Seattle Seahawk's NFL red t-shirt. A retired 64-year old US Air Force Major and Colonel Wickersham's Executive Officer for the AFBM, Peterson was a former C-130 pilot. He was born and raised in Anchorage, Alaska, and the dependent brat of a Lt. Colonel. He had flown 27-missions during Desert Storm. During his time with the service, he'd been assigned in Germany, Japan, California, and Arizona, and was married to Alicia Lee (Rogers), who has been with him for just over 40-years. Resembling the dimensions of the Iron Giant, Peterson has long rail-thin arms, which ended in unusually big hands, long fence post looking legs that ended in huge size 14 4E feet, and a bald head. He could easily grasp a regulation basketball or a triple-decker all meat sandwich in one hand, even with all the veggies thrown in. He also had a large scar on his left shoulder from a childhood incident and still refused to talk about what had happened to him back then. They had one son who was now a Navy Lt. Commander and an F-14 pilot aboard the USS Enterprise. Their 34-year old daughter was unmarried and a teacher at Delta Junction, Alaska. Upon retirement, Allen was awarded the Legion of Merit, but he had also earned seven Air Medals, his Senior Aviator Wings, and was known to be extremely intelligent. But sadly enough, after Desert Storm, he had suffered a problem with booze and took retirement when offered by a caring commander, but he had sobered up afterward to save his marriage and had recently earned his 5-year reward with the AA.

Major Norm Johnson came out of the kitchen with a metal tray stacked high with ham and turkey sandwiches and three glasses of iced tea. A big smile on his face, he set the tray down on the coffee table and made sure each man had a coaster for his iced tea. Norm loved moose season, and the happy expression on his face showed it. Even if no one bagged a moose, he enjoyed the time out here with his two best friends. The only thing he hated was his nightly mad dash for the outhouse in hopes the mosquitoes wouldn't carry him off, and he didn't find a bear waiting for him inside, which had happened one time before to another guest. Norm was 63 years old and retired from the Alaska Air National Guard as a Chief Master Sergeant in Law Enforcement/K-9 qualified. He sat down on a dumpster dive special love seat. The blue cushions came from two other disposed of love seats, and the main part of the furniture piece, which was crème colored, had to be vacuumed several times before the Colonel's wife would allow it in the cabin. But he liked it, and everyone thought it was comfortable. Wendy had added extra pillows and finally accepted it.

Major Johnson was the Operations Officer for the AFBM. He was born in Dillingham, Alaska. Being of half Eskimo and half Aleut blood, he was one tough little fellow, and from the get-go, he had to prove himself on both sides of the family and in school. From all this scrapping, he was bound to become a Marine. Resembling a city fireplug, with not much of a neck and currently weighing in at a chubby, but no one would say it to his face, 214 pounds, Johnson had served with the 9th Marines in Vietnam. One of his two Purple Hearts was for a bayonet wound across his right cheek. He was also awarded a Bronze Star for Valor from that operation. Since he retired from the US Air National Guard, he'd put on another 14-pounds, and Silas had had a few sterns words with him about his pudgy look.

Norm wore his favorite light blue and dark blue patchwork long-sleeved wool shirt and faded blue jeans with knee patches. He walked about in thick blue wool socks after leaving his green insulated hunting boots by the back door. He grabbed a sandwich and a glass of iced tea, took a big bite, and then set back to wait for his commander to begin the meeting. Tonight, it was AFBM business, and tomorrow they were off moose hunting. The standing rule was no matter who got the moose, they all shared in the carrying, butchering, and eating. Two years ago, they all got a moose and were busy for a week in getting the meat carried out, ready for hanging, and even had to shoot an overly curious black bear to keep it away from their kill. They tried to warn it off several times, but it just wouldn't leave and was now a rug mount at ADF Headquarters in Anchorage.

As they consumed their sandwiches, Silas finished cleaning his rifle, loaded it, and placed it by the back door. He wanted to keep it ready in the event a bear got nosey and tried to break into the cabin. It had happened a few times over the years, but they'd been able to chase them off with a couple shots. Each of the men carried the cabin's Mossberg 12 gauge shotgun out to the outhouse for added security but had never had to use it. But there were a few times Silas threatened to cut loose on a swarm of mosquitoes in hopes of bagging a few big ones and mounting them.

"You've looked at the numbers all evening, Al," Silas said between sips of iced tea. "Do we have the numbers for the operation or not?"

Allen thought about it for a moment before answering and then said, "No, Colonel. We do not. As of now, we're a good 15 troops short. We need additional ground troops; people with combat experience if this operation is to be successful." Allen made sure he used the coaster for his iced tea, not wanting to face Wendy's wrath for leaving stains on the wooden coffee table.

"Norm and I worked over this operation for a month or better, Sir, and we first saw the need for 150 troops. But per your request, we've cut it down to 120 personnel. But those numbers are shy by 15, and we need to have that number by February to begin training for the operation or cancel it altogether."

"No!" Silas exclaimed, and he shot up out of his chair. He glared at both men for a moment and then walked over to the stove to toss another chunk of dried spruce into the fire. "We will not cancel the operation. We'll step up our recruiting. I know there are a lot of men and women coming home, getting out, and some are deciding to remain here in Alaska. Some of these troops are Alaskans. We've got to reach out, squeeze the ADF dry of possible applicants, but we will move forward even if our numbers are shy of the mark."

"It will not work, Colonel," Norm said. "We have to have 120 personnel to cover each and every position, or we risk a collapse in the operation and people getting hurt. We decided early on that the last thing we wanted was the spilling of blood."

"Yes, we did agree, but we have to think positive. Put your people out, hit the American Legions and VFW's. They're out there, and we have to find them before February."

Allen looked over at Norm, both men wondering what else it would take to find additional personnel and still maintain the secrecy of the operation. The whole operation's success lay in its secrecy, and one bad apple could ruin everything, and people could get killed.

"C'mon, let's get some sleep," Silas said. "We can discuss this some more tomorrow night. You know we almost never get a moose on the first day, and I could use some shut-eye. This whole getting old bit is for the birds. Next year we use a helicopter."

"To shoot from or lug the critter out with?" Norm asked.

"Both! Hang those Fish and Wildlife jerks. I have to think about my poor back." Silas checked the ground floor. He then walked outside to make sure the generator had plenty of fuel while he swatted the enemy and made his way to the outhouse for his late-night ritual. He had finally made a decision; next year, he'd bring the wife along to do the cooking and keep her side of the bed warm. He was getting too old for this he-man in the woods stuff. He'd leave that for the younger kids. Besides, his old stomach wasn't handling the moose meat that well anymore. Not just moose meat, but all red meat. He knew pretty soon he was going to be one of those fish, chicken, and veggie people, and that thought saddened him. To live in Alaska and not enjoy a great moose steak was unthinkable.

Taking the lower bunk in the first bedroom and leaving the top bunk to lay out tomorrow's hunting ensemble, Allen thought over the operation. He looked at it from every point; from entry to securing the hostages, to blowing the bridges and closing off the runways. The major problem was going to be the one-man scenario, some clown trying to play hero and turning the operation into a blood bath, and the ADF taking all the blame. They had to watch for that one or two-man team that thought they could take on a small army of armed men and women. They also needed to be extremely particular in selecting their hostages; no pregnant women, no old people, no kids under 18, no sick or disabled people. But he knew they'd have the numbers to choose from and the right place to hold them. That part wouldn't be a problem. The next problem would be getting the word out to the world and making sure the world was listening, and for that, they might have to deal with their longtime enemies; Russians, the Chinese, and North Koreans. Even the Iranians would help spread the word, but would it come quick enough before the US can put a strike team together and attack. That was the question that haunted him as he finally drifted off to sleep.

# 4

# HITTING THE CLUBS

*Apartment # 3, First Avenue and Dunkel Street*
*Fairbanks*
*2:10 P.M. 25 September*

Clay was fortunate to live within walking distance of a grocery store, several fast-food eateries, and a decent steak joint, and an American Legion Post. There was also a Yellow Cab service, which was where he was able to land a job. This was only his second day in his new apartment, having grown extremely weary of paying the city's high prices for hotel stays while he waited for something to open up. As usual, the Feds had forgotten to look into the current state of financial affairs in Alaska, which for Fairbanks and Anchorage wasn't all that stable. Both cities were college towns, and besides that, they both had massive military installations. This meant the students and servicemen and their family members, who were already struggling with Alaska's high prices, often had to work two jobs to stay out of the red, grabbed up all the decent employment positions. Even with his exemplary military history and a college degree, Clay couldn't land a job and still stay in the immediate Fairbanks area to fulfill the needs of his undercover assignment.

Clay could've taken one of several positions with various interior native corporations, but the jobs meant living out in the villages or in the field. He was offered positions in the oil fields, working security, and along the Trans-Alaska Pipeline, but these positions also interfered with what he was in Alaska to accomplish. So, he finally responded to a Yellow Cab Company advertisement in search of drivers. He had to get his Commercial Driver's License, but he had maintained his Alaska residency and still collected his yearly Alaska Permanent Dividend, which he promptly signed over to various educational charities. He sure didn't need the money, and he liked to think it was helping someone, the way his parent's money had helped him.

Once properly licensed and a criminal and driver's background run and satisfied by the Fairbanks Police Department, Clay spent two nights working with another driver at no pay. He then rented his own cab for the midnight to noon shift for five days a week. He could've gotten it for six days a week, but he knew he needed some time off for his undercover work. But it worked out pretty well for him, much better than he expected. As a cab driver, he responded to taxi calls to not only the regular bars and fraternal clubs, such as Elks, Eagles, and Moose, but he was also handling calls for Both American Legion Posts and the Veterans of Foreign Wars. He was getting to know the bartenders and, in a short time, a lot of the veterans.

On his two days off, he spent one evening at the VFW and one evening at one of the two American Legions. Though he soon realized taxi drivers, especially those starting out, didn't make a lot of money, he now knew a good tip went a long way in helping these drivers eat their next meal. But so far, he hadn't made any contact with anyone from the Alaska Defense Force but had made eye contact with several good looking women. Most of these, he found out, were married, waiting for their men to return home from an overseas assignment, and he avoided these ladies like the bubonic plague.

While Clay was busy trying to catch up on his sleep on Wednesday afternoon, a hot red 1968 Chevrolet Camaro pulled into the main gate at Eielson Air Force Base, 22-miles east of Fairbanks. Rebuilt from the ground up, this cherry of an automobile sounded like a rumbling herd of finally tuned Harley-Davidson hogs and ran with a custom rebuilt 327 under the hood. The leather interior was red and white, and the 4-speed floor shifter was a Hertz with a red cue ball on top. The owner had gone one step further and installed a Bose sound system, with a 10-CD changer in the trunk beside the bass woofer. For tires, it ran on the rear classic L-50 x15's, shipped directly from the tire plant at St. Louis, Missouri, giving it that certain racing look, and it was fitted with five-spoke Crager Mag Wheels all around. Now this car never saw a day of snow, being parked inside a heated inside storage facility from September 30th through May 15th, but strangely enough, the Security Force Senior Airman who manned the front gate hardly noticed this beautiful muscle car, covered in a minimum of 7 coats of wax, for behind the wheel was his vision of a stunning goddess.

Golden blonde hair cascading down to her hips, she had deeply tanned, blemish-free skin and large eyes the color of cobalt blue. The day was still warm, so she was wearing a white halter top to show her tan off and a pair of faded cut off blue jeans. The young man was at the point of proposing marriage when she broke the spell by asking for a visitor's pass.

Had the lady had a base sticker on the front bumper of her car, the Security Forces Senior Airman would've simply waved her through. Occasionally, they do stop a vehicle now and then to check for proper identification unless they're on alert status and then every vehicle was stopped, inspected, and ID was required.

"I am sorry, Miss, but you'll have to pull in over in front of that trailer over there," He pointed to a 10' x 14' size metal-sided trailer, "... and ask for a pass in there."

"Oh, I haven't met you before. I'm just here to pick up my little brother at Civil Air Patrol."

"I'd remember you, miss, but you'll still have to go over there for a pass."

"Okay then," She said in a flirty voice. "I'll be seein' you."

The Senior Airman stepped out to stop the rest of the traffic from driving by to allow the pretty lady the opportunity to drive across the lanes and pull up in front of the Pass and Registration trailer. The Senior Airman enjoyed working at the Main Gate, especially when he got to meet such attractive young ladies. He hadn't noticed a wedding band or engagement ring, not that he was looking for one and hoped she might stop by one her way back out. He then watched as she climbed out of her Camaro, and his heart nearly stopped as she gracefully walked up each of the three steps to the front door of the trailer. Suddenly, he wished he was one of those geeky clerks working inside there today. Only while she was inside did he take notice of her car, and his eyes grew even wider.

Normally the main gate at Eielson Air Force Base was a two troop post, but for the next hour, the Senior Airman worked it alone. His partner was at a doctor's appointment, and they didn't have enough personnel on duty to handle the second position. But rarely did anything occur on the Main Gate, except for the occasional drunk driver slamming into the concrete bunkers in place in front and behind the wooden gate shack. In the past, there had been protests for different reasons held on the outside of the gate, but it had been some time since the last protest and long before any of the Security Force personnel were currently assigned here.

SSgt Emy Sanders of the Alaska Defense Force and assigned to the Intelligence Section for the newer organized AFBM, leaned against the wooden counter and waited to be noticed by one of the two personnel. One was a woman, and one was a man, both in woodland utilities and somewhere in the mid-20 range in years. Emy was playing an act, one she was very good at. 25yrs old, she had already served 4 years with the US Army as a Military Policeman, with one combat tour in Iraq. She dreamed of employment with either the Fairbanks Police Department or Alaska State Troopers, but they were not hiring at the moment. Born in Tanana, she was raised in Nenana and enlisted in US Army in Fairbanks. When she came home, she had joined the Alaska Defense Force because she didn't want to go back to the sandbox and saw too many National Guardsmen being sent over for a second and even a third tour of duty.

The Colonel knew how well Emy was appreciated by the male soldier and used that as a factor as he prepared for the upcoming operation. Several times Emy had entered Eielson Air Force Base, under the pretense she had come to pick up her little brother, Stephen, who was on base to attend weekly Civil Air Patrol meetings. In fact, Stephen was on base for these meetings, but he had no relationship to Emy and was the grandson of another one of the Colonel's senior NCOs. While on base, Emy used her cell phone to send out various calls to Major Norm Johnson to make reports. She also photographed key points of the runway, tarmac, and flight line activity for the AFBM with her miniature phone. She was never in a restricted area and always appeared to waiting for little brother and in such an obvious vehicle as her eye-catching Camaro. Not something a Soviet or Chinese spy would be driving, which was why it was used.

Emy loved the car and hated that she had to give it up soon. It was time for it to go back into storage to protect it from the cold, ice, and snow. She hoped one day to buy it off its owner, but that was extremely doubtful; her father had spent three years rebuilding it as a special wedding anniversary gift to his wife.

With her Visitor's Pass in hand and a brief flirtation with the clerical geek behind the counter, Emy waved to the gate guard and drove down Flight Line Avenue. She made it look as if she was on the phone, but in fact, she was taking photographs the entire time. After she picked up Stephen at Building #1121 on the flight line, home to the Civil Air Patrol and Aero Club, she pulled back onto Flight Line Avenue and headed south instead of going right back to the gate. She went all the way down to the Control Tower & Base Operations; Bldgs # 1215/1216 and then turned around in the Base Operations parking lot. This allowed her an opportunity to take additional photographs of the area. After leaving the base, she then proceeded southeast on the Richardson Highway, which happened to run parallel to the south side of the flight line, and there were no trees to block her view or from taking additional photographs, which was done all the time by both locals and tourists. This time she used a more professional digital camera with a telescoping lens and shot quick photos over her left shoulder. People had been photographing Eielson from the highway for over 40-years. The more classified aircraft were kept from view, where security was tighter, and K-9 units were involved.

There were some who believed Eielson Air Force Base began as an auxiliary field, only for military fliers who were having trouble reaching trying Ladd Army Air Corp Base during the Tanana Valley's heavy fog. Ladd is now known as Fort Wainwright. There are others, though, who stick with the Air Force version that simply states the government was looking for an interior landing field that could handle the newer and larger bombers. Whichever the case, the first plan was to build a field 29 miles south of Nenana, but that didn't work out, and extending the runway at Ladd was prevented by Mother Nature; Alaska's Chena River wouldn't allow it. So, Eielson was born, which was named after the famous Alaska aviator Ben Eielson.

Over the decades, Eielson had been home to an assortment of aircraft, from prop-driven fighters and bombers to jet tankers and massive reconnaissance birds used to monitor Soviet submarines. F-4 Phantom fighter/bombers were used here as alert birds, launched on two minutes notice to respond and chase Soviet aircraft back out of US air space. As a result, Eielson had become quite more than simply an auxiliary airfield, but a thriving proud member of the Alaskan Air Command and under the Pacific Air Command. Along the way, its personnel had become part of the growing citizenry of Moose Creek, North Pole, Salcha, and Fairbanks.

The 354th Fighter Wing was stationed at Eielson, which included the 354th Fight Wing Staff Agencies, 354th Logistics Group, 35th Medical Group, 354th Operations Group, and 354th Support Group. Eielson also played host to other tenant units; 168th Refueling Wing of the Alaska Air National Guard, Detachment 460 Air Force Technical Applications Center, Arctic Survival School of Detachment 1, 66th Training Squadron, Air Training Command, Detachment 632 of the Office of Special Investigations and 3rd Air Support Operations Squadron, and one of the better-known outfits in Alaska is the Detachment 1, 210th Rescue Squadron, Alaska Air National Guard.

The famous A-10 Thunderbolt, also known as the Warthog because of its appearance and fierceness, was stationed at Eielson and used by the 355th Fighter Squadron, but recently moved to the lower 48. There was a lot of speculation about the return of the Warthog since it was a primary infantry support bird needed by the army to combat enemy armor. The F-16 Falcon (or Viper) is used quite effectively by the 18th Fighter Wing.

Standing a very fit 5'7", Emy was more than happy to get Stephen off her hands. She knew the kid had a childish crush on her and was growing weary of manually adjusting his eyes all the time. Then he'd laugh, and five minutes later, he'd be glaring at her again. She finally told his father, who took the boy aside and sent him to his mother. That would be the end of that. She hoped.

Emy had made a promise to the Colonel that if the Fairbanks Police or Alaska State Troopers opened up their hiring lists, she would not seek employment with them until the AFBM operation was completed. She knew he needed her, and that alone felt pretty cool, but she was getting tired of living at home with mom and dad. Driving the Camaro was over for the season, she wasn't going back to school, and she couldn't leave the area because of the needed training for the operation. She had a rifle squad to prepare, and at this point, she wasn't all that sure they were ready for anything like the planned operation and was doubtful they would be. She knew all the reasons why the operation was necessary and agreed with them, but she still wasn't as sure as the Colonel if they could carry this operation off without someone being killed.

Emy's folks had left Nenana, where her father had worked as a mechanic/welder on the river barge traffic, and moved to Fairbanks, where he had taken a job with the Riverboat Discovery Tourism Trade on the Chena River. He was now about to retire, but all along, he had remained a staunch member of the Alaskan Independence Party and had been a good friend with the party's founder, Joe Vogler. Her parents owned a very nice home in the Nenana Subdivision, off behind Airport Way, and she had her own room and a second bedroom she used for her various hobbies. She was into military action figures, combat gaming, and collecting historic firearms. Her father had presented her with her paternal grandfather's 45-70 Winchester, and it kicked like a Missouri Mule. She owned a replica of the Colt 1911 she had carried in Iraq, while most of the female MPs were forced to carry the 9mm. She also owned not one but two semi-automatic M-4's and a collection of vintage .38 caliber revolvers of various makes, along with several lever-action Winchesters and Marlins, and two ancient Henry rifles. On the top shelf in her hobby room, she had every military action figure the McFarlane Toy Company put out, well over $2,000 worth, and the value was always growing.

Dad and Mom kept hoping she'd bring home a nice young man, but it was always guns, maneuvers, and her toys. He began to wonder if she'd become a lesbian in the army, but his wife had said no, having already covered that subject with her during an embarrassing moment in the kitchen. She said Emy didn't quit laughing until she split her favorite skirt, spit out a mouthful of tuna fish sandwich, and then ran to her room and laughed some more.

It was after that conversation with her mom that Emy realized it had been a very long time since she'd had a date with a guy. Oh, she had some drinking parties with buddies from the unit or her new ADF friends, but not one single guy dude to sit and maybe hold hands... I need a date!

She was working part-time at the airport, working private security at the security scanners, and couldn't think of anything more boring. It was either this, drive cab or dance topless, and cab driving was beneath her and the other vocation, her father would disown her. But much like cab driving, she spent her shift listening to people's complaints. Except this time, it was as she ran her hands over the female's bodies, tried very hard not to smile, and be very gentle with the frightened children.

Emy thought this whole thing was stupid. Anyone who had anything they wanted to bring across our borders could easily slip across through our northern or southern borders quite easily. If they wanted to blow up a plane, they could rent a hotel room outside LAX or any number of airports and use an RPG or three of them to take out a DC-10 taking off or arriving. All this did was anger the citizens and try to make them think the government was doing something. She saw a lot of this sort of thing in Iraq. She never felt anyone truly wanted to win the war, much like she heard the Vietnam vets speak of in the VFW's and American Legion Bars. Yeah, that's where I need to go tonight, and I'd better take a cab home. I feel a good drunk coming on, and I don't need a DWI on my record to block my chances of becoming a cop...If we even survive next summer, and I'm not in Leavenworth Federal Pen on an all-expense 20-year vacation.

Out of her geeky looking security uniform, which looked as if it came from one of Walmart's overseas bins, and into her more relaxed faded blue jeans and Seattle Seahawk Football jersey, Emy locked the front door behind her and quietly left the house. A friend from work waited for her at the curb to give her a ride down to the Back Door Lounge. She often began there and would then end up at either the American Legion or

VFW. She liked to be somewhat on the comfortable side before all the war stories began. Nowadays, there were vets from Korea, Vietnam, and one or two guys who actually owned up to going ashore at Grenada, then Desert Storm, and the two wars that brought the US back into the sandbox. Most of the regulars knew her and how she had served as a combat MP in Iraq, how she had earned a Purple Heart from an IED, and a Bronze Star for Valor by pulling her supervisor from out of the bottom of their burning overturned HMMWV. She'd been put in for a Silver Star, but someone back in the states didn't think women belonged in combat, and a Silver Star might highlight their heavy involvement as MP's. She cared, but she and her supervisor were both alive; that was the main thing. Whenever the challenge coins came out for the next round, her Bronze Star coin usually kept her from buying. But with this war going on so long, she'd been buying more and more lately. The last time some guy from Anchorage tossed out a coin, it was for his Distinguished Service Cross, and she felt proud to buy him a drink. But she saw it in his eyes; they were dead like. He had that infamous 1000 yard stare made famous in Vietnam. She wondered if she had acquired it too, but no one had commented on it.

Sometimes these military coins were for the people who gave you the highest-ranking coin, and there was always some clown in the group with a general's coin. Or highest medal, not their own, and once she had seen a Medal of Honor coin tossed on the table. It made for an interesting game and kept the drinks flowing, which helped hide the wounds, and before long, everyone was either an Audi Murphy, John Wayne, or George Armstrong Custer. She had one 101st Airborne veteran who claimed to be a direct descendent to Chief Crazy Horse, and she thought he had the look.

The American Legion on South Cushman usually closed at 2 a.m., while the one on 1st Avenue wrapped things up depending on the crowd. The VFW stayed open until the last drunk was dragged out feet first by a counselor of the AA, and that's where she was headed tonight. Liquor laws in Alaska said the bars had to close by 5 a.m. and could not re-open before 8 a.m.

The Yellow Cab that picked her up had a new driver, and between the bar and VFW, they shared looks in the rearview mirror. She didn't feel like talking, and because she smelled of booze, he didn't feel much like starting up a conversation with her. Clay never liked intoxicated women, even good-looking drunk women, and this one was probably another loyal wife who was out partying while her devoted husband was off fighting to defend her growing bar bill. He had listened to too many sob-stories of young troops who received "Dear John" letters in the mail.

He dropped her off at the door to the VFW and didn't bother to get out of the taxi to open the door for her. He told her the fare, which was $7.60, and took her crinkled up $10 bill through the passage window. With all the robberies, the taxi driver association had gotten the owners to purchase bulletproof windows that separated the passengers from the driver. There was a small pass-through slot for money. But as she climbed out, she told him to keep the change, and for some reason, she couldn't explain why, she grew angry and flipped him the bird with the middle finger salute, slammed the car door, and stormed into the VFW.

Clay looked down at the $10 bill and felt like tossing it out the window. But he had rent to pay on this cab and couldn't be tossing good money aside. Why such a beautiful woman was behaving like such a jerk was beyond him, and then he suddenly wondered, Did she get the government telegram today? Was she informed her husband, brother, or maybe even her father was killed in action or in some training accident?

He sat there for a moment, waiting to see if anyone was coming outside in need of a cab. He then decided she was probably simply a boozer and at least happy she wasn't driving tonight.

Perched on a tall bar stool at the left side of the nearly empty bar, a Long Island Tea set untouched in front of her. Emy felt teary-eyed and wasn't sure why. She couldn't understand why she was so nasty with that good looking cab driver. She hadn't flipped off anyone since one of the Marines in Iraq gave her a hard time. Then to make matters even more memorable, that same Marine corporal visited her in the hospital on base, and they shared a few moments together. He had apologized for his conduct, having learned of what Emy had done and remembered what his mother would've said to him had she still been alive for being so rude to a woman. They had a good laugh, though it hurt a bit as some of the stitches stretched, and then he left. After coming home, she learned from the corporal's buddy how he'd been killed by a sniper a month later. She cried that night while her mother held her. It was the first time she had cried since coming home.

Emy pushed the drink away. She had had enough for one night and looked at her wallet, counted her money, and saw that she had spent nearly $50 and felt like crap. Shaking her head, he looked over at George, the bartender, and said, "Georgie, would you call me a cab, please. I'm done for tonight."

"Sure thing, Emy…would you like some free hot coffee? We use regulation GI grounds to give you that home town smell." George reached over, picked up the VFW cell phone, and made the call to Yellow Cab. Most of the bars preferred Yellow Cab after dark. The cabs were easily identifiable, and after a couple cab drivers in Anchorage had used their cabs to commit rape of their female passengers, bar patrons simply felt safer in them in the dark.

"No coffee," Emy replied. "I hope to get some sleep, but I'll probably wake Mom up when I get home, and then we'll sit down and have one of our long talks. Second thought, give me the coffee. I need to be prepared for that old woman. She can blindside me and the strangest times. Last time it was about how old she was getting and her desire for grandchildren. Do I look like I'm ready to have kids?"

"No comment," George answered.

"Good answer," Emy said.

A moment later, Emy heard the horn honk outside and knew her taxi had arrived. She wasn't even thinking of her last driver when she walked outside, opened the rear passenger side door, and climbed in, only to find Clay glaring at her.

Suddenly, without being able to stop herself, Emy burst out laughing hysterically, but before Clay could react, she vomited all over his back seat, and the vile odor filled the taxi. Clay opened his door, ran inside the VFW, and advised the bartender what had happened. George came outside with an armful of clean bar towels to clean Emy off while Clay worked on the upholstery. He kept some upholstery cleaner and towels in the trunk, along with some lemon odor spray to kill the stench.

"Man, what should I do with her?" Clay asked the bartender. "You got anyone inside who can take care of her?"

"All I got are old boozers waiting to die," George replied. He looked her over and decided, "I don't think she needs to go to the hospital, and she lives right here in town."

Emy was sick and just semi-conscious, but she was able to hand her license to Clay, and holding a towel in front of her mouth, she whispered, "Take me there... mom an' dad... they'll take care of me."

"All right," Clay agreed, "but we're going with all the windows down, and lady, this is going to cost you extra!"

Emy responded with a nod of her head, and then she leaned back against her seat. George took his towels and walked over to the trash dumpster, and tossed them inside. He went inside and washed himself up before announcing, "Last call!" George had gotten weary of drunks 35-years ago, but by then, he didn't know what else to do for a vocation. He'd worked as a bartender from one end of Alaska to another, from Unalaska to Nome, across to Skagway, Juneau, and Ketchikan, to Valdez and Anchorage and back to Fairbanks, where he'd received a Medical Discharge from the Army and retired on 50% disability for mistakenly standing in the way of an AK-47 bullet in the Battle of Hue, South Vietnam in 1968. He was an alcoholic, a heavy user of marijuana, and had recently learned he was dying from Liver Cancer. So, he decided he was not going to bother with washing those foul-smelling bar towels and, in fact, treated himself to the Long Island Tea Emy had left behind. He hated to see good booze wasted.

Though the drive to Emy house took less than 8-minutes, for Clay, the minutes slowly ticked by, and he was breathing through his mouth. He knew his driving was done for the night, and he'd be busy the rest of his shift trying to clean up his cab and trying to get the odor out of the back seat. He had to turn the taxi over to the day shift driver, and he would not be very happy with the shape it was in now. Very rapidly, he was learning there was a lot more to this taxi driving than he ever thought there was. He couldn't wait to see the face of his so-called doctor at Bassett for his visit next week when he briefs him on the people of the night he meets. Every two weeks, he was going to Fort Wainwright for his official visit, sometimes for medication refills, lab tests, x-rays, and mental check-ups, and other times to actually visit the doctor. But in each case, he'd be in a room with his case officer, a senior FBI agent, who would record whatever Clay had to report. Which hadn't been much so far, but they knew it would be slow going at first, and that's why they wanted him up here so fast.

Clay pulled up into Emy's driveway and noticed in his headlights in the carport in front of a two-car garage a vintage Camaro body shape under a gray cloth cover. He thought about leaving the taxi running but turned to look at his unconscious passenger and decided it safer to turn the engine off as he went to the front door to wake up the house. It only took a moment before mom and dad were at the door, saw the cab, and dashed out to see if their daughter was okay. Only when they reached the cab was Clay able to explain what had happened, and being her parents, he tried to make it easy on them with, "Could be food poisoning. It comes on pretty quick, and once they upchuck, they begin to feel better."

But dad knew better. He had a nose. "She's drunk and baptized your cab, right?"

"Yes, Sir," Clay said, almost apologetically, and then helped dad carry his daughter inside the house.

"We'll take her from here, son. But uh, how much does she... do we owe you?"

"Look, I'm done for the night, and that's the truth," He had to stay in the role. "I gotta clean this heap up for the next driver, or I'm out of a job."

"You can do it here if you want," Dad said and pointed toward the end of the house garage door. "I've got power washers, steam cleaners, even power waxers... you name it, and I got it."

"Is that Camaro out there yours?" Clay asked.

"You knew it right away, didn't yuh. Most Camaro lovers would," Dad said. A smile on his face, he waved him toward the garage, "C'mon, my wife can handle Emy while I get you started, and we can talk cars later."

"Sure, anything that saves me money is okay with me."

Clay was having his second helping of pancakes, with real homemade boysenberry syrup, when a very subdued Emy walked into the dining room. She wore a floor-length white terry bathrobe; her hair still wet from her second shower, and what Clay thought to be well-faded two-piece light blue flannel pajamas under her robe. She also had white bunny slippers on her feet. Mom came into the dining room with a steaming mug of hot coffee and handed it to her daughter. "Come, honey, sit down and meet Clay. We've gotten to know him, and you two have a lot in common."

She glanced over at Clay, trying to decide what his ethnic background was. At first sight, she took him for an Italian or possible Greek, but then she went with Plains Indian or possibly an Alaskan Interior tribe, but not a full blood. She was pretty good at picking people out, which helped her with her job, and she had nailed several insurgents because of it and been awarded an Army Commendation Medal for snagging a carload of Iranians insurgents attempting to get on base overseas. They were found to be in possession of automatic weapons.

Emy sat down beside her father, opposite Clay, and couldn't help but notice the man had a pretty good appetite. She kept looking at him over the rim of her cup as she listened to her father and him discuss cars. When she heard how her dad had removed the tarp off the Camaro so Clay could see it, she knew her Dad liked him. A lot of people came by the house who heard about her father's muscle car, and he'd never give them a view of it. He'd tell them to wait for next summer, explaining how the taking the tarp off and on could scratch the paint- which was hogwash. He just kept his baby private and only let her drive it to support the party and help the Colonel. She knew how he missed Old Joe Vogler.

"Hope you don't mind, honey, but Mom took Clay over to show him your medals."

"Awe, Dad!" Emy complained. Clay could see she was embarrassed, but he also saw how proud her parents were of her duty to country and display of valor.

"It's okay, honey," Mom said. She had sat down beside Emy and grasped her right hand. "Clay here, he was US Army too. He was a Captain with... what'd you call that group, young man?"

"I was with the 82nd Airborne. I went into the sandbox as a 1st lieutenant and got tossed out on my ear as a captain. Couldn't make my gold leaf, so they offered me a 70% discharge for my wounds, and I accepted it." Clay pointed towards the living room. "You should be very proud of those awards, Emy... if I may call you that? Not a lot of women were allowed to see combat, much less win an award for valor. The Purple Heart part, we all got those for forgetting to duck."

Emy nodded her head, agreeing with him, and then she said, "I'm glad you're still here, Clay. I wanted to apologize to you for how I acted last night. I behaved like an ass, and when I climbed back into the cab and saw it was you again, I just couldn't hold it in. After that, well, I paid for my sins."

"All is forgiven... your parents told me about working out at the airport. All I could find was driving a cab. Even with my DD Form 214 and my college degree...I attended the University of Alaska...the one here in town, but I'm still a half breed from Minto, stuck between two worlds that still don't get along that well, even now. I've got cousins out there that won't acknowledge me and family on my dad's side who hate having a breed for a grandson."

"Sounds like some sour grapes there, Clay. College up on the hill gave you a great education, the military a lot of experience, and even better, the leadership of good men and women. Now is a new chapter in your life, don't enter into with a chip on your shoulder. Nothing good comes from it. I've known a lot of people from all racial and religious backgrounds, and I still say a jerk is a jerk, and the rest can always be your friend. Now admittedly, I don't understand these Muslims you two had to deal with, but... well, I'll shut up. I'm entering an area I'm not up to par on. I'd just prefer Alaska for Alaskans, whatever color or creed."

Clay looked at Emy's dad for a moment, unsure exactly what to take from all that. He glanced over at Emy, thought of her war record, and for a brief moment, wondered if she was a member of the Alaskan Defense Force. But she knew better than to step too hard and let it drop. "How do you feel now?"

"Like I should've known better...But how much money did you lose last night? I must have cost you a dozen fares or better. From what Mom says, the car really stunk!"

"It did," Clay said. "We came here with all the windows down, and that was after the bartender cleaned you up, and I worked on the back seat."

"No photographs, right?" Emy asked. "It would look pretty bad for me out on YouTube or Facebook."

"Nope, I missed my chance," Clay said with a laugh. "I could've sold them down at the airport for $10 a copy."

"So, Clay, what sort of medals did you come home with?" Dad asked.

"Dad!" Emy couldn't believe her dad had asked Clay that. "You'll have to forgive them, Clay. He's not prior service and doesn't understand the whole humility thing."

Dad stood up and walked around the table, pointing toward an antique buffet in the living room. It held several very nice car show trophies. "See those. I'm proud of those because I rebuilt that Camaro from the frame up. I did everything on it. I love looking at those trophies, and I love my car… not quite as much as I love you two. But those are my medals. That's why I have your medals out there on display. I'm proud of them. I never served, but you chose to and did us proud. You nearly got killed, but you saved someone's life and caught some bad guys in the process too. Humility is fine, but when asked, it's nice to reply, so a man knows the answer."

Clay could see Mom and Dad's eyes were locked on his nervous look of apprehension, waiting for a reply or told to mind their own business. But he needed to come up with something, or he'd never be invited back inside this house, and this might be his first and only opening into the ADF. "I was awarded three Purple Hearts; one for being shot and another two for RPG shrapnel…that's a rocket-propelled grenade… They shoot them off like a small bazooka… sort of." He looked at Emy and then continued. I won a Silver Star and two Bronze Stars, but I had very good men with me and feel those medals also belong to them. I also have my jump wings and my Combat Infantrymen's Badge."

"Wow…" Dad said, but I like best of all what you said about the others being involved. Now that's humility, as I understand the word."

Emy grinned and then said, "You officer types, always gettin' the best medals for yourselves."

"Ma'am, if this wasn't your house and you hadn't been so sick, I think I might've taken offense to that remark. "Clay then looked to Mom and said, "That was a mighty fine breakfast, but now I must leave. I've got paperwork to do and another shift to pull tonight." Clay stood to his feet, shook hands with Dad, and grinned across the table at Emy.

"Here, let me walk you to the door," Emy said and added, "...an' no remarks about my slippers. I've had them since Junior High, and my feet still fit."

"Wouldn't think about it, Miss; I personally happen to like those cute little bunny slippers," Clay said, just as he made a dash for the door before she could whack him with a pancake turner.

After Clay left, Emy turned to her father and asked him, "Did you pay him for his lost time, Dad?"

"He wouldn't let me, Emy. But he loved my shop. That man knows his ways around a set of tools, and he knows cars. I bet he could've taken that Camaro apart and rebuilt again in less than 24 hours. He has the eye, Emy."

"Wish you could've paid him, though. He's on disability, and even as a captain, that's doesn't mean he's making a lot of money."

"I know, honey," Dad said. "That's why I invited him over for this week-end's barbecue. I want the Colonel to get a gander at him. He's an Alaskan, he's tried and true, and he's already been off to see the elephant."

"Oh, Daddy, you got that from some movie."

"Sure did, but I understood what it meant. He's a man, and any man will enjoy a good brew, a good barbecued steak, and a good gathering with some pretty great folks."

"What do you think of him, Daddy?"

"It's not what I think of him, honey, it's what you think of him that counts, and yes, that line came from some movie too. Fact is, every line, every remark, has been used in a movie. We can't get around it because that's what we say. And you're dodging the question?"

Emy smiled, turned from her dad, and walked out to the kitchen to help mom clean up. Time for another mom and daughter chat, so dad decided he'd go out to the garage and play with his tools. Truth is, he did like the man, and he sincerely hoped the Colonel would too.

# 5

# SEEING THE SHRINK

*Bassett Army Hospital*
*Fort Wainwright, Alaska*
*Room 318 - 1622 Hours (4:22 P.M.), 30 September*

Clay was a bit bleary-eyed, having been awakened 25-minutes earlier from only 6-hours of sleep. But he was off tonight and was looking forward to hitting the sack early. He was supposed to be here seeing his doctor for a check-up over concern due to some pain generating around his chest wound's scar tissue, where he'd taken the AK-47 bullet nearly three years earlier. But actually, he was here to brief his FBI handler on his progress in working his way into the Alaska Defense Force Militia. Up until this week, Clay had little to report, except for a few drinks with men he suspected of as members and how he didn't believe anyone was watching him. This would be the first move the Alaska Defense Force would do if they were interested in Clay for their special unit if they had one. Someone would be following to see if he was someone other than who he said he was. A lot of people were being used in this operation to provide him a good cover, but for the moment, Clay was meeting with only a Dr. Adams.

"How are you feeling, Clay?" Dr. Adams asked. The middle-aged man entered Room # 318 and closed the door. He locked it to ensure they would not be disturbed and then grinned as he lugged with him his heavy black briefcase across the room to sit down beside Clay. They ignored the exam table and only used the two chrome metal stiff back chairs in the room, with gray felt material stretched over thick cardboard and fiberboard. There was also a small rollaway table in the room for the doctor's tools or the nurse's equipment. But Dr. Adams used the table to hold his digital recorder, which he removed from his briefcase, along with his digital camera. He took two photos of Clay, which were to be accomplished on each visit for his own case file. He used these to show any evidence of visible stress to the operative while on assignment.

Clay estimated Doc Adams to be in his late fifties to early sixties. He was partially balding with white and grayish colored hair, now thinning across the crown of his head. Doc's face was circular in shape, causing Clay to think of a small pie pan, yet the rest of the man's body was quite thin and lanky, at around 160 pounds. Doc's hazel eyes were heavily bloodshot, surrounded by an array of wrinkles and a flock of crow's feet. His cheeks were beginning to droop to become heavy jowls and were splattered with reddish age spots of various sizes. He wore very thick brown framed trifocal eyeglasses, and he had a mustache that drooped down well past the corners of his mouth. Doc had also apparently forgotten to shave this morning because his chin had stubbles showing. Doc was wearing the hospital white coat, with his blue officer's name tag pinned to his right breast area. He had the silver leaves of a Lieutenant Colonel pinned on his collar, but Clay doubted this man was really an officer. He would never get away with such a long mustache, and he was simply too old for a Lt. Colonel in today's Army. The FBI made a key mistake in selecting this man for his handler, but again, he doubted anyone was going to come on base to check him out on these hospital visits. At least the man was wearing a blue stethoscope around his neck to show he was a doctor. He hoped the people would simply believe he was a reserve officer or possibly National Guard if they even took time to notice.

"Do you have anything to report, Captain?" Doc had turned his digital recorder on, took a seat, and waited, hoping his trip up from Seattle and Anchorage hadn't been a waste of time, like the previous three weeks. Yet, he couldn't really say that. He did like Clay, and as a clinical psychologist, with a large amount of training in suspect profiling, he did enjoy learning more about the Athabascan people and adding what he learned here to his notes. He was putting a new training manual together for the Federal Bureau of Investigation and planned on using some of what he has learned from this case into it.

"Yes, sir, I may have made a connection...at least with a member of the Alaska Defense Force." Clay went on for the next 25-minutes, explaining what had happened the other night with Emy, her parents, and their views and the coming barbecue. Clay hoped this barbecue would lead to something, for he had grown weary of seeing the sorry shape some of his cousins from Minto and other Alaska Natives communities became when they come to Fairbanks and got all boozed up. A lot of them travel here from dry villages, where liquor is not allowed, and they spend all their time and money on brew. He'd found them living under the various bridges, which cross the Chena River in town, even large groups living in hotel rooms or unconscious on the street. Fairbanks Community Patrols would pick the unconscious ones off the street and haul them to shelters, or the combative ones were transported to the Fairbanks Correctional Center for a Title 47, which involved a 24- hour hold. This allowed the state to protect them while they were unable to care for themselves. During the winter, the Community Patrol was extremely busy, trying to pull the drunks off the street before they froze to death, and they were not always successful.

Clay knows his people; the Athabascan and other Alaskan natives needed help, and a lot of good charity and church organizations were out there to assist them, yet so many of these Alaskan Natives didn't want any help and their poor conduct brought about such a pathetic example of the Athabascan Indian or the other native groups. They pay their taxi fare, and he hauls them from one bar to another; usually, only the bars which still keep serving these intoxicated natives. But, since coming home, he had seen that there were now some bars that won't serve drunks anymore, mostly for fear of losing their liquor licenses. The intoxicated person will complain, sometimes violently, but the bartender is protected by Title 4 of the Alaskan law, which covered the liquor business. No intoxicated person was to be served, of any color or creed.

However, some of the bartenders would continue to put a drink out even when the patron was unconscious and even lying flat on the floor. Then Clay is called to haul the drunk to some hotel room, often with the help of four-guys carrying the unconscious man or woman out and tossing them into the back of his cab. He's handed the money and directed where to take him or her. Clay would first make sure the passenger was still alive and not in need of a visit to the Emergency Room. He had already taken three passengers to the Emergency Room, not that the staff was all that happy to receive them. A security officer had to be summoned to stand-by in the event the unconscious person suddenly came to and started swinging. When Clay took them to their usual hotels, he'd turn them over to the more sober people of the room and notice how 10-14 people were often sharing the room. He had run into three of his cousins doing this, but they hadn't recognized him, and he didn't bother to stage a reunion. Fairbanks had several hotels the Alaskan Natives used for their weekly visits, coming from over a dozen dry communities and the owners seemed to care less how many people were put into a room as long as the money was paid.

Even with some of his family members here, Clay knew if he drove out to Minto right then, he'd find most of the community dry and a good fair share of them living a Christian lifestyle. A flame of the Holy Spirit had come to Minto, setting off a revival, and a lot of people had given their lives to the Lord. But a few had held out to their traditional beliefs, and some of them now go to Fairbanks or even Anchorage for their fun.

Doc Adams could see his young officer was under a lot of stress. He wasn't agreeable with the plan to bring Clay back into his own area for this undercover operation, knowing how Clay would be feeling the extreme effects of cultural differences of going from the Middle East to Tennessee and on to Alaska in such a short time period. Here, he'd b thrown into a situation where he could be dealing with his own Athabascan family ties. Every rule he knew of was against it, but they refused to listen to him. He had argued in vain how this was not the same as when Clay operated in Libya or Egypt, for here in Alaska, he'd be dealing directly with family, where he was already known as a breed, berated by old friends and even family. It would cause a great strain upon him. In only this little time, it was having this effect. Clay had shared briefly about his feeling for seeing all the drunkenness and misbehavior among his people and how the Whites and Afro-Americans on the streets took advantage of them or hurt them.

Doc needed to temper Clay down a bit and began a series of questions about his own life, "Clay, I've seen from your medical file you had some difficulty with alcohol in the past. Have you had any problem lately, any desire to take a night off and get intoxicated...wasted?"

"Sir, I'd be lying to you if I said the old desire never crept up on me, but I am still able to call upon the Lord to defeat those attacks by the enemy."

"Yes, it does help to have faith, especially in our line of work. A lot of good agents or other law enforcement officers are not able to handle it well on their own, and they suffer grievously for the lack of it."

"Were... or are you a drinking man, sir?" Clay asked. He also noticed the recorder was still going. Doc Adams never turned it off during their meetings and wondered if he would now. But he didn't.

"I've fought my share of demons, son. Cost me my marriage and nearly my job. Now I am a member of Alcoholics Anonymous and have my 15-year coin. Whenever I get the compulsion to have a drink, I pull out this coin, and it keeps me dry for another day." Doc Adams showed the coin to Clay.

"What about faith, sir...beyond the higher power the AA teaches on?" Clay handed the coin back; it was the first 20-year AA coin he had ever seen. He wondered if the AA had their coins before the military began using theirs. He'd heard from a lot of Vietnam veterans who said they never had coins in their day, how it was a new fad.

Doc Adams grinned and started to shut his recorder off, but then stopped and looked back at Clay. "I am of the Jewish Faith... though it has been a very long time since I last entered a synagogue to pray, and I know you are a Christian. Our common religious enemy is the Muslim, yet he follows the same God of Abraham as we both do. I think you'd agree it makes for such a confusing world."

"What is your opinion concerning the fanatics...the terrorism?"

"Clay, I do not believe in the slaying of innocents...of women and children. Only God the Father can order such a thing, as He did in the Old Testament when He ordered the destruction of whole cities. He also ordered the death of a lot of Israelites who refused to obey His laws. But Christians have also done this to Muslims and Jews, and now this also involves what some of my Israeli brothers and sisters are doing to the Palestine Nation. Or what the alleged Christians do to each other because of a difference of skin color." Doc Adams lowered his head and was silent for a moment, and Clay remained quiet also. Then Doc lifted his head and, with saddened eyes, looked into Clay's face and said, "No, sir, all we do is carry forth the battle standard of Satan when we do his work and not God's."

Clay stood up and walked to the side of the room, looking at an aged Department of Defense eye chart, and then he turned to face Doc Adams, "That was quite a mouthful, Doc...you sure you wanted it recorded?"

"I learned long ago, it is better to be honest, and then you do not get trapped by lies, but that is a difficult rule for one carrying out your duties. But my best advice is to not get too attached to this Emy. She is only your assignment, not your future. When this case is brought to closure, and a conspiracy is proven, you will have to testify against her and her parents, and she will hate you until the day you die. Do you realize that?"

"Yes, Sir," Clay replied. "Sitting there at breakfast with the family, I knew I might be put into a position that would involve sending them to federal prison. But I also have a job to do, and though I have trouble with the Lower 48 at times, especially when they interfere with Alaska's future, we're still part of the United States, and I am proud of our country's history." Clay set back down and added, "Is that what you wanted to hear, Doc?"

Doc Adams had that fatherly grin on his face again and reached across to pat Clay gently on the top of his left knee. "You're doing fine, but take it very slow at that barbecue. You've worked enough of these operations to know how easy it is for an operative to get too pushy with too many questions from the beginning and end up dead. Simply enjoy the food, meet the people, and leave the rest to them. We have time, no matter what Washington thinks. I doubt anyone is going to do anything up this far north during an Alaskan winter. Besides anything else, you'd never get any southern reporters up here to cover the news. Those people with all the flashy dental work, expensive hairstyles, and $5,000 monthly clothing allowances love their comforts, and freezing to death is not in their contracts. No, if anything is going to happen up here, it will be in the summer. Still, it's the target or targets we have no information on, and this we must obtain before the snow melts."

"I see you watch a lot of cable news, Doc. Our local news people are more homey-like. We've got a few people who've grown up on our TV news, going from young '20s to early '50s. We even had one who left the news to become a church pastor. No, we rarely see an outsider newscaster up here unless the Pope is coming through to meet the President, which is pretty rare, or the Iditarod Dogsled Race is on, or we suffer another oil spill or massive earthquake. We may be the largest state in the US, but we don't make enough news unless it's on the grand scale. I think that last time we had the big commentators up here was when former Governor Sarah Palin was running for Vice President, and now she's become one of them."

"Do you want her back?" Doc Adams asked in jest.

"I'd have to think a bit on that one, Doc." Clay stood to his feet, shook hands with Doc, and agreed on another meeting a week from now in the same room. "Hey, Doc, where do you go from here? Do you stay in Fairbanks for a bit or fly straight out?"

"I'll be in Anchorage in about three hours from now, Clay...Tomorrow, I'll be in Seattle. But I'll be back up here next week. You and I are working together on this one. No one else will be here to see you. In the event they are, you make sure they have those two names you received in Washington, as you were instructed. If not, take whatever action you need and get out. If you do not believe you can make it off base, turn yourself over to the MPs and demand they turn you over to the Provost Martial. Then you will have him contact J. Edgar Hoover Office in DC and not any of the Alaskan offices... only because the offices up here won't be able to help you if this operation is compromised. Okay...you got it?"

"Yes, Sir...I got it. See you next week." Clay shook hands with the Doc and was out the door. Half an hour later, he was back at his apartment with a take-out dinner from Burger King. He was a Whopper fan but also liked the Big Mac. Driving cab and not working out, he had noticed he was beginning to put on a few pounds and needed to watch out with these fast-food meals. He was drinking either too much soda or coffee to stay awake at night and eating far too many doughnuts. He'd failed to get any jogging in as he had promised himself. He needed to find a job that was more physical, possibly working in one of the lumber yards or some kind of construction, but it seemed all the jobs were taken up by active-duty servicemen needing extra work to make ends meet and college kids between classes. It saddened Clay to see how low the pay was for the enlisted personnel, especially up here in Alaska and down in Hawaii.

## THE BARBECUE AT EMY'S HOUSE
## SATURDAY AFTERNOON

For the better part of the last two hours, Emy had spent her time working in the kitchen to help her mother prepare the side dishes for today's barbecue. The first thing they did was clean up Dad's mess. He'd spent an hour last night making up a gallon of his special raspberry chipotle barbecue dressing for today's event, and there was sauce splattered everywhere, on the walls and over the countertops. It was his annual end of summer gala event, open to mostly hunters, their wives and kids, and a few well-chosen friends. There were also a few car enthusiasts added in to keep the conversations rounded out. But job talk was forbidden.

Emy's mom had painstakingly baked fresh dinner rolls to feed 75 people, with enough deviled eggs to fill up the extra refrigerator in the garage, a longtime favorite of the old man's and on the menu for every holiday, and she only used organic eggs. Emy had started slow cooking a five-gallon vat of barbecued red and black beans late last night, and it was still simmering away at 2 p.m. On a large side counter set 5 cakes, three of them being chocolate with chocolate and cream cheese icing and two double-layer white cakes with white and cream cheese icing, which was a favorite of the Colonels. Emy had worked on a large Blueberry pie and 3 deep dish apple pies, all homemade, and she was worn to a frazzle. Her apron was covered in the various ingredients she had used today, and her hair was highlighted in white and wheat flour, while her face had splotches of cake batter and icing. She always wondered how her mother could do this every year, not to mention all the different family holidays. There was also an assortment of cupcakes for the children, and Emy had just finished icing them.

Assigned guests were requested to bring in either homemade or store-bought potato salads, tossed green salads, coleslaw, macaroni salad, shrimp salad, and three-bean salads. There would be two families who always brought in fresh corn on the cob, which was shucked in the kitchen and placed in a massive propane boiler. The boiler was set up beside the red cement brick barbecue and ready to go. The massive Barbecue was built out on the back deck by Emy's father and the envy of the neighborhood. Three years earlier, the family had put a shingled roof over the 10-year old deck, held up by redwood and cedar support beams, and the barbecue, which was built from the ground up, was vented up through the ceiling. The following year, the family had framed screening installed to surround the deck, preventing the mosquitoes and other unwanted guests from interfering with their activities. From the ceiling were hung electric Japanese style lanterns in various colored screens. With the coming of the first snow, framed pieces of fiberglass were inserted over the screens to keep the snow from covering the deck. Though it was not heated, this kept the snow from piling up against that side of the house and allowed them access to the deck long before they would've normally have had.

The deck was three feet above ground and aligned to the house through back double-sliding doors. It was 28' in width and 40' in length, and the deck provided a sizeable room for summer activities and had a set of 4-stairs 6-feet wide down to the backyard. Emy held several parties here during high school and during a couple of her military leaves. She even had enough room to have a small live-band during her last party, which nearly sent her father over the end and brought the Fairbanks Police Department to his door when complaints continued coming in after 2 a.m. of noise disturbance. One of the officers had gone to high school with Emy and knew she was home on leave and an MP, so no action was taken, and the party winded down almost instantly.

There were six large spruce wood picnic tables, stained a cedar red color to match the deck. Several lounge chairs were scattered about and nearly 20-feet of foldable serving tables to hold all the food and needed utensils. For the meal, Emy's dad was already barbecuing two rather large moose roasts, having started at 10 a.m., over a slow roasting flame. There would be king and silver salmon steaks, halibut fillets, caribou steaks, and reindeer sausage, a dozen chickens spilt into pieces, London broil at least 3 inches thick for the beef lovers, and pork steaks for those who couldn't eat beef because of dietary problems. He had enough meat and fish here to make any grown man salivate, and the odors were already carrying across the neighborhood, telling the people it was time for the annual end of summer barbecue and wishing they'd been lucky enough to have been invited.

For his contribution, Clay was asked to bring a case of assorted flavored sodas and a bag of ice, so he walked over to the nearby Safeway, selected two flats of mixed cans of drinks, and piled two bags of ice on top. He then used his new cell phone to call the Yellow Cab dispatcher and request an employee's special ride. If a cab wasn't busy, drivers received free transportation if the other driver was willing to cooperate, and this was almost always the case. But along the way, the taxi may be dispatched to a call, and the off-duty man or woman would have to wait a bit before getting to their destination. In Clay's case, the cab was parked nearby, and the driver, who barely knew Clay but was a fellow Athabascan, transported him directly to Emy's house without any side trips.

Clay was surprised by the number of cars parked along the street outside Emy's house. The parked cars made it look as if a hundred people or more were in attendance, and once Clay was inside, he discovered he was pretty close in his estimation and probably on the low side.

Emy wore a blue summer dress and looked as if she had come right out of the wheat fields of Kansas. She answered the door, relieved Clay of the ice, and took it out into the garage to place it in a very large 22 cubic foot floor freezer. Another young man Clay had never seen before suddenly showed up and took the soda away and carted it toward the deck outside. Clay looked out through a rear dining room window and could see this was where the masses were converging. He thought about waiting for Emy, who seemed to have disappeared, but then her mother appeared to grab him by the arm and lead him through the kitchen and out onto the deck. The picnic tables were full of families, with kids from babies and toddlers, pre-teens and teenagers to young adults, and then the old farts. Most of the men-folk stood around talking, and they ran from the early twenties to senior citizens, each one with a beer, mixed drink, or a non-alcoholic beverage in his hand. Clay also noticed a good-sized group of men who stood around the barbecue. Emy's father basted the two massive roasts on the iron spit, which was being turned slowly by an electric engine. Clay had never seen such a large barbecue pit before; he figured it was holding more than 60lbs of meat on its rotating spit.

Clay was startled by this whole affair. It had been a long time since he had attended a GI barbecue, which was roughly the same size as this one. But for the last 6-years, he'd been pretty much of a loaner and on assignment, so this rubbed up against his comfort zone somewhat.

Emy suddenly appeared at his side with her left arm draped through his right and a big joyous smile on her face. "Can't you feel it?" She asked. She glanced around the room and then was suddenly gone again, leaving Clay there wondering what she was talking about. He'd been to a lot of barbecues in his life, some rowdy and some downright homey, but the twitter she caused to his stomach was something brand new. Then he spotted her. She stood beside her father and pointed back at him. Dad turned and casually waved with a huge blue barbecue mitten on his right hand. Clay waved back. He didn't want to approach unless he was summoned; there were a lot of men around he didn't know and didn't want to make it look like he was pushing his way in. By the looks of the men-folk, he saw a lot of servicemen or prior servicemen and women in this large group. The short haircuts and tattoos were always a giveaway, then their stance and finally the look in their eyes. For the ones who had seen close combat, there was always that particular look in their eyes that could never be faked. No actor had ever been able to reflect that particular blank look, and he hoped they never could because to him, it was born of pure honesty. For war was truly terrifying and horrifying, a point in a man or woman's life when she was quickly changed in the blink of an eye and could never go back to who they were a moment before. For those who were in combat too long, they now drifted about with the infamous 1000-yard stare. All too many Vietnam veterans came home with this look, and now, it had become apparent in the veterans returning home from the sandbox- especially after their second and third tour of duty.

Then it came. Emy's dad waved Clay over with a simple gesture of his blue mitten. For the briefest of moments, Clay stood frozen; he struggled with a desire to leave the house and just tell the FBI he couldn't do this job. The idea of putting Emy and her family in prison sickened him, but besides him never earning his major's gold leaf, Clay still had his oath to consider, serving and protecting his country against domestic terrorism. Slowly, Clay made his way over. He only stopped long enough to grab an ice-cold cola, pop it open and take a long sip. He really wanted a beer or something stronger but knew this wasn't the time to get careless. The crowd of men separated and allowed room for Dad to take his barbecue mitten off and shake Clay's hand, to welcome him officially to his house. Clay was then introduced to several of the older men standing about while Emy went outside to join in the on-going volleyball game in the backyard.

"Clay, this is Silas Wickersham... these gentlemen are Allen Peterson, Norm Johnson, Sid Linker, and Greg Slocum...and here we have Charlie Yoder, Chad Kenders and Steven Rouse." All of the men stepped up and shook hands with Clay. He needed to wipe his right hand off on his jeans to dry it; damp from holding the ice-cold can of soda.

The first thing Clay noticed was Kenders, who appeared to be half native, and Slocum, who Clay felt was most likely Athabascan. Between the coastal natives, Aleut, and the Indian, there were some noticeable physical differences between them. Add in the half-white or half Afro-American or other minority influence, and there are very noticeable differences. Clay had known of at least two Japanese men who had married Athabascan women and one woman from Indonesia who had married an Athabascan missionary back in the 1960s, and their grandchildren were spread all over the interior. Being Christian, they were no longer welcome back in the Muslim world of Northern Indonesia, so the family had to finally stop their visits.

"Mr. Jefferson, or might we call you Clay?" Silas had stepped up and was facing Clay.

"Clay is fine, Sir." Clay recognized authority in this man and also a lot of pain. He recognized the eyes of an old warrior, one who had led men into combat and had written too many letters home to their loved ones for when their young man had fallen. He also noticed the Texas A&M University ring on his right hand, knowing this college was well known for its Army ROTC program.

"Well, Clay, from what our gracious host tells me, you've only recently returned from over there and have received your Honorable Discharge with a high disability rating. On behalf of myself and the others here, I wanted to thank you for your service to our country." Silas again offered his hand, and Clay grasped, while the others came up and patted Clay on his shoulders.

Silas then pulled out a business card from his wallet and handed it to Clay, "I own Wickersham Chevrolet on South Cushman, and we offer a 20% discount off the sticker price for combat veterans. If you need a car or a job, you come see me. Emy told me you were driving Yellow Cab... that's no job for a former US Army Captain with your awards for valor. No, you come see me, and we'll see about a job... all right, Clay?"

"Yes, Sir," Clay said, and then he looked down at the business card, which had all the lettering in gold.

Emy's Dad stepped up then and reprimanded Silas for talking shop at his barbecue, "You know the rules, Colonel. Now you've got to take over here, while I see about the rest of the meat. If I don't get some fish on here, the wife is liable to skin me."

Silas looked over his shoulder at Clay as he pulled the barbecue mitten on, "I'm a retired Colonel, Clay. US Army... commanded a company of the 173rd Airborne in Vietnam in '68, spent some time in Germany and General Staff in DC, then up here finally with the 6th Infantry-Buffalo Soldiers out of Fort Wainwright. Then I pulled the pin and my Wendy Sue, and I have been up here for 35-years. That's her sitting over there, gabbing with a table full of grey-haired lovelies." Silas pointed with his barbecuing brush, with sauce droplets all over the deck and his people darting this way and that to get out of the way.

Clay looked over and saw the senior ladies and wondered what it was like for them to spend their lives following their husbands around the world, to raise their kids in often terrible conditions and have to play out the role of the Colonel's Lady and stay shy of post-politics.

Emy was back again to stand in front of him and ignore the looks of the other men around her. All her attention was on one man, and this tended to make Clay uncomfortable. "Did you meet everyone?"

"Not everyone, but your dad introduced me to this group here, and I believe I was offered a job at Wickersham Chevrolet." He pulled the business card out and showed it to her.

"Oh, that's good. He gave you one of the gold ones. He has two types, and he saves this one for important people. Besides, this was the group I wanted you to meet. The rest of the people are great and all, but they're just people. This group here, they're important, and I am hoping you might see why sometime."

Clay looked into Emy's eyes, "You're a very strange lady, and being a pessimist, I keep asking myself, why all this attention to me?"

For a brief moment, her grin was gone, and then it was back, and her eyes lit up again, "You're a pessimist, and I'm an optimist. You helped me out, even after I slammed you bad, and a lot of men would've either ignored me, hurt me, or even taken advantage of me. Yet, you played my knight in shining armor and brought me home. I thought you were worth having as a good friend… got it?"

Now Clay was grinning, "Yeah, I got it, but I'd better be buffing up my armor if you keep having nights out like that."

Her grin was gone again, but there was no bitterness in her eyes. She was suddenly very serious and reached out to grab his hands, "For the first time in a very long time, Clay, I feel very safe. You've done that for me. I'm not sure how, but I'm glad it was you in that taxi that other night." Then Emy was gone again, back to the kitchen to help her mother and leave Clay there with a twitter in his stomach, his mouth hanging open and strange warmth in his chest. Right at that moment, Emy's Dad came up behind Clay's blindside, and Clay suddenly jerked around in a flash with his hands up in an offensive posture. Then he saw Dad standing there with a surprised look on his face, and he immediately lowered his hands.

"Easy, Lad… It's only me," Dad said. His hands were also up, but in defense, concerned that Clay might lash out. He'd seen one too many veterans respond with violence for no apparent reason, and he should've known better than to come up behind Clay without announcing himself. He hadn't been home from the sandbox that long to have adapted to civilization.

"I'm sorry, Sir... just... just combat. It does that to you, an automatic reflex to stay alive." Clay dropped his hands and reached over to pick-up his soda.

"My fault, Clay, I shouldn't have surprised you like that. I simply wanted to have a chat with you about Emy while she was away helping her mother."

"Yes, Sir, that would be fine." Clay directed Dad over to a set of lounge chairs in the corner of the deck against the house, and the two of them sat down on the blue over-stuffed chairs. They set their drinks down on a small white plastic table, and Clay waited for Dad to begin. Outside on the lawn, the joyous game of volleyball had transformed into a combative game of who can knock the most players out with spiked balls, gang tackles, and body blocks under the nets. The smaller children were on the sidelines rooting for their favorite team or player. There would be a lot of bruises and black eyes before this game was over.

Dad took a sip of his mixed drink; vodka and grapefruit juice, sat it down again, and began, "Clay, Emy, which I short for Emily, but she's never liked that name, is our only child, and as you know, she has been through a lot. We didn't want her to enlist, but she felt it was her duty, and then she went into the MPs, which caused her mother to have nightmares for weeks. Worst of all was when she volunteered for an assignment over there...then I had the nightmares. She was always the tomboy. Could've been a model with her looks, maybe even gone into acting, but no, she wanted the Army. She never seemed to have time for boys either, missed out on a lot of dances because she didn't want to dress up in what she considered a clown suit. I began to think we had dropped her on her head once too often." Dad looked into Clay's eyes, cleared his throat, and in a strained whisper of a voice, he said, "You did something very nice for my Emy, and she appreciates it. Her mother loves you for it, and in my own way, so do I. You'll always be welcome here, Clay. You can use my tools in my shop, and you're always welcome here for our celebrations. But Clay...

Clay, if you ever hurt my baby girl…there is nothing this side of Heaven that can protect you from my wrath."

"Sir!" Clay glared at Dad, shot to his feet, and spilled his can of soda.

"Sit down, Clay. Don't get excited."

Clay didn't know what to think and remained on his feet, "Sir, as hokey as it sounds, my intentions are strictly honorable…in fact, I had no intentions."

"Dad!" Emy screamed. Her voice carried, and it could be heard throughout the house, deck, backyard, and most of the neighborhood. Dad suddenly noticed that his daughter was no longer in the kitchen but was now standing only a couple feet behind him. Her face was flushed red, her hands were on her hips, and her icy glare was directed right at him. She was not happy. To make matters worse, everyone on the deck had become eerily silent.

Who needed reality TV? Clay thought for some strange reason. Then Dad suddenly realized he had really messed up when he looked over to the kitchen door and saw the look of doom on his wife's face and the threatening tapping of her right toe against the floor. It was the couch tonight for sure and maybe the whole week.

# 6

# INSIDE THE AFBM

*Wickersham Chevrolet Dealership*
*1400 South Cushman Avenue, Fairbanks*
*4:18 P.M., 3 October*

His hands somewhat sweaty, partly from nervousness, and the rest from the long walk down to the dealership, Clay was pretty sure why he'd been called by Mr. Wickersham and was asked to come by this afternoon. He'd been expecting the call, having not made one himself. He wanted to wait on the old Colonel but would've made the call in another few days. He simply didn't want to seem overly aggressive. But, as the last couple of days went by, he began to wonder if he should make the call and his concern about the case began to gnaw on him. He never enjoyed this part of undercover work, waiting for the opening or, for that matter, the long stakeouts that could take up an entire 3-day weekend. To get by, he continued to remind himself this was going to be his last Black Ops undercover assignment for where he was needed in such a role. Going in guns a blazing was one thing, but all this secret agent stuff should be for one of those three-letter acronym outfits: CIA, FBI, ICE, or ATF. He was also surprised to find how concerned he'd become over Emy, knowing this attachment was a major mistake. Their parting words at the barbecue and the silence between them since then really bothered him. He saw how embarrassed she was by her father's intrusion, even though Clay had tried to calm her down outside with an attempt to explain how a father's interest was to protect their child. But that was the wrong move. Her right eyebrow shot up, she snorted, stomped her right foot, just missing his own foot by mere inches, and it caused all his bright shiny armor to fall to the ground.

Her eyes flared, she then stomped off without a word, and he walked back to his apartment in silence, which was approximately a good 4-mile hike. He did have a chat with the Lord along the way, but that was all in his head. At too often, he'd seen the strange looks people got when they walked down the streets when he had had verbal conversations with God. But, Clay was all alone this time, yet he didn't want to take a chance on someone driving and reporting his rantings with no one accompanying him. It was safer to pray in his head, and during this walk, he was hoping the Lord would give him some understanding of women. Oddly enough, he actually imagined he could hear his grandfather's laughter in his head, and then he gave up.

Silas Wickersham's office waiting room was a very nice affair; four walls in real light walnut paneling, with nice comfortable black leather couches on each wall, and the latest in various entertainment and car magazines sitting on two expensive-looking coffee tables. There was also two wall mounted shelving units that held yesterday's and today's Fairbanks News-Miner and copies of the Anchorage Times. From the ceiling and in the corners were two colored ceramic hanging lanterns, which provided suitable reading light, and the floor was carpeted in all-purpose gray matting. He was surprised by that at first, expecting more expensive carpeting, but then he remembered this was a car dealership and mechanics, parts men, and salespeople were probably coming in here all through the day to see the boss-man, bringing in grease and grime on the soles of their shoes and boots. The carpet needed to be steam cleaned probably every weekend, or even every night if a mess is made. There were large framed posters on the walls of the newest cars and even a couple classic cars. Clay really appreciated the one of this year's black Corvette, which resembled more a racing car than a street model. There was a poster of the new Suburban and a silver mini-van. What also surprised Clay was the absence of a secretary's desk or window to her or his office. There was also a lack of music being placed in the waiting room. Nor was there a coffee machine. Still, the room was quite comfortable, and he was able to relax.

Clay had received the call for the appointment yesterday afternoon, only moments after he had awakened from a 6-hour sleep. Today wasn't much better; he caught less than 7-hours of shut-eye. But, he was used to this when working an operation. Yet, going from one operation right to another without a short leave, at least, the stress was wearing on him. At least he had one or two evenings at the Fairbanks Health Club, where he had gotten a steam and a swim in. Too much coffee or soda to stay awake for his lousy taxi shift, plus no time for long-distance running to giving way to his fast-food meals, his weight gain was starting to get out of hand. He had noticed his new ring of fat around his belt line. He was now expecting a chew-out from his weekend visits to the Doc on Post.

Besides his physical health problems, he was also concerned about his spiritual health; he had missed every church Sunday since coming back to Alaska. Church fellowship, when possible, always helped him fight the stress of military life, but he was always working during Sunday morning services or mid-week night services. He didn't worry about his attendance interfering with his undercover role because a lot of Alaskans attended church, and veterans seemed to be drawn to services when coming home from the sandbox wars. Lots of questions to ask the various pastors, priests, rabbi, and even the imams.

While in Egypt and on the operation to help rescue Christian missionaries out of Cairo, he was able to spend some time with them in Bible study and prayer. This had surprised some of his teammates, seeing their gung-ho and fire-breathing Captain actually kneeling in prayer. Had it not been for a CIA agent turned traitor, the operation would've come off perfect and made headlines for a successful rescue.

Prior to this, the Christian churches were protected by the Egyptian dictator, but when he was overthrown by the Muslims in that province, they began moving in on the missionaries and Egyptian Christian churches. Sadly, one of the CIA agents, a man born and raised in Oakland, California, had turned to Islam without the knowledge of the CIA. These were the same people who didn't know Communism had failed in the Soviet Union and the Berlin Wall had come down. The man had turned the team's secret location over to a mob of Egyptian Muslims, not for money but for his new-found belief.

Led by a fanatical cleric, the mob attacked the Delta Force safe house. A firefight broke out, and during an exchange of automatic fire, two missionaries and two of Clay's teammates were killed. Yet, under Clay's leadership and the Delta Force support system, the remainder of the team and surviving missionaries were able to escape safely. Several other Christian Egyptians also escaped Cairo in the days to follow, knowing they were now identified as troublemakers by the traitor. As a result of the CIA operatives treachery and the fatalities that resulted, the operation was listed under a news blackout and highly classified. The surviving missionaries and Egyptian Christians were asked to refrain from commenting about it to anyone, and with the support of the US State Department, the Egyptians were granted asylum and relocated into Egyptian neighborhoods in the USA. Clay wanted permission to go back and look for the traitor, but this action was refused, and he was sent to Kabul, Afghanistan, for another Delta Team operation.

The door into Silas's office opened, and a very attractive woman stepped out to welcome Clay and invite him into the office. "Please come in, Mr. Jefferson. Mr. Wickersham is expecting you." Clay gave her one last look and then stepped through the doorway. She was just shy of being a 6-footer and had her shoulder-length shiny brown hair worn loose. Her make-up was applied lightly, and she wore small silver loop earrings, two-sets to each ear, and a matching silver necklace draped around her long neck. She was attired in an expensive three-piece outfit; a long sleeve white shirt, royal blue vest, and skirt. Her shoes appeared to be very nice, but Clay always had trouble describing woman's shoes unless they were tennis shoes or combat boots. He had heard in a movie; it was always good to comment on a girl's shoes when going on a first date, and he always wondered why? Those are sure nice biker boots you got there, babe... or nice tennis shoes, honey. The whole thing sounds really stupid.

He put her age at about 35 years old and quickly noticed an expensive wedding ring on the correct ring finger, and she wore a very attractive silver bracelet to match the rest of her jewelry. Being this good looking, Clay was sure she was approved by Mrs. Wickersham before being hired. Clay then noticed she had a separate office on the other side of the door he had followed her through, but the door was half-closed, and all he could make out was a coffee machine and one-third of a basic office desk.

"Clay, if you do not mind my using your first name...we keep things pretty friendly here in the shop; I am so glad you were able to find time to meet with the boss today." But, before he could reply, he was shown into an office half-again bigger than the waiting room.

Mr. Silas Wickersham was standing-up from behind a monstrous wooden desk, his big hand being offered. "Thanks for coming by, Clay. I was hoping you'd take me up on my offer. As I said at the barbecue, I really like to employ veterans, especially young officers," Silas said in a friendly, fatherly voice.

Clay thought his office was large enough to land a Blackhawk helicopter in, and he had to lean over to shake the man's hand. Silas then came around to the left of the desk and added a friendly-like left hand to place over Clay's right shoulder, to add to a gesture of goodwill. *Man, with a welcome like this, he must think I'm lookin' to buy one of those fancy Corvettes outside. Sorry, Colonel, I'm not interested in a car. I can only drive up here 4-months out of the year and then put in heated storage for the other 8 months. I'm actually a Ford man, but I'd better not say anything yet and ruin the moment.*

"Take a seat, Captain... there's some things I'd like to discuss with you, and one of them is your new job here at Wickersham Chevrolet. Would you like some coffee, maybe tea, or a soda?"

"No, sir...I'm just fine," Clay replied. He glanced about the room and was surprised by the complete lack of military memorabilia anywhere in the room. He was expecting Army plaques, awards, and an array of photos, even possibly a sword or two, some service trophies, and a frame holding his well-earned medals. But no, he had nothing to show his time with the military, and that made Clay wonder, why not? He did have several expensive pieces of original Alaskan artwork; two well-known large wolf paintings by Jon Van Zyle and the third painting of a grizzly bear done by an artist Clay couldn't read. There were several shelves on the far wall which held pieces of carved walrus ivory and half-a-dozen scrimshawed orca whale's teeth. Clay could tell from the yellowing of the ivory how some of the pieces were quite old. The desk took up most of the room and was filled with photographs, though Clay couldn't see them very well from his side and suspected them to be of the Colonel's family.

There was an office chair for the secretary to sit in while taking notes and two very nice, overly stuffed brown easy chairs in front of his desk. Clay was now using one of these and had sunk right into it. For additional space, Clay was to learn Silas had a large conference room behind his office, and each sales representative had their own cubicle to work out of and as a really nice break room, which was used by all the office staff and sales staff. The parts department and mechanics had their own break room, which came with a full-sized pool table for lunch hours and a locker room with 6-shower stalls.

"Sir... or do you prefer to be called Colonel?" Clay asked.

"Between us, Clay, you can use either one or even call me by Silas. But, out in front of people, I prefer Mr. Wickersham... until people get to know you as a member of the Wickersham family. Now as to why I asked you here..." Silas sat down in his high back black leather swivel office chair and continued, "...as I told you at the barbecue, I felt it was a poor use of manpower to have a former US Army Captain driving a taxi in Fairbanks. Not that I am faulting our city's cab drivers in any way. They have a tough and often dangerous job, but not for one of your education and training. I believe I could make better use of you down here with my company if you feel you could work for an old geezer like me?"

"Sir, I appreciate the offer, but I am no car salesman. You'd probably lose money on me and Sir, let's face it, I am an Alaskan Native, and this could-" Clay was shut off by Silas's interruption.

"Clay, I've noticed you seem to have a real problem with your heritage. You carry it around like a 200-pound rucksack on your back or maybe better yet a flashing advertisement sign over your head, saying, 'I'm a half-breed!' You have got to let it go, man. You are who you are, and you cannot do anything about it. You can go around being a breed, or you can be proud of your Alaskan Native heritage. I know it's been tough on you. I've heard the stories of others like you and what they and you have all gone through here in Alaska. But, it's ending now, and people are changing rapidly. We're learning to accept people for who they are, for what they produce in our current economy, and to add to our lives. It's how they get along with others, can they change and learn…oh, my spiel goes on forever. I use it for my new salesmen. But it is all true," Silas sighed.

"You've got to drop that rucksack and move on, Captain. You met two of my good friends at the barbecue, both Alaskan Natives and both either half-white or half-Afro-American. Talk to them; they've adjusted and are doing quite well in helping others. We still have a lot of Alaskan Natives who have a hard time dealing with alcohol. They have the same problem all over the United States. The only answer is Christian living and avoiding liquor and narcotics. It is not easy, and too many of our returning troops have come home with severe problems, much like what happened during and after Vietnam. It is up to us, the veterans, to help our buddies… well, that was a mouthful, and I need to show you what I have in mind for you."

Silas stood up and directed Clay out of the office and back out onto the mechanic's bay. Here Clay saw the massive bay, which was painted a very light blue and covered in grease spots and splotches of grime. It was lined on both sides with car lifts, and the structure was open and over two stories high, with windows at the top of the walls to let the sunlight in. Each side of the bay had 10 car lifts. The walls were lined with toolboxes, diagnostic machines, tires and tire machines, and an array of air and water hoses. There were batteries of various sizes, cables, and mats, 55-gallon drums of assorted greases, and people running around to and frow. At the time, 8 of the lifts were in use. Toward the front of the bay, where Clay stood, was a large brown painted wooden counter 4-feet high, where four men in coveralls were hustling about. They handled the paperwork, the phones and yelled out orders across the bay. Here the appointments were made for work, and parts were ordered. At the end of the bay was a massive garage door, which was closed for the moment.

"Clay, we have a large parts department here...one of the biggest in Fairbanks. I have it split into two sides. One side is open to the public, which allows the customers to come in and purchase parts they need for home repairs. The other half is used by my mechanics to get the parts they need for the repair work they're doing here in the bay or outside in my yard. At any one time, they can be working on 30-cars until the cold weather drives them inside, and the numbers are reduced, and the work piles up outside. During the summer, we can turn a vehicle around in about 4-days, quicker for minor jobs. But come winter... a vehicle can take up to 10-days or more once it's brought to us because of the backlog. We simply don't have the room. It's too cold to work on them outside, and I have limited space. I can't afford to build another bay for some time, so we listen to the customer's complaints and do the best we can."

Silas then pointed toward the massive garage door and said, "I also have a body shop and paint shop outside, where I have another twenty men and women employed. The body shop people all work one shift in the summer and two shifts in the winter. Do you know why?"

"Winter brings on more accidents... people sliding on the ice and more fender benders."

"That's correct. Our body shop makes a small fortune in the winter, but we're always arguing with the insurance companies, and a lot of my money goes to my lawyers."

"Quite an operation you have here, Sir. This must bring back some memories of your Army days."

"Often does," Silas said as he glanced around and made sure everyone was staying busy. "Altogether I have employed here a total of 103 employees, and that includes my secretary, of course.

"Clay, I have a Parts Manager, a Sales Manager, and a combined Finance and Business Manager, but I need someone on this floor to make sure things run smoothly here. Now, I've heard about how good you are with tools, and I've done some checking into your service record...something I needed to do to ensure I was getting the quality I insist in my staff. Anyhow, if you're offended by my background investigation, get over it and consider becoming my Shop Manager. My last Shop Manager resigned a couple weeks ago and headed south. I haven't found a replacement until you came around. Based on what I've seen and what I've found in your records, I believe you are the right man for this job. The pay is good, you'll start off at $27.50 an hour, and the hours can be long, but it also comes with pretty good benefits. My employees have a great insurance and retirement package.... One of the best in the city. So, what do you say?"

Clay sucked in a breath of air and glanced about the bay. Working full time with tools and on cars would be a sweet job, and he'd be close to the man he believes is a key player in this Alaska Defense Force. He brought his right hand up and said, "I need three days, Sir, to clear my contract with Yellow Cab, and yes, Sir, I'd like to join your staff."

"Don't worry about your contract. Yellow Cab gets their discount on vehicles and parts right here. I'll call over and make things nice. You be here in the morning at 8 a.m., and I'll introduce you to your team. We'll issue you some coveralls, and you can get your hands dirty."

"Thank you, Sir...I'll be here," Clay said enthusiastically. He had a big smile on his face, which he believed the old Colonel would expect to see.

"By the way, Clay, how are things with Emy since the Barbecue? The only reason I ask is that...well, I'm sort of like a grandfather figure or a Dutch-uncle in her life, and I dearly care about her. She was pretty upset the other night."

"We haven't spoken since that night, Sir. I've called, but she won't speak to me."

"Don't give up. I saw the way she looked at you, and I've never seen her look that way before at any other young man. Right now, she's embarrassed and blaming her father for interfering in her life. But, dads do that. It's part of being a dad. We care so much; we often blunder while trying to protect our children. Don't worry; she'll get over it."

"I hope so, Sir... I really do."

"Good! You two will make a good couple." Silas punched Clay lightly on the side of his left arm and walked back to his office, which left Clay there alone. For a long moment, he watched the crew members do their work and could see the Colonel had hired a lot of well-trained mechanics. He suspected a good share of these people had come from the military. He then spotted a few females in the bay, their hair and faces splotched with grease and coveralls filthy in grime. Clay loved female mechanics. He always thought it was the better of two worlds; girls and wrench turners, and he suspected Emy was a hotshot mechanic herself.

As he glanced about, he also noticed there were at least 10-security cameras inside the bay and a couple extra in the parts shop. Clay wondered if these were for security at night or were they in play for the boss to keep an eye on his employees. But, he knew this system might work for the feds also if Clay could have the Feds hack into the system and possibly overhear the worker's conversations. Nighttime operations might provide additional evidence if the Colonel was, in fact, running this area's section for the Alaska Defense Force and having some of his meetings right here. But it was the ADF, or possibly a rogue militia unit that he was here for, but he still wasn't sold on the idea that old Silas was involved with this. I'll tell the Doc what's happened so far and suggest they look into hacking the building's security system. They're so advanced now that Silas's security boys would never suspect they were now providing action flicks for the feds.

*BASSETT ARMY HOSPITAL*
*FORT WAINWRIGHT, ALASKA*
*ROOM # 318*
*1625 HOURS (4:25 P.M.), 11 OCTOBER*

Doc Adams took notes today, even though his digital recorder was on. He'd already taken his photographs of Clay, and they were into their interview to the point where Clay described his new job and a couple of the problems he had with his personnel.

"It's not a big thing, Doc, and I'm working real hard, trying not to lose my temper. Last thing I need is to get arrested for assault or disorderly conduct at work. But, I've got this one clown who keeps pushing me about the whole racial crap, and my button is getting thinner every day. Now I know I've been trained to handle this, but you people never gave me any downtime between operations....time to unwind a bit. Besides Tennessee, with those racist bastards, I've spent two years undercover in Egypt and Libya. Before that, it was Afghanistan and Iraq, not to mention all the schools the military sent me through. I'm tighter than...I'm tired, Doc, and this guy might end up in the hospital if he doesn't back off."

"What's he doing?"

"He's an Assistant Parts Manager, who I guess had high hopes for my position. Now he probably thinks by taking me down; he can walk right into it. But, he has no idea who he's messing with, or what the Army has transformed me into."

"Can you talk to Mr. Wickersham about it?"

"That's showing weakness on my part, and I'd rather not do that."

"What's the solution then?" Doc Adams jotted down a few notes and took a sip from his Starbucks 16 ounce travel cup. He was a Peppermint Mocha fan and usually 2-3 times a day. There was a Starbucks located on the first floor of the hospital in Seattle, and they had one on nearly every downtown corner.

As for Clay, he liked commercial coffee, but he preferred the hard and gritty G.I. coffee. Its after-effects could last nearly a whole day. He also enjoyed some of the coffee the locals served in Egypt and Afghanistan, except they usually served it in small cups, and you often drank it black. He quickly learned he needed to play it safe with some of the sweeteners and creams they might offer you. Rarely did they tell you what sort of critter the milky substance came from or what was being used for a sugary substance. But, one didn't wish to offend anyone when the boiling hot drink was offered, so you took a single sip to save your lips, tongue, and throat from being boiled. But, if Clay liked it, he would finish off the cup, and this gratified the local who provided the service.

Clay glanced up at the Doc and said, "I guess I'll just have to keep enduring it until he gets tired of pushing his crap," Clay said wearily. "Funny thing, Doc, it's not about me being a breed either. He thinks I'm some kind of camel jockey and probably a Muslim terrorist hiding out in some hidden cell awaiting word to strike. Can you believe it? He keeps coming up to me and shouting out in a few words of Farsi he knows, hoping I'd respond. I don't even think he knows what he's saying because he sure would be surprised if he did… especially talking that way to a man. I'm not going to gratify him by identifying my race, but when he does find out, he sure is going to feel stupid."

"Doc Adams laughed. "How about the Colonel? Anything new there?"

"I'm not sure," Clay replied with some slight hesitation. "He's been in the bay a lot lately, watching me or the mechanics, and I've been invited out to lunch with the staff day after tomorrow. Most likely, it's simply a businessmen's lunch to discuss company tactics. But, I have this feeling… I can't explain it, but I have this feeling of expectation."

"In your job, Clay, I'm not surprised you wouldn't work by such inner feelings. You're out there by your lonesome; you've got to ride those hunches. Like, what's around that corner, who can I trust… such things are quite normal for an undercover operative. But how are they working on your other venture?"

"My other… what venture?"

"Ms. Emy, of course," Doc Adams replied with a grin on his face.

"Oh, her," Clay responded with a shrug of his shoulders and a shake of his head. "We've finally spoken on the phone once, but I felt like I was speaking to the town's librarian. I never knew such coldness… No, that's not true. The Muslim women in Iraq and Afghanistan really hated us. You didn't know real hate until you saw it in their eyes when they knew you were an American and not some French or Canadian. I was with the Airborne and then Special Forces, but you already know all that. Anyway, quite often, we'd say we were Canadian or even Alaskan when buying stuff. For some reason, they never put Alaska and the USA together. Still, it was easier to work with the men… they weren't as honest as the women with their hate. But as to Emy, we haven't crossed the ice bridge yet, and I'm not sure we ever will."

"Stay in there, soldier," Doc said. "From what you've told me about her, she's worth it."

"Hey, Doc, did you forget why I'm here? I could very well be the one who sends Emy and her family to federal prison for life and has to live with that cheery thought."

Doc Adam's face filled with a deep frown, and he looked about the room, "Sorry, Lad. I forgot where I was for a moment. I've become a little too close on this one, much like yourself. Felt like I was back in my office in Seattle, giving advice to a lovelorn patient who suffered from PTSD or alcoholism. It happens now and then, Clay…comes with the job. But don't worry, won't happen again…Still, you need some contact with her as a link, and it may involve you doing a bit of the old James Bond love 'em and leave 'em routine."

"I think I need to go to Disneyland for a couple weeks after this. Everything will make sense there after these last few years, and the Mad Hatter and the March Hare and I can have some tea together."

Doc grinned and then said, "Remember, Clay, if your combat antenna is telling you something, then be prepared at this luncheon for anything. This could be about cars, and it could be about the Alaska Defense Force, or it could be something even deeper. Be gentle, hesitant, and soft-spoken, avoid liquor, try not to get stuck with the bill, and make a mental note of what is said and if it concerns what we need to know about. If it's about cars, I am interested in the newest hybrid models…" Doc shook his head and added, "Sorry, that wasn't funny."

"Doc, I know how to work my job, and I'll move along slowly with Emy." Clay was silent for a moment, and then he shook his head and grinned, "Sir, you would not believe the army of protectors that girl has. I'd be afraid to wrong her for fear you'd never find my body again. No one would!"

With a raised eyebrow, Doc made a few written notes and then said, "I know you are a highly trained operative, Clay. But you've been overly stressed, and as I've said before, you should have never been placed on this assignment in the first place. I've said this to my bosses, of how you're worn out. I even added how I was too. I'm getting too old for this kind of work, and I'm beginning to believe you will be my last governmental assignment. But, as to you, you're stuck being the best man for the assignment. Now, when this is over, you can hit Disneyland or Disney World, but for me, it's time for a few years in sunny Florida, or maybe some time in Hawaii. I've earned it, and they owe me. But I'll stick it out until we're done here.

"Now, if you need me to, I'll stay in the state and be available for when you start getting close. You can contact me 24/7. Here is my number for all emergencies, and it's simply a VA recording line, so you can get away with carrying the number without a problem. If you call, I know it's time for a rush appointment. You've either got news, or you're hiding somewhere, and we need to pull you out ASAP."

"Thank you, Doc. I'll let you know," Clay said. "Actually, talking with you does relieve some of the stress. I'm ready to go back in and face the dragons. I know if anyone died because I couldn't handle it anymore...I'm done, and that means the Army, too."

Twenty minutes later, Clay was walking out the front gate of Fort Wainwright and on his way to a public parking lot. He had a dealership loaner to use for his doctor's appointment, but it didn't have a base decal to allow him onto the base, and he didn't feel like going through all the paperwork to get a guest pass. So he parked it and walked the half-mile to the huge Army hospital. Periodically, the Army MP's Explosive sniffer dogs came around the parking lots outside the gate, which was legal because the parking lot being on federal ground. Clay remembered when the front gate used to be more open and just about anyone could pass through as a short cut to North Pole or to visit people on post. But, that was all before September 11th, 2001, and the 9/11 disaster. Now there were concrete barricades on both sides of the gate shack to protect the gate guards, and the MPs wore camouflaged fatigues and were armed with M-4 automatic rifles.

*PRINCESS HOTEL - OFF THE CHENA RIVER, FAIRBANKS, ALASKA*
*PRIVATE CONFERENCE / LUNCHEON / DINNER ROOM*
*11:48 A.M. 15 OCTOBER*

By invitation, Clay had ridden to the staff luncheon in Silas's brand new cobalt blue Suburban. It came with a deluxe package and every do-dad added on. A ground crew had recently washed and waxed it, so it really shined, and Clay was surprised to see Silas actually driving it. Clay had expected him to be chauffeured around by one of the workers and was additionally surprised to see they were the only two in the vehicle. Clay had never been inside the

Princess Hotel, other than the lobby when he had picked up some passengers to take them to the airport to catch the Alaskan Airlines or Delta redeye flights out at 1 a.m. He thought it was a beautiful hotel and knew that with winter on its way, things were slowing down. There was already a frost to the air, with morning temperatures down below freezing and ice showing up on the windshields of the vehicles parked outside in the lot. There had been some snow flurries, but the snow wasn't sticking yet.

When they arrived in the lobby, Clay looked about the room and was glad Silas had given him time to change out of his coveralls and into his street clothes. Though at the moment he didn't think his clothes were suitable for the dining room of the Princess Hotel; most of the men eating here were in suits, sport coats, and ties, while the women wore very nice dresses or skirt& blouse outfits. But, Clay was dressed in blue jeans, a blue flannel shirt, and his grandfather's moose-hide vest.

Clay figured they were early because he didn't see anyone else from the dealership, and then Silas lead him to the elevator. A moment later, they arrived on the 3$^{rd}$ floor, and Clay found himself being led into a large private conference room. Once inside, Clay began to recognize some of the men and women he had met at the barbecue, and suddenly, his combat antenna stood up and began to buzz with a 100-volt charge. At times like this, he wished he'd had his pistol with him, but that would've blown his cover. Yet, right at this moment, he felt so naked and disarmed, and he didn't like it at all.

"Clay, I believe you've met all these people. But, in the event you've forgotten their names..." Silas began pointing to the people sitting around a large conference table. "... Allen Peterson, who is a retired Air Force major; Norm Johnson, a retired Alaskan Air National Guard Chief Master Sergeant; Sid Linker, former US Army Captain; Wendy Butler, Principal of Tanana Middle School; Greg Slocum, holds a degree in Economics and works with a local investment firm; Charlie Yoder, former EOD Sergeant with US Army, a K-9 dog handler and owner of the Fairbanks Electrical Supply Shop on South Cushman. Now, this is Sandy Benders, who recently received her college degree in Forestry and is hoping to wrangle a job with the Department of Forestry here in Alaska. Then here we have

Hannah Mayo, attending UAF and in her 3$^{rd}$ year, but also an Army veteran, who served two tours in Iraq."

Silas then led Clay to the far end of the table and introduced Chad Kenders, "Chad is our resident elf and former lieutenant in the Alaska Army National Guard... the elf business is due to his work at the Santa Claus House in North Pole. We have Steve Rouse, former US Army Airborne E-6 with 3-tours in the sandbox and now retired on service disability...And now you have met my staff."

Clay didn't say a word and exchanged non-committal looks with the people who sat around the big table, nodded his head, and then looked to Silas and waited for an explanation.

"Take a seat over there, Clay, that empty seat to the end chair. That's where I normally sit when I'm holding court." Silas couldn't help but notice the look of confusion on Clay's face, and this is what he expected.

"Now, I will endeavor to explain all this....and please wait a moment though, while the waiters bring in our lunch. Some of these people here have schedules, and we only have a short time to meet here."

Clay wasn't sure how he did it, but suddenly the doors opened, and four tables with silver buffet trays were wheeled in by four waiters. A fifth table was then brought in, which contained non-alcoholic drinks and glasses filled with ice. There were elegant tableware, white cloth napkins, and Clay saw the food was top of the line from the hotel's luncheon menu. Roast beef, ham, turkey, and five kinds of cheeses. There were four different kinds of bread for sandwiches, heaps of fresh veggies for either a side salad or a sandwich and various dressings, bowls of assorted chips, and fresh fruits. To add to all this was trays of assorted delicate desserts, and it all had Clay licking his chops, but of course, he wondered if there were any donuts?

Once they all had their plates full and returned to their seats, Silas looked over to Norm Johnson, his security expert, and asked if everything was taken care of.

"Yes, Sir...jamming device is on. The whole room was previously searched for cameras or recording devices. We're up and running," Norm replied.

"Thank you," Silas said and advised everyone to fill their plates as I talk with Clay, here." Then, with everyone moving toward the tables, plates in hand, Silas began to advise Clay about the Alaska National Guard. Suddenly, Clay thought he was in the wrong room, and Silas was a recruiter for either the Alaskan Army or Air National Guard. This was not in his game plan, but then he noticed a change in Silas's tone, "... The Guard is certainly up to the task, but not completely, not with Congress reducing its funding. If our state came under attack, if we were invaded by land, sea, or air, the Guard would not be able to defend our people. Even with the current strength of the US Military forces present here, which is currently downsizing...again, Alaska would be defenseless against a major foe such as Russia or China....even North Korea. Now, this is why the State of Alaska has allowed a legal militia to be formed, which is called the Alaska Defense Force.

Okay! Now we're talkin'! Clay had to fight a smile down, but he'd done this work before, and he now waited.

"Currently, our Alaska Defense Force has less than 1500 people, with each troop an owner of his personal weapon and responsible for his or her uniforms, often his ammo. We conduct training, which includes live-fire courses for sidearms, rifles of semi and fully automatic weapons...fully licensed of course, along with group tactics. We also have purchased an assortment of vehicles to assist us, from military auctions, of course. In the event our Militia is called upon to assist the Guard for any state or national emergency, we want to be prepared. But unlike the Alaska National Guard, our Alaska Defense Force cannot be sent overseas to fight in a war...like Afghanistan or even Korea. Do you understand all I've told you here so far, Clay?"

"Yes, Sir," Clay replied. He wasn't sure if he should say more, so he stayed quiet for now.

"Colonel, some of us have to leave very soon," Allen Peterson said. He knew he was to be the one to speak up, being the 2nd in command for the AFBM.

"Yes, yes, of course. You all know me; once I begin rattling on, I forget all about the clock. Well, then, finish your sandwiches, and I do hope everyone has had a good lunch here and enjoyed getting to know Clay a little better. He and I will have another chat back at the office, and we'll all get together later to discuss matters at hand. I'm only sorry we couldn't have had the time to speak at length, but that is my fault. Pressures of the job. But, gentlemen and ladies, I do thank you."

There was a chorus of "Thank you, Colonel," as everyone wrapped up what was left of their sandwiches and left the room one after the other. Only one or two bothered to say goodbye to Clay, and then suddenly, Clay realized only he and Silas were left alone in the room. They both remained in their chairs, as Silas set back and patted his stomach and removed a splotch of mustard from his shirt, "I really enjoy a good roast beef sandwich with all the fixings, but the wife hates the messes I make."

"Yes, sir...it was a very good lunch." Clay wished he had longer to prepare his, but he was suddenly the man of the hour, and his sandwich was nearly empty of all the goodies offered by the hotel. He had wrapped up three-quarters of his sandwich to take back to work with him. He also noticed the security equipment had quickly vanished, too.

"So, have you formed an opinion about this bunch of mine?"

"Sir, I have to admit I am somewhat confused."

"How so?" Silas set forward and reached for his glass of iced tea.

"I expected a staff meeting with your staff from the dealership and ended up with these people. I must admit I find them to be a well-rounded group of Alaskans. You have men and women, Alaskan Natives, whites, and Afro-Americans. Most, if not all of them are of a higher education, have former military experience, and seem totally loyal to you. I also gather from you bringing me here, you're interested in my joining this Alaska Defense Force militia. Am I correct, sir?"

"Yes, Clay, I am. I am the Assistant Militia Commander for the Alaska Defense Force, and I desperately need a good training officer and also one who can pull duties as a 2nd Assistant Operational Officer. A man who has an understanding of combat tactics. I've been watching you, and the men and women in the shop already respect you because you get right in there and get your hands dirty instead of standing back and shouting out orders. You know how to accomplish the necessary paperwork without filling my box with useless junk. I'm already impressed, and you've only worked for me for a week. "

"Colonel, does my job have any bearing on my decision to join your staff with the militia?"

"Cut right to it...I like that. But no," Silas replied. "Truthfully, I'd be disappointed, but you're a good shop supervisor, and I am not going to lose you because you're wary of playing soldier. But, I'd keep working on you, and in time, I might turn you around to my way of thinking."

Clay used a thick white cloth napkin to wipe his mouth and pushed his chair back to stand up. "Sir, I may not have anything left in me to help your militia. I'm tired, my body is pretty well shot up, but I love Alaska and well do my best to defend it." He hesitated briefly to show he was thinking and then replied, "Yes, sir. I'd appreciate it if you'd let me join up. I'll do whatever I can to help with your unit."

"Great!" Silas exclaimed. "I have all the paperwork in my office safe. We can fill it out, give you the oath and send everything down to Anchorage. You'll retain your current rank as Captain. Now, as to weapons, do you have any?" Silas was now standing, a smile now on his face as they slowly walked toward the door.

"I have no rifle, but I have my grandfather's pistol...a Colt .45 Model 1911...only thing I kept after he died. Oh, that and a family drum."

"That's a great pistol, and we have lots of .45 ammo," Silas replied. "We'll see about picking you up a rifle for cost. You'll need a new M-4, semi-automatic, of course, and with as many magazines as we can get. There always seems to be a shortage of magazines. We purchase our .45 and M-4 ammo by the truckload and have it hauled up here by the Guard for most of the Militia. Juneau often has to have their weapons and ammo brought up by ferry from Seattle."

"What about uniforms, Sir?"

"Not a problem, Captain. We have our own supply of woodland camouflage, which we obtained from the Guard some time ago. Let Sally have your sizes when we get back to the office; besides being my secretary, she also handles supply needs for the Militia."

Once back in the Suburban and still parked outside the Princess Hotel, Silas sat behind the steering wheel but didn't start the truck. He turned to face Clay and asked, "Captain, what do you know about Alaska's statehood and how it came about?"

Wow! Things are happening way too fast now. I've got to watch my Ps & Qs with this old man; he's a sharp one. I have to remember everything said here. No note-taking, everything by memory until I meet with Doc Adams in the event they search my apartment... but the old mind isn't all that sharp right now. Worn out... Need a break so bad. "Statehood, Sir? Only that it came about in 1959, we're the 49th state, and before that, we were a territory. My people on the native side used to say this was all God's land...or the Supreme Being. I've heard a lot of different God names as I was growing up. But, my people never felt that our land was owned by the Russians, nor the Americans."

"What would you say if I told you the whole election process for Alaskan statehood was a farce, completely illegal under United Nations' Law and also unethical by civilized standards this USA was built on?" Silas had a serious expression on his face, so even though he had heard this all before in DC, he knew better than to make light of the matter. Even if hearing about it for the first time, his boss's expression should've been a warning not to make jokes, and Clay didn't.

Clay squirmed in his high-backed bucket seat for a moment, thought of his response, and then replied, "Then, Sir, I'd have to say I'd need to know a whole lot more information before drawing any conclusions."

Silas nodded his head and grinned, "Spoken like a former officer of the US Army, Clay. We were instructed well not to jump to conclusions and make snap decisions, and I was curious about the response I'd get out of you. Though you replied the way I expected you too."

"Sir, you've been testing me, challenging me, and observing me, and I am curious as to why so much careful investigation when you knew I had held a position of responsibility with the service?"

"You answered your own question, Clay," Silas replied. "You were up for your major's gold leaf but failed to achieve it and were asked to take a 70% disability retirement instead. I was concerned you were too worn out for what I have planned for the Militia's future. A man can take only so much, and you've had more than your share, and anyone can attest to this. You've had people under your command killed and wounded, you yourself were wounded three times, and you spent more than your share of time in the sandbox. I needed to know if you still had some of that Army grunt in you. That officer's integrity and do or die attitude that carried you over the top against impossible odds, yet able to tone it down when it was needed and even play the politician when required."

"Yes, Sir...I think I do, or I wouldn't have taken the job or even returned home."

"I agree," Silas said. "I also had you challenged on the floor, had one of my men go after that chip on your shoulder, and you didn't strike back or come running to me. I know full well you could've taken him out back and thrashed him near to death, but you did your best to ignore him because he didn't work for you. He will now, though. He's part of the militia force and will be assigned to your training staff. He's actually a pretty good guy, but he was following my orders, and Clay, you're right, I have a very loyal group of troops. The best in Alaska, and they're all true-blue Alaskans, whether or not they were born here or not. They love this state, as much as you or I do."

"Sir, what about this whole statehood thing you brought up? Was it simply a question, or was there more to it than that?"

"There is, but we'll get into it later. I have another meeting right now and need to drop you off at the dealership."

An hour later, Silas, Norm, and Allen were sharing a park bench at a near-empty Pioneer Park off Airport Way in Fairbanks. They were in the area of The Salmon Cook-Out, which was now closed down for the season, but the 9-foot dirt walls surrounding the cook-out prevented them from being listened to by directional microphones. There was nothing they could do about microwaves or satellites, but last they heard, the FBI up here wasn't using anything like that outside of the Anchorage area for monitoring organized crime.

All three men set atop the table, their feet on the benches; two men on one side and one man on the other, and they spoke over their shoulders. Silas arrived first, and he was the first to speak, "What do you think?"

Allen Peterson spoke up, "Our search of his VA records is sound. We have his tribal records, birth records, and GED records. We also have his college and ROTC records. There's nothing to hide, everything is in the open, and the Feds just aren't that smart. The boy was raised in Alaska. He's half-Athabascan and was raised by his maternal grandfather in

Minto. He became an Army Officer through ROTC. He wasn't well treated by family on either side because of his split heritage but seemed to have had found a home with the Army. He came home first for his grandmother's funeral in Minto and then his grandfather's. He was 82nd Airborne and also served with the 10th Mountain Group for a short time. He served as an advisor with an Iraqi infantry company that saw a lot of action with them and was wounded. He was wounded twice more before he came home to a medical discharge. For whatever reason, he wasn't put on the Major's promotion list, and as to why, I haven't been able to find out, but I am betting its basic politics. The kid saw too much action, is highly decorated, and of mixed blood, and this offends some general officer. We've all seen it before. Fine to have them serve and all that, but not all that quaint to have them in the Officer's Club wearing field grade rank. Better to save those gold leaves for some senator's kid or that son of an industrialist, who might add some campaign funds to some general who's about to retire and wants to go to Congress."

"My you've gained an attitude since retiring, Allen," Silas said.

"Colonel, it's the same reason you never got your star. You were always there to protect your troops, and a lot of generals never liked that quality in you. They felt you selected the little people over them, and you paid for it," Norm said in stern words.

"Be that as it may, we're discussing, Clay Jefferson here. Norm, what is your view of the young Captain."

"We've thrown a lot at him in a very short time, mostly to see if he could handle it, and he has. I've known a lot of the Athabascan people...nix that, I've known a lot of Alaskan Natives and have found them to be some of the most trusting, loyal and courageous, caring, and considerate people I've ever had the good fortune to encounter. At the same time, if they have a drinking problem, we can't trust a one of them. I've read where he was in the program and beat it, found religion, and I have no problem with walking with the Lord. In my view, it shows even a higher character for the young man. Still, I think before we bring him into the inner circle, let's give him a few more weeks working with the regular militia and see how he operates. His injuries may prevent him from being able to carry out the role we have planned for him in the operation."

"I can agree with that," Silas said and then stood up to stretch. "I like this kid, gentlemen, and I can see him having a future with us and possibly with Emy. I hope we haven't messed that up for them, but this operation and our expected results are bigger than all of us, though I would like to see them coming out of this together as a couple. Her mom is still not talking to me, which has Wendy Sue giving me a hard time at home. I'm too old and too out of shape to be playing cupid, so one of you is going to have to wear that funny outfit."

Norm and Allen looked at each other for a brief moment and then burst out laughing. It was time to get back to work, and Silas still had another three appointments this afternoon before he'd be able to drive home and see if he had a warm meal or cold meatloaf sandwich waiting for him.

Clay responded to his page, and he met Silas at his office. The militia documentation was pulled out of the safe and additional paperwork removed from a file cabinet devoted to Militia business and stacked on Silas's desk. Once he was given the oath and the paperwork was signed and notarized by Sally, Silas gave Clay a copy of their current training schedule, location for indoor and outdoor shooting ranges, and times they had set aside for them. He was also given a complete list of the Fairbanks Militia force by name, rank and social security number, phone number, plus street and mailing address. It was at that moment that Clay learned he was also responsible for turning out a weekly Militia newsletter, with attached training schedules for every activity called for that coming week. The Militia personnel were supposed to receive their newsletters on the Thursday prior to that coming Monday, which began that week's schedule. Clay suddenly realized he was already behind.

"Sally will give you a helping hand; she's been doing it for the last few weeks, but I need her back in the saddle with her normal duties, or this place is liable to fall down around my ears. She knows where every skeleton is buried in this town, and I rely on her to keep the upper hand. Her father was a Superior Court Judge here and before that, a District

Court Judge. He was also a town Magistrate, while still going to law school and for a while the only legal criminal attorney in Fairbanks prior to World War II."

"I'm surprised she didn't become a lawyer, herself," Clay said."

"She is," Silas replied. "But she stuck to business law and married another lawyer. They had a pretty large firm here until he died of a heart attack, and that was enough for her. She was old friends with my wife, and Wendy knew I was looking for a secretary. She came to me, and I hired her on the spot. She has saved me from so many court battles just by reminding me to sign my name here and there and not making any promises I didn't plan to keep. I also enforce the Lemon Law strictly. If they bring back a used car within 30-days, they get their money back and no complaints. Oh, I may try to talk them into another car. But they get that money back. I've got really great PR with the Military, and I'm not about to lose it over a $3500 Chevy mini-van."

"I thought she was about 35-yrs old...I'm usually pretty good at estimating ages."

"Tell her that, and you've really made her day, Clay. Now being a gentleman, I will not share with you her true age, mostly because I don't remember the exact year, but it would get back to Wendy Sue, and I'd pay for it. No, she takes very good care of herself, but her one husband was her only husband, and she now spends her time with two Newfoundland dogs, a temperamental Siamese cat that even those massive dogs avoid, and some really expensive saltwater fish that resemble rainbows."

Before he left the office, Silas presented Clay with a piece of paper, and on it was written the words, "Jaybird's Wing World- North Pole - 9:30 p.m."

"Sir?"

"Captain, my best advice is for you to be there. We gave you a loner, you have gas money, and I know you can afford a basket of wings at Wing World."

"Yes, Sir," Clay said with a hint of smile forming on his face. He had a fairly good idea this rendezvous had nothing to do with dealership work or militia duty, but a certain young lady with beautiful blonde hair and eyes that sent his stomach to twittering. Is it smart? If I don't go, what might happen in my dealings with these militia people? I'm so close, I can feel it, but at what cost and who will have to pay the piper?

"Thank you, Colonel." Clay opened the door and started to walk out, but Silas stopped him.

"And about that loaner, Captain... I dearly hope in the very near future you decide to actually purchase one of my fine new vehicles. I am paying you now."

"Yes, Sir," Clay said in a laugh. "I'll check out the new car lot as soon as I get the newsletter out, but it seems I have a meeting on for tonight."

Silas closed the door and shook his head, "I knew this whole Cupid thing Wendy Sue dreamed up was going to cost me money. I'll go ask Sally, see if there is some way to declare it on my taxes... welfare of my employees."

# 7

## "EMY"

*Jaybird's Wing World*
*North Pole, Alaska*
*10:46 P.M. 18 October*

The first few moments between them were tense and awkward, with several apologies battered back and forth, and then the smiles broke out, and they relaxed. After an hour of conversation, they were on their second helping of barbecued wings and onion rings, at Jaybird's, a well-known Alaskan eatery, with a special sweet and tangy Gold Rush sauce to dip everything into. They had a quiet booth in the corner of a nearly empty restaurant, and Clay had already gone through a handful of napkins to wipe sauce off his hands and face.

"I'm full. How about you?" Emy asked. She glanced back and forth between Clay and the television monitor mounted in the corner of the room opposite them.

The eatery had several monitors of assorted sizes mounted for the customer's pleasures, and at the moment, all of the channels were on the NFL Network, showing the highlights of last Sunday and Monday Night's games. Afterward, they would be showing the highlights of the Sunday day games.

"Look, Seattle is playing Thursday night. Maybe you can come on over and watch the game with Dad and me. Mom hates it, so she usually goes out shopping or visits a friend at one of the senior centers. She and her friends used to schedule cards for football night, but too many of the regular players moved away, and the card games stopped. But, Dad and I go all out with popcorn, pop, and some deep-fried wings. Maybe he'll barbecue something if you'll be there. What do you say?"

"Do you think it will go better than last time?"

"We made up, didn't we? Emy asked. "Dad and I have buried the hatchet, and even Mom lets him sleep in their room again. So, come on over and show my parents everything is okay between us. Besides...I'd like you to be there."

"Before we leave this joint, I wanted to ask you something," Clay said in a low tone. "The Colonel...my boss arranged all this, and don't get me wrong, I'm glad he did, but are you part of this Militia...this Alaska Defense Force?"

"Yes, Captain, I am. I was already called and was told you signed up for the Militia, and I was overjoyed to hear it. Now I'll have to address you by your rank when we're out in the field or training class, but I don't mind. I retained my NCO status, but I am hoping to eventually work my way up to 2$^{nd}$ lieutenant someday, but I'm in no hurry for the moment. For now, though, I'm with A Company and leading a squad of pampered overweight weekend warriors."

"You'll find I'm a pretty tough training officer, Sergeant. So stay sharp."

"It's a good thing the Militia doesn't have any regulations about enlisted and officers being...sort of involved." Emy tossed her napkins down, stood up, and waited for Clay.

"They call it fraternizing, Sergeant, and I agree with you." Clay then looked down at the barbecue sauce splotches on his shirt. "I need to make a stop and wash-up. You can watch some more football, and I'll see you in a moment." Clay first stopped at the register to pay the bill and then walked into the restroom to wash the sauce off his face and inspect his clothes for droplets. He grinned when he looked down and saw a droplet of Gold Rush Sauce on his shoe. "I'm a real pig."

Washing up, Clay looked in the mirror and thought about what was happening; I really hate doing this... I feel like a big-time chump. Yet, I care about this girl, I may be falling for her, and on the downside, she could very well turn out to be a traitor or even a terrorist. I can't believe this. I'd rather be in a firefight with a mob of fanatical Muslims than hurt her...or her dad.

It was Emy's suggestion to follow Clay back to his apartment, and she was really surprised, almost shocked when he declined her offer. She was actually offended but gave him a chance to explain himself before breaking both of his knee caps. "Listen, Emy, let's not rush this thing between us. We're both adults, sure, but we've also been through a lot, and I'd rather enjoy this gradually...letting it blossom slowly. This is really different for me, and I want...If it's real, then we'll make a connection that will last forever. Does this make any sense to you? I don't need an overnighter, which could ruin our friendship. Can you understand that? You mean more to me than a roll in the hay."

"A roll in the hay... ?" Emy said. "I haven't heard that said in a long time." She looked hard at him for a moment and then asked, "Clay, are you a Christian?"

Oh boy! How do I answer that? I've never been asked that while working undercover, except by those missionaries in Egypt. Why would she ask this now, just because I don't want to go to bed with her? He gambled and went with the truth. "Yes, Emy, I'm a Christian, though I've had a hard time walking the walk and talking the talk as a soldier. I gave my life to the Lord while attending college at UAF."

"I suspected as much," Emy said. "You're always so nice, respectful, and I don't think I've ever heard you take God's name in vain... And not trying to be vain, I know I'm a good looking babe, and I'm stunned by your refusal to have...what was it?... 'A roll in the hay with me'... But, it explains a lot, and I can respect it."

"What about you, Emy?" They were leaning against Clay's loaner in Jaybird's parking lot, under the glow of a parking lot light. The air had turned cold, and the temperature was now around the freezing mark. Clay had a windbreaker on and had retrieved a jacket for Emy from her car.

"I'm pretty much a nothing, Clay. Oh, I went to Sunday school as a kid and Vacation Bible School, but once I became a teenager, I was more interested in cars, sports, and my hobbies. I worked with my dad when I wasn't in the books, so I never had time for church. Mom attended, but I don't remember where. She tried to get me to come but then gave up."

"What about in the military?"

Emy hesitated and then replied, "Saw too much, I guess, and the Base Chapel services were so…mellow-like. I had trouble believing in a God who would allow all this death and destruction and all the hatred. I just couldn't accept it. Nope. But, I can accept your desire or need to…and I'll wait for you. Remember, you're my knight, and I hope to be your princess." She punched him lightly in the stomach and said, "Got it, buster!?"

"You have a delicate way about expressing yourself, Sergeant Sanders."

"So, will I see you early Thursday evening at 4 p.m. for the game?"

"Probably closer to 6, and only then if the boss lets me off. Weeknights are not the easiest nights to get off early. Our workload is picking up, with the roads becoming icy. Snow is around the corner, and I'm thinking 12-hour shifts for the winter…lots of overtime."

"You want me to give him a call, see if you can be excused for the game?"

"No, I can handle this matter myself and remember, we have training on Saturday morning at 7 a.m. I'll give you a call Friday night, and maybe you can pick me up, and we can go out for donuts and coffee on the way out."

"What is it with you and donuts? If I didn't know you better, I'd suspect you were a cop."

Clay could imagine his heart missing a beat, and then he replied, "The Lord's food for soldiers, cops, street cleaners, and wayward sailors."

"You're crazy!" Emy exclaimed and turned to head for her car. She then looked over her shoulder and said, "Drive home safely, Captain. I have plans for you, and they do not involve you putting your car around a light pole."

"The Colonel wants me to buy a new car, so you'll probably have to help me pick one out. I hate to break it to him, but I've grown up a Ford man. But having a Ford on his lot would be a sacrilege, and someone, probably one of the dealers, would set fire to it."

"You're right, don't say a word. We'll look at his lot and find a nice family vehicle, room for lots of kids. She had a big smile on her face, then moved up and kissed him on the lips. Though it began lightly, it quickly turned into a patient exchange. "That was nice," she said and then turned away and made a dash off to her vehicle. Clay was left standing there with that awkward mouth open look on his face and his arms slightly extended from just holding her.

Then he thought, Kids!? We've just had our first real kiss. Could she be feeling the same flutter I've got in my chest right now? We've only had our first date…sort of. Yet, when I look at her, I'm ready to just sink into those eyes of hers. Oh man, I'm in real trouble here.

Driving back to his apartment, Clay kept wondering, I've known this girl such a short time…we've seen each other only a few times, and let's not forget she upchucked on the back seat of my cab after flipping me off. Now I'm her knight in shining armor- again, and she's talking about kids! Oh, I know she was joking…Yet, strangely enough, it doesn't feel all that weird after talking it out in my head. She's beautiful beyond comparison, loves to work on cars or anything needing tools, loves guns, she's a decorated veteran with wonderful parents…Her dad has the most beautiful Camaro I've ever seen…Hold it, kid, you're really blowing it here, Clay. You've got to keep that Camaro out of her good points pile, not fair to you or her, and it's because the old man will never give it away. When he goes to prison, he'll leave it with his wife.

Clay pulled out his handkerchief and wiped his face. Think rationally, boy. You cannot be already falling in love with her, you've never believed in love at first sight, and you've counseled a lot of young troops to stop doing what you're doing right now. Get your head working and not your carnal desires… and yet, I know it's happening, but I can't believe it's happening to me. If I don't get control of this, I'm looking at a lot of hurt. Chances of us having a real love-thing, possibly a marriage and even a squad of beautiful children… it's ridiculous! But, I bet her parents would be wonderful grandparents… even when I visit them in prison! Clay pushed down on the accelerator, and his speed increased to 65 mph, which was pushing it for this 6-cylinder loaner with nearly 200,000 miles on the odometer.

By the time he got to his apartment, Clay was really stressed out. He stripped off his clothes, threw them into the corner by his full dirty clothes hamper, and climbed into the shower. The hot water made his scars stand out, but the heat relieved some of the stress. With eyes closed, he stood under the nozzle and allowed the hot water cascade down his neck and back. Slowly, he began to relax, and only then did he began to shampoo his hair. Later, once he was dried off, he set his alarm and was asleep within a moment of hitting his pillow. Thankfully, he didn't have any nightmares tonight, but he did see a pack of small unidentifiable dark-haired children running across someone's lawn, and when he awakened to the alarm, he knew where the suggestion for that dream had come from. He recalled how Grandpa had said his Germanic side reportedly supported a lot of dark-haired relatives and ancestors, but one of the little girls in his dream was a red-head. His own father was born a dark blonde, but by the time he was 10-years old, he had transformed into a light brown-haired young man. This made him wonder, with his own hair following the traits of his mother's family, how would it mix with Emy's red hair if and when the two of them had children? Oh, man...I've got to quit thinking about this.

Getting dressed, Clay shook his head, having a hard time believing he was even beginning his morning with such crazy thoughts, knowing that on any operation, even one like this, he could end up very dead if he fouled up and didn't keep his head in the game. Besides that, he knew the reality of this could also endanger Emy. If they somehow figured out who I actually was, they could very easily believe Emy was now playing a mole for the government. That I had turned her with my spy skills. So, can I keep this platonic, stop everything cold? But, would that then cause Silas to suspect... Maybe, he'd think I wore soft shoes, that I was gay? Oh, I've really got myself into a mess. He'd probably toss me out on my ear, and I would've fouled up the whole job.

Thursday night was a scrub. Clay didn't get off work until 10:40 p.m. and only had time to call Emy before going to sleep. She was, of course, disappointed, and he was beat, plus the Seahawks lost to make matters worse. Then on Friday, he had his upcoming meeting with Doc Adams and spent several minutes in the room alone, going over everything in his head before their session began. He didn't want to waste the Doctor's time and was relieved when he could recall nearly everything that had happened since the last appointment. Doc Adams was surprised by how fast the Militia was moving on Clay, but at the same time, hoping this meant something was either happening, or they could wind this case up before Christmas as a No Threat. Doc hoped to put in his retirement papers but didn't want to abandon Clay until this operation was over. A new man could upset everything and blow the operation and even endanger Clay. No, he would hang on and hope for the best. He also had his other patients that might feel abandoned if he just up and pulled the pin on them. But, Doc knew that time was rapidly approaching. By the time he was getting home at night, the exhaustion he felt was getting hard to handle, and his sleep was restless. All signs that he needed to take some time off and head for sunny Florida.

The session lasted longer than an hour, with the digital recorder running all the time and Doc Adams making several pages of his hand-scrawled notes. Then he surprised Clay when he turned off the recorder and asked him about Emy, "I've decided to keep her relationship with you as private as possible, something between us. I will keep it in my notes, but only my impressions of your mental and physical health brought about by this relationship. In the event, I hope to write a book. Of course, I'd never use your real names, dates, or locations."

Without the monitor running, recording his every word, Clay began to relax some as he began describing what had happened at the eatery in North Pole afterward and the suggestion of an overnighter in their future. How he refused taking her up on it that night, which had surprised her and then her questions about his faith. He had been honest with her, to some allowable degree, which had surprised him. He even told Doc how she had shocked him with the brief mention of children.

Doc grinned as he made a few notes. He was actually somewhat surprised by Clay's refusal for a lovemaking session. Mainly because he couldn't think of too many men he knew who had the strength of will to turn down such an offer. "Clay, you may not wish to hear this, but I believe you're falling in love with this lady. It shows all over you, and I also believe this can compromise your assignment. Do you agree?"

"It could if I allowed it to. But, I am more interested in finding a way to get her out of it, if indeed she is involved in a terrorist plot. This Militia itself is lawful and not a problem, but I feel there is something lurking underneath it, and Emy is a part of it. I'd like to go deeper, become a part of it, and find a way to pull her out before we bust them. If I can take her out of it, maybe..."

"Clay, you have one chance in ten of accomplishing that goal. But, you are in deep, and it would be nearly impossible for us to get anyone else in this deep in time to stop whatever it is they have planned. The thing you have to do is focus. If you love her and want to save her, you've got to do your job. Or you'll be sending her postcards in a Federal Facility some-where, and you could be looking at a Bad Conduct Discharge. Plus, I'm risking your life by leaving you in place. Do you realize this? Still, a lot of lives could be at stake here. I'll have to let your superiors know all this and let them make the decision. But, being a mission-minded group, they'll decide it is worth one life to save many."

"Doc, I knew all this going in. I lost two of my men in our last opera-tion...they were 'expendable,' and they knew this when they volunteered. I'm also expendable, Doc....especially if my job can save lives. Oh, I still don't know what this militia has planned, but it is something big, and it's very important to them...something surrounding the 1959 statehood vote.

"Will, my advice is to move slow with Emy, especially concerning pressing what she might know concerning future actions by the militia. If she tells you anything, then she's volunteered it, and you might not have to feel so bad concerning future events. I doubt it, though. But, Clay, you're an experienced operative. You know what you have to do, but my concern is also what happens to you once this operation is over. I seriously believe you are going to need at least a month of leave time, outside this state, to handle the after-effects of this Op. Unless events transpire that prevents Emy and her father from serving any jail time, I believe this could be your last undercover detail for a very long time. I'll be recommending you need to return back to regular Special Force assignments. Where you can be a Captain again."

Clay got off work Friday night at 8 p.m., and though he was invited out by several people to share in a beer, he declined graciously and drove home. Tomorrow was going to be a very long day, and he wanted to be at his best in meeting these people. According to the Colonel, nearly half of the Fairbanks Militia Unit would be out for this Training Day. A lot of them wanted to meet their new training officer, including the unit's top non-commissioned officers.

Instead of waiting for Emy to call, he telephoned her at her home, chatted with her mother for a moment, and then spent the next hour on the phone with her. Oddly enough, Clay couldn't recall the last time he'd spent longer than ten minutes on the phone with a girl without becoming bored to tears and making up some excuse to hang-up. They agreed for her to pick him up after she stopped for coffee and donuts. They had a 22-mile drive, so she thought he could probably consume 3 or 4 cake donuts by the time they reached their destination. She had learned his favorite to be a white cake donut, with white icing and covered over in chocolate sprinkles, and one of the local bakeries usually had a dozen on display early in the morning.

"You know, Clay, eventually, you're going to have to start some kind of exercise program… either with the Fairbanks Athletic Club or one of the others. But I will not be dating a tubby!"

"A tubby," Clay replied. "I'm far from being a tubby, but I do admit I am in need of some exercise. I used to jog quite a bit and hit the free weights two to three times a week. I also enjoy swimming, so I joined the Fairbanks Athletic Club. They have a great winter program, a pretty nice Olympic-sized indoor pool, and an indoor track."

"Yeah, I used to be a member before I left for the military," Emy said.

"So, Sergeant, how come we have to come out by Eielson for our training classes? I would've thought we could've gone out behind Fort Wainwright." Clay pulled an iced donut ring out of his white bakery bag and took a nice bite out of it, and then remembered to wipe his mouth with a paper napkin.

"Across from Eielson is this massive piece of land owned by the state and federal government. There are a few homesteads on it, and recently, there have been some land sales by the state. But, there is enough land still out there to hide Los Angeles in. About like the land distance between Fairbanks and Minto, say 90-miles, and just as flat and most likely the same number of waterways. We have our pistol, rifle, and machine-gun weapons courses out there, along with compass courses and other spots for field training exercises. Occasionally we operate with one of the National Guard units, and we've even conducted emergency exercises with the Royal Rangers from the Assembly of God Church and the Boy Scouts of America. A lot of our people will get out there to hunt for spring bear and the occasional moose, but I think it's been pretty well hunted out for moose."

"How about firefighting? Does the Militia ever get called in for that?"

"It has in the past, but it's on a case by case situation. Some of our guys have their red cards as trained firefighters, and others don't, and the command doesn't want to risk those. But, if the City of Fairbanks was at risk or Nenana, then the whole unit would be hitting the road in force. We'd probably even get the troops from Southeast Alaska in that event. Everyone loves a little excitement."

"What about these machine-guns you mentioned... how'd the Militia get licensed for automatic weapons?"

"Remember, Clay, this is Alaska... where nearly everyone owns at least one firearm and probably two or more. We have no concealed carry permit law in Alaska. You simply can't carry a gun into schools, state and federal buildings, liquor establishments, and banking institutions. Some people think we've gone back to the old west, but the federal government makes sure we stay in line with all automatic weapons and silencers. Now, as to our Militia, we have several federally licensed Class III dealers and collectors of automatic weapons. We have one man who collects tripod-mounted World War II American, Japanese, and British machine-guns, and another collector of German antique machine-guns. One of our people is licensed for Vietnam era M-60 machine-guns, and he has several of them; licensed for each one at a costly price to the federal government I might add."

"What about fully automatic M-16's and M-4's, Sergeant," Clay asked in his Captain's voice, which made Emy a bit uncomfortable.

"It's all legal, Clay... Captain. The M-4s and M-16's that are fully automatic have federal stamps and are owned by licensed people. There is nothing in the law that says a person simply firing the weapon on a range has to be licensed, and believe me, we have researched that from cover to cover. We also have two .50 caliber sniper rifles, and some of the guys like to carry those new Ak-47 semi-automatic rifles you can get for a pretty reasonable price. Now, are you going to tell me we have grenades, maybe a few mortars and a tank standing by?"

"Enjoy your donuts, Captain. I think you'd better wait until we arrive to see the rest of the inventory. I wouldn't want to ruin your appetite." She shot him that raised eyebrow he remembered from that day at the barbecue and returned to her driving. They didn't say another word as they drove east along the Richardson Highway.

Within fifty yards of turning left for Eielson AFB main gate, Emy turned right and pulled off onto a well-graded dirt road. A cloud of dust followed behind them as they proceeded south along its single lane. For the next couple of miles, they suffered a washboard effect brought about by the heavy equipment used to keep the road built up and clean the snow off during the long winter. This, of course, brought memories back for Clay, picturing the long, seemingly endless desert roads overseas and even his dirt highway out to the Community of Minto. He was really glad he hadn't brought the loaner out, its poor shocks wouldn't have survived this dirt road, and he would've been stuck calling for a wrecker and probably stuck with the bill for repairs.

Clay heard the whump-whump-whump sound of a Chinook helicopter flying over. The huge hot dog shaped helicopter with dual rotor blades flew at less than 200 feet above the ground and appeared to be going in for a landing at Eielson Air Force Base. Clay knew these Chinooks were stationed at Fort Wainwright, in support of the infantry, and he had flown in them on numerous occasions in the sandbox, and they always seemed to have made him nervous.

As he thought about Fort Wainwright, Clay recalled how the post had grown to near a full-strength division of 20,000 troops back in the 1970s. Every barracks was full. Fairbanks business people were overjoyed by their sales receipts, and the bars were hopping. Then the downsizing began with a new political party in the White House. All-too-soon, Fort Wainwright dwindled down to approximately 6,000 troops, and most of these were support personnel for the single regiment of infantry and a couple heli-copter aviation units. He had no idea what their strength was now or how many troops were now stationed at Eielson AFB, but he knew Fairbanks and North Pole were not looking all that prosperous at the moment, and a lot of people were concerned over the expected move of even more aircraft to the Lower 48. The civilian-owned fuel plant constructed here in North Pole to take the North Slope crude oil pumped up from the ground and transform it into high-grade avionics fuel had been closed down. It had once employed over 200-people, and now only a half-a-dozen security guards wandered about the grounds and worked the entry gate. Most of the structures had become scrap iron and was being driven out to the state's various auto wrecking yards. Most of the steel would be purchased in small parcels by civilians to turn them into small structures or even yard projects, such as homemade windmills, to help lower the electrical costs.

Clay had heard that some of the steel sheets were helping a man build his own aircraft. Alaskans were known for their ingenuity. He had seen the circular house in Fairbanks that set upon a 5-story tower, and the house slowly circled, like the massive Seattle Space Needle did. Plus, they had constructed a small elevator inside the tower to bring people up into the house. Clay imagined the builders had the most awesome view in the entire Fairbanks area.

After another mile, Clay began to see a long line of vehicles parked beside the road, lining both sides adjacent the training field. A makeshift parking lot was packed and off to one side of the roadway, and Clay easily spotted a small fleet of diesel tractor rigs hooked up to 40-foot long empty flatbed trailers.

"Looks like they pulled all the stops out for you, Captain. The Colonel wanted you to see the whole Fairbanks Command, including our troop vehicles...which, you might notice, is an assortment of retired military armored personnel carriers." She pointed out, gesturing with her right hand over the steering wheel, to a row of older model APCs. "But believe me, Clay. The engines inside those brutes have all been rebuilt, and they could run the butts off anything Fort Wainwright has right now. Our civilian engines would put the Army's to shame... Oh, I'd estimate we've got better than 100 horsepower over theirs, maybe more."

They drove up, and Emy turned the ignition off. Clay grabbed his fatigue cap and climbed out of Emy's family 8-passenger Chevy van. Normally her mom's rig, she used this today to haul out her weapons and try as she may, Dad wouldn't let her bring the Camaro out. Clay was in full woodland camouflage, his name tag and captain bars in place. Instead of U.S. Army or National Guard, the cloth tag over his left pocket simply had the letters ADF sewn in black thread. The words were too long for the allowable size, and they wanted something more than simply-"Militia." The Colonel and other officers were not present, so a senior NCO called the crowd to attention and saluted Clay. Clay returned the salute in a crisp fashion and then said loudly enough for everyone nearby to be able to hear him, "Unless the Colonel disagrees and counters my order, there will be no saluting on the training grounds during a training day. Experience shows that accidents have happened when enlisted personnel and even officers are worried about rendering a proper salute and not ducking to avoid having their head knocked off or their butt run over."

"Yes, Sir," The senior NCO replied, and he nodded his head in agreement. "I believe that to be a sound order, Captain. I'll pass it on to the Colonel for confirmation." He approached Clay and offered his hand, "Captain, I'm Glenn Whitehead of Salcha. I am the unit's 1st Sergeant, and I am also retired Air Force. I put in 28-years and pulled the pin right here at Eielson as an E-9. You let me know if I can do anything for you, day or night."

"Thank you, First Sergeant. I will." Clay had learned a good 1st Sergeant was worth his weight in gold. It was his responsibility to handle the enlisted men's personal and military problems and take care of them before having to bring in an officer if possible. He had to be a counselor, a chaplain, a dad, and a knuckle-buster for his troops. Clay knew from Whitehead's service records he was 67-years old, a tough as a rail spike driver, and at 255 pounds, could probably still play a tough game of no-holds-barred combat football as a nose tackle. In the military, combat football resembled Rugby, in that they wore no pads, had few rules, and nearly everyone got bruised up. Most of the games were created in Vietnam, where the grunts, back on the rear bases, would play tackle football without pads and usually during monsoon season. The mud would quickly become over a foot deep, and one of the biggest concerns was not drowning at the bottom of any pile. When possible, officers also played, and rank met very little on the playing field.

"We have a good bunch of people here, Captain, and I personally believe the Colonel is tops in my book. I served in Vietnam, Thailand, the Philippines twice and then in Iraq, and by large, he's the best and most caring commander I have ever worked for. The men and women love him; that's why you have so many people out here today. He says jump, and they say—"

"How high," Clay finished the old military saying, which got a grin from the senior NCO. "I can see that, First Sergeant. Even with the no salute order, I am betting they'll still salute him."

"Yes, Sir, they will." First Sergeant Whitehead first glanced about and then nodded his head in farewell. He then walked off to see if the Colonel had arrived, while Clay went over to inspect the vehicle fleet. Clay also wanted to see the firing range and meet his range instructors.

The fleet of civilian diesel tractors included half-a-dozen Kenworth 10-ton rigs and a newer Kenworth 15-ton beast. The flatbeds were old and empty, but they had previously held (5) older model Vietnam era 706 "rubber ducky" amphibious armored personnel carriers. These vehicles traveled on 4 huge tires; they could carry up to 6-men and usually had a mounted M-60 machine-gun on top. Clay noticed that each of these was painted in woodland camouflage, and though they did have the machine-gun mounts on them, the vehicles did not display the weapons. He was surprised to see how good of shape they were in and then noticed the paintwork on the bodies was quite recent. Next to these were (2) track-driven APC 113 armored personnel carriers. They too were equipped with machine-gun mounts and had also been recently painted in the woodland camouflage pattern. Clay suspected the paint and bodywork were accomplished in the Wickersham Body and Paint Shop. There was an assortment of other vehicles, and most of these had a matching paint job, and we're all in pretty good shape. A lot of expense went into this, making me wonder what the Colonel has planned for this armada. With a gifted welder and knowledgeable armorer, those weapon mounts could easily switch from an M-60 to an older model .50 caliber machine-gun. Those APC 113's could also handle the weight and recoil of a 20mm automatic weapon, possibly even the newer 25mm cannon if the frame walls have been reinforced.

"Captain, the Colonel is down at the pistol range, and he'd like for you to please join him," 2nd Lieutenant Rouse said.

"I'll be on my way if you can point me in the right direction," Clay said.

"Over that way, Captain, you can just make out the firing range towers to the southwest. The towers were two stories high, a simple two-by-four construction with a ladder on one side and painted white. There was a tower for each of the rifle and pistol ranges."

"Thanks, Lieutenant." Clay watched the lieutenant walk off, pulled out a small notebook from his left shirt pocket, and turned it to where he had Lieutenant Rouse's information and reviewed it; 28 years old and recently assigned to C Company as a new platoon leader. Currently, he works for North Pole City Roads, Parks, and Recreation. A good-sized man, he was a hair over 6'4", was quite wide at the shoulders and a tad bit overweight. He refused to re-enlist after serving 3-tours in Iraq and chose the Militia over the Guard to prevent a return trip to the sandbox. Born and raised in Healy, his father had worked in the Healy coal mines, and this was a job Rouse wanted to avoid. He's also reported to be of good character and of sniper caliber with an M-4 or the .50 caliber sniper rifle.

When Clay reached the pistol range, he found 8 shooting lanes in operation for today's training, with target lanes set up at 25-yards, 50-yards, 100-yards, and even a couple targets at 500-yards and 1,000-yards. Each target was the standard military shooting paper target, which showed a black center and an area where the head would be. It was supported by a plywood backing and a 2" by 4" framing to lift it to the expected height of an enemy soldier. Shooters would shoot from standing, off-hand, kneeling, and prone. Clay was impressed.

The Colonel and his senior staff were up on the line and apparently awaiting the arrival of their new training officer so he may get qualified before instructing the others. "Captain, we just want to make sure you can shoot before giving our men lessons," Silas said in jest. He knew Clay's records listed him as an expert shot in all standard-issue weapons, but his records had also shown his expert status with the sniper rifles and many of the foreign issue weapons. Clay wasn't happy to see this was all listed in the records Silas was able to get his hands on. But then he knew, most combat officers serving in the sandbox would have this training, and growing up a hunter in the Alaska wilderness, he would've become an excellent shot.

"I am ready, Colonel, just as soon as I load my magazines."

"We've already taken care of it, Clay. We have several troops who carry the Model 1911, and we keep loaded magazines ready to go on the range to speed things up. Same thing for the Glock Models 17 and 22... it saves time."

Clay walked up to the ammo table and found four loaded magazines for his Model 1911. He inspected them first and then inserted one into his weapon, without chambering a round. Three more were placed into his belt pouches. He then approached a firing lane to the left of the Colonel and to the right of Major Peterson. He then adjusted his canteen belt to a comfortable fit. Normally, he would be wearing a tactile holster rig, which would also be strapped to his right leg. But, for now, he would use the Army's regulation holster for the large Colt 1911. Clay noticed the Colonel was also using a Colt 1911, while Peterson shot a Smith & Wesson .45.

The instructor in the tower, who was using a handheld bull-horn, was First Sergeant Whitehead, and it didn't surprise him to see Emy standing up there beside him with a pair of binoculars in her hands. Clay took a moment to decide how well he should shoot today, but he decided to go for it and impress both his lady friend and the others. They might listen to him if they know he can shoot well.

Instructions were given, and permission to load the first round was authorized. The officers placed their ear protectors on; either soft foam inserts or full shooter's ear protectors that resembled old-fashioned stereo headphones. Whitehead directed them to fire the first four rounds in the two-hand combat grip and begin shooting when he blew the whistle. Clay loved shooting and was often at the range 3-4 times a week when on post or at a forward base. By the time he had emptied his four magazines, he knew he had outshot everyone in the senior staff, and by the end of the day, everyone would be suitably impressed, and this included his fair princess. He completely blew out the center of the 10 spot and made a large hole for where the man's nose would be.

By the end of the rifle shoot, Silas was standing beside Clay and shaking his head, "Clay, I was told your grandfather had taught you to shoot, but I had no idea you could shoot this well. You embarrassed my best sniper, and I thought he was one of the best shots in Alaska." Clay didn't want to have to tell him that the men in Delta were some of the best shooters in the world, and it came from a natural talent and a whole lot of practice, practice, and more practice.

"I think the troops are ready to listen to you, Captain. So what's next on your itinerary for today?" Silas stood beside his new training officer and had his right hand on top of Clay's left shoulder as the men compared some of the troop's targets.

"Colonel, you brought all these combat vehicles out here for something, so let's see how our troops handle some combat deployment drills from a slow-moving APC. We can have a few sergeants shooting into the air to add to the moment with one of those old machine-guns you have over there to get the blood flowing... make it real. But I really don't want to see anyone run over. So, first, we do it from a single parked APC and show each troop how it's done. Okay with you, Sir."

"You're turning out to be a good training officer, Captain. I strongly believe fate may have brought you to us." Silas began to round up his company commanders for the exercise.

Clay watched him walk away and wondered, Colonel, was it your fate or my own? When this is all over, we'll know for sure, and one of us is going to be extremely unhappy with the outcome.

For half an hour, Clay had each company train its personnel with a single parked APC. They'd load up with 4 to 6 troops, then an order was given, and they exited the vehicle. At first, it was done slowly to get the order down and then in a rush. The first move was to roll to one side, the first man going left and the next going right. Once away from the vehicle, they would remain in the shooter's prone firing position and await an order from their squad leader to move out. They were to keep their magazine out of their weapons and not have a round chambered. Sergeants were directed to check each soldier's weapon, and sure enough, 3 rifles were found with live rounds chambered. These men were sent off on 2-mile runs to help them remember their misdeed. Then the exercise was started with moving vehicles at 5 mph for the next two hours, switching off between wheeled and tank tread APCs, and surprisingly enough, not a single soldier was run over or injured. There were a few bruised up elbows and knees, but nothing that needed a visit to the emergency room.

Clay brought all the troops together and wasn't surprised to see the female and male troops equally sore. "I wanted to do it this way first to show you how the real thing can be harmful to the body. I presume, a word I normally do not like to use, but it appears a lot of you veterans have been out of the service long enough to forget how tough training can be, especially on our older bodies. So, I recommend that both female and male troops go to Fred Meyers or whatever sport's store you favor and purchase elbow and knee pads. They are to be either be black or covered in woodland colors. I have yet to see green pads at the stores, only white or black. You will not wear white ones, even if you plan on wearing them under your clothes. From my experiences, your fatigues will get torn, and then you'll have these white-colored pads sticking out for all to see.

"When I'm conducting training, I conduct it as if we are involved in the real thing. The only factor I allow to remain is weapons and knife safety. You'll soon be learning what I mean about knife safety, for with the month, I expect each and every one of you to have on your uniform a seven to eight-inch sheath knife. As you can see, I wear a Marine K-Bar knife taped to my combat suspenders. I wear it upside down for an easy grab, plus I feel the Marine K-Bar is the finest general-purpose combat knife in the world. But, I know that Buck makes a fine sheath knife also, but you must purchase one without the silvery handle. The French also make a fine combat knife, as well as the Israeli, India, and several others. The blade needs to be thick enough so it will not snap in half. Now, I'm not all that crazy about the Smith and Wesson Bowie knife, but I've known soldiers who preferred them, and I will allow it if you can remove the silvery pieces or darken them somehow.

Now, as to other knives, I will insist each of you will carry a hidden boot knife in each boot, and you will learn how to throw them for a distance of less than 12-feet. You will also be learning knife fighting techniques. A couple years ago, such boot knives and what I was taught saved my life. Other soldiers I worked with in the sandbox have had similar stories to tell. You will learn how to throw the knife and fight with it. So, you will find knives that can be safely worn and hidden in your boots, and that will be throwable. A dozen companies make such knives, and you can find them at various stores in town. In one month from today, inspections will be conducted to see if you have said knives in your possession. If not, long-distance running will be in your future. Please believe me, the Chinese and Russians who have designs on our lovely state all train with knives....from fighting techniques to throwing them. The Chinese officers still carry a short sword, and it is not for just looks.

"Now, as for all of you who served in the sandbox, I am sure you'll recall all of the bad guys who carried swords and knives." Clay thought over what he had just seen and then remembering one last thing concerning the knives, he added. "Listen, I know these additional items I am requiring, between the knives and the pads, cost money, and maybe you cannot afford it. Come see me between now and 30-days from now. I also want to add, remember to remove your boot knives once training days have ended. You might get pulled over by a local police officer or State Trooper, and if this leads to a pat-down search and your boot knives are found...you could be arrested for carrying a concealable weapon. So please, remember to remove them once we're done, and I also hope to remember to advise you of this when we are done. Now any questions?" He was surprised when there was none.

To finish off the night, Clay ordered an 8-mile hike back out to the highway, which was immediately greeted by a lot of boos; that is until the Colonel slung his rifle and began walking away from them and heading north up the road. That stopped all the complaints. The companies were formed up by platoons, and the two majors led the way in a two-column loose formation. Major's Peterson and Johnson were right behind the Colonel, and Clay was a couple steps behind them. Along the way, Clay filtered back through the formation to talk with the troops. He wanted to get their ideas about what they would like to see for their training days, and he obtained several good suggestions, which he promptly wrote down in his small notebook. By the time they reached the highway, the tractor-trailer vehicle fleet had pulled up behind them, now loaded down with the APCs. The 15-ton Kenworth had an empty flatbed, and once it got turned around out on the highway, it began shuttling the weary couch potatoes back to their cars and trucks. The tractor had to make two trips to get everyone back to the parking lot, and then it loaded the remaining 2-APC 113 track vehicles for the journey back to Fairbanks.

Clay was curious, but he hadn't asked as to where the APCs were stored. He was pretty sure the trucks belonged to a commercial trucking line, and the owner was either friends with the Colonel, or they were hired out by a local dealership. For a moment, he also wondered if there might be some connection between the truck-line with the Alaskan Independence Party. He knew one of the trucking firms in town was owned by some hard-core right-wing Christians, but he was simply letting his mind wander at this point. Toss it out and let's see what sticks to the flypaper, Grandfather always used to say.

Clay rode back to the parking lot in the cab of the Kenworth so he could chat with the driver and learn how the big beast was operated. He had driven the smaller tractors, but never one of this size, and he was surprised by how similar it was in its operation. Double-clutching was the same for both and the same with the usage of air brakes. He liked big trucks and, at one point in his young life, thought about becoming a trucker, but his Grandpa had talked him out of it. The driver here was an older guy named Matt Davis, who had been driving trucks for over 50-yrs and all of it in Alaska. He'd driven the Haul Road to Prudhoe Bay so many times he no longer bothered to keep count. Matt knew every turn and was smart enough to know that he could never take any Alaskan road for granted.

Once Clay and Emy had cleaned and put their weapons into their various weapon carriers, they loaded them into the van, finished off two bottles of water, and then finally climbed aboard. It had been a long day for both of them, and next time she was going to bring knee and elbow pads along. She was mad at Clay for not having warned her about the exercise involving the disembarking of a moving APC and rolling across the hard dirt ground. But he told her that would've been unfair to the others.

"Are you dating the others, Mr. Captain… Sir?"

"No, but when I'm a Captain…, I'm a Captain. I have to go by the rules, even if it upsets you."

"Does that work on our dates too, Captain…dear?" Emy asked, batting her eyes at him.

"I'm not a Captain on our dates. I'm just a love-struck Indian boy from Minto in search of warmth and compassion, and the love of a good understanding woman…who can cook like her mother."

"Right! The only thing you love, Mr. Captain, sir, is my dad's Camaro, and I'll have you know I can cook, though not as good as Mom. But, she got a lot of years on me in learning."

"Well, that's true… to a certain degree on the cooking part and maybe the car too, but I can't kiss and hug a Camaro, or at least get any satisfaction from it."

"You keep this up, and you can't kiss and hug this girl either. You're beginning to sound like a General Motor's Hallmark card."

"Do you want to stop by McDonald's?" Clay asked. His stomach was rumbling, and he felt like a Big Mac, maybe a couple of them.

"No, I do not want to stop at McDonald's. Here I am dating a retired Army Captain who works as a manager for the largest car dealership in Fairbanks, and he wants to take me out to McDonald's. You're a cheap-oh, Captain Jefferson! So, no, I'm going to drop you off, and you will pick me up in two hours and take me out for a nice formal dinner. You select the location, but there will be no pizza, no fast food, or any place that gives out toys with their meals, neither will it be a place that offers donuts or ice cream for dessert and no oriental buffets. I want a nice place where you will be showing me off, and I will even wear one of my best dresses for you. So, plan on wearing your sports coat and a tie, or I will slam the front door in your face. Fail to show up at the appointed time, and I will have a contract out on your life by morning, and I do know a lot of men who carry guns and who dearly love me. You understand me... Captain, Sir...dear?"

Almost exactly two hours later, when the doorbell rang, Emy opened the front door and was stunned to find a black limo waiting outside on the street. It was too long for the driveway. Clay stood off to one side of the doorway in his best finery, with a tie on, freshly showered, and a white orchid corsage in his hands. Emy's mom was in tears, and Dad struggled to keep from blubbering. This was the night she never had in high school, and it was with the man she was beginning to love, and as an added plus, they approved of him. What could be better? The corsage was carefully pinned onto her blue satin dress by Mom, and unable to speak, Emy was escorted out to the vehicle by a young man who even remembered to shave, again. The fancy-dressed Chauffer also wore a black tuxedo and was there to open the door for them. Once they vanished inside, the parents at the front door were now shaking their heads, as they had suddenly wished someone had bothered to run and gotten the camera.

Because of who Emy was, being much of a tomboy, she had not been asked to a Senior Ball or any of the other fancy school dances. Though she had attended a few of them with groups of other unattached young ladies, who would usually find a dance with one of the unattached boys. Later, at least they could say they had danced and, in some of the cases, had had some fun. For Emy, she thought high school was a total drag and hadn't realized she was thought to be one of the most beautiful girls in their class. But, her mind was devoted to other things, and she didn't experience 'life' until she joined the U.S. Army and went to war. When she came home, her social life revolved around things she could do on her own. Her physical scars and her mental ones kept her from the dating scene until she looked into Clay's eyes. Then a whole new world opened up to her. Except, Clay turned out to be a Christian, a man with ideals and set standards, a man she had some trouble in understanding.

"How'd you do this in two hours?" Emy had never been in a limo before and was busy opening all the cabinets and playing with the various buttons. The driver didn't care, it always happened, and if he went along with the youthful behavior, the tip was always better.

"Charge card," Clay said. "We have a dinner reservation at Pikes, it is their limo service, and I have something special planned for right afterward."

"What?" She had a hopeful vixen-like gleam to her eyes and a smile on her face.

"No, not that," Clay said. "Your old man would have a shotgun wedding waiting for me when I got you home. No something else... something very special for a very special lady who's raced into my life like a Japanese bullet train."

Dinner was a fantastic affair, and Emy had no idea a formal dinner with only one couple could last so long. Afterward, the limo transported them to the airport, where a charter flight awaited them. Clay had scheduled a one hour flight over the Fairbanks area and southern region of the Tanana Valley. It was a beautiful cool summer night, the skies were clear, and Emy couldn't remember ever having such a romantic night in all her life. It was approaching 3 a.m. when the pumpkin-limo pulled up to the front of Emy's house. She was asleep. Her head rested on his shoulder, and she was covered by a fake-fur throw provided by the limo.

"I'll be right out; just give me a moment."

"Not a problem, Sir." The Chauffer came around and opened the door wide so Clay could carry her to the door, but then she awakened, and he slowly lowered her to her feet. "Once again, my knight has returned his princess to her castle."

"I've got to get a couple of hours of sleep before Football Sunday. If I fall asleep on your couch, your Dad will skin me alive."

"He'd understand. You gave him the prom night I never had, and it was all a surprise. I think I love you, Clay Jefferson, Captain... Sir," Emy whispered.

"I will see you soon, my princess." Clay kissed her lightly on her lips and turned to dash back to his limo. At what it was costing per hour, every minute mattered. This was an expensive date, but one he was so long overdue for. He had never mentioned it, but he had never gone to a high school senior prom either. Most of the dances he attended in college and in the service were mixers, with a bunch of buddies all coming together. To the best of his knowledge, this was his first real formal date, and it had come off just right.

On NFL Sunday, every single team Dad swore was going to win was completely slaughtered. By the time the Sunday Night game was over, he could only shake his head, kick his footstool across the room and finish the bottom of his 10th can of beer before he stumbled off to bed. As for Clay and Emy, they sat on the couch and held hands. They could have cared less which of the teams had won or were even playing. They had both fallen sound asleep.

After Dad came into the bedroom, grumbling about the game, Mom put away her books, climbed out of bed, and put on her robe. She then went out into the living room, straightened everything up, and turned the TV off. She then woke the kids up and led her daughter off to her bedroom. When she returned to the living room, she was surprised to find Clay off the couch and in the kitchen. He was getting ready to do dishes, but she wouldn't hear of it. "You get on home and get some sleep, Clay. Workday tomorrow and knowing your boss, you're going to be hitting the ground running."

"Yes, ma'am," Clay said. "Our shop will be backed up before noon, and if I get home tomorrow night before 10 p.m., I am doing pretty good."

"You like working for Silas, Clay?"

"Yes, I do… he took a real chance on me, and I'll always be grateful. I see what he does for the veterans in Fairbanks and around the state. I've never heard a bad word spoken about him, and I fear for the person who tried."

"Well, you get along and drive slow. There's a lot of nuts out there after Sunday Night Football."

"You don't have to remind me, ma'am…"

"Oh, God, I'm sorry, Clay, I forgot about your parents."

"It's not a problem, Mrs. Sanders. But it's a poison, and it destroys a lot of people…from both sides. I always pray how someday we'll get it beat, make it right, but we will probably have to wait until our Good Lord returns for that to happen."

Mom walked up, put her arms around clay's shoulders, and hugged him. "You're an answer to my prayers, Clay. For my Emy to become romantically involved with a Christian man. I can't tell you how happy I am to have you in our family...even as a friend."

"Don't try to kid a kidder, Ma'am. I saw the Bride's magazine underneath the coffee table, and I know where your mind's been drifting off too lately. But please, ma'am, don't rush her... or me, we've got a lot of healing to do before making a serious commitment like marriage."

"Clay, what happened to her over there? She won't talk to us about it, and I have trouble understanding. I've checked out movies, read books, but I can't make a connection."

"There isn't a movie or a book that can help, except the Bible. But she won't accept that right now. She saw too much pain and suffering... too much fighting over religion and the innocents who suffered for it. She saw that our government, the politicians, not the people she supported, had failed to come through with fighting the war as a war—much the same as we did in Korea and Vietnam. We haven't fought a real war as a war since World War II. The politicians keep us from winning, and that can be real tough on a patriot's heart... especially one who has lost a friend or loved one, or like herself, have become wounded and paid a dear price. Healing must occur from the inside, and this is still going on for me too, and I am not healthy enough to go into a forever-type relationship until I am healed. It's not fair to my future spouse or myself...I've just seen too many problems with married couples from the troops coming home.

"Mrs. Sanders, you're a Christian... were you aware that even in many of our Christian churches, divorce has reached the 50% mark. We are now equal with the secular world in destroying our marriages."

"I had no idea."

"That's why we both need time, and I pray I can help, with your prayers, to bring your daughter into the King's Kingdom. I desire a Christian marriage when it happens; I do not wish to be unequally yoked."

She looked toward her daughter's bedroom, closed her eyes, and lowered her head. Then she opened them, patted Clay on the arm, and hurried him off. "Get some sleep, Clay. We will see you when you have time."

"Oh, I'll make time."

"I think you will too."

Clay nodded his head, offered up a smile, and turned toward the road. He hadn't called for a cab. He thought he'd walk down to the neighborhood 7-11 and call from there. He needed the fresh air to think about a few things; his job, his mission, his Christian walk, and his blooming love life. *At times like this, I can almost wish I was back in the sandbox and just shooting at people.*

# 8

# THINGS ARE BECOMING ALL TOO REAL

*Wickersham Chevrolet Car Dealership*
*Executive Office Of Silas Wickersham*
*South Cushman, Fairbanks*
*11:17 A.M. 22 October*

The office's thick winter brown curtains were currently closed, which had dimmed the illumination in the room as Silas had only his desk lamp turned on. The two overhead lights and the table lamp in the corner were all turned off, so Silas, Allen Peterson, and Norm Johnson could review numerous still photos of Eielson Air Force Base's flight line on Silas's large flat screen wall monitor. With his feet propped up on the top drawer of his massive desk, Silas used his hand control to adjust the TV monitor and computer set-up. He moved the photos forward after the three men had discussed each one. The office door was locked and even dead-bolted. A black metal box on the desk was a new-fangled toy Silas had bought, which was advertised as a sonic radio wave scrambler and, when activated, was supposed to distort their conversations in an area the size of this office and even somewhat larger. They were using this in the event someone was using a directional microphone to spy on their meetings. A vibration scrambler was also in place on the two office windows, similar to the ones used by governmental offices in Washington DC and in American Consulates around the world. Silas had obtained the sonic radio wave scrambler through an underground source in Canada at a nasty price, and tests had shown it to be effective. Both Allen Peterson and Norm Johnson had purchased two each, ever hopeful of someday being reimbursed for their AFBM costs. They had set them up in their offices and their homes, for when they had meetings there.

Silas was dressed in his favorite navy blue sports coat with gold-colored buttons, a light blue long sleeve shirt with button-down collar, a loose-fitting black tie without a tie tack, black pants with a sharp crease and a two-inch cuff, and comfortable looking LL Bean brown leather Velcro loafers. He wore a wideband gold nugget Rolex on his left wrist, which was worth more than most of his new cars on his lot, and a very attractive handmade gold nugget wedding band on his left ring finger with a 1-carat diamond sunk in the middle of it. This was his 25th Anniversary present from Wendy Sue. When they got married, he wore only a simple gold band. The Rolex watch was his 60th birthday present from his whole family, and he figured it probably took everyone's efforts to afford it. On his right hand, he wore his Texas A&M College ring, and he was also wearing a pair of heavy, black-rimmed bifocal eyeglasses to help him see the details on the screen clearer.

Allen Peterson was leaning forward in one of Silas's easy chairs, trying to make out one of the details in a photo of the Colonel. A retired C-130 pilot, Peterson wore a US Air Force faded blue flight jacket with his leather name tag on it and his senior flight wings engraved in silver right above his name and rank. After retiring, he had taken his coat to a tailor and had a large and colorful C-130 Hercules stitched on the back, with the words Desert Storm written under it in three-inch lettering. He was proud of his limited combat service, having flown 27-missions and taken a total of 63-hits from flak, rifle fire, and RPG shrapnel. Under his coat, he wore a dark brown wool sweater and had gray slacks for pants. His footwear consisted of black Wellingtons, their heels scuffed up, and the boots in need of a good shine. He was also wearing a black wool driver's cap on his head, but at the moment, it was slid back, which often was a sure sign of his frustration with something. His black leather Thinsulate driving gloves set on the corner of Silas's desk, right next to Norm's gray wool gloves.

Though Norm Johnson had retired as an E-9 from the Alaskan Air National Guard, he was still a Marine at heart. He had served with the 9th Marines in Vietnam, and today he was wearing a threadbare red Marines t-shirt, with the yellow globe and anchor emblem on the front and barely legible from being washed so many times. He was divorced and still mixed his colors and whites together for adverse effects, but his uniforms and formal wear were always dry cleaned at the Korean dry cleaners down the street from his place. Being part Aleut on his dad's side and part Inupiat from his mom, he was brought up having to fight both sides of the family. So his dad thought the Marine Corps was the perfect spot for him and took him to the Anchorage recruiter.

Norm came out of Vietnam with 2-Bronze Stars for Valor and 2-Purple Hearts. He only left the Marines to get married to his Aleut girl-friend, who refused to leave Alaska. He joined up with the Alaska Air National Guard because they had units closer to her family. But then, she had enough and found someone new, and he stayed on with the Guard and got a job with the Anchorage Police Department. After 16-years with them, he resigned because he didn't like the way the department treated the Alaskan Natives and didn't see much chance of promotion in the newer department. The guard was different, and he rose up the ranks. Upon retirement, Silas had sought him out to join the ADF and offered him a commission as a captain. Within 2-years, Norm had become a major. When not working with the ADF, he was fishing or hunting in Southwest Alaska or down on the Aleutian Chain, and he still did some guide work for people from the Lower 48 now and then. He had been wearing a blue and green wool patchwork insulated blue jean jacket when he arrived, but he dropped it on the floor beside his chair, and his faded blue Levis looked as if they had come from his Marine Corps days. He always had trouble with his feet, coming home from Vietnam with a bad case of trench foot, and more often than not, he wore white tennis shoes one size too big. But, once the snow hit, he then switched over to over-sized tan and brown laced-up Sorrel boots.

Silas then handed out a small collection of photographs. "This is the latest batch of photos from Emy Sanders, and as you can see, they still haven't moved any of those KC-135 tankers off the flight line," Silas said. The photo showed the Eielson Air Force Base flight line from the northwest angle, highlighting the positioning of 6 US Air Force refueling tankers operated by the US Air Force Reserve Units from the Lower 48. The crews and their aircraft would routinely transfer up here for a 30 to 90-day temporary duty assignment from their home bases to gain experience in arctic refueling operations for the various fighter aircraft stationed at Eielson.

"If it's like the Open House we had here two years ago, they'll have those tankers, and also those newly arriving B-52's moved to the south base area for the Open House," Norm said. "They'll be too many people wandering around the tarmac to leave them there. Security Forces will be spread thin as it is; they don't need to add to their headaches."

Silas pushed a couple buttons, and Base operations and the Tower were shown from the Richardson Highway. "That girl's a pretty good photographer," Peterson said. "She might even consider a career in photography."

"Allen, how many people do we have planned for the tower and Base Ops?" Silas asked.

Peterson picked up his black spiral notebook, leafed through it, and then replied, "We'll have a platoon commander in the tower with a 3-riflemen force, one of them being a sniper armed with a .50 caliber rifle for long-range shots. This will then give us one sergeant and a full 9-man squad in and around Base Operations. The Sergeant will, of course, be in direct radio contact with our Command Center and the Tower above..." He hesitated and then suggested, "Colonel, I still say we should move the Command Post to Base Operations."

"I suspect they'll be thinking the same thing, Allen. I want them thrown off for as long as possible. We'll keep our Command Post secret for now, but may change the location the closer we get to S-Day."

"Sir, what about Clay? Are you ready to bring him on board? The troops sure like him, and from what I hear, we should be hearing wedding bells real soon between him and Emy," Norm said. He reached over to the desk and grabbed for a cold open can of Coke, and took a large gulp. It was one of his few remaining vices. His health forced him to give up liquor and tobacco, and his temper usually kept the women away. He was known to finish off half-a-case of Coke a day and more if watching sports on TV. He also had a craving for Snickers Bars, but his doctor told him he had to make a choice because his cholesterol was too high. "You have too much sugar and fat in your system, and it's causing problems with your weight. So either chose the Coke or the chocolate." So, he chose the soft drink, but every now and then, he was seen with a half-consumed Snickers Bar in his hand.

"I'm thinking about it, gentlemen…but how about our other manpower problems?" Silas looked over at Peterson with a raised right eyebrow. "Numbers, Major?"

"We've added a few troops, Colonel, but we still need half-a-dozen more people, and our selection pool has gotten mighty thin. Just too many drunks, dopers, braincases, and gun-happy grunts coming back from over there. Finding a well-balanced troop is like me picking the next Iditarod winner." Each year men and women raced their dog-teams across a grueling course of ice and snow, through Alaska's treacherous mountain ranges, from Anchorage to Nome. A lot of the teams never finish for one reason or another, and the winner is awarded a new truck and a very large cash prize.

"Keep at it," Silas ordered. "I know another Stryker Unit is coming home in November. We may have the numbers we need from them. There is bound to be some Alaskans in a unit that size."

"I hope so, Colonel," Norm replied.

Silas switched the computer and wall monitor off and pushed his chair back. He stood up and walked over to turn the overhead light back on and pull a single set of curtains back to let in some daylight. He then returned to his desk, took the photo disc out of his computer, and handed it to Peterson. "You guys have plans for lunch?"

"I'm meeting with that gentleman in Delta Junction concerning the amount of Ammonia Nitrates we will need," Peterson said. "Next week, I'll be on my way to Seattle to confirm the purchase of a barge of diesel fuel to arrive at our agreed upon date in Nenana."

Silas looked thoughtful for a moment, pushing his glasses back on his forehead and nodding his head while the other two waited in silence.

Then he spoke with a small degree of hesitance, "Are you sure about this farmer, Allen?"

"We've run a thorough background on him. His family has owned this farm for over 60-years, and he's a long-time member of the Alaska Independence Party and the National Rifle Association. Word around town is how he's not all too fond of the IRS over a dispute from some 10-years back, and we know he's an old friend of Joe Vogler. He also lost a grandson two-years ago in Afghanistan, which has him pretty teed off against Washington. Sales receipts for the last five years show how much ammonia nitrates his farm purchases, and this year he's simply willing to do without some of his fertilizer. Of course, if we don't use it, he'd like it all back."

"Yes... I sincerely hope we don't have to use it. If we do, it won't matter... for anyone," Silas said quietly, almost like in a prayer.

"Colonel, I haven't asked before now, but... well, Sir, all of this is costing a lot of money. More than what you have or what our whole Militia could put together. I mean, just bringing that diesel barge up from Seattle is... and why are we doing that?" Norm asked.

Norm was showing new worry lines on his forehead, and this had both Allen and Silas concerned, knowing the old man's health wasn't the best at the moment. Still, the AFBM needed Norm, and Silas couldn't talk Norm into stepping down without his old buddy losing it completely and possibly opting to kill himself for feeling useless. The ADF and AFBM were his life, and they both knew depression was a constant problem for him.

Silas shook his head, "I swear, Norm, whenever you wear that Marine T-shirt, you get dumber than a rock!"

"Colonel, I resent that!" Norm said. On his feet, he glared at his Colonel, with his hands balled into fists and his shoulders hunched over.

"Oh, I'm only joshing you, Norm... you were getting too serious there for a moment and your blood pressures up, again. I could see it in your face. You know I love you, now calm down and let me worry about the money issue."

Norm glanced over at Allen, who nodded his head in agreement, which got Norm to relax his hands and slowly sit back down. "All right, Colonel... but I am still concerned about the costs involved here. There's a lot of funds going out, and I'd like to know who's backing our play. I would feel like a fool if we ended up owing the wrong people when this was all over."

Silas moved up and gently laid his right hand on his old friend's left shoulder, "Trust me, Norm. This is the better way right now... that only I know where our money is coming from. Our benefactors need to be kept secret. In fact, they demand it... It's the only way they'd agree to help us. But understand Norm and you too, Al, I would never hurt you or anyone else in the Militia or the Alaska Independence Party. You must know I would never hurt my beloved Alaska by tying in with an unethical or illegal source. If nothing else, Wendy Sue would either leave me or kill me... No, when it is revealed, you'll know your trust in me was verified." Silas removed his hand and returned to his chair.

"Now as to the fuel barge... by purchasing it down there in Seattle, no one will even notice it. Fuel is always being transported up here by barge, and it was Clay who gave me the idea, of course, without his knowledge. The fuel will be towed up by a tug with records showing the fuel's destination as the Community of Minto. Truck rigs will rendezvous with the barge in Nenana, where our people will meet it and transfer the fuel over into one hundred 55-gallon drums. This keeps the authorities from knowing a large purchase of diesel fuel was made here in Alaska. Since 9-11, they keep records for the same, but no one will notice nitrates purchased by a farmer who gets the same amount every year and fuel ordered for a native community. Then combined with the nitrates, the fuel, and the ignition sources being created for us by our EOD personnel, we will have enough explosive power to level nearly half of Eielson Air Force Base, and the threat of that, my friends, will get someone's attention."

By 8 p.m., the Sanders' house was reasonably quiet. The TV was off. Dad was asleep in his chair and snoring up a storm. He had a nice thick brown wool throw draped over his stomach and legs. Clay had finally sat down on the couch, worn out from so many hours of host and KP duty. Eyes closed briefly when he was startled by a full dinner plate in the hands of a fair maiden that dropped over him from behind.

"T'is time my Knight Protector doth consume thy vittles," Emy said. The plate had sliced white turkey breast, heaps of homemade cranberry sauce, a small mountain of mashed potatoes covered in Mom's secret homemade gravy, a helping of Wendy Sue's 3-bean salad, someone's really tasty homemade turkey dressing with walnuts, and an ear of corn freshly husked and smothered in real butter.

Emy vanished briefly and returned with his cutlery, a large clean blue dishtowel in place of a napkin, and another tall glass of iced tea. Clay believed he had easily consumed a gallon or more of iced tea today, but this was his first real meal since early this morning, and he was quite hungry. But he wasn't able to finish it. It was after 10 p.m. when he said his goodnight to Emy inside the house. It was much too cold to be standing around outside on the porch, so he ran to a waiting Yellow Cab for a ride back to his apartment. He didn't know the driver, but the man was Middle Eastern, and for a moment, he thought about conversing in Farsi, for he actually did know the language quite well. No, Clay decided to just enjoy the ride in silence, for it had been a noisy day. It cost him $5.75, and he tipped the driver another $2.25. He understood now how hard a cab driver worked and was really happy not to be driving a cab in these temperatures. He'd grown up in this weather, but his body had acclimated to the desert regions of the world, and it would take all winter for him to change back. He shivering was evidence of that.

A week earlier, Clay had hoped the Friday after Thanksgiving Thursday would also be a company holiday and was thinking about taking Emy out to Chena Hot Springs. But not at Wickersham Chevrolet Car Dealership; the only people off today were the ones who had made previous arrangements so they could leave the area and have the holiday with family members outside of the Fairbanks region. In Clay's shop, he was short 5 mechanics; 4 men and 1 woman. With only three hours of work into the day, Clay's set of coveralls were a mess with grease and oil splotches from having helped out with the jobs. Every lift was busy.

The tire shop was also under Clay's supervision, and last Monday, he had lost one good man to a Workman's Compensation Injury; a tire machine had rejected the tire for some unknown reason, and the tire flew upward, striking the employee in the face. He suffered facial and neck injuries and was treated in the Emergency Room at Fairbanks Memorial Hospital. He was home now on Workman's Comp paid leave, while a professional safety company hired by the dealership's insurance company inspected the tire machine for mechanical problems or to see if it was operator error. Thankfully, they had three other machines, and the work could go on. This was Clay's first stab at filling out all the paperwork involved with an on-site employee injury, and he hoped it was his last.

Since coming to work, he had finished up one oil change of an F-150 Ford Pick-up, helped with the tune-up of a custom-built 8-cylinder Jeep Wrangler, and assisted in running down an electrical problem in the body frame of a recently purchased new Camaro. Clay loved the look of the new Camaro but could already see what the early signs of winter were doing with these sporty cars. They were not built for Alaskan roads or the extreme weather conditions. The new Camaro already had a pitted windshield, and some of the fiberglass was getting pretty scratched up.

The work in the body and paint shop was picking up, causing Clay to move some of the outside workers into those shops to help out. He couldn't have people sitting around, though; at the moment, it appeared all of the salespeople seemed to be spending most of their time in their cubicles due to a lack of customers. During the month of October and November, Permanent Dividend Funds were paid out, and for a few short weeks, the sales of new and used cars was up, but already the number of customers had dropped off rapidly.

With the snow came the extra work of keeping the vehicles cleaned off and the pathways between the rows clear for the customers and the movement of vehicles. When the temperatures dropped below minus 20 degrees, the batteries went dead, and a special cart had to be brought out with a battery charger, turbo-heater to warm up the engine, and a three-man crew to get the vehicle up and running to move into the garage to make it presentable for the customer. But with so few customers, this was only happening a couple times a day.

Then at midday, Clay heard his name being broadcast over the shop's PA system, "Will Mr. Jefferson please see Mr. Wickersham immediately in his office." It wasn't hard to recognize Sally's voice. She handled all the paging for the boss, while a girl from the part's department did it for the rest of the dealership. It was proven a female's higher voice transmitted clearer over the system, which is simply one of the reasons most police and first responder dispatchers were female.

Clay looked down at his coverall, he hated to show up looking so filthy, but the call said immediately. Clay told his assistant he was off to see the boss and not to bother him unless it was extremely important, "Don't call unless a lift fails, the roof gives way or terrorists are holding the car dealers hostage...second thought, let them have the dealers." There was a certain amount of attitude between the nicely dressed car dealers who worked upfront and the oily shop workers. The dealers worked on a commission basis and drove nice dealer loaners, while shop employees worked on hourly wages and were not allowed to drive any of the dealership vehicles off the lot, the exception being Clay, who was given a loaner for a brief time.

After he brushed off his dark gray coveralls and wiped his gritty hands with a soiled rag, he walked into Silas's outer office and was surprised to find his inner office door wide open. He walked to the doorway and saw Silas behind his desk, diligently at work on a stack of paperwork. His glasses were stuck perched upon his forehead, and Clay thought he resembled a middle-aged bookkeeper. His left hand held up his chin, with his left elbow braced against the desktop for support. His right hand held a black ink pen, and he appeared to be checking over a report form in front of him. Silas was again wearing his favorite open dark blue sports coat with gold brass buttons, and a button-down dress shirt of a soft baby blue color, except this one, came with narrow white stripes and had a stiff button down the neck. The shirt's top button was unbuttoned, and his black tie hung loose. He wore gray dress slacks and brown Velcro flap-over soft leather slippers with rubber soles. By the door, Silas kept a pair of tan and brown winter Sorrels for when he went outside. For extreme weather, he kept an aged pair of white "bunny boots" arctic footwear in his office closet. They were referred to as bunny boots because of their appearance; white rubber and enormous in size. Some people had also called them clown shoes, but they kept the foot warm in sub-zero temperatures, and the military had used them in Alaska for a long time.

Clay cleared his throat to announce himself, which only prompted a casual wave from Silas to bring him into the office. He then pointed to the nearest chair, but Clay objected, "Colonel, I'm filthy with grease."

Silas looked up for the first time and noticed Clay's condition, "I'll either clean it or have it replaced, now sit down and give me just a moment to finish up here."

Unable to accept those terms, Clay went into the outer office and picked up two car magazines. He brought them back inside and used them to line the chair as best he could to protect it. He then sat down, but he didn't relax.

It took only a moment longer for Silas to jot down a few more numbers and sign a couple of documents. He then hit a button, which summoned Sally, who entered through a side door. She said hello to Clay, removed the documents from Silas's hand, and returned to her office to leave these gentlemen in privacy. "Clay, would you close my door please and lock it... throw the deadbolt, too. I'd like some privacy for our chat." Silas always liked to use the word "chat" instead of having a talk, and Clay wondered if it was something he had picked up while working with the Australians in Vietnam. But he carried out his orders and then returned to his chair.

"I hate working the books. I leave most of it for the accountants, but I've been burned before by bookkeepers. In fact, one of them is down at Spring Creek Maximum Security Prison in Seward, serving out a 9-year sentence for embezzling my dealership out of $250,000 over a three-year period. Now I check over everything, and this time of year, it usually gives me a stomachache. Wendy Sue is worried I have an ulcer, but I told her I'm too old for those childish things."

"What's the problem, Colonel? The shop is working around the clock, and I could probably hand out more overtime if you authorized it."

"The problem isn't the shops, Clay; it's the sales floor. Comes every winter and lasts from late November through late March and sometimes early April. People simply do not come out in such in-climate weather to buy cars. They'll call for a tow or want their vehicle fixed and even have them repaired following accidents, but no buyers. It's a problem all dealer-ships deal with up here in Alaska, especially in Fairbanks, and it means layoffs. I cannot afford to keep so many people on over the winter. As it stands, I'll have to place most of the dealers on salary for the winter, or they'll starve, and I can't afford to lose my good dealers. One or two of the slackers will have to go, but they were leaving anyway. Not everyone can sell cars, and these guys need to find another occupation. Maybe write a best seller or become a book agent. People are always writing when they're cooped up for the winter."

Clay shifted around in his chair uncomfortably and then asked, "Colonel, are you trying to tell me I need to go job hunting tomorrow... I can probably get my old cab contract back."

Silas glared at Clay with a blank expression on his face, and then he burst into a grin, "I forgot for a moment you came from the military and not another executive position. But no, Clay, you're management here and would only have to go if you and I had a major disagreement over some-thing, and we were unable to work it out. No, it means three of your mechanics have to go. I've got to let loose some other people, but those three people are your concern. We have a 'last to come-first to go' policy here, and these are the names." Silas handed the paper with the three names to Clay. "I'll provide letters of reference for each of them, and if they haven't found employment by spring, they're to come to see us in early April for a re-hire date. They can collect unemployment right away since they're being terminated by no fault of their own and if they have any questions, have them see Sally to make an appointment. Also, Sally will provide you with the letters of reference to give them by the end of the day."

"Will they finish out the month, Colonel...it's only a few days."

He thought about it for a moment and remembered how each of those men was in his Militia. He replied, "Yes, they can finish out the month."

"All right, Colonel, was there anything else?" Clay stood up and waited. He was concerned with how pale the Colonel looked today and hoped it was only due to the cold.

"Yes, I am having a late lunch with Peterson and Johnson. I'd like you to join us at 2 p.m." Silas stood up and walked Clay to the door, unbolted the deadlock, and opened it.

"That would be fine, Colonel. I can turn things over to the chief mechanic for a couple of hours. Where shall I meet you?"

"Come to my office, and you and I will drive out together. We're meeting them up on Chena Pump Road." Silas patted Clay on the back, sent his shop supervisor on his way, and returned to his reports. He needed to find a new source for some of his older model parts. People were beginning to associate old clunkers with the words "vintage" and "antique." Parts had gotten expensive. He liked to keep his customers and maintain their trust because he knew a lot of used car buyers would return at some point to purchase a new automobile, and he wanted them to buy it from him. Silas also had another agenda in mind, and it involved the trust of the people of Fairbanks. He held a secret ambition that only his single benefactor and Wendy Sue knew about; Silas desired to be the first President of Alaska.

For at least half-an-hour Clay spent washing up in the men's shop locker room. He hoped in vain to get all the grease off his hands and arms and out from underneath his fingernails. At home, it usually took 20-minutes in a hot shower and his small scrub brush, but here he didn't have the hot shower. That's one of the things he needed to talk to Silas about; hot showers in the locker rooms. They already had installed eye washing stations for emergencies, so he figured the plumbing was nearly in place. He needed to have a plumber come in and give him some estimates to present to the boss and then talk it over with him.

Clay wanted to appear in some reasonably acceptable form of cleanliness when going out for lunch with the boss. Chena Pump Road was on the western side of Fairbanks, a very long stretch of roadway with multiple subdivisions that bordered the eastern side of the Chena River. With the Chena Pump House closed for the season, Clay suspected they were going to a private home for lunch, but the Colonel hadn't bothered to say who. So, after climbing into the Suburban with Silas, the two of them headed west on Airport Way. Eventually, they were traveling west on Geist Road, but instead of turning south along the Chena Pump Road, Silas continued driving straight ahead and up the hill into the Chena Hillside

Subdivision. This was an extremely large, rounded hilltop overlooking the Chena River, where dozens of very expensive homes had been built, and others were still under construction. The Chena Volunteer Fire Department was also located on this hillside, much to the delight of the homeowners and their insurance carriers.

"Colonel, are we picking anyone else up?" Clay asked. A hardened combat soldier, he had become a bit antsy by this time and was not one who enjoyed surprises.

In the background, the radio was playing old country hits. The colonel advertised over all the stations in town, but his favorite had always been the country stations, and at this time of day, they played the older hits of the 1960s. "No, Clay, but we're going up here to Major Peterson's place for lunch. I didn't say anything earlier because I've noticed how tongue-tied you seem to get around my two majors, but you've been invited, so relax."

He tried, but Clay couldn't relax, though he was trained well enough to make himself appear he was relaxed, and he went into that mode. Yet his mind ran through his options in the event his cover was blown. He couldn't imagine what other reason the Colonel would've lied to him, and the excuse stunk up the truck. He also watched the Colonel, who didn't appear he was taking Clay somewhere to be tortured for what he knew and then executed. In fact, Silas appeared quite relaxed and was even singing along with the song. Clay actually hated country music, a favorite of his grandpa's, but he didn't say anything. I sure hope my security detail isn't asleep on the job or stopping at McDonald's for lunch. I haven't seen them yet, but I'm told they're around, but a lot of good they're going to do if I get my head blown off in Major Peterson's house. Hopefully, the CSI people can find my blood on his rug, and it won't all be in vain.

They climbed the hillside and were now on the backside when Silas pulled left into a long unpaved driveway. The house was two stories high, with red cedar siding and a high pitched roof over the living room and dining room areas. The house had reddish-tinted metal roof panels, and Clay counted two smokestacks that shot up through the roof. The front room had two large picture windows, which allowed the people inside to have a grand view of the Chena River below and the Alaska Mountain Range off in the distance. Clay would later be told how, on a very clear day, the Petersons could see the majestic Denali, also known as Mt. McKinley. The house was 3500 square feet and came with a two-car garage, and though the snow was deep, the driveway was cleared, and Silas had no problem pulling in with his Suburban. Clay also saw a newer model gray Suburban in the driveway with the engine running. There was also a pick-up truck parked inside the garage.

With the temperatures so low, Silas would leave the truck running while they had lunch. He and Clay zipped up their parkas and dismounted for the short walk to the front door. The frost from their breath quickly turned the wolf hairs on their parka hoods white while waiting for someone to come to open the door. Allan welcomed them at the door, and Clay saw that Norm was already here. In the absence of Norm's older big 4x4 Ford F-350, he suspected the other major had come by taxi. With the cost of fuel for that beast, it was probably cheaper to use a cab. He saw that Norm was drinking his soda from a clear glass stuffed with ice, and on the coffee table in the living room was a red plastic circular ice chest with assorted sodas, and beside it were several glasses full of ice. Mrs. Peterson had played host and prepared a nice meal of assorted sandwiches and fruits. Once everyone was seated, with Clay sharing a couch with Norm and both Silas and Norm in easy chairs; Norm's was an overstuffed recliner, Silas was using the wife's well-padded rocker. Mrs. Peterson came in from the kitchen and said her goodbye to everyone, donned her parka, slid on her boots, grabbed up her black leather purse, and was gone. Clay realized the running gray Suburban was hers.

Silas, with a sandwich in hand, looked over at Allan and asked, "Are we alone?"

"Completely, Colonel," Allen replied. He then put his soda down, walked over to his living room closet, opened the door, reached up to the top shelf, and pulled out his own sonic wave scrambler. He brought it down and set it on the coffee table and plugged it in, which activated it. After that, he went over to the front door and deadbolted it. Then before returning to his seat, he went upstairs for a moment and came back down wearing a brown leather shoulder holster harness, with his Smith & Wesson .45 in it. Only then did Clay notice that Norm had pulled a Glock

Model 17 from beside him, previously hidden between the cushion and the side of the couch, and laid it on the arm of the couch.

Oh Boy! Things are getting' real sticky now. I might be able to take out one, maybe two, but if the Colonel is armed, I'm gonna catch a round for sure. Sure enough, Silas leaned forward and pulled a Smith & Wesson 5-shot Chief's Special .38 caliber revolver from out of the small of his back. He had carried it in a special holster he had made for him out of moose hide and clipped to the inside of his pants.

"Am I in some kind of trouble here, Colonel? Seems no one bothered to mention to me I needed to come armed to this luncheon, and except for tossing my sandwich in your face, I'm a bit outgunned here." Do I wait for the fat lady to sing or go for Norm beside me...I think he's probably the most dangerous and a far better shot than Peterson is. But before Clay makes his move, Norm held up his left hand and said, "Relax, Captain, these aren't for you. Besides, with your background, we're way too old to handle you. If we had problems to work out, we would've brought a couple squads along to hold you down."

"Then what's with all the artillery?" Clay asked.

"We always want to be ready, Clay. For what we're about to tell you, the government for the United States would love to break in that front door without a warrant, citing the Patriot Act, and arrest all of us. We'd be hauled away and most likely not even be seen for 90-days, while experts of the FBI, NSA, DSI...you name it, tried to pick our brains apart," Silas said. He then pointed to the scrambler. "This highly expensive device is to stop directional microphones from picking up and recording our voices. We are hoping it will also work for microwave and satellite surveillance, and as of yet, we haven't been raided or arrested."

"Well, Colonel, you certainly have my attention, and now that my stomach is unwinding, I will attempt to finish my sandwich and listen as to why I am here and what all this is about." I'm gonna live! Better yet, I've reached the inner circle...now maybe I'll find out what this is all about.

"Clay, what do you know about Alaska's history, and I'm not just speaking about the Athabascan people?" Silas wiped his face with a paper napkin and pulled a small blue spiral notebook from the inside left pocket of his sport coat.

"The basics, I guess…how our ancient peoples came across the ice bridge and settled this land, while others eventually continued on to the Lower 48 to become Native Americans of the Lower 48. Our Alaska has the three main native groups of Aleut, Eskimo, and Indian, which, unfortunately, as with the Native American Indians, our three people groups seem to have a lot of trouble getting along. I've read of the great Indian wars of the west and how the great Iroquois Nations were found and governed. But Alaskan Indians were more interested in hunting and fishing than fighting. We tried to get along with the white man right from the beginning, when they first came over from Russia and later from Europe, and it cost us dearly. How the Russians had laid claim to Alaska, then sold it to the United States, without even talking it over with any of the Alaskan Natives. That's about as far as I go on the history, Colonel, but I'm still interested in what this has to do with all the guns and this James Bond doohickey."

"Give me a moment for a quick history lesson, and then we'll talk," Silas said. "First off, true it was the Alaskan Native who was here first. But in 1741, the Danish Navigator Vitus Bering was commissioned by the Czar Peter the Great of Russia to land on the Alaskan Islands. The Bering Sea and Bering Strait were named for him. They then established the first white settlement on Kodiak Island in 1784 and, in their arrogance, believed they now owned the land…all of it. In effect, though, Russia did legally own some 7.4 acres of land in Southeast Alaska, on the Island of Sitka. They had purchased this small parcel from the Indians, where they had built a fort, and later, a famous battle was fought there. When Russia sold Alaska to the United States, they had no legal right to do so, other than those 7.4 acres. The remainder of Alaska was owned by the various tribes, but their tribal rights were totally ignored. The USA paid Russia $7,200,000.00 for 591,004 square miles, which comes to basically two-cents per acre. A ridiculous cost, even in those days. Alaska also comes with 6,640 miles of coastline.

"We jump ahead now to the great gold rush of 1897-98, where thousands of people come north from the United States to find the mother lode in Nome and Skagway. Most of them end up going home broke, and all too many never leave Alaska alive. Then in 1903, the USA and Canada settle a borderline dispute and begin working toward making Alaska a US Territory, which finally occurred in 1912. We all know Alaska became a state in 1959, oil reserves were discovered in Prudhoe Bay in 1968, and the rush was on for black gold. With the boom came the need to move the crude oil, and the great Alaskan pipeline was finished in 1977 from Prudhoe Bay to the Port of Valdez.

"Our most western point is only 51-miles from Russia's coastline. But, 2 miles separate our former Defensive Early Warning site on Little Diomede Island in the Bering Sea from Russia's Big Diomede Island. When the ice bridge is formed every winter, we all know that anyone can easily walk across from Alaska to Russia or back the other way. The Alaska-Canadian Highway, built by mostly Afro-American soldiers in World War II, is 1,422 miles long and runs between Dawson Creek, British Columbia, and Delta Junction, Alaska—"

Clay held his hand up, "Colonel, I don't mean to interrupt, but I know all of this, and I'm not sure the point you are trying put across..."

This time Clay was stopped, interrupted by Allen. "Let him finish, Clay. The Colonel always has a point as you will see," Allen said, and the Colonel nodded his thanks.

"As I was saying, Alaska's constitution was first adopted in 1956, three years before statehood was voted on. We have a governor, lieutenant governor, 13 commissioners appointed by the governor. Based on our population, US law allows us two US senators and one US representative for serving us in DC. In Juneau, our state capital, we have 20-state senators and 40-representatives. Local boroughs number 12, but that number is due to change at any time.

"In 1971, the Alaska Native Claims Settlement Act came to be, giving $962.5 Million in funds and 40 million acres of land to the state's Alaska Natives. Some viewed it as a way of buying the state from them when it was previously never purchased. Not all of the Alaskan Natives accepted these funds or the acreage. Some of the communities did not have corporations in place to accept these funds. Then in 1976, the Alaska Permanent Fund came to be, where 1% of the net profits from oil revenue were broken down every year and issued in part as a dividend to all qualified Alaskans who had applied for it.

"Then the worst happened; President Jimmy Carter in-acted the infamous Antiquities Act, where he stripped Alaskans of over 1 million acres of public land and transformed it into National Park land, wilderness lands, and refuges. One such refuge is the great Arctic National Wildlife Refuge, a hotbed of contention. Here it is believed, ANWR is sitting upon possibly the largest oil deposit in North America, and this act prevents Alaskans and citizens of the US from profiting from it. While we are paying up to $5 for a gallon of gas, having to tolerate those people overseas who hate us for our religion and something that happened more than 2,000 years ago, they could shut the flow of oil off at any time, while this oil sits below the ground for us to take."

"Yes, Sir," Clay replied. "I've read all of this and agree with our need to drill in ANWR, but until Congress allows it, this will never happen, and the Environmentalists have an extremely strong lobby."

"Exactly, and that is my point and why you are here this afternoon. These same lobbyists own a good percentage of our DC politicians through bribes, campaign donations, and promises of future jobs. What if I was to tell you there was a way to get around Congress to free up Alaska and let Alaskans run our own affairs?"

*Easy boy don't jump! You don't want to lose this one now because you didn't set the hook. Move slow, let them reel you in, and remember, you're a former Captain in the US Army, act somewhat offended by all this.* "Colonel, you're speaking of the US Congress here, right?" Clay moved toward the edge of his cushion, his eyes having that glare of offense, but not too much. "Sir, I'm not a bit happy with our political state and our country's current downward spiral, but I'm not sure what we can do about it up here in Alaska."

"What about Alaska for Alaskans, Clay?" Allen asked.

But before Clay could reply, Norm interrupted, "How often have you seen the federal government either ignore us completely, when we need something we've been promised or then simply do what they want with our natural resources and our Guard units, while we're supposed to stand up, donate our men and women and wave Old Glory to the tune of these highly paid lobbyists. It's oil and defense contractors that are keeping us in the Middle East, Clay."

"Norm, you're a former Marine, and what I am hearing here surprises me. I'm a patriot, and as for Old Glory, I love the history of my country. From the mid-1700s through today, our country has worn the white hat. We've been the 7th Cavalry for the world, and from what I'm hearing here, you'd like to think of a way to separate Alaska from the USA. Am I right?"

"Relax, Clay," Allen said, "...though I find it amusing to hear an Indian praise the laurels of the 7th Cavalry. Much less all the broken treaties the US has swept aside as the federal troops moved one Indian tribe after another onto the federal reservation to make room for white man's civilization." Allen stopped for a moment, seeing how red in the face Norm was getting. He hated it when they brought up the indignities suffered by the American and Alaskan Native People at the hands of the white man.

The room was quiet for a moment, and then Allen continued, "Clay... no, we're simply talking here, and you haven't heard the rest of it yet. Give the Colonel a chance to finish."

"Let me tell you about our vote for statehood, and you tell me what you think of the process undertaken by our Alaskan politicians," Silas said. He stood up and walked about the room as he spoke. He needed to digest his sandwich, and walking helped. The old stomach had given him some problems, and pretty soon, he would have to go see a doctor, and he wasn't looking forward to someone poking around in certain areas with all sorts of new-fangled tools.

"As I said, they adopted the Constitution three whole years before the vote was taken, giving certain people a lot of time to set the thing up to go their way. The political party in power had its key people in place, and that's all they needed to get the ball rolling up here. They held the key positions in the various committees both here and in DC and were connected with the right amount of US senators and representatives. They also certainly had the money needed to get their plan through.

"Now you may not know this, but the voting for statehood was to be regulated by United Nations Law, which at the time required several options to be placed on the actual ballot for the voter to vote on. The first option was a vote for statehood; the second option is a no vote to statehood, and Alaska remains a territory; the third option was for Alaska to have the opportunity to pursue alignment with another country...say

Canada, with which we share a good-sized border with; the fourth option was to obtain sovereignty and allow Alaska to become its own country. Now for some strange reason, which was never explained or even cleared up, the ballot only had two options on it; statehood or no statehood. They would either become a state or remain a territory. The voters, the citizens of Alaska, were not being allowed the decision of the other two options, and this was conducted by UN law and apparently ignored. There was also no opportunity offered for a second election to right things. To make matters worse, the ballots were only printed in English. A lot of Alaskan Native People could not write, much less read the English language in 1959."

Silas looked Clay in the face, "Did your grandfather vote for statehood?"

It took a moment for Clay to remember his Grandpa's words about those days, and he seemed to recall how he hadn't voted and didn't know very many people who had. "No, he didn't."

"I didn't think so. I don't have the numbers, but a lot of the Native Alaskans I've spoken to who lived outside of the main population areas were not able to vote. We've also learned how the US government committed some very unethical acts during these times. True, they were not technically illegal because voter registration laws were still not worked out or implemented, but the US Military brought up thousands of troops for short temporary duty assignments during this brief period, and they were not only told how to vote by their officers but transported in groups down to the polls. Some say there were several beer parties held on base afterward as a way of rewarding the troops before flying them home the same week. These short term assignments must have cost the American taxpayer a fortune in travel expenses and TDY pay for the troops."

Good, God! Grandpa said they pulled a lot of high-jinx back then, especially against the native people, but I had no idea to such a degree. And I have little doubt the Colonel is telling me the truth; it's probably easy enough to check if I look in the right places. But I can tell the Colonel has more. Goes along with the "No native allowed" bars, bathrooms, and restaurants of the 1960s.

"Between the time of the creation and adoption of the Constitution and the vote for statehood, the US government came to the conclusion that with Alaska's limited population, the new state government might not have the funds to operate. So, working in tandem with the statehood committee, they came up with what is termed the 90/10 statehood compact. Now understand, most states receive a low percentage of funds from the US Government, about 33%, for the mineral wealth taken from their ground in the form of gold, silver, oil, natural gas... the list is long. So, Congress, in its infinite wisdom, proposed and made a compact with the statehood committee to pay Alaska 90% instead of 33%, giving the state the needed monies to operate with. Now, this was a great encouragement to go for statehood. As a territory, they weren't receiving anything. Not even the 33%. But like a crooked used car dealer, our US Congress immediately backed out on the deal once statehood was signed into law by President Eisenhower. Currently, I believe there are several native corporations suing the US government over this 90/10 issue, but they'll be tied up in court for decades.

"Now the founder of the Alaska Independence Party, Joe Vogler, tried to press the United Nations into hearing his proclamation and evidence to force a second statehood vote, but he got nowhere, and he quickly became a thorn in the side of the US government. Somewhere along the line, he became too much trouble, and Joe was murdered. Supposedly he was killed by an unstable friend, but from what I've been able to piece together, the murder investigation was a shabby one and accomplished all too quickly for a homicide. The killer confessed right away, a plea deal was used, and the man sort of vanished into the penal system. Sort of a Ruby to Oswald thing, or maybe an Oswald to Kennedy thing; I'll let the pro's figure it out. But it stinks. Joe is gone, and the US Government is happy... well until this 90/10 stuff started showing up in local federal court and it's sort of hard to murder off a whole native corporation and not catch the eyes and ears of the International news services."

"Wow... I am... I am... Colonel, I'm still wondering why I'm here. Not that I don't mind hearing all this, and I so dearly hope some of my family is involved in this legal action."

"Has any of this made you angry, Clay?" Norm asked.

"Major, it's real hard to get me angry anymore. I've seen a lot, bought way too many of those proverbial t-shirts, worn 'em out, and burned 'em to ashes. So, sometimes, I no longer know what to think. But I love Alaska, there is no other place like it in the world, and I would die to protect her."

"I hope so, Clay," Silas said in a serious tone of voice and added, "... because I am about to brief you on an extremely sensitive matter and the true reason behind your presence here today... and it may involve you risking your life... for Alaska."

# 9

# THE NEXT STEP IN THE GAME

*Bassett Army Hospital*
*Fort Wainwright, Fairbanks, Alaska*
*Room # 318*
*1631 Hours, (4:31 P.M.) December 3rd*

Doc Adams's note pad now was full, and he interrupted Clay for a moment with an upraised hand, while he switched to a second spiral notebook. This one was red and somewhat larger than the previous one. He then braced this new one on his knee, opened it to the first page, and made a couple notes on top. Doc then nodded to Clay to signify he was ready to continue.

The doctor's treatment room was overly warm today, causing both men to sweat. Fort Wainwright's massive coal-fired steam plant heated nearly all of the Army's buildings, with the radiating moist heat piped out through miles of large pipes and into the various structures around the base. Smaller pipes then broke off from the main one until even smaller ones delivered the heat into the baseboard heaters in separate housing units. It was an inexpensive way of heating the post. The coal was shipped up by train car, carried north via the Alaska Railroad from the Healy Coal Mines approximately ninety miles to the south of Fort Wainwright.

During the colder weather, the steam plants on the post, at Eielson Air Force Base and for the City of Fairbanks, created clouds of microscopic white ice crystals, and this formed what was known in Alaska as ice fog. This fog, thicker than the worst fog London or San Francisco had to offer, often caused some serious accidents. Generally, as it grew colder, the upper air forced the colder air down to the surface, which meant the ice fog didn't descend upon the highway or open areas around the valley until minus 35 degrees or lower. Above that temperature, the clouds of vapor coming out of the plants simply filled the skies over the Tanana Valley with icy wisps of air.

His white handkerchief soiled from usage to wipe the sweat off his forehead and cheeks, Doc Adams stopped his writings for a moment to again wipe the area over his eyebrows and clean his eyeglasses from sweat droplets. He had already removed his white doctor's smock but was compelled by pride not to remove his dark brown and tan striped wool sweater. Had he remembered the steam heat of this old hospital building, he would've worn one of his vests. But he was not going to sit here in front of Clay in a stretched-out white t-shirt. Doctors simply didn't do that. He was wearing his black slacks with two-inch cuffs and had given in to removing his Sorrels, leaving his feet in thick wool blue socks. The Sorrels were placed over by the door, where they were leaving a puddle from the ice and snow outside. When Doc came inside the hospital, the outside temperature was dropping, and the 40-foot tall electric signboard on Airport Way had shown it to be a minus 51 degrees. Thankfully, the taxi he had taken was nice and warm, and they had no problem getting on post, though the driver, a Muslim, was wearing an off-white turban, and this surprised Doc. But then he figured the MP's and civilian Department of Defense Police had seen the man often enough. But he knew that made him just as dangerous, if not more. Insurgents or terrorists, whatever word they were likely to use, would use someone who was known by the front gate defenders and who might gain easy entrance. Doc would make a note of this and pass it down the line to the MP Provost Martial. Doc Adams could envision the next terrorist attack would come in a fleet of Yellow Cabs, and all these Muslim drivers were up here making test runs. A lot of explosives could be packed into a large cab.

Clay's heavy blue parka with a wolf fur bordered hood lay on the floor, his new black Sorrel boots melting on the floor next to Doc's pair. He was in a brown leather vest, a heavy blue and black patch long sleeve wool shirt, and blue Levi's, with a three-inch cuff. He needed to have the Levi's hemmed but just hadn't had time to get it done. He was wearing a pair of calf-length gray wool boot socks, but the left one was beginning to show heel ware and in need of mending. Clay was in the process of rolling up his sleeves while Doc switched over to his second notebook. The steam heat was getting to him, too, and the next thing to go would be the vest. They both had good-sized water bottles with them, and they had finished nearly half of them already. They wanted to open the door, which led directly into the large hallway, but the highly sensitive nature of their meeting prevented this.

"All right then, let's go over that last part again," Doc said. He held his pen in his right hand, and Clay noticed from their first meeting he was one of those pen chewers and probably used it to help him concentrate. But he knew some used it as a stress reliever, and he wondered, which one might Doc be? Clay saw Doc glance over at the recorder, knowing he was ensuring it was still operating and then returned his attention to Clay.

"They had me rattled there for a moment...I was thinking seriously about making my play to escape, fight my way out, and make it to the post, but then everything changed. The Colonel started making sense in his sort of way, I mean. I'm saying that with all the causes out there, lawful and unlawful, the Colonel, as a spokesman, has a way of making everything sound reasonable and plausible. I must admit, he had me agreeing with him on those last two points he finally got around to. If the statehood committee did conduct the election that way, it was conducted illegally and no bones about it. If the military got behind it, the whole thing stinks. Then we have this whole 90/10 thing, but I can still see that as a civil matter against the feds and one that can hopefully be settled in court... even though it might take another twenty years and a federal court may be biased."

"Tell me what you feel, Clay... as an Alaska Native?" Doc had the end of the pen between his teeth, his left leg crossed over the top of his right leg, and his left toe-tapping away to some beat in his mind.

"I'm angry, Doc," Clay said, and he stood up suddenly and walked about the room, which didn't allow for much strutting one's anger off. They also had the exam table to deal with, so Clay gave up, tossed his hands up in frustration, and slumped back into his seat. "The whole thing just pisses me off. What the government did to my people, the Aleuts, and the rest of the native people…They imprisoned the Aleuts in World War II, and they exploded a nuclear bomb underneath the land near Nome, supposedly to get some idea of what might happen if they used such a device to build a big harbor up there. They also put nuclear isotopes inside the native women without their knowledge to see what would happen to them… can you imagine how a white woman or her husband would feel to find that out? They'd be blowing something up, but not the native people.

"This is our government! The United States of America and the politicians use us as test-tube experiments, and yes, I am really angry, and I found myself walking right into the Colonel's charm… except, I was able to remember who I was and why I was there. I also remembered who I owed my allegiance to. I'm an Alaskan, but I am an American first and above all, a Christian. I've bled for my country, fought for my country, and watched my buddies die for this country. So, if this is what you're wondering, Doc. I know where I'm at and where I need to be, but I'm still angry about how my beautiful Alaska was mistreated by people in power.

"But, Doc, I'm a history nut, and I know it's just not minorities who've been hurt, oppressed, and killed. I've read how white men and women were enslaved, shipped over to the colonies from England and France to be slaves, and many of them died in chains. So seldom do our schools teach on this. It is not a question of race, creed, or ethnic background. It comes down to greed and simple evil in mankind to control the fate of others. To enslave or kill those who do not agree with them, and I am afraid the Colonel may be marching down a path he has no idea of the price he will have to pay or the cost those who serve him will have to give up. But yes, Doc, I am angry."

Doc Adams needed to get Clay calmed down before his operative lost it, knowing this would be listened to many times back in DC. "Talk to me about this AFBM."

"As I said earlier, it is called the Alaska Freedom Brigade Militia, or

AFBM and simply pronounced as "Fam" among those involved. This is a secret part of the Alaska Defense Force, also known as the ADF, and it is led by Colonel Wickersham. The other members of the ADF, including the Commanding Officer of the entire Militia, based in Anchorage, do not know of its existence. Colonel Wickersham has approximately one hundred and fifteen personnel, which includes a Major Allen Peterson as his Executive Officer and Major Norm Johnson, his Operations Officer. I've recently been accepted into the inner core as we hoped and have continued on in my job as a Training Officer and Assistant Operation Officer. They've told me they are still short of personnel for their one hundred and twenty-member goal, and their target date is sometime in July. They trust me to some degree, but I haven't been given the target yet or actual date, but I do know the AFBM has six personnel with Explosive Ordinance Disposal training from the military. Nearly all of the AFBM are the best the ADF has to offer and come with some very fine US Army, Marine, and Air Force Training behind them. We have many combat veterans, some from as far back as Vietnam, and I can tell you they are loyal enough to follow the Colonel into the fiery pits of Hell."

"You mentioned earlier about the AFBM having an array of military equipment; let's go over that again, please."

Clay nodded his head, took in a deep breath, and then continued with his briefing, "We have a well-armed fighting force of nearly 115-men and women, with armored personnel carriers, adequate military training, and personal drive to carry out some form of domestic terrorism. They have six fully operational armored personnel carriers; two APC-113 on dual tracks, four APC- 706 wheeled 'rubber ducky" vehicles; all 6 from the Vietnam era, and each one set up with mounts for automatic weapons. I have also heard they have another rubber ducky being worked on to be ready for use by summer. As you are already aware, they have several Class Three dealers who possess automatic weapons: M-4s, M-16s, M-60's, World War II-era .30 and .50 caliber machine-guns. Some foreign machine-guns from Japan, Germany, England, and France. I know of no grenades, LAWS, or AT4's. I have heard nothing of Semtex, C-4, or Claymore mines. But with one hundred and fifteen-troops, this makes for a sizeable armed force."

"Let's now got to the points that struck a nerve with you, what the Colonel is most likely using to recruit his personnel," Doc Adams said.

"Statehood vote," Clay immediately replied. "Colonel wants the United Nations to use its authority to ensure a lawful election. He desires it under UN guidelines and Alaska residency laws, the same way Joe Vogler wanted; a true vote for statehood by legal Alaskan residents. One vote in which the US Government will honor and ensure all Alaska communities will receive ballots and interpreters to be provided for those Alaska Native elders who still fail to understand English. I know of several elders who still don't speak a word of English, trying to hold on to their dying language. I'm not sure they've ever learned to read it."

Clay looked over at the recorder and added, "DC is going to flip with they read this report, but I need to add a warning here, Doc."

"A warning?"

"Recently, the feds and Alaska State Troopers arrested and brought to court several militia members on weapon charges. They were originally charged with Conspiracy to Commit Murder of some judges and state troopers, but some of the charges were dropped because the District Attorney botched the case. Though these people were not part of the ADF, they've gotten a lot of Alaskans riled up and on their side to some degree. While a good share of the state thinks these guys are some idiotic clowns and they were found guilty, some Alaskans feel the federal government got scared and stepped in too fast and too hard. I'm not sure how much traveling you've done around the US, Doc, but Alaskans are the most hardheaded and stubborn people you'll ever come across... We have to be to handle this country and its wildness. We're isolated, the weather and land are unforgiving, but we have a lot of pride, and we love our freedom above all else. Too much government is going the wrong way. If the Feds and the state come in here and arrest the AFBM right now, you're looking at a lot of trouble.

"Not only that, Doc, but a lot of people are going to be killed. Give me some time; this S-Day, as the Colonel calls it, isn't supposed to happen until summer. I have all winter. Have the bosses in DC give me the time to work this case. If they come in now...too many innocent people are going to die, the bosses will be tied up in dozens of sessions before Congress, and the President will have to be thinking about a new job. You'll have Ruby Ridge and Waco times ten before it was over."

"Besides keeping you on the case, what would you recommend at this point, Clay?"

"Increase the manpower of the FBI office in Anchorage, but only add a couple more agents to the Fairbanks office. If the AFBM gets wind of something, they'll go underground and possibly hit somewhere else at a later date. Maybe divide into smaller teams and hit all the military installations at once or the federal buildings. Simply a platoon of AFBM could secure the Federal Court House in Anchorage and hold the judge's hostage or blow the place apart with what's in the building. Take your store-bought cleaning fluids... a good EOD man can make a bomb out of just about anything found in a building's cleaning or utility storeroom.

"Washington needs to move slow; they've been embarrassed enough over Ruby and Waco. Let me find out more, especially if the AFBM finds out you're on to them and does go underground. I want to learn where the illegal automatic weapons are hidden and who is the money man supporting the Colonel. There's just too much money involved in this operation, and I know the Colonel couldn't be carrying it on his own. I'm curious to see if another country is behind this, like Russia or China. I know China played this game in Africa and South America too."

"I'll add in my two cents, Clay. I think you're right. We now know we have an extremely dangerous situation here involving a large armed force, possibly in possession of explosives if you're right about the EOD people and those automatic weapons you spoke of. The threat situation is high. But and this is a big but, we do not know the target or when this event is to occur, except sometime in the summer. You are in a perfect place to learn these things. I also know about the current legal matter involving those militia members and the general atmosphere favoring them, mostly because of Alaskan's desire for freedom and less government interference. Also, it should be noted, the personnel involved in this domestic terrorism do not possess nuclear, chemical, or biological weapons of mass destruction.

"So, in wrapping this week's session up, I'd recommend we leave Operative Jefferson in place and continue on with this operation. If and when we learn of the target and the date, we can then reassess the situation and look at our options." Doc Adams turned off the recorder but kept his notebook on his knee.

"Now, tell me about your love life."

"You go right for the throat, Doc."

"Recorder is off, this is just you and I talking...Think about me as your big brother, and you're asking for advice."

"Doc, I hate to break it to you, but you're old enough to be my Dad, and I'm giving you a few years there on the good side."

"Cold, down and dirty, Clay, and here I'm working for you so you can stay around here and enjoy Emy's companionship, and you go and slam me. I'm hurt, young man."

"Doc, you're like a rattler...a nice rattler, but I doubt you can be hurt, and I think you probably got one heck of a bite if you need to strike."

"Wrong there, my boy. I can be hurt, and I've been hurt, but yes, I've got a real cold side like the snake you mentioned, and that's to protect me from being hurt again. It's too easy to get involved with my operatives. I've tried to quit this business before and even fled to Europe under another name. But I knew too much about the right people, so it was either a bullet behind the ear in London, a hit and run accident on some back street in Paris or come back to DC and play nice. I even have a contract and signed in blood that says I can't write a book about my life until five-years after I retire. By then, they expect me to be dead of old age, or one of my old patients had found me and didn't want his story told, and I disappeared. Or I got disgusted with the whole mess and simply tossed my computer files in the river and walked away."

"Just who have you worked with, Doc?"

"Remember that old saying, 'if I told you I'd have to kill you,' well it's true. Wouldn't be me, I'm too passive, but someone would. Poison in your toothpaste, sniper from some car...you know the game. So skip it, Clay. But I will tell you, you're my last operative. I'll do some government PTSD cases, drunks, and other addictions, but no more operatives. I can't handle the excitement...or the worry."

"Thanks, Doc...I know you meant that for me," Clay said, and he patted Doc on the knee.

"Well, as to Emy, we're moving along. We're all looking forward to Christmas. I've been invited over for both Christmas Eve and Christmas morning. I'm still looking for her Christmas gift, which is driving me batty. I'm trying to talk her into attending Christmas Eve services at my old church, but all I've gotten was a 'maybe.' Now, every time we walk by a jewelry store, she wants to stop and look at engagement and wedding rings. No hint here; she drags me over and points at the ones she likes. The girl has expensive tastes."

"Wish I could meet her. From what you tell me about her, I like her. Somehow, just speaking off the collar here, I hope we can find a way to get her out of this. The whole family is easily looking at twenty-years for conspiracy and worse if they carry out the act."

"I'll drag her kicking and screaming away from whatever it is before I let her do anything that stupid. I might be angry at the government, I might be an Indian, but domestic terrorism is still terrorism, and it's not the way to go."

"Glad to hear you say that, Clay." Doc Adam uncrossed his knee and stood up to stretch. He then walked over to pick up his boots and brought them back over to the chair to put them on. Once they were on, he wiped his forehead and face with the damp handkerchief. He knew now to ensure there was a box of Kleenex in this room whenever they met.

## BACK AT THE DEALERSHIP

When Clay got back to the dealership, he found Silas in the shop area, talking to a few mechanics. After Clay changed back into his filthy coveralls; one set was good for only two days if he stayed busy; he came out and saw that Silas was still there and wandered over to the group.

"You people are sure you want your Christmas party here instead of somewhere else this year?" Silas asked the men and women around him, which had grown in number since Clay had first come in. "Colonel," a tall mechanic with a greasy blue baseball cap, was speaking and waving his hands about, "...no sense on the extra cost of renting someplace, not when we have the whole showroom floor and shop area to move about in." A female mechanic then added, "You'll have the place all prettied up for the holidays, and all we need to do is bring in the food."

"Sure, Colonel," a militia sergeant and parts man said in a raised voice. "...this way, you can spend more money on beer, and our Christmas bonuses get fatter."

Silas shook his head, "Joey, the only thing getting fatter around here is that tire around your tummy." Silas then spotted Clay and waved him over and pointed at Joey, "Captain, this NCO is not how I imagined my noncommissioned officers to look. Do you think you could run twenty-pounds off him by summer?"

With a raised eyebrow, Clay's glare shot in Joey's direction, who was now trying to back into the crowd to avoid the attention, when Clay replied, "Consider it accomplished, Colonel, I'll be putting a few of our personnel on a new exercise routine of which I will be joining with them three times a week at the Fairbanks Athletic Club down the road. I've arranged with the club for veterans who are serving with the ADF on a regular basis to attend special three-days a week lunch hour work-outs on free passes for the purpose of getting in shape. On Wednesday, this will involve swimming, so if you need a pair of swim trunks-get them. I will be posting a list of those personnel who will attend this activity on Monday, Wednesday and Friday, or be considered AWOL. This will begin the first week in January, so for you married people, please notify your wives and or husbands of this activity. If I need to call them to verify this, I am willing to do so. We certainly do not want your spouses to suspect you're sneaking away to meet some sweet thing for a one-hour getaway at the hotel down the street."

"Thank you, Captain," Silas said. He then bid his farewell to the troops and began making his way to his office, but grabbed Clay by the elbow along the way and stopped by his outer office door for a quiet conversation. "That was a good idea about the gym work-outs. If those men need an extra hour, I'll keep them on the clock. But, Clay, I want them in shape by the end of May."

"Actually, Colonel, I went to the club to check out their prices for my own needs." Clay patted his stomach. "I've put on twelve-pounds since coming home from overseas and need to start jogging again. The club has an indoor track, and I really love to swim. While I was there, I got talking with the guy behind the desk, and he ended up being a Desert Storm vet and now a member of the Alaska Air National Guard. I told him about the ADF and how I was the new training officer, and my concern for the shape of some of my troops. Before long, we'd worked this whole thing out for these free passes. He's hoping it may lead to some extra memberships once the troops begin their programs. I signed Emy and me up for a one-year full package, mostly out of a way of saying thanks to him. But I need the workouts. I love weightlifting, and they have one of the finest gyms in Alaska."

Silas grinned, thought about something for a moment, and then said, "I'll give you a little perk... you lose twenty pounds by first of June, and I'll reimburse you for your membership fee."

"For both of us, Colonel?" Clay asked with a sly smile on his face.

"Only as a wedding gift, Captain," Silas replied. He had the last smile at Clay's expense. He walked on by and went into the outer office, but then remembered something and turned around to catch Clay before he walked off. "Clay, have that list of names to Sally as soon as you can. I want her to make a copy to be put in their personnel files. If they lose the weight, I'll figure out some kind of special reward for their efforts."

"Yes, Sir... but, Colonel, what will the sales staff say about having the party here instead of a nice restaurant?"

"Like the man said a moment ago, we have the room, we'll have the decorations up, and you know those greedy dealers will be expecting fatter bonuses for the money I'll be saving. But the joke will be on them. This has been a tough year, and they'll be lucky they receive any bonus besides a frozen turkey, a cheap Christmas stocking filled with candy canes, and a couple Walmart gift certificates."

"The business is looking that bad, Colonel?"

"No, but we're right at that fine edge between the black and red inks.... a part of winter, Clay. Don't let it worry you; seven more months and the fourth of July party will be a smasher. We'll have more sales, people are happier, and our main shop is busy with clunkers breaking down. I just wish those people in Detroit would go back to making their engines the way they used to. One-hundred-thousand miles and the beast was ready for the heap, but now they're going two hundred-thousand miles or better. Bodies are junk, but the mechanical side is outstanding. Too bad the union laborers have their wages jacked up so high the average customer is now paying for cars what we used to pay for houses fifteen-years ago. That's completely absurd, but it's what we're stuck with."

"I know, sir. I'm still amazed at what I paid for on that one-year-old used Camaro, and that was with the employee and veteran's discount. I can't help but think we're only hurting ourselves in the long run. Higher wages at the plants bring higher costs to the dealerships, and it's passed on down to the car buyer. No one wins that way."

"I forgot to ask, have you had any problems with the car?" Silas heard his name being called, and he glanced over his shoulder to see Sally standing in the doorway that led into his inner office. "I'm sorry, Clay, I'm being summoned. We'll have a chat later."

Clay had walked the new car line for several days but couldn't find anything that satisfied him. He knew he needed wheels, mainly because it would look funny for him to be using a taxi all the time, and he really didn't want to invest in a new ride, knowing he'd be leaving Alaska again once this case was wrapped up. Then his eyes widened in delight one morning when an Army private came into the dealership to return his one-year-old Camaro. A former US Army E-5 Sergeant, he had bought the Camaro when he reenlisted. But then he got himself into trouble, lost all of his rank, and could no longer afford the car payments or locate anyone who could purchase the vehicle from him. He was doing a voluntary repossession, which would be harmful to his credit for the next eight years, but he had little choice. He told the Sales Manager that with the loss of his rank, he couldn't even afford the monthly car insurance payments.

By late afternoon the same day, Clay owned the navy blue Camaro, with a black interior and a killer sound system capable of shaking the whole vehicle with the bass speaker in the trunk. It was a four-speed automatic and came with a big block eight-cylinder engine, which the GI had added to equal the power of four hundred HP. The tires were custom ordered L-60 from St Louis, with vintage chromed Crager-Mags, usually seen on the Camaro's of the late 1960s to mid-1970s. Clay was in love, and he would find a way to ship it where ever he was going or store it near the John F Kennedy School for Special Forces. Clay knew of several of his Green Beret and Delta Force buddies who had their cars stored in heated garages, protected by twenty-four-hour security.

The Party came and went, one week before Christmas, and when Silas finally got all the receipts for the party piled up on his desk and totaled them up, his face took on a certain pale ghoulish-like look; as if all the blood had suddenly rushed out of his head and poured from his pores to puddle at his feet. He pulled from his desk the written estimate Pike's Restaurant had provided him in Mid-November, which was the opportune time to reserve a location for a Christmas Party. He compared the estimate to his actual costs and saw that his attempt to save money had cost him an extra one thousand-six-hundred and ninety-four dollars. This did not take into account the employee gifts, which was always an eighteen to twenty-pound frozen turkey or ham dinner package from Fred Meyer's Meats and fifty-dollars in gift certificates from Walmart. General employees did not receive cash bonuses, but management did, and this year he provided along with the dinner packages a five-hundred-dollar bonus for each member of his management staff, and this included his car dealers.

At the party, the employees exchanged gifts. They used the name drawing tradition, but it was done by departments. In this way, a mechanic or parts employee was not expected to have to buy a gift for a car dealer or a supervisor. Silas never participated in this since he already handed out gifts to everyone, and he always had a special gift for Sally. This year he presented her with a diamond and precious jeweled broach, which was picked out by Wendy Sue. She had noticed how Sally admired it one time while the two ladies were out window shopping to keep the cabin fever from grabbing hold. People who stay closed in all the time because of the severe cold tend to go a bit batty, and in Alaska, it is referred to as Cabin Fever. A lot of the locals will brave the harsh weather to keep this from happening and simply browse the stores. With the massive Fred Meyers and Walmart stores, along with Sam's Club in Fairbanks, this gave the people of Fairbanks plenty of room to stretch their legs and check on the latest sales. There were even people who would put on their gym wear and do laps around the stores in the early morning hours when they first opened.

It wasn't until Christmas Eve when Clay finally decided on his Christmas gift for Emy. But he wanted to do something for the entire family, and at seven p.m., a U-Haul truck drove up to the front of the Sanders' house, followed by an older Suburban with a load of six- young men. Clay had paid six of his single employee's twenty-five dollars each to help him for one hour. They all volunteered, but he knew they could use the extra money and made sure they took it. The back of the U-Haul was opened when Clay jumped out from behind the steering wheel and slammed the door shut to keep the heat in. According to the Airport Way electronic sign, the temperature when he went by was a minus forty-four degrees. He had his heavy blue parka on and a dark blue Navy style beanie-cap over his head and covering his ears. He was also wearing thick leather insulated mittens.

"Let's get this unloaded and you all inside before we all freeze to death," Clay ordered. All of these men not only worked for him but were enlisted men in the ADF and AFBM. Under a thick pile of U-Haul gray blankets were four boxes of assorted sizes, and two of them were of a very large size.

"We'll put the bigger boxes in the garage, but I'll have to get it open from inside. The smaller two will go inside the house and watch where you step. Mrs. Sanders has the whole house decorated to the max, looks like a Macy's Department Store Window. "

When he saw the confused look on their faces, he shook his head and added, "Your lack of education is showing. Macy's is the store made famous in 'Miracle on 34th Street' and where they fly the big balloons on the Thanksgiving Day Parade."

"Oh, yeah...I remember that movie...Shirley Temple, right?" One of the men asked as he pulled a blanket off the biggest box.

"Never mind, it's too cold out here to give you a movie lesson. Let's move!" A forklift from U-Haul was placed under the biggest box, and once untied from the sidewall, it was lifted and carried over to the truck's lift-gate. Mr. Sanders wasn't sure what was happening outside, but He recognized the U-Haul truck and went to the kitchen door by the carport to see who it was. He then found Clay standing there with a big grin on his face. Dad opened the door, and Clay shouted, "Merry Christmas!"

"Clay, we were beginning to wonder what happened to you. You missed dinner, but Emy has a plate in the refrigerator for you. And you'd better make amends with my wife before she skins you." Clay began to come in the house and then remembered, "Mr. Sanders, would you open your garage for me? I have some men out there who need to bring some boxes in." Clay then dashed in to beg forgiveness of Mom and give Emy a kiss on the cheek. Instead, he got walloped in the face with a couch pillow. "You were supposed to be here at five o'clock, and I know the dealership closed today at three p.m., so where have you been?"

"Is your daughter always as testy as this, Mrs. Sanders?" Clay asked.

"I'm not speaking to you," Mom replied. "I made your favorite dishes at whats-her-name's request, and you fail to show up. So, you two work it out." She went back to watching a Christmas program, the one where some Grinch-thing stole Christmas cartoon.

Clay looked about the room, admiring how beautiful and tasteful it looked. From one corner to another, it was Christmas, and lights were shining everywhere. The manger scene had six-inch tall figures, which were all hand-painted. In one corner of the room, near the deck doors, stood the eight-foot-tall natural Spruce Christmas tree filled with family ornaments and colorful in blue, green, and red lights. A top of the tree was a beautiful angel and beneath the bottom layer of branches was a wide assortment of finely wrapped gifts of every shape and color of wrapping. Clay knew he could never learn to wrap a gift so well and suspected it was simply a woman thing.

"Clay," Mr. Sanders bellowed. "What are your men bringing into my garage and into my wife's kitchen?"

"Hold that question, Sir. I need to pay off my elves." Clay went into the kitchen and gave the men the money they were owed, and they agreed to get the U-Haul back to the rental store. He wished them all a Merry Christmas and watched them leave before turning to a confused looking Mr. Sanders. "Your question, I believe, Sir was about those boxes... am I correct, Sir?"

"I think so, but I have had some of my wife's special eggnog tonight, so I might be a little confused...though I do see the boxes at my feet."

"Merry Christmas, Mr. Sanders, from my family to yours." Clay reached into his Parka's inside coat pocket and pulled out a plastic bag containing an assortment of documents, from a sales catalog describing the various pieces to their various warranties. The only thing missing was the sales receipts.

"Clay, as far as I know, you're the only member of your family... Honey, would you come out here."

Mrs. Sanders and Emy walked into the kitchen and then out into the garage after Dad pointed that way. "What did Santa here bring us," Dad asked.

"Sir, I'm over here a lot and watch television with you all the time. I noticed your TV is getting a bit long in the tooth as my Grandpa would often say and thought you needed a new one." Clay pointed to a photo of the television flat-screen monitor on the front cover of the sales catalog and smiled as Dad's eyes grew wider and wider, "Oh, my lord, that beast is seventy-inches in size. You bought us a seventy-inch TV, Clay?"

"Yes, Sir, and it comes with all the bells and whistles, including the wall mount, which will take both of us to put up. The entertainment center also comes with a Bose Surround Sound Theater DVD/CD system, so I picked up a Blue-Ray system too."

"Clay, do you have any idea what you've done to him?" Mrs. Sanders asked."

"What ma'am," Clay replied. He wasn't exactly sure how to answer that question.

"Every man in the neighborhood will want to be over here to watch football, and with this monstrous thing, the players will be almost life-size."

"I was also thinking, ma'am, you can put on those Christian seminar DVD's and have your Bible studies here during the week. You'll be the envy of the ladies." He knew that got her thinking too.

"Politics, Clay, you really have a natural talent... and thank you. Yes, the ladies and I will love it. Plus, I can truly fill our home with the Lord's music with such a sound system.

"Clay!" Dad shouted. "How could you do this to me? Football yes, but Christian music bouncing off my walls; I'll never get another nap again.

Clay looked over at Emy and noticed the strange look on her face, she seemed to be pouting, and he wasn't sure why. He mouthed the words, "What's the matter?" But all she did was shake her head and turn away to go back into the kitchen. Clay looked over at Dad, who was already busy unpacking the sound system, leaving the TV and wall mount for tomorrow. Mom was sitting in her chair, reviewing the catalog and warranties. She was always the practical one of the family and kept the files for all the appliance warranties.

Clay walked out into the kitchen and found Emy standing at the sink and looking out the window, through the carport, and out into the street. It was cold, so the ice fog was dropping low, and their neighborhood now resembled the streets of San Francisco on a foggy evening.

"What's the matter, honey?" Clay asked.

"Nothing," She replied in a light voice.

"You're not glad I got your parents the entertainment center for Christmas?" I thought she'd be overjoyed; she likes football as much as her father does. But it seems I blew it somehow. Maybe she thinks I spent too much, but she knows I can afford it... at least for now. If I keep spending it this way, I'll be broke soon enough. That new M-4 cost me nine-hundred dollars, and with the extra magazines and other equipment I needed, I was well over a thousand dollars... So what's with her? Why do women have to be so hard to read?

"Clay, the gift is fantastic...it's almost overboard, but I know how much you love my parents and how you wanted to please them. I understand how long you went without parents and how difficult this has been opening up yourself to them, but it's... I was expecting something...forget it. I don't want to spoil this for them, and I'll probably get the old TV to put in my room... a plus all around...right?" Emy stood on her tiptoes and kissed Clay lightly on the lips, and went back into the living room to watch Mom and Dad play with the sound system.

Within the hour, Mr. Sanders had talked Clay into helping him set the whole monstrosity up on the wall, and that meant locating the wall studs to ensure they simply didn't put big holes in the sheetrock and the weight of the massive television pull the whole wall off.

By midnight, they were done, and everything was mounted and in operation. Dad had two new hand controls to play with, which totally confused Mom, but Clay promised to show her how they each worked. Dad, with a weary smile on his face and a sore back, said his thanks and goodnights before limping off to bed. Mom came over and gave Clay a big hug, "You made him very happy, Clay. He's always wanted one of those big screens, but money was always needed elsewhere." She hugged him again and said, "Merry Christmas." She started to walk away and then turned to face him and Emy, "You sure you don't want to use the spare bedroom or the couch… you're going to be back here at ten a.m. anyway for Christmas morning madness?"

"I still have a few things to take care of, Mrs. Sanders, but thank you. I'll be here on time. I wouldn't miss one of your breakfasts for anything."

"Well, okay then, good night," Mom said, and she walked away with a bit of a cringe of pain to her side from her husband over-enthusiasm into installing this beast in such a hurry. She suggested they call the professionals, but her husband would hear of it, and now they were both going to wake up in the morning in need of a good helping of Aspirin with their coffee.

Emy turned to Clay, "Why don't you stay? Kind of silly to leave now… you afraid you might try to sneak into my bedroom in the middle of the night?"

Clay frowned at her and then replied, "You know I hate it when you talk like that. I've never looked at you that way or for that purpose."

She dropped her head and shook it slowly, her hands at her side, "I'm sorry, Clay. Guess you Christians would say my physical side is weak… or something like that. You know I'm no virgin, I've never lied to you about that, and I enjoy sex, but I love you, and I don't want to be with anyone else."

"I love you too, Emy, which means we wait. I have to be true to my Lord first and above all. I pray someday you will feel the same way." He brought her hands together, lifted them up, and kissed her fingers. "I will see you in about nine hours. So please get some sleep; those lines under your eyes are not attractive."

"Oh, you!!" Emy walloped him in the chest, her favorite spot to hit him, and then made a dash for her bedroom, leaving Clay standing alone in the living room. He looked around, enjoying the atmosphere of the decorated room, and walked into the kitchen to use the phone and call a cab to take him back to the U-Haul shop to get his car. The salesmen had allowed him to use one of the employee plug-ins so he'd be able to start it. At these low temperatures, within two hours, the car battery could be zapped of juice, and the vehicle would not turn over. Clay's Camaro had an electric battery blanket, an engine heater, and an oil pan heater, all going to a three-way electric box attached to the body under the hood. An electric cord then ran for 5-feet from the box, through the grill, and was rolled up inside the fiberglass bumper. He carried a 50-foot extension cord that would run from this cord to the plugin provided by the U-Haul Shop. All over Alaska, people plugged their vehicles in when the temperatures dropped below 20 degrees. Some people waited until below zero, but for an outsider coming into the state during winter for the first time, it appeared everyone was driving electric cars.

The Camaro turned over just fine, though the interior of the vehicle was also in the minus forty-degree temperature, and it took several minutes to get the heat up to a tolerable range, and the windows defrosted. Clay was thinking about getting one of those interior heaters, but he was still reviewing the pros and cons of them.

When he got back to his place and plugged his car in, he walked into his nice and toasty apartment, tossed his parka on the chair, and walked over to his dresser. He opened the top drawer and pulled out a small velvet jewelry box he had picked up only a couple of days earlier. For the last forty-eight hours, he was debating with himself as to whether or not if he should or not?

# THE FIRST REAL CHRISTMAS IN A LONG TIME

*The Sanders House*
*Christmas Morning*
*Fairbanks*
*11:14 A.M. 25 December*

Brightly colored gift wrap and lengths of shredded ribbon were scattered about all over the living room floor and Mr. Sanders, who was sitting in his chair, attired in blue wool flannel two-piece pajamas underneath a thick dark blue terry robe, was busy admiring his new set of power tools from his wife. This was a special floor kit of battery-operated hand tools, and he couldn't wait to get out into the garage to see how they worked. Mrs. Sanders was dressed in a flowing green, blue, and white robe over a light blue gown had her hair covered by a white and blue scarf, and wore silver and pearl earrings in her ears. She was reading the warranty paperwork for her new commercial-grade six-quart Kitchen-Aide Mixer, which had come in cobalt blue. She had also received a completely new set of dishes from Emy because the old set had suffered from heavy wear, and there were a lot of nicks and cracks. The previous Thanksgiving bash had taken its toll.

Clay set on the floor cross-legged, putting together his new radio-control 1968 red Camaro, which came with a hand controller. He could tell this was not the cheap twenty-nine dollar and ninety-eight cent toy he'd seen in the stores, but the more expensive model, which included all the batteries and could do everything but stand on its rear bumper and salute the flag. This was a gift from Mom and Dad, knowing he'd have to wait until summer to use it out on the parking lot. Still, they figured he could probably play with it down at the dealership shop and showroom to gain expertise.

Emy sat at the other end of the couch from her mother and right above Clay. She had received box after box of clothes; sweaters, blouses, and skirts and then opened one gift to find a collector's vintage GI Joe doll from Clay. He had bought it at an auction on E Bay for a bit more than he planned, and she really loved it. The twelve-inch GI Joe had come with an M-1 Garand Rifle, his complete uniform and helmet, and a footlocker with several items in it. It wasn't a first issue GI Joe, which was worth up to thirty-thousand dollars, but it was quite old. In her way of thanking him, she thumped him on the head with a couch pillow.

Once he had his car and hand control together, Clay asked Mr. Sanders if he could take it out into the garage to see if it worked all right. He also asked Dad to accompany him. When Emy got up to join them, Clay asked her to remain with her mom, "I'd like to be with your Dad for a moment, okay? It's a guy thing."

"Sure, go, do your guy thing!" Emy said in a tone, which carried a bite with it. She's fought that guy thing in the military for four years and was really wary of it, plus she wondered what her boyfriend had to talk to her Dad about?

Mrs. Sanders looked up from her warranty paperwork in time to see them walk out into the garage. She had heard the conversation and had some idea of what Clay wished to speak to her husband about. Being a gentleman, in fact, a former officer and a gentleman as verified by Congress, he wanted to do the right thing by way of their daughter. She grinned and then covered her face with the paperwork so Emy wouldn't see her smile. She didn't want to ruin the fun if she was right.

It was nearly 20-minutes later before the two men came back into the kitchen, where Dad grabbed a pitcher of iced tea in the refrigerator and poured a glass over ice cubes for him and Clay. They then came into the living room, and Dad called out to Mom, "Honey, what say you and I go upstairs and grab our shower. I'm beginning to feel like one of those loafing couch potatoes Emy used to bring around here."

"Dad, some of them were between jobs, and they were hungry…"

"Just kidding, Honey," Dad said as he walked out of the living room. Then he turned, waiting for his wife and said, "Any of your friends were always welcome here, even their appetites… even that galoot."

"What's a galoot?" Clay asked.

"I'm not sure, but in that tone, I'm thinking he means it in a nice way. Must be a term he picked up from one of those westerns he watches. John Wayne, Audio Murphy or Robert Taylor comes on, and it drives Mom right out of the house."

"Yeah, I've noticed your dad really went in for the old movies, especially the black and white ones. He's got me hooked too. John Wayne was the king of western movies; I read somewhere he did something like two-hundred movies before the cancer took him."

Emy grabbed Clay by the hand and led him back to the couch, sat him down, and landed right beside him with a soft thump. He draped his left arm around her, brought her close, and kissed her with gusto, bringing a grin to her face. "Was that a John Wayne kiss?"

"Nope, his were fast and hard, like this." Clay gave her a quick but meaningful kiss. "Women knew they were kissed by the Duke and never forgot it."

"Well, I prefer a long soft kiss if you don't mind. You're liable to bust out my front teeth with one of those Duke' kisses, and I'd look pretty funny."

Clay pointed toward the Christmas tree, "I notice there's still a gift over there; you might go see who it's for…might be for me." Emy pushed off of him to stand up and took three steps to the tree, dropped to her knees, and reached underneath to find a medium-sized box wrapped in blue velvet-like wrapping paper and white satin ribbon. The bow was silvery and was large enough to take up one-half of the top of the box. The address label said it was to Emy and from Santa Claus.

"Such a beautiful box; I almost hate to open it." Carefully, she removed the ribbon and untapped one end of the paper to pull the box out. Once removed, she noticed the box was a plain cardboard box with no markings of any kind. She brought it to her right ear and listened to it, wondering if anything inside would be making any sound, and then as an afterthought, she shook it gently. But it still didn't make any sound. So, she pulled off the top of the box and was surprised to find a smaller box inside- which was also unmarked. She looked over at Clay, who was shaking his head to say he had nothing to do with this and held his hands up to emphasize his innocence. So, she kept going and went through seven-boxes until she reached a small white box. Then her heart jumped, but she didn't want to hope too much. Knowing how Clay thought about things, this could be a bracelet, a necklace, or even a broach, but she pulled the white box out and removed the jewelers' box from within it. Now Clay was grinning wide as she slowly opened it and found an extremely beautiful engagement ring inside.

"This was my mother's ring, Emy. I had to have some work done on it and add a few precious stones to honor your birth month...but...will you marry me, Emy?"

She looked deeply into his eyes and studied his face, remaining silent for a moment and glancing back and forth between the ring and Clay's expectant expression. "You must have wanted this some time ago to get this beautiful work done."

"Truthfully, I didn't make my final decision until last night. I wasn't sure I would be good enough for you, knowing how I carry along a lot of baggage. But last night, I prayed, as I do every night, and I felt I received my answer for us to become what the Bible refers to as One Flesh...one being instead of two. We join together for eternity in all ways."

"But Clay, I'm not saved, as you would say, and I'm not sure I'll ever be. Doesn't your Bible say something about being unequally yoked...Christian and not Christian being forbidden?"

"Not forbidden, but unwise. But I still have hopes you will come around, just as I did. Until then, I will continue to pray for your heathen soul. So, what's your answer, Sergeant?"

"I've been in love with you for so long, almost from that first shameful night. You've been my knight protector, and now you will be my king. Yes,

Clay, I will marry you." She fell into his arms, and they kissed until they heard Mom and Dad entering the room, clapping their hands. Mom came over, wanting to see the ring, oohing-awing, while Dad shook Clay's hand and pounded him on the back with his left hand. "Welcome to the family, Clay!"

Doc Adams is gonna kill me! He's is just gonna kill me. If he doesn't pull me off the case, he's liable to do something else drastic. Knowing the kind of hardball these feds play, they're liable to even go so far as to threaten my Emy's life if I blow this now over love for one of the terrorists. I just can't believe this has happened to me or how I allowed it to happen as if I had no choice in the matter. Someone sprinkled some kind of magic love dust in my face, and I was helpless. It's going to get dicey; I wonder which side of ol' Doc I'm going to see now

# 11

# WEDDING, OR PLANNING A D-DAY INVASION

*Sanders' House*
*Fairbanks, Alaska*
*March 20th*

The Wedding date, how big a wedding and who to invite was a matter debated back and forth between Emy and her parents over the dinner table and in the living room until it got so bad Clay was making excuses to stay away from the house. Finally, a decision was made based on compromise, setting the wedding date for June Sixth. It would be held in the backyard, with Clay's pastor handling the official side of the ceremony. No more than one hundred and fifty people would be invited, and then came the matter of selecting the one-hundred and fifty. Clay made it easy on them by choosing not to invite anyone from Minto and only ten-people from his church. This gave the Sanders a choice of one hundred and forty people to choose for their mailing list. Being a wise man, Mr. Sanders decided to stay out of this part altogether so he could tell all his friends who were not invited; he had no choice in the matter. Now it was time to figure out the wedding colors, style of wedding dress, and the wedding cake. When Mr. Sanders estimated the costs for the wedding, he made a single attempt at suggesting elopement and nearly had to sleep on the couch. His wife did not think his suggestion was at all very amusing. Clay even offered to cover half the expense and was promptly turned down, but by protocol policy, he would be allowed to cover the costs of the wedding ceremony rehearsal dinner- to be held at Pike's Landing.

Clay had taken one piece of his future father-in-law's advice to heart, "the wedding belongs to the wife and her mother, just stay out of the way and be around to say 'I do' at the appropriate moment.'" Whenever Clay came over to the Sanders home, it was wedding this and wedding that, and he was beginning to think an overseas assignment to Afghanistan could be sounding pretty good about now.

## WICKERSHAM CAR DEALERSHIP
## MARCH 21$^{ST}$

Silas sat behind his desk, an open can of Dr. Pepper in his right hand as he reviewed the training reports Clay had just brought him. Clay, wearing his oily coveralls from three hours of helping rebuild a short block engine with two recently hired mechanics, finished off a can of Pepsi and waited to hear what the Colonel had to say about last weekend's training session. They had held the training out at twenty-two mile Richardson Highway, so Clay could set up a series of combat courses for both rifle and handgun and run squad-sized units through. But he was unsatisfied with the results and recorded it for the Colonel to review.

Silas set back in his chair and studied Clay for a moment, who looked back at him over the top of his Pepsi can and waited for his boss to speak. He had learned enough about the man over the last few months to remain silent until Silas opened the conversation.

"You were clearly not impressed with our troops from what you wrote down here. I can understand the shooting scores and the need for more practice, but we all know ammo costs money, and we have a training budget I need to stick to if at all possible. But there's something else here, Clay... I'm reading between the lines here, yet I feel you're hedging about something and not coming right out and identifying in your report. I am curious what it is."

"Can I be candid, Sir," Clay asked. He reached forward and tossed his empty soda can into the office's black metal trash can.

"Of course," Silas said. "I always expect my employees and my officers to be honest with me. Whether it's about the dealership or our militia, and I thought by now, you would've realized it."

"Old military habits die hard, Colonel," Clay said. "Junior officers are usually compelled to stand around, observe and keep their mouths shut unless called upon directly. Even then, a response is to be brief and to the point."

"Yes, I seem to remember... All right, Captain, I am soliciting a response, but please, in some detail."

Clay thought about how to frame his reply for a moment and then stood up and walked over to a dry erase board Silas kept mounted on the wall in his office. He often used it to keep track of projects, but today it was empty. Grabbing a black dry erase marker, Clay quickly wrote out a diagram of the local unit's chain of command, going down to squad level. He didn't list names, only platoon and squad numbers. He then circled several positions and stepped back. "Colonel, these are your problem areas as I see them. You have two lieutenants who know almost nothing of leadership in how to best use their NCO's. They bypass their NCO's and go directly to their troops, which upsets their NCO's and creates a void between the lieutenants and their sergeants. These NCOs I've circled should be back in the ranks. They'd actually be happier there. They dislike the responsibility and can't shoulder it very well either. Rather than act like an NCO, they behave like a buddy, and a squad becomes a headless click of high-school students. This is causing a breakdown of leadership in these platoons, which affects the ability of your whole unit."

Silas studied the drawing from his chair, then stood up and walked over to the board. He picked up a cloth that hung from a thumb-tacked string and wiped the board clean. "I had no idea, Clay."

"I believe, Colonel, part of the problem stems from so many of these soldiers having grown up together. It can be hard to give orders to your buddy. Part of the problem could come from the idea of how the unit is only a volunteer thing and not a real Army unit, where they were paid twice a month, housed and fed. I know a lot of these soldiers would follow you anywhere, Colonel, but I am not sure they all have your vision... at least not the way you explained it to me."

Silas returned to his chair, sat down, and gazed at Clay, who remained standing. "What is your recommendation, Captain?"

"First off, I believe a series of weekend drills. The first one with officers only... the second one with NCO's only, and the third one with the whole unit. Part of the training will involve leadership training, military exercises, and marksmanship, and this may mean you will have to buy the ammo yourself, Sir. Then we finish off the weekend with an inspiring speech from you and an oath of loyalty taken by the troops. This will give those who want out a chance to leave honorably, and you will then know the ones who stay will stand with you." Clay walked over to Silas's desk. "Sir, you haven't taken me into your confidence of what action, if any, you intend in the foreseeable future, and I can understand. But you will have to know who will stand with you, when and if a snafu develops in your operation and people begin getting hurt. Who is weak, and who is strong?"

Silas thought about it for a moment and then nodded his head, "All right, Captain. Arrange the retreats for May. We'll hold the officer's weekend at my cabin on Chena Hot Springs Road. The NCO training and Unit training will be at twenty-two mile Richardson. Order what ammo you need and have it billed... have it billed to the Militia for annual qualifications. I'll put the money into the account from my personal funds to cover it and advise Anchorage the extra expenditures was due to poor shooting scores. They won't even care as long as the money comes from somewhere."

"Sir, what about the food costs... at the officer's weekend retreat? "Clay asked.

"My dealership will cover it, and I'll probably list it as a community expense. I learned early on in the car business how to play the tax game."

"I'll handle it, Sir."

"No, you will get with your Operations Officer, and the two of you will handle it. I'm not going to have my shop supervisor burned out because he's been burning the candle at both ends. Now get out of here; I've got cars to sell and a dealer to fire. I hate deadwood, and I'll only carry a dealer so long before I let him go. Besides, she was never cut out to be a dealer... too soft-hearted."

"Don't women make good car dealers, Colonel?"

"You bet! Normally they go right for the throat faster than most men when dealing with finance companies and banks, then turn around and give their best smiles to the customer sitting across the desk from them. This one, though, she just didn't have the predator instinct."

Clay grinned and left the office; he needed to go check on his floor and make sure no one had dropped a lift on someone's foot.

*SPRING - BASSETT HOSPITAL, FORT WAINWRIGHT*
*MARCH 24TH*

The outside temperature on the post was holding at minus eighteen degrees, and inside the hospital lobby, the steam heat from the post's massive coal plant was sixty-five degrees. This made for a sudden change in air temperature when Clay came through the double sets of doors and quickly took off his winter coat. With so many retirees in the Fairbanks area, it wasn't unusual to see men on post, especially the hospital, PX, or commissary, with hair was too long or wore beards. So, Clay had no trouble fitting in with his blue plaid long-sleeved shirt, brown down vest, and insulated Carhartt Bibs. He was letting his hair grow out, but only his sideburns and mustache were out of line with military standards. The Colonel had been giving him the once over every now and then but hadn't come right out and said anything. A lot of the militia troops were in major violation of military standards, but it wasn't enforced too strictly. Though Clay knew Silas disliked any facial jewelry for men, while in uniform or any facial tattoos.

Clay was on his way to the elevator to make his appointment with Doc and wasn't looking forward to it. He had to explain why he thought it okay to become engaged to a suspected domestic terrorist, for whom he was investigating, and Clay, who had racked his brain for days with a good story, couldn't come up with anything Doc would understand. He knew he was finished and would probably be hanging his career up too, if not on his way to Kansas for an extended stay in Leavenworth Federal Penitentiary for wayward GI's.

Halfway through the lobby, he was bumped into by a uniformed nurse who dropped her clipboard and a couple books. Being a gentleman, Clay knelt down to help here. In the process, she slipped a folded piece of paper into his hand very expertly, thanked him, and then disappeared down the hall. He knew better than to open a paper out here in the open and went to the second floor by the stairs and found the men's room at the far end of the hall. Secluded in a stall, he took a seat, took the paper out of his pocket, and opened it. The first thing he noticed was the name of his two Washington DC officers, Thomas Cleffinger, Deputy Director for the FBI, and Bradley Carlson, Supervisor with Homeland Security.

With those two names on it, he knew the note was okay. He was directed to go to skip his appointment with Doc and meet with another agent tonight behind Clay's church at ten p.m. and to come alone. They know where I go to church? Do they know I'm getting married in June? Do they want an invitation too? Or is this the kiss-off, and will I know my shooter… maybe one of my bud's from Delta?

*DOOR OF HOPE CHURCH*
*OVERLOOKING FAIRBANKS*
*10:03 P.M.*

Emy wasn't happy when Clay had to leave the house early tonight, she wanted to discuss some of the finale wedding plans, but Clay wanted to scout the area out before the meet. The temperature had gone up, and it was snowing, and climbing the hillside to reach the Door of Hope parking lot was no easy feat.

He drove through the deserted parking lot at nine-fifteen p.m. and again at nine-forty p.m. and found no sign of anyone having recently been there. With fresh snow on the ground, it was easy to check the tire imprints, and his was the only tracks since he first arrived. Armed with his pistol, he walked around the church, looked for a sniper, and was relieved to find he was all alone. But when he came back at 10:03, he found fresh car tracks and a new model Ford sedan behind the church with the engine running. Clay, who drove in with lights off, left his vehicle out front and walked in. Again, he checked for a sniper, but with so much snow falling, it would be hard to see anyone. He took his time, and with a drawn gun, made his way up to the back of the car. First off, he checked to ensure the trunk was closed. During a police officer survival course he took, he was killed by a shooter who sprang up from a not so closed trunk and hit him with a Nerf dart. He then inspected the back seat and saw only the driver was in the vehicle.

The driver's window came down, and he recognized the voice of Mr. Bradley Carlson of Homeland Security. "Clay, would you please quit playing commando games and get in this car. I'm freezing my butt off here."

Clay was relieved. He knew if the government wanted him dead, they wouldn't have sent Carlson up here to do the job. Thinking back, he knew the nurse could've got him with a quick and almost painless jab of a needle while they were on the floor picking up her books.

Clay ran around to the passenger side and climbed in, holstering his pistol under his coat and shaking Carlson's hand. "What's wrong with Doc?"

"He had a heart attack and died in his sleep three nights ago, and before you ask, yes, it was a real heart attack. The old man should've retired about twenty years ago, but he loved the game and was still one of the best at it as a handler. I'm not sure what he told you about himself, but Doc worked with North Korean spies and Vietnam prisoners of war. The agency had sent him to medical school to add to his other expertise. I can only imagine what he's seen and heard over the last few decades. But it all went with him. We don't have any of the work he did with you except for the initial contacts, and that's why I'm here. We've got a lot of work to do before I fly out in the morning. I have to be brought up to date so Washington can decide on whether or not to cancel this operation."

Clay thought about it for a moment. He could get Emy out of it now and her parents by simply telling them his time up here had proven to be much ado about nothing, but when the Colonel's plan was carried out, whatever it is, and people died, he'd have to live with it. Clay knew, and he couldn't do that. "Doc was supposed to be sending you weekly reports, and I'm not sure why he wasn't. Maybe it had something to do with his advanced years and his health problems. I knew he was old, but not that old. But this operation has revealed a major domestic terrorist organization here in Fairbanks. This is a rogue militia force, which I am now an officer in, inside the legitimate Alaska Defense Force, and it numbers one-hundred and twenty officers, NCOs, and troops. They are motorized and extremely well-armed with high explosives and automatic weapons.

He had just startled Mr. Carlson from Homeland Security, who was now all ears and no longer freezing.

"I was made the unit's training officer for both the Alaska Defense Force Northern Unit and, more recently, for the Alaska Freedom Brigade Militia or AFBM. This could become your worst nightmare, Mr. Carlson."

"And the good doctor was sitting on all this. We've searched his office and his condo, but we've found nothing concerning his meetings with you."

"He recorded every meeting we had…I wonder what happened to those recordings."

"We may never know," Carlson said. "Okay, I've got two thermoses of strong black coffee, my own recording machine with satellite transfer to Washington DC…even Radio shack doesn't have that yet, and four belly bomber burgers with all the fixings. So let's get started."

At 5:14 a.m., Mr. Carlson turned the recorder off and rubbed the sleep from his eyes. "So, you're convinced that if we moved in right now and made massive arrests, we'd end up with Ruby Ridge and Waco all rolled into one."

"Sir, Fairbanks, for as spread out as it is, is a tight town, and Alaskans love their freedom and especially their privacy. If you were to start making arrests, word would be out quicker than you could get your people moved around. Weapons would either vanish, along with the troops, and you'd never find them out there in the wilderness. They know this land, and your agents don't. I doubt you'd be able to find non-law enforcement Alaskans willing to track these people down either. There's a lot of people up here who support this sovereignty issue, wary of the US government stepping in with their clodhoppers and telling the state what to do and how to do it. I'm not sure, but if this was to be handled wrong, you could initiate the war over statehood you wanted to stop in the beginning.

"No, until I can learn the date of the event and the target, I'd say simply prepare your people. But hands off until then, Mr. Carlson... nothing is going to happen until summer anyway. No one does much of anything up here in the wintertime."

Carlson nodded his head, "I can't make any decisions, and you know that, but I will pass along your recommendation and my support of it. I would prefer taking down the whole unit with charges we can confirm. They botched the last militia trial they had up here because they moved too fast. Something about the cold up here... gets all the federal prosecutors' brains chilled, and they jump before they're ready.

"So, now I have to find another handler for you... be about a week. I'll have him or her bring their car to the shop and demand to see the shop supervisor. They'll toss my name into the conversation, and you two work it out on meeting locations and times. But I want weekly updates and reports on this training you're doing."

"How do you like the snow?" Clay asked. The car had seven-inches of snow on it, and both men had to get outside to clean it off so Carlson would be able to leave.

"Alaska is a beautiful land, and between you and I, the US should stay out of most state affairs. It would make things a whole lot easier for the federal government to operate."

*WICKERSHAM CHEVROLET DEALERSHIP*
*SOUTH CUSHMAN, FAIRBANKS*
*APRIL 2ND*

"Hey Clay, you got a moment?" Jeremy Packa asked. A longtime mechanic for Wickersham, Jeremy chose the vehicles he wanted to work on unless things were backed up. He was checked out on every piece of equipment on the floor and knew more about cars than anyone in the dealership. He also made as much money as Clay did, plus Jeremy earned extra with his overtime.

Dressed in oily gray coverall with Wickersham Chevrolet stitched on the back and Jeremy Packa stitched on the front left breast area, Jeremy's reddish-blonde hair was equally oily, and the rag he wore to keep the hair out of his eyes was 10-30 weight for weeks of usage without washing. His tan work gloves were now mostly a stained dark brown, and his steel-toed black leather boots had suffered abominable damage. He also had a foul mouth from his four years with the US Navy.

"What's the problem, Jeremy?" Clay was standing by the parts' counter, reviewing an order a customer had complained about over the phone concerning a charge for a part installed yesterday that was never installed or requested. They got home and checked the paperwork, checked under the hood, and became upset.

"I got this broad out front who wants to see the shop foreman about her car. She's upset about some work we were supposed to have done, and I told her she's got the wrong place. But she's not happy, so I thought you being a real smooth talker and all with the ladies, you could get her—"

"Yeah, I got it. Her ears started burning from all those big words the Navy taught you."

Jeremy shook his head, "I knew I should've stayed at sea. You meet a better sort of people on the ocean. You Army grunts are a bunch of—"

Jeremy got cut off when Clay pointed toward where Silas's office was. "I'll take care of her, Jeremy...now go wash your mouth out with soap."

Jeremy walked off laughing. He liked Clay, even though he was an Army grunt.

Clay walked out through the doors and found a tall lady in a heavy blue wool winter coat, over a white ski sweater, and black woman's slack tucked into calf-high insulated black leather boots. She had long brown hair with gray highlights and a longish face, with a pointy nose supporting a pair of gold wire-rimmed glasses. Clay estimated her to be in her early 40's and she was holding a pair of insulated black leather gloves in her hands, smacking them together to illustrate her impatience.

"Ma'am, I'm Clay Jefferson, the shop supervisor. I understand there is some sort of problem."

"Yes, I should say so! I brought my car in here a week ago and talked with a Mr. Carlson, who promised me he had it all fixed. Now it's broken down again, in my driveway and I have to use a taxi to get around town. I was hoping to have a nice chat with Mr. Carlson and give him a piece of my mind concerning promises made to women. I paid you people four-hundred and seventy-five dollars!"

*Mr. Carlson...so, you're my new handler. Are you FBI, Agency, or Homeland Security?* "Ma'am, we have no Mr. Carlson here, but I believe he works for the Ford dealership up the street. I think you came to the wrong place by mistake. We sort of look-alike... South Cushman is one big car lot."

"Oh, my...I am sorry. I thought this was the Ford dealership. I told my taxi driver to take me to the Ford dealership, but I don't think he speaks English very well. Cars all look alike to me."

"Well, why don't I walk you outside and have a talk with your driver. I might be able to explain to him where you want to go, and please let me cover the extra charge."

"Wow, a man of chivalry, and here I thought it was a dying art." She buttoned up her coat, put her gloves on, and walked outside. Clay held the door open for her and followed her to the taxi.

He opened the door for her, and she slid in. "Don't worry, the driver works for us. My name is Leslie File. Mr. Carlson sends his regards, and your recommendation is being considered. I'll meet with you once a week. What day is best, and where?"

Clay had been considering this since he left Mr. Carlson but wasn't expecting a woman. "Can you get on Post?"

"That's not a problem."

"Let's continue our meetings at the hospital... Psychology Wing. I go in for my PTSD. You can pose as a doctor, nurse, or whatever. But get a room so we won't be disturbed...Doc cleared it with Hospital Administrator. Say, Thursday at 3 p.m. I know you have my phone number, but it could be wired. Call me as if you're the reservations office at the hospital to confirm my appointment on Wednesday like they always do. They don't trust me completely yet, and they have the personnel to wire whatever they want. This is a very dedicated and very possibly a dangerous group."

"Yes, I read your report with Mr. Carlson. I'm impressed with what you've been able to do. I'll see you soon."

Clay closed the door, gave her a casual wave, and walked inside. The air was still pretty cool, and the heat on the showroom floor felt good. He was standing there watching the taxi drive toward the Ford dealership when he felt someone approach his blindside, and he turned to find Silas. "Is there a problem, Clay?"

"Yes, Sir," Clay said. He had a smirk on his face. "But it's not our problem. She's on her way to the Ford dealership now, had gotten them confused with us, and it appears English was her driver's second language. Apparently, a mechanic at the Ford place is about to get the tongue lashing of his life."

"Well, I'm glad it wasn't us. I saw Jeremy out here with her, and I could tell his use of the English language was quite a shock in itself. I had to get off the phone, but then I saw you come out and handle it. By the way, how are things looking for our leadership training weekends?"

"Everything is set up, announcements made, and ammo on order. We should have everything a week or two before the weekend we need it."

"Great," Silas said. "You're doing a fine job for me, Clay, and I appreciate it." Silas began to turn away, and then he remembered something and asked Clay, "How are the wedding plans coming along?"

"I'm taking my future father-in-law's advice and staying out of the way. I think scheduling the wedding for June 6th is prophetic; it feels much like the planning of the D Day Invasion."

"One very special day in a young woman's life, and she wants it all perfect. But I'd stay out of her way too. On another thought, how are you doing with your PTSD support group…is it helping with the nightmares?"

"Thank you for asking, Colonel," Clay replied. "Yes, it helps, but the nightmares come and go. I'm sure you understand."

"Yes, but you handle it better than most, Clay, and I would have to say you owe that to your faith in God. Am I right?"

"Yes, Sir," Clay answered. "Good Lord has brought a lot of healing to me; I now wait for my Emy to find her faith. It can be so hard after experiencing what we did over there. The Barbarism and brutality of man can cause a might rift between God and man. But He is always there."

"Amen to that." Silas put his right hand on Clay's left shoulder in friendship and then returned to his office.

*THURSDAY 3 P.M. BASSETT HOSPITAL*
*PSYCHOLOGY WING/EXAM ROOM*
*APRIL 5TH*

Leslie File wore a white doctor's smock, white pants, and white jogger's shoes. A lot of nurses and doctors had switched over to the more comfortable joggers in the last several years. She had a blue stethoscope draped around the back of her neck and an official hospital ID card pinned to her right breast area of her smock.

"Is it Mrs. or miss?" Clay asked.

"Make it simple and call me Leslie. Personal information is not needed at this time. Except to say, I work for Mr. Carlson at Homeland Security, and you are not my first operative. I know your entire personal history, for which I might add, I am greatly impressed with your service record. But having said all this, let's turn on the recorder and begin."

Leslie used a similar device to what Doc had used and now turned it on and began with a question concerning Clay's latest moves within the AFBM.

"As the militia and AFBM training officer, I've advised the Colonel of several areas of concern involving leadership. I've done this in hopes of gaining further trust in hopes of learning targets and target dates. I know with the size force we have, it will be large. He wants to make a big splash in the worldwide news in hopes of gaining sympathy from the United Nations. His whole goal is to bring about a second statehood vote. He feels if another legitimate vote was taken today, under UN law, the people of Alaska would vote for sovereignty and become a free nation and ally to the USA and Canada. He would rent the military land to the US for $ 1 a year in order to keep its protection, but Alaska would then have a real say in what happens here."

"Let's go back to the leadership problem areas you mentioned..."

*MILITIA TRAINING FIELD*
*22-MILE RICHARDSON HIGHWAY / ACROSS FROM EIELSON AIR*
*FORCE BASE*
*MAY 23RD/ SATURDAY MORNING 9:40 A.M.*

Over the weekly meetings with Leslie, Clay had come to respect the woman's insight and keen intelligence. He was relieved when Washington DC had taken his recommendation to hold off on massive arrests and had moved twelve-new FBI agents and six Homeland Security Agents into the Anchorage offices. Alcohol, Tobacco, and Firearms (ATF) moved a special weapons team in under the guise of spring bear hunters up from California. A Federal Fish & Game Officer was posing as their guide. Three other teams of Homeland Security Agents and the FBI Hostage/Rescue SWAT were on standby in Seattle. The feds were doing everything they could not to alarm the AFBM or even the Alaska Defense Force of the extra federal presence. Men and women who usually wore suits to the office were now wearing typical Alaska wear for the season. Tourist season was just beginning, and a lot of extra people in Anchorage was no big thing.

The Officer retreat had come off quite well, except for the two lieutenants who were reduced in rank to Staff Sergeants and placed in non-leadership positions. They attended the NCO weekend and actually had a pretty good time, and there been no apparent hard feelings. But this meant two new lieutenants were needed to balance. The senior officers discussed it, and two senior NCOs, with good leadership skills, were promoted and made platoon commanders.

Clay looked out over the formation of the Alaska Defense Force Northern Command. They were formed up by squads, then by platoons and by companies before Colonel Wickersham. The tents were all up, breakfast was completed, and everyone was heavily dosed down with mosquito repellant. According to today's training schedule, they would begin with weapons training by platoons, while the other soldiers were working on hand-to-hand fighting drills, exercising, obstacle course Clay had set up, a three-mile compass course with a full pack. Special teams had been chosen to work with Explosive Ordinance Disposal personnel, anti-tank squads, and heavy weapons squads. This made for a very busy day, and the training field was packed with active personnel and the background filled with the near-constant sound of weapons fire.

Clay had used his US Army retired government identification to go to Eielson Air Force Base and notify the US Air Force Security Force commander of the training day and all the weapons fire. The commander knew the Militia was in legal possession of automatic weapons, but it left some of the entry controllers at the perimeter posts with an unsettling feeling to hear what sounded like a prelude to World War Three out there across the highway.

At six p.m., or 1800 hours military time, Colonel Wickersham had a big surprise for his troops. A three-ton truck arrived, and within forty-five minutes, the men were licking their chops as they watched several cooks barbecuing beef and pork over propane grills. Foil-wrapped potatoes and corn on the cob, already cooked back at the restaurant, were staying warm in the campfires built up by the troops. Clay made sure to pick up all the weapons, securing them into the weapons truck, before the iced-up kegs of beer were unloaded from the big truck. One-hundred and twenty men and women were very appreciative after a long day of training, and best of all, there had been no injuries.

Clay and Emy's future wedding was toasted several times, and then the Colonel was saluted with raised plastic cups of cold beer from a boisterous crowd. From the looks of this group, Clay knew the Colonel had all the troops he needed for whatever he had planned. But outside Emy and her parents, and his own hide, his other major concern was finding out who was putting up all the money for this operation. That tingly feeling on the back of his neck was making him real unhappy. It was the kind of weird ticklish feeling he got right before a good plan fell apart. The last time was with those CIA clowns, and it made him wonder if the CIA was backing this plan, trying to stir things up here in the far north and maybe agitate old Mother Russia and bring back the Cold War. He knew the CIA hadn't been happy since the Great Wall came down, and a civil war up here in Alaska could very well create the very needs to bring back the old CIA glory days of skullduggery and mayhem.

*THE WEDDING/SANDERS' HOUSE*
*JUNE 6TH*

Clay made it through the ceremony without fainting or stammering his words, and he only had one drink at the reception, which was the Best Man's toast. Colonel Wickersham, Clay's Best Man, was quite a romantic, as he presented his oratory to a crowd of nearly three hundred people, most of them standing elbow to elbow in the backyard of the Sanders' home. By the time the reception was over, the final beverage figures totaled out to five twenty-five-gallon kegs of beer, five cases of imported French champagne, five-cases of assorted bottles of liquor, twenty-cases of assorted sodas, and ten-cases of bottled water. The caterer provided twenty-trays of assorted meats, cheeses, fruits and bread, sauces, and nuts. The wedding cake, which was supposed to feed three hundred people, didn't make it, but thankfully there were two very large sheet cakes on the side to help out. Being summertime, there was also fifty-gallons of ice cream in assorted flavors. With all the food, drink, plastic, and paper-ware, plus caterers' cost and the wedding dress, Mr. Sanders was looking at a final bill of over twenty-five thousand dollars. He was in shock, but then he remembered how beautiful his lovely daughter looked as she walked up the aisle to be married to that vile man he had foolishly allowed to enter his home not so long ago. I should've shot him when I had the chance!

*CLAY & EMY'S APARTMENT*
*FAIRBANKS*
*JUNE 20TH-SATURDAY MORNING*

Clay was still asleep, and Emy was up making morning coffee when there was a knock at their door. They were living in Clay's apartment but looking for a larger dwelling since coming home from their all-too-brief of a honeymoon in Hawaii. Emy glanced out the window and saw it was Norm Johnson, dressed in a black t-shirt and blue jeans. The Fairbanks temperatures were in the high 80's, and their apartment was being cooled by two rotating fans. Emy grabbed up her robe, pulled it on, and tied it closed. She then opened the door, greeted Norm, and invited him in for morning coffee. "He's not awake yet, Norm, but I'll roust him out."

"I really hate to disturb you two, but the Colonel's called for an emergency staff meeting. Something's come up... maybe another Exxon Valdez disaster, but he wants us out at his cabin ASAP."

Emy nodded her head, pointed to the coffee maker, which was nearly finished in its brewing cycle, and went toward their single bedroom. "Clay, wake-up… honey. Clay…" She sat down beside him and gently shook him from a sound sleep. He was supposed to have the weekend off, and they had stayed awake until the wee hours watching movies and cuddling on the couch with a bowl of buttered popcorn.

Clay woke up with a start and automatically reached for the pistol he normally would've had under his pillow but had placed in his dresser before moving Emy into his home. Mom & Dad Sanders wanted them to stay with them, even offered to convert the garage into an apartment, but Clay explained how he needed his freedom to move about at night. He often did his running late into the summer nights or early morning hours, and when his nightmares hit, he was up late watching TV. Emy had witnessed one of his PTSD nightmares in Hawaii and had held on to him as he fought his way through the hellish episode, leaving him in a thick layer of night sweats.

"What's up!?" Clay asked as he wiped the sleep from his eyes and scooted himself up into a sitting position. He then heard someone on the other side of their apartment and asked, "Who's out there?"

"Norm Johnson, Clay. He's here to pick you up. The Colonel's called an emergency staff meeting out at his cabin and wants all his officers. Norm is here to pick you up."

Clay sucked on his top lip, bringing some moisture to his dry mouth, as he considered this. Whenever he was called for one of these surprise meetings, a scare ran through him, that his true identity had been discovered. But he didn't want to alarm his new wife. "Tell Norm I'll be right out."

She gave him a quick morning kiss and added, "Make sure you brush your teeth, buffalo breath."

"And I got married for this!?"

"No, you got married for this." Emy sat down on his lap, wrapped her arms around his neck, and gave Clay one of her best thirty-second heat-filled kisses, an Ann Margaret and Elvis Presley from Viva Las Vegas style of moment.

"Oh yeah, now I remember… Why don't you tell Norm to go have breakfast at Denny's and come back in an hour or two?"

"No, lover boy… Your Colonel is calling, and Silas Wickersham hates to be kept waiting." She got up and left the room, leaving a bewildered undercover operative sitting in bed with a thousand thoughts racing through his brain. But the first thing he needed to do was take a shower and then find out what had happened to his pants. Emy had taken it upon herself to check his pockets for change whenever he came home, put the findings in a coin jar, and then if she felt the pants were in her opinion soiled enough, toss them in the dirty clothes hamper. The apartment didn't come with a washer and dryer, so they had to use Far North Laundromat down the street. If his wallet and comb were on his dresser, then his pants were gone, and he needed to find a clean pair. He had also learned how his young wife was removing cash from his wallet and had to check it to ensure he had enough to pay for his lunch before he sat down at a restaurant and ordered. She had learned it from her mother to remove the extra small amounts of cash and save them up to make sure they had cash at the end of the month. She was also stashing money into a new savings account they had just opened. Emy hadn't said anything to Clay, but she wanted to buy a house and needed some money put aside for furniture and appliances. They could use their military time to receive VA assistance in the home loan and shouldn't have to worry about a down payment. But a home needed far more than simply floors and walls, and she wanted at least a three-bedroom because she wanted children; another topic the newlyweds had only briefly discussed.

"Good morning, Norm," Clay said as he entered the kitchen area and took the blue ceramic coffee cup being handed to him by his wife.

"Sorry to wake you up, Clay. But the Colonel telephoned me at five a.m. and put an alert call-up into place. For some strange reason, you weren't answering your phones, so I was sent over here to collect you. He's holding the meeting out at his cabin, and before you ask me, I don't know why we're going there, and I'm too tired to play guessing games with the old man. So, I am here, and we need to get going. If you're hungry, we can stop by one of the fast-food joints and pick up something."

Clay looked over at Emy, "Do I have any money left?"

Emy turned a shade of red and then grinned, "You have $20 in your wallet and both bank cards."

"Well, it seems I won't starve, at least." Clay looked over at Norm to explain. "Emy's mother taught her to keep tight control over the purse strings in the house, and though I make really good wages, I often feel like a pauper. But I'm ready. He gave Emy another kiss and then asked Norm, "You want me to take my car out, too?"

"Naw…with the cost of fuel, we're better off with one rig, and the road to the cabin will already be filled with the other staff members. Thinking about food, maybe we should get something for lunch too; I imagine we might be out there all day. You know the Colonel; once he starts talking, it could make for a very long day."

*SILAS WICKERSHAM'S CABIN*
*CHENA HOT SPRINGS ROAD*
*JUNE 20TH*

The dirt road leading up to the cabin was blocked bumper to bumper with assorted trucks and all-wheel-drive SUVs; enough vehicles to show Clay how it appeared the entire officer staff of the Alaska Defense Force Northern Command Militia was most likely present. Clay carried a Glock 19 9mm pistol in an inside the pants holster in the middle of his back and had it covered over by a dark blue t-shirt. He was wearing brown jeans and a pair of Sear's black and white tennis shoes. He knew the cabin would be full, as it was during the officer's retreat, but the meeting was being held out back. To help with the mosquito problem, Silas had three of the propane anti-bug deflectors going, and they were doing a reasonably good job at keeping the enemy at bay.

All the officers, from platoon commanders on up, were sitting in cloth camp chairs. Silas had picked up fifty of them last year in garage sales and had them stashed away for just such a meeting as this. He had used them for campfire and bonfire nights, and at five-dollars apiece, they were quite the bargain. The men and women were set up in a half-circle around an unlit fire pit. Clay saw he was the last one to arrive and ignored the smirks he received from his fellow militia officers. He also noticed the Colonel had a large black chalkboard set up, five-feet wide by three-feet tall. It was currently blank.

"Well, I see that our recently wed training officer has arrived," Silas said. "Now be kind, gentlemen, and ladies, our young captain was supposed to have today off, but his unkind employer has called upon him once again." Silas looked at Clay and asked, "Is Emy mad at me, Clay?"

"Don't expect any Christmas cards this year, Colonel." This reply brought about a polite chuckle from those in attendance. Donuts and sweet rolls, along with coffee and tea, had been served. Silas had lunch being prepared at the Chena Hot Springs Resort, and he had only two hours and fourteen minutes of time to conduct the first briefing before mealtime. A second brief would follow, and then the troops would be released to go home.

"Now then, as to why you're all here... You've all taken an oath of loyalty to Alaska, to our Militia, and to me. Most of you, but not all of you know about another faction inside our Militia, and this is why you are out here today." Silas went on with the same sort of speech he had given Clay not so long ago in Major Peterson's home. The officers remained silent, but a few became agitated as they learned about the election process of 1959.

"Several years ago, without the authority of the State of Alaska or the Alaska Defense Force, I created a smaller militia faction known as the Alaska Freedom Brigade Militia or the AFBM. Now before I go any further in discussing this faction, I will ask that if any of you have the slightest objection or feel uncomfortable with what has been said here already, this is the time for you to leave. Nothing will be said against you, and I will respect your honesty. Your rank and service with the Alaska Defense Force will continue on, and this I promise you. Not everyone agrees with another person's vision, and this is the moment to bow out. We will take a break of ten minutes for all of you to consider this and talk among yourselves. If you wish to depart, please advise either Major Peterson or Major Johnson... we will try to get your vehicles moved out during the lunch break, and in the meantime, you can relax in the cabin."

Clay was not surprised when they returned after the break that not one officer had gone against the Colonel. Before continuing on, he then administered an oath of allegiance to Alaska and the AFBM. This was one of the parts of working undercover Clay disliked so, giving his word or taking an oath and knowing both were lies.

"All right then... I should advise you now that each of you has had an extensive history check conducted on you. From criminal records, work history to credit scores. If you notice anyone missing here, it was because they may have failed one of these areas and were not selected for this special militia force." Silas picked up a long wooden pointed wand and waved it over the officers. "This is why you have worked together over the last twenty-four months, in preparation for the upcoming operation. Only three people have known about this plan, Majors' Peterson and Johnson, and me. In the next week or so, you will learn the complete details of this operation, from what it involves and the possible consequences that may result.

"However, over the next few hours, we will discuss tactics, equipment needs, and issuance, deployment of manpower, and usage of high explosives as a justifiable deterrence. As to our target and why it was chosen...I have selected Eielson Air Force Base during the 4th of July Celebration and Open House. The Thunderbirds will be providing an air show, and more than fifteen thousand people are expected to be in attendance. All we need is five-hundred well-chosen healthy hostages to be held inside the main hanger in order to gain the eyes and ears of the world news organizations. Such an act will allow us time to present our petition to the United Nations, as Joe Vogler attempted so many times and was blocked by the United States. We are out to right a wrong and bring about a second and lawful election for statehood. We of AFBM declare sovereignty for our beloved Alaska."

# PART II

# 12

# THE CLOCK IS WINDING DOWN

*The Meeting at Silas Wickersham's Cabin*
*June 20th*

C lay had been sitting through his boss's meeting now for over two-hours and was feeling pretty restless at this point and struggling to conceal it. A big part of him would have liked to have jumped up and shout out, "You're all a bunch of traitors!" But he doubted he would be allowed to leave had he done so and probably would've ended up in an unmarked grave outside. This was rapidly becoming one of the hardest assignments in his long career as the day of the attack grew ever closer. Keeping the expression of one of being in favor of this upcoming operation was proving difficult, and he was now experiences bouts of nervous tension, which he fought hard to pass off as excitement for the upcoming invasion of Eielson Air Force Base.

As with the others in the main room, Clay was also carrying a concealed pistol in the middle of his back, covered over by his black t-shirt with the imprint of an Alaskan State flag on the front.

Earlier, all of the officers, from platoon commanders on up, had been sitting in cloth camp chairs, set-up in a half-circle around an unlit camp-fire pit out in front of the cabin. But Silas had moved the meeting inside because of the growing mosquito problem and watching his staff busily swatting themselves in an attempt to deter these miniature vampires.

Once inside, Silas had asked Clay if his new bride was angry about Clay having to attend this meeting, to which Clay had replied, "Don't expect any Christmas cards this year, Colonel." His response produced a polite chuckle from the others. Once everyone was settled, a serving tray was brought out, and Clay was happy to see there were donuts and other Danish, as well as tea and coffee being provided. He had missed breakfast and was now hungry. Silas also had an early dinner planned for his staff at the Chena Hot Springs Resort down the road, following this afternoon session. The Springs was a well-known tourist stop, with rental cabins, a lodge, and a restaurant, and also came with its own private landing strip for small aircraft.

Silas continued with his speech he had started outside, "As you know, this airbase is also right outside our training area, and we can continue to gather there and prepare for our operation without bringing suspicion on what our actual plans are. We have an established shooting range out there, so the base Security Policemen are used to us. But, as you know, we are not allowed to have automatic weapons, only semiautomatic. So, we cannot use our newly acquired fully automatic weapons in this area. We have chosen another location off of Circle Hot Springs Road for firing of the new weapons and ensuring our grenades actually work. Some of our older Vietnam era explosives have failed us in the past, and we cannot afford for this to happen when we hit Eielson.

"Our Armored Personnel Vehicles bought for the ADF will be tarped over and carried by flatbed out to our training area so that we can finish up our training in the use of these beasts. Each APC will eventually be armed with their assigned automatic weapon. The APC 706 vehicles will be armed with M-60's, much like the weapons the amphibious Rubber Duckies carried in Vietnam and the early days of Desert Storm. As to our two APC 113s, they will be better armed. One will carry our newly acquired 20mm Gatling Gun, and the other 113 will be carrying our new addition… a 25mm cannon. Both of these weapons were quite expensive and put a severe dent in our operating budget, and to protect you all and our benefactors, I will not divulge where I made my purchases.

"Now as to the plan... " Silas handed his wand to Major Peterson and walked over to a six-foot-long by three-foot-wide piece of brown fake-wood paneling and proceeded to turn it around and place it back onto the three-legged wooden frame holding it four-feet above the floor.

Silas then accepted the wand back from Peterson and pointed to a large map pinned to the wall panel. "This is a blow-up of Eielson Air Force Base's Flight-line. Primarily it shows where Base Operations is situated, and you can see the three large hangers and the two active runways, which are the primary and secondary strips... Oh, and the taxiway." Silas then removed a black felt marker and made a square out in front of Base Operations and two large arrows, one pointing away to the east of Base Ops and the other pointing to the west.

"For those of you who might not be aware of it, the base's control tower stands right above Base Operations. These two arrows I have just drawn make up the areas where the vendors will be putting their tents, where they'll sell food and their giftware from... souvenirs and such. American and Alaskan flags, all kinds of junk the public likes to buy to commemorate the event.

"I've attended the last fifteen Open Houses at Eielson, and it never changes, so I expect the same set-up for this July 4th. This squared-off area will be where the VIP tent is located, and they'll be two sets of stands for the families of the VIPs so they can sit and enjoy the air show, while the VIP themselves will mostly be inside the tent hobnobbing with each other. We can expect the Borough Mayor, both the mayors of North Pole and Fairbanks and very probably the Alaskan State Trooper commander for the Fairbanks area and both the Police Chiefs for Fairbanks and North Pole. I also imagine Fort Wainwright's Commanding General will be there since the army will be setting up static displays showing off their different helicopters and weapons for the taxpayers to see they're getting their money's worth. That's how it always happens. Last year I was in the VIP Tent, more for my car dealership and how much money we donate to the local charities than my service to the Alaska Defense Force.

"At the extreme eastern edge of the runway is where the alert hanger is, and they keep six birds ready to launch in the event the Russians or someone else violates our air space. The first two birds would be launched, and then four others would take-off behind them if needed. Approximately, twenty-minutes later, a KC-135 would take off to refuel these fighters, who'll be burning a lot of fuel to get to our west coast to intercept any violator of our state's safety zone... or whatever else they call it. In the past, our pilots have encountered Russian fighters or their Backfire prop-driven bombers and escorted them back to international air space.

"Now back here, on the northeastern edge of the map is where all the other fighters are parked, along with the other tankers. Transient aircraft are usually placed on the flight-line near Base Operations, and for this air show, this will also include the Thunderbirds after they arrive from Elmendorf Air Force Base. Each year the two bases switch off to see who will host the air show first. Sometimes, the Thunderbirds will arrive just in time, but there have been other times they arrived at Eielson the night before and launched their show in the early afternoon. As it stands right now, they'll do their show is scheduled for 3 p.m. or 1500 hours.

"At my last count the Air Force Security Police Squadron numbers approximately one-hundred and sixty-four SPs, but they'll add another fifty- Security Police augmentees, who come from other squadrons but train with the regular SPs in the event an emergency arises. Similar to when our members of the ADF supports the Army and Air National Guard. So, this could mean we could be facing as many as two-hundred or more SPs, but probably less because their midnight shift flight will be now off-duty and sleeping in preparation for that night's mid-shift. Plus, we will, of course, have the element of surprise on our side.

"Based on what I've seen of past Open Houses, the Army likes to put on a show also, and I'm hoping that in the first few moments of our attack, the guests will now think that we're just part of the show.

"Any questions so far," Silas asked.

Captain Sid Linker raised his hand. A former U.S. Army Captain, Sid had served in Vietnam and was now the school principal for Tanana Middle School in Fairbanks. His position with the ADF has him now in charge of A Company. When Silas pointed his wand at him, Sid stood up and asked, "Colonel, I'm concerned our old APCs might give us away. The military quit using these beasts when the Stryker Vehicle came out. I believe only the Marines still use the 113s now and mostly just stateside."

"You're right, Captain, but in all the racket and seeing us charging forward, I doubt the SPs will react right away. I believe if we move fast enough, and with the element of surprise, we will be amongst the civilians before the SPs can respond. By then, they'll not dare fire, for risk of causing civilian casualties. But, it is a good question, and we may have to look at this action again prior to the 4th of July. Any other questions?"

Clay then stood up, and when Silas pointed the end of the wand at him, he asked his question. "Sir, once we leave the woods, how much time do you expect it will take us to cross the highway and both runways to reach the VIP tent to secure these civilians?"

"Another good question, thank you, Captain Jefferson.... I believe once we're in position, approximately 500-yards from the southern edge of the highway, I feel we can secure the tent by 1305 hours... with the attack beginning precisely at 1300 hours. I can only imagine all the adrenaline the troops will be pumping, and it will be hard to slow them down once our invasion begins. But, each squad will have their assignments, and I believe we can carry this off without too much difficulty. Next question?"

No one else held up their hands, knowing they would be briefed on everything the plan entailed several times over the next week or so. With July 4th being their D-Day, they now had all of thirteen days to put everything together and complete their training.

Silas put his wand down on a coffee table and then addressed his people, "My basic plan is to take and hold five-hundred well-chosen hostages inside the Eielson's main hanger, in order to gain the eyes and ears of the world's news organizations. Our VIPs will be among this number, and this will include the crew members of the Thunderbirds in the event they do land at Eielson on July 3rd. We will also choose only those civilians who appear healthy... no handicapped people and no seniors. Also, no children. Though we will use teenagers, children can easily become more difficult to handle. But, based on prior Eielson Air Shows, gathering up 500 hostages will not prove difficult. And please remind our personnel that though they will be looked upon as hostages during this stage of our plan, they are also mostly our fellow Alaskan citizens and will be politely treated when at all possible. We will have provisions and water for them, plus the open house will have ample porta-potties, which we will have nearly two dozen of them moved into the hanger to be nearby for our guests.

"I know this may appear to be a drastic act, but I feel such action is necessary to cause the United States and the United Nations to listen to our demands. I also believe that such an act will allow us time to present our petition before the United Nations, as Joe Vogler, founder of the Alaska Independence Party, attempted to do so many times before and was always blocked by the United States government. We are out to right a wrong and bring about a second and lawful election for statehood. We, the members of the AFBM, are about to declare sovereignty for our beloved Alaska, to create a new country. But, as with any free society, the final outcome will be decided by the voters of this state. They will make that final decision. Only this time, all of the Alaskan communities will receive ballots, interpreters will be available if needed for the native villages and townships, and the ballots will ask all four questions as they should have in 1959, instead of only two."

But what Silas was still withholding from all but his two senior commanders was that he sincerely desired to become the first President of Alaska, for he was convinced the citizens of Alaska would indeed select to go their own way as a new sovereign nation. But he also knew many of the Alaskans would strongly desire to remain a close ally to both the US and Canada.

Silas was also thinking about putting Clay on his senior staff when he became President, possibly even making him his Army Chief of Staff in Alaska's new army. He sincerely doubted that any of the senior officers stationed in Alaska would consider staying around once Alaska had become its own country. He was also not too sure how Canada would feel about this new change but had been unwilling to take a chance on making contact with them out of fear they would then advise the United States' government.

Clay sat spellbound, unable to completely grasp the plan that Silas had outlined. He was also struggling with his thoughts over what this investigation he was on could mean to his brand-new marriage to Emy and her parents. Clay had been so openly welcomed into their family; he was now fearful that when this whole thing ended, he just might lose his wife. He was also at a loss as to what he would tell Agent Leslie File, his new handler when they next met. Based on his schedule, their next appointment was only a couple days away.

With his stomach churning as he wrestled with this planned operation and what could happen if such an attack took place, Clay could well understand his wife and her devotion to Silas. He was such an old family friend that Silas was much like an uncle to her. Clay also knew that if Emy survived the attack, she could be brought up on federal charges of treason, conspiracy, and kidnapping, plus even murder if anyone lost their life on July 4th. She could easily be locked away for life, as well as her parents, who could be seen as conspiring with Silas.

Clay felt sick, but being a seasoned operative, he was able to hide his distress and simply nodded as Silas made his various points. He then saw that Silas was again pointing his right index finger straight at him, "Clay, our training officer will be setting up three more training dates over the next thirteen-days...We will spend the night of that third training day in our training area on July 3rd. We will then hold a final inspection and briefing to ensure everyone is prepared for this operation.

"But remember, we still have thirteen-days to ready ourselves. I am sure you men and women, and the troops who serve under you, are up to this challenge. We have the manpower and equipment to launch a surprise attack, and I am hoping many of the visitors massing upon the flight line will simply believe this is part of the bigger show, allowing us to move in without having to hurt anyone...hopefully. We will all be extremely careful not to shoot anyone unless we are fired upon. But the civilians are off-limits unless one has picked up a weapon from a downed SP and enters into the battle. Then he is no longer a civilian but an enemy soldier. Now, does anyone have a problem with that?"

No one offered any objection, though Clay really wanted to. He had seen overseas how fast a well-planned operation could become a screwed up mess, and people often started dying by the numbers. But he knew right now was not the time for him to blow his trust with Colonel Silas Wickersham.

Clay knew the wooded ADF training area pretty well by now, which held several miles of dirt roads and wide broken fields and wooded areas across from Eielson Air Force Base. He had seen why this area had been chosen for ADF maneuvers and training. He thought it was a perfect spot for training purposes for its remoteness, but also could be easily reached from the Richardson Highway. There were farms to each side, but at least a mile in distance, plus an Assembly of God summer camp, where their Royal Rangers, similar to the Boy Scouts of America, held their weekend campouts. Here the ADF and now the AFBM could train and even shoot their semi-automatic weapons without alarming anyone.

Clay also knew that for whatever reason, Eielson Air Force Base, whose southern base perimeter ran along for miles of the Richardson Highway, had no actual perimeter fence and relied solely on ground sensors and radar to protect its southern and eastern perimeter. There was always a Security Police mobile patrol on the flight-line, ever on alert in the event some terrorist, a nut, or an intoxicated driver decided to enter the base illegally. Clay also knew from working with the SPs when he first arrived in Iraq of how SPs acted as the mobile infantry for the Air Force.

Eielson's base perimeter was also protected by a single large main gate, usually manned by two-Security Policemen, and Clay knew the combat veterans inside the AFBM would have little problem dealing with them. For on July 4th, the base entryway would be completely open to visitors for the Open House and the Thunderbirds' Show. The flight line would be filled with dozens of vendors and numerous military static displays, which would draw thousands in from Fairbanks and outlining areas on a sunny day. Personnel from Fort Wainwright would also be arriving for the show, as the Thunderbirds were well known for their aerobatics.

Clay had once read how nearly a million people had attended a 1976 Open House at Edwards Air Force Base on the Upper Mojave Desert of Southern California. NASA had placed the Space Shuttle Enterprise, atop a 747, on display. There were also three of the scientific wonders- "lifting bodies," which had been used in the testing and planning for the Space Shuttles. These strange aircraft, manned by a single pilot, closely resembled numerous sightings of UFOs over the years leading up to the Space Shuttle Enterprise's official naming ceremony in Palmdale, when the public was first able to see the Enterprise.

So, Clay knew Silas's numbers for possible visitors could still be on the low side, and they could have as many as 50,000 or more people coming from town and the outlying areas to watch this show, and this gravely concerned him. He knew how easily the situation could grow out of control, and hundreds could fall victim to a battle being fought on the base flight line. Not just the police or reserve civilian police officers, but in Alaska, a lot of civilians were able to legally carry concealed handguns, though they couldn't legally carry them onto the base as federal law trumped state law. Still, Clay knew there would be some people who were liable to still carry their concealed firearms, federal law or not.

Clay was also struggling with his own thoughts concerning statehood. The more he learned about the bogus statehood election in 1959, the stronger he felt about the need for a possible second election. In his research, Clay had verified many of the Colonel's talking points and how the Alaska Statehood Committee had done a poor job on that Election, especially over the 90/10 decision.

He had to smile, though, when he learned of how the U.S. had been conned by the Russians over the purchase of Alaska. For when the US bought Alaska from Russia for over seven-million dollars, it turned out that Russia had only legally owned a small portion of the Southeast Alaska Island of Sitka. But the U.S. had thought they had gained the whole of Alaska and, in the process ignoring the many native tribal groups who had lived upon the land. The United States had moved in on it and not so gently shoved the Alaskan natives aside, as it had done in the Lower 48. But, due to Alaska's terrain, its massive size, and harsh snowy winters, even today, there were still very few roadways in the State of Alaska. There were no roads going to outside coastal communities to the west from Alaska's vast interior, except via Anchorage and the Kenai Peninsula. Also, there was only a single mostly dirt highway going to Prudhoe Bay on the northern coast. This was one of the reasons the state's population was still under eight-hundred thousand people, and most of the outer communities remained primarily native Alaskans.

Clay actually went back and forth with himself as to whether he thought Alaska becoming a separate country would be a good thing, and it was truly affecting his outlook on this whole investigation. Though, he did not agree with Silas's plan to invade Eielson for fear of the battle that might ensue. He wished that Silas would take this Joe Vogler's plan back to the UN, but he also knew it was now far too late for that. For in thirteen days, the AFBM would be staging their attack, and he would be caught right in the middle of it.

He could now imagine his beloved wife and her parents being rounded up as traitors and being held for trial, with him being the prosecution's primary witness. A small part of him, the one part which actually fought with his PTSD and his six years of combat and secret operations against the enemies of the U.S., would have preferred just bagging it all and walking off into the Alaskan wilderness with his wife. Maybe even returning to the old Athabaskan Village of Minto, where he was raised.

But he knew that eventually, the federal authorities would hunt him down. Then there was also the reality of his love for his new wife, as he looked into Emy's beautiful eyes and thought of all their plans for a future together...

Yes, it was really tearing him apart, and he couldn't tell anyone, not even Agent File, what he was thinking. He knew File would relieve him on the spot and probably have him taken him into federal custody, which would immediately lead to Emy and her parent's arrest and that of the whole AFBM force. It might also cause the Alaska Defense Force to lose their legal standing with the U.S. militaries for allowing this terrorist splinter group to form within their ranks. A side of him thought that would be the best thing, stopping a battle from occurring and so many lives placed in jeopardy. Yet, then Emy would know he had been lying to her. He just had to come up with something else, and that turned him to doing some intense praying, asking the Good Lord for help.

Outside the Chena Hot Springs Lodge, Clay was struggling with a strong urge to head for a stand of trees and upchucking his meal. He knew this had to be his worst intelligence op ever, even worse than the CIA op that ended up with the killing of some of his good friends. In that case, he was as much surprised as everyone else when the one agent blew the whole operation. He knew he was facing even a worse catastrophe in this Eielson AFB attack and just couldn't decide what he needed to do, so for now, he put off doing anything and knew that would probably prove to also a bad decision.

*Should I take a chance and tell Emy everything, but what do I risk if I do? Will she feel more loyal to her parents, to Silas and the AFBM... even to Alaska, and might she report me. Or even kill me in my sleep and make it look like suicide. Oh, Lord, what have I gotten myself into? I should've demanded a vacation after that last operation in Tennessee... Not volunteer for this damn assignment. But, that wouldn't have stopped this attack from happening. Silas has his grand goals in mind and one-hundred and twenty-three troops behind him to carry this out. My beautiful Emy still could face being harmed, and if she survived intact, face imprisonment for her traitorous participation... I just wouldn't have known her if I had not returned to Alaska for this operation. But, I also would've learned of what had happened to my beloved Alaska, which I might've been able to stop had I accepted this damn assignment.*

*Lord, I need some real heavy help here in dealing with this and bringing it to a safe conclusion. Please, Lord, show me how to proceed,* Clay prayed as he stood outside the lodge while the other remained inside enjoying a good meal.

Clay knew another briefing would probably be held for the senior NCOs to better prepare them for this operation, and they, in turn, would brief their enlisted personnel under them. Each member of the AFBM would give his oath of allegiance prior to receiving the overall plan. Silas had already explained to them on how the Alaska Statehood Committee had played false with the citizens of Alaska. The more he thought about it, the more he leaned toward Alaska independence, but he would want to remain a close ally to the US and continue to defend both Canada and the US in the event an enemy planned to attack the North American Continent.

He was proud of his service to the country, but Alaska was still his home. He began to wonder if this was what went through General Robert E. Lee's mind when he refused to take up arms against his beloved Virginia and joined the confederacy?

*I'm thinking too hard on this right now? Do I need to listen to Silas and see what he is truly saying and hopefully learn what other intentions he just might have? I know he's a highly decorated senior officer from the Army and has made millions through his car dealership, but lately... lately, he's been a bit frazzled, and he's out of the office more than he's in. Is there something else going on here? Do I need to start tailing him to see what he's doing outside the dealership and who he might be meeting with...Now, where did that come from. Is that you, Lord? Are You giving me direction, or is my leaking brain misleading me? I need some coffee!*

Inside the lodge and in a private dining room, which had already checked by the unit's security officer, and men were posted for added security, Silas was again chatting with his officers, "Several years ago, without the authority of the State of Alaska or the Alaska Defense Force, I took it upon myself to create this smaller militia faction... One that you know I named the Alaska Freedom Brigade Militia for that very reason... to free Alaska from the clutches of the United States government. We now number one-hundred and twenty-three members. It is this smaller unit that you have worked and trained together for the last twenty-four-months in preparation for this upcoming operation.

"Now, over the next thirteen days, you will also learn the complete details of this operation and what it means to you and all of Alaska. You will also learn of the possible consequences this op-plan could cause to each and every one of you if we fail. I'll be very honest with each of you, this event could lead us all to lengthy prison terms, or worse, very possibly to our deaths or serious injuries, in the event we fail in catching them by surprise.

"However, over the next few days, we will discuss tactics, our equipment needs and issuance, the unit's deployment of manpower, and also the usage of high explosives as a justifiable deterrence. As to our target and why it has been chosen... I had selected Eielson Air Force Base because of its 4th of July Open House. As you know, the Thunderbirds Aerial Demonstration Team, flying their F-16s, will be performing, and this will likely bring thousands of civilians to the base for the air show.

"I'm predicting anywhere from fifteen to possibly more than twenty-five thousand civilians to be in attendance...maybe even more. But, all we will need is five-hundred well-chosen people to become healthy hostages, who will be held in Eielson's big hanger, in order to gain the eyes and ears of the world's news organizations. Such an act will allow us time to present our petition to the State of Alaska, Washington, D.C., and the United Nations.

"We are out to right a grievous wrong and bring about a second and lawful election for either statehood or for Alaska to stand on its own as a free and sovereign nation. We, the members of the AFBM wish, if possible, to declare sovereignty for our beloved Alaska…But, it will, of course, be up to our voters to make that decision."

Clay knew he needed to have another meeting with his FBI handler, Agent Leslie File, to provide her with all this pertinent information. But, what was he to do about his new wife, Emy, and her parents? He had a nightmare just last night where he saw Emy locked up at Leavenworth Federal Prison, awaiting her execution. He woke up bathed in night sweats and was extremely relieved to see Emy lying beside him and snoring lightly.

Silas continued, "Now I'll offer this once more. If there is anyone here who cannot faithfully carry out his assigned duties with the AFBM, speak up now. I cannot let you just walk-off, but I will provide you with your own tent to use out at the training grounds, under guard, of course, and give you a letter stating you had refused to join with us. Once the operation is done, no matter how it ends, you can at least have this letter to provide to the authorities." *Though I doubt the US would honor any letter from me…I just hope no one wants to bail out now.*

But to Silas's relief, no one had raised their hand or stood to their feet. He knew then that all of these men and women would be faithful to the cause. As for Clay, he sure wished he could have had a few minutes to talk with these people to explain to them how foolhardy this plan was. Clay knew a lot of innocent people could possibly die from their actions on the 4th of July, and many more wounded during the battle for the flight-line. He had been to these Open Houses before and recalled just how many armed soldiers and SPs would be walking about. Once a firefight broke out, Clay knew the flight-line would be covered in blood and screaming people shouting for help. He just couldn't figure out why these NCOs didn't see that either. But, then Clay realized they looked upon Silas as being a sort of prophet, the man to lead Alaska, even though, as far as Clay knew, Silas hadn't said a word about what was to happen afterward when they had gained their sovereignty.

Clay had known a few such men, who felt destiny was leading them toward fame, riches, and glory. In the Middle East, he had encountered several tribal leaders who felt they were the rebirth of Muhammed, and several members of their tribes believed this and were prepared to die for their leader as suicidal martyrs. But, with the exception of some of the individual men he had known in the past, this was the first time he had seen so many veterans in one group wanting to change the way the United States was.

Oh, he knew American history did identify such characters, and like Silas, they were charismatic, wealthy and had often shown how they sincerely cared for their fellow Americans. But in truth, they had only thought of themselves and how they could profit from their schemes and plans.

Silas had loaned and given money to them, helped celebrate their kid's birthdays, and even provided dinners or a night out on the town for when that man or woman in his command who was about to celebrate a wedding anniversary. Clay had only recently learned that Silas had issued car loans directly to some of his people who couldn't finance a vehicle through a bank or loan company because of their poor credit history, or they just didn't make enough money for the loan company to okay. No, the more Clay thought about it, the more he felt these AFBM members would probably follow their Colonel into Hell.

# FAMILY ISSUES

*Jefferson Household*

That same night, as Clay lay in bed beside Emy, he thought about telling her about tonight's meeting with Silas and then explaining to her about just who he actually was. But, as he contemplated this, he also knew that Emy would, of course, be extremely concerned with what might happen to her parents. Clay also knew how loyal she was to Silas and the other members of the AFBM, for she had explained to Clay on numerous times of how she thought a lot of them were like family and how loyal she was to them.

With his thoughts now racing, going from one extreme to another, he knew how easily he could lose her, and even worse, she might actually go as far as trying to kill him in his sleep. *Then she'd just tell the good Colonel about what she had learned from her dear and now dead husband.*

Will that thought sure didn't make it any easier for him to get back to sleep, and for a brief moment, he considered getting his pistol out of the dresser drawer and placing it under his pillow. But then he realized he needed to trust in the Lord, as he had learned to do on his other dangerous assignments. Still, he wanted to kick himself for getting so heavily involved with her, knowing full well going in of what sort of complications might develop, and clearly, now they had.

Clay had been involved with other girls before, and a couple of those times, he had considered them to be serious, but in those cases, he had never considered marriage, and mostly that was due to his chosen career. His Christian walk also prevented him from entering into a relationship the Lord would frown upon, so he never lived with any of these ladies. He had also learned as a young adult, the best thing he could do when the nightmares came was to grab his Bible and read the Word of God, followed by praying. As a result, he had earlier picked up the title of being a Bible thumper. However, Clay was still a warrior, and no one who ever knew how Clay operated in the field ever referred to him as a Holy Joe.

To make matters worse, Clay knew he was now scheduled to meet with Agent Lisa File at Basset Hospital. Agent File, out of the Portland FBI Office and also assigned to Washington D.C., had replaced Doc Adams. Though he had learned the old man had died due to overwork and advanced age, at first Clay suspected Doc had possibly been murdered, but the intensive autopsy had shown his death was, in fact, by natural causes.

Clay didn't know this new handler all that well, and she might pull him out of the operation if he decided to tell her everything, but he knew that would most likely result in his wife's arrest and very possibly her parents. He could imagine himself being called to the stand to testify against his in-laws, and that realization caused his stomach to turn backflips, which was making it tougher to fall asleep. Still, Clay also knew that for withholding all that, he knew he too could be arrested for Treason, Conspiracy, and even Murder. He knew the murder charges would come forward if anyone, anyone at all, was killed in the attack on Eielson.

Lying there in bed, now very much awake, his mind filled with doubt and running arguments with himself, he felt as if his life was being ripped apart by angry monkeys, and his heart was breaking. He also couldn't figure out how Silas could possibly believe he could take over Eielson's flight-line and hold all these hostages, with only one-hundred and twenty-three AFBM troops. Clay knew the Air Force Security Police on the flight-line that afternoon could easily number close to over one hundred person-nel, plus they would have the support from the Army's Military Police and other armed troops working the military's static displays. There would also be half-a-dozen Alaska State Troopers, not counting off-duty civilian law enforcement here to attend the Open House. The Alaska State Troopers and even the Fairbanks Police knew these Open Houses were a good place for AST and FPD to advertise and hand out job applications and info brochures.

*No, something else has gotta be going on here... Silas wants to hold all these hostages in order to get the feds and the United Nations to listen to him... if they will or not was up in the air... But, they might simply blow him off as a radical, and the military, assisted by local police, would then work up a plan to free those hostages. Then the whole thing could blow up in our faces as in a major firefight breaking out, and the results could be catastrophic!*

*Silas has got to have something else in mind to force a vote in the UN... and in Congress... But what? Those explosives he talked about... just maybe, he could have the hanger packed with C-4... or simply crates of dynamite... or worse. Maybe he's been able to get his hands on some sort of weapon to threaten the military with. There's always a lot of biological weapons for sale in Europe and occasionally even in the Middle East... plus there's Africa. Could that be it, and he's keeping it real quiet because it might cause some of his troops to fall away or even fight him? No one really wants to see their own children withering on the ground because they were just exposed to a biological weapon.*

Clay really didn't like the idea that Silas had gotten his hands on some kind of weapon of mass destruction... possibly either chemical or biological device. Clay knew a large hanger would make a perfect spot to detonate or release such a weapon. *But where would he have gotten it? Even an explosive device made with dynamite and gasoline could do a lot of harm inside a large hanger. If only I hadn't been so stupid to have fallen in love with Emy, but I did, and I can't risk her being placed into custody, or worse, but can I trust her? Would she stab Silas in the back and endanger her folks for me? Can I take that chance? Oh, Lord, I'm in real trouble here... I need your help!*

Clay finally gave up on trying to sleep and quietly slipped out of bed. Once he was sure Emy was sleeping soundly, he then walked into the bathroom, quietly closed the door, and washed his face from the sink. He thought about a hot shower to help him relax, but that might have awakened her. Then after checking on her again, he walked quietly into the kitchen for a glass of milk. His stomach was too restless to eat anything, and he now realized he would have to schedule another meeting with Silas to see if he could learn of what the Colonel really had planned for the 4th of July. He needed to know as many of the facts as possible to make his decision on what actions he would have to make. He also struggled with the idea of just running away and fleeing to Minto, handcuffing his wife and holding her in her grandfather's house until July 5th. But he knew that was a stupid idea, and he would still have to face the authorities, not to mention having to deal with an enraged Emy.

He knew the feds would run him down easily enough because of his records, the original set, which showed he was raised in his grandfather's home in Minto. They would most assuredly incarcerate both he and Emy. and quite possibly take both of them out and bury their bodies somewhere out in the tundra, so their arrest didn't embarrass the Feds.

No, he needed to make that meeting with Leslie File, and between now and then, he would have to decide what his next steps would be. He wasn't scheduled to see File until 2:15 p.m. at Basset Hospital on Fort Wainwright, plus he still had to work the morning shift at Wickersham Chevrolet. Silas knew about his PTSD appointments at Bassett and actually encouraged Clay to attend all of his VA appointments. Clay had been honest with Silas to some degree, telling him of how his prior doctor had died, and he was assigned a new female psychologist to help him with his Post Traumatic Stress Disorder.

"Oh, I'll give you the time off, no problem, but you just make sure you make those appointments and any therapy groups they want you to attend. I've seen how well such sessions have helped many of our veterans, and Emy would probably shoot me if you missed these sessions and became a drunk or a stoner. So, you take the hour or so off and make sure you meet your obligations, besides… it's covered by the government," Silas had said to him

Clay had a scheduled 9:25 a.m. appointment with Silas to discuss a couple of shop problems. But now Clay hoped he could also learn more about any sort of massive destruction weapon that he might have in the hanger to keep the hostages under control. Clay hoped such information could possibly be used as a bargaining tool to help him save Emy and her parents from going to trial.

His wife was awake at 6:45 a.m. and had made him a breakfast of waffles smothered in applesauce and four links of caribou sausage, which was one of his favorite dishes. Then he left for work. He had seriously considered telling Emy about the whole undercover role over breakfast, but he had chickened-out. He just didn't know if he could've handled her choosing her parents and Silas over him, and at the moment, he just couldn't afford that happening. There was too much at risk, and he felt much like a rubber Gumby figure being stretched apart. He was also concerned she might then lie to him, and then after he left for work, she might have telephoned Silas and spilled all the beans.

Clay was also hiding a secret bank account, where the military was depositing his captain's pay, along with the stipend the FBI provided. Which just gave himself another thing to be worried about, hiding this extra pay away from Emy. Thankfully, he was making pretty good pay as a shop manager, plus his VA retirement pay for him being carried temporarily as 70% retired. This pretty much meant they didn't have any financial concerns; except he was still lying to her.

Tomorrow was another training day out at 22-mile Richardson Highway. They were scheduled to practice quick deployment procedures from their armored personnel vehicles. They would also be practicing shooting and quick take-down arrest techniques. Clay knew the Colonel had said how he didn't want any servicemen or guests shot down if at all possible, but there was bound to be numerous scuffles in disarming the base police and Army personnel.

AFBM members were being told to shoot to wound only if they must fire, but Clay knew the adrenaline would be pumping, and accidental killings were bound to occur. Still, Clay would do what he could to make the shooting practice be as real as possible. He didn't want his men to be responsible for the shooting of unarmed men, women, and children. Clay also knew there would be hundreds of cameras on the flight-line, and the AFBM would clearly lose their battle with the press if they had photographs of female and child victims being gunned down by militia members.

However, due to the closeness of the range to the highway, the troops could only practice while firing on semiautomatic. The AFBM knew that any fully automatic fire was bound to bring the SPs or State Troopers out to investigate. So, for practice on fully automatic fire, and the use of crew weapons such as the M-60s, the 20mm Gatling Gun, and the 25mm cannon, they were now using a hidden range out off of Circle Hot Springs Road. This was a good 60-miles northeast of Fairbanks and miles away from the nearest homestead. The weapons were concealed under the floorboards inside a 29-passenger bus that was also used to haul the shooters out to the hidden rifle range. The men handling the automatic crew weapons were all combat veterans who had used such weapons in either Iraq or Afghanistan.

The six-706 Amphibious "Rubber Ducky" Armored Personnel Carriers and the two APC heavily armored 113s had been kept in a warehouse owned by Wickersham Chevrolet and guarded by members of the AFBM. All of the machine-guns would remain inside their APC vehicles, along with ammo and grenades, which contained either tear gas, smoke, or were of the more lethal fragmentation type. The ammo for the riflemen assigned to each of the eight APCs would also be stored in the vehicles. The troops assigned to the mounted machine-guns would undergo driving practice out at the training grounds across from Eielson, in the event the assigned drivers were possibly wounded or killed during the attack. Of course, added precautions were needed to hopefully prevent the authorities from knowing the AFBM was in possession of these automatic weapons, but it was common knowledge of how the Alaska Defense Force had purchased these former military vehicles in a federal auction.

Six ten-ton Kenworth tractors and their forty-foot flatbed trailers were used for hauling the six-Rubber Ducky APCs to the training grounds. Two much heavier 15-ton tractors were then used to haul the two-heavier 113 APCs. They had been removed from the warehouse this last week and hauled out to the training grounds to enable the men to have time to practice rapid deployment from them prior to the Open House.

All of the troops inside the AFBM were to be armed with M-16s that could fire on semiautomatic or for a brief three-round burst on fully automatic. The troops were also to be armed with a semi-automatic pistol.

Silas had made several large purchases of both Glock and Smith and Wesson handguns over the last year and actually received a tax credit for donating these weapons to the ADF Militia. Each troop would also carry in their field backpacks MRE meals for at least 3-days, a first-aid packet, two-extra full canteens of water, besides the one on their canteen belt, and gas masks, in the event the military attempted to gas the hanger. Also, in the event the need arose, certain troops, trained in the use of the same, would also be armed with tasers to help in the control of the hostages.

The troops with tasers would also be part of an advance troop of a twelve-member scout squad, whose assignment was to quickly secure the VIP Tent and take as many of these people, including members of the Thunderbirds, if in attendance, as hostages. With these VIPs being state and local politicians, plus high ranking military officers, Silas had hopes in taking such high-value targets as hostages would help put a stop to any shooting from taking place in a possible dangerous rescue attempt by U.S. Armed Forces.

*AT THE 22-MILE AFBM TRAINING SITE*

Two well-armed uniformed AFBM guards were standing post at the road's access point to the training field. With several farms nearby who used this entry point when exiting the highway, the militia's gate was located just over a mile south from the highway, and the site took in just over two-hundred acres. Both of the militia members were in possession of hand radios in order to stay in contact with Silas or the on-duty security officer in the event of any problems. The guard would also report any military or civilian law enforcement personnel who might show up and was requesting entry.

There were also two-four man perimeter patrols walking about the training area, also with radios, in the event someone might try to get close enough to observe the AFBM training. Though sometimes it was just hunters who were not aware of this area belonging to the militia. Clay had also stationed a seven-member squad to be on standby with a Rubber Ducky as a quick reaction response team, who were ready to respond if any emergency arose.

Yesterday afternoon, Clay had been busily working with a training class of twenty-eight AFBM personnel, conducting hand-to-hand fighting techniques for disarming military and law enforcement personnel. He was also continuing his training in the use of various knife fighting skills, but he was now actually working with rubber training knives. He didn't want to risk anyone being injured so close to the 4th of July.

Meanwhile, Emy was following Silas around, temporarily assigned as his aide and runner. She also made sure the old man didn't become dehydrated by this June heat and was always pushing a canteen at him.

When he saw Emy with the Colonel, Clay fought to keep his expression from appearing troubled. He had to keep his thoughts and concerns buried deeply as he struggled with what actions he should take to stop this attack from taking place. He also wondered if he should just let the operation continue on, dueling it out with the idea a new statehood election was warranted and then kicking himself for thinking this way. He only hoped for the moment he could keep his inner turmoil hidden from the other AFBM members, and this, of course, also meant his wife.

At that moment, he was in the midst of showing his class a move taught to him by the Turkish Special Forces in using the butt of the knife's handle to strike the temple area of a guard, either right or left side, which would then disable the man and render him unconscious.

"Our Special Forces people teach this, but the Turks have gone a step further in how you handle the body of the troops you're disabling to ensure you do not just drop them and make noise. This is a completely silent move if you do it right. And if it's forced upon you, your knife or bayonet is in such a place as to insert it under his ear and rip outward, killing him quickly and silently. But, you should try first to disable him by rendering him unconscious; the lethal move is liable to spray blood all over you, and blood stinks."

"Captain, what about a simple slicing of his throat from one ear to the other?" A staff sergeant asked.

"Have you ever completed such move before, Sergeant?" Clay asked.

"No, Sir... But I have seen it done in the movies, and it looks like a quick and silent kill."

"That's Hollywood... The move I just showed you will keep the combatant from being able to make any noise. But, the older move, still used in Hollywood, allows for the man to make gurgling noises, which can make your presence known to other enemy troops. Hollywood would probably have to turn a PG-13 film into an R- rated movie if they used the move I just showed you.

"You first want to disable him, knock him out with the blow like this. But if you must kill, you want the blood spray to go away from you. Otherwise, you'll be smelling his blood on you until the mission is over and you risk exposing yourself by the death sounds he is able to make while choking. Believe me, people do not die as quickly as Hollywood hopes you believe. No, knock 'em out quick and continue on your mission. Only kill when you have to... understand?"

"Thank you, Sir.... But, Captain, have you ever used this move in actual combat?"

"Sergeant, I wouldn't be teaching it had I not seen how well it works. I also don't recommend using your knife or bayonet in an attempt for a quick kill to the heart or the kidneys. Nine times out of ten, you'll miss the mark because of the adrenaline you're pumping. Forget Hollywood and use the techniques you're being taught by your training officers...like myself." Clay grinned and then advised the troops to pair off and practice with one another to ensure they had the move down. Several times he had to make adjustments for the men and women having some degree of trouble with the exercise.

Clay had known from experience that with such limited training, most of these men would flub it on July 4th and would probably end up either clubbing their victim over the head with their bayonet or resorting to the butt of their rifle. Otherwise, some of them were liable to be locked in a death match with the SP or soldier they're trying to subdue. From watching these guys train, he could tell who had prior combat service and the ones who were new to all this.

From the various pair-ups, Clay knew several of these people would probably end up shooting their targets out of fear of risking their lives in a wrestling to the death match-up. To this, he could only shake his head as he pictured how many people might actually die out there on the flight line.

That afternoon he had expressed his doubts to Silas in how some of these troops just were not ready to make the attack on July 4th. Silas had disagreed with him and told him to keep working with them. "Look, Clay, I cannot shorten our strength by removing some of our younger or unqualified troops. We will need every one of them that afternoon. But, if you feel we need to move a couple of them around to less… aggressive assignments, I'll see what you have in mind. But keep working them hard, and hopefully, you will have them ready. Remember, Captain, you were green once too."

Clay agreed with Silas to some degree and kept pushing his new troops hard. Working over their fighting techniques and making the new ones spend extra time at training. Yet he knew that just one more week was simply not enough time to turn these virgins into hardened killers.

*SILAS'S BACK-UP PLAN*

Clay had been right about Silas having obtained a weapon of mass destruction, but it was not a biological or chemical weapon. No, Silas had been secretly working with a foreign power, the People's Republic of China, and their Communist Party. The weapon, a 5-megaton A-bomb, had once belonged to the USSR, but when the Soviet Union fell apart, many of their nuclear weapons had suddenly disappeared. A Russian black marketeer had obtained several of these weapons and had sold them. Silas had hawked nearly everything he owned, mortgaged his home, his cabin, and his car dealership to cover the $20 million price tag for the device and his operational plans. The device was packed into a large metal conex and shipped across the Pacific by ocean barge to the Port of Seward. Here, it was then loaded aboard a 40-foot trailer and transported to Fairbanks, where it was stored in one of Silas's warehouses.

The Russian nuclear physicist bought and paid for by the Russian Mafia, had accompanied the stolen A-Bomb to Fairbanks and had been tinkering with the weapons timing system since his arrival here. He had now just finished assembling the weapon and had carefully inserted the timing device into the bomb casing. Then with the nervous help of two Russian Mercenaries, both former Russian Special Forces troops, they had placed the bomb inside the shell of a now-defunct wheeled-portable diesel-generator. Wet concrete was then placed around the bomb in hopes it would make it tamper-proof. Once the cement was dry, the whole contraption was then chained onto a twenty-two-foot flatbed trailer, now repainted and bearing forged Air Force ID numbers.

The generator was already painted Air Force blue, having been stolen from a shared U.S. and Japanese Air Force Base near Tokyo. The flight-line tech who had sold them the generator was paid a handsome $15,000 for his part of the theft. Since being stolen, the generator was provided with fake U.S. Air Force identification numbers, which made it appear to be just another authentic USAF Diesel Generator assigned to Eielson Air Force Base. Except to make room for the large bomb, the engine for the generator had been removed. As a finishing touch, the generator was now concealed under a large gray tarp now strapped in place.

The Generator had arrived in Alaska via a Japanese 747 cargo carrier, boxed up to appear as containing four large air conditioners. The nuclear weapon's grade material for the bomb had been shielded in a large box heavily lined in lead. The plan called for two of the six Russian merce-naries to sign for the large wooden box, posing as warehouse workmen, and then by using a large airport forklift, they loaded the box onto the twenty-two-foot flatbed truck. They showed their fake documents to the Fairbanks Airport Security personnel and then drove the generator to the Wickersham Warehouse in the Fairbanks Industrial Park off of College Road. The trailer, which would carry the generator, now with the bomb inside, displayed stolen USAF license plates and forged ID numbers. These plates had been removed from a tractor and trailer rig that was decommis-sioned from government service and awaiting auction. Both the tractor and the trailer now showed current USAF license plates for Eielson Air Force Base. A young airman assigned to the storage yard was paid five-thousand dollars for carrying off his side of the operation in obtaining the license plates Colonel Wickersham needed for the drive between Fair-banks and entry onto Eielson AFB.

Once the rig was mobile, on July 3rd, the tractor-trailer rig would be driven by two of the Russian Mercenaries, now wearing Air Force uniforms and posing as USAF enlisted personnel. Their orders were to drive the rig east on the Richardson Highway to 27-mile and then turn left onto a dirt road. They were provided with a hand-drawn map for them to follow. This hard gravel roadway led first to an Alaska Pipeline Pump Station, but then a side road headed northeast and went to the rear side of the Eielson AFB Reservation. This route allowed them access to the base without having to drive through the base's front gate and risk exposure.

They would be driving late in the evening and continue on the old dirt road that once led to the decommissioned Nike Missile Batteries that had at one time defended Eielson Air Force Base from possible air attacks. All the batteries had been torn down, but a lot of hunters used this back road that traversed a series of rolling hills and tundra flats for their moose and bear hunting.

The mercenaries were to show their fake paperwork that allowed them to drive onto the flight line, and as ordered, they parked it as close as possible to the large hanger. Birchwood Hanger was where the hostages were to be held. The tractor would then be disconnected from the trailer, which would hold the mobile generator. They would then drive off the base the same way they had come and then abandon the vehicle on a North Pole back road near Chena Lakes and camouflage it so it wouldn't be seen any time soon. The men would then change into civilian clothes that they had brought with them and hitchhike their way to the North Pole Shopping Mall. Once there, they would call the special number and arrange to be picked up by one of the other mercenaries, driving a rental vehicle.

With the bomb in place, the nuclear physicist and the mercenaries would then fly out on the evening of July 3rd to Anchorage and then disappear. The Russian physicist was ordered to eventually return to Moscow, Russia, after a week of visiting friends in Europe. The mercenaries were well paid for their services and would soon be headed off to different destinations for a couple weeks of relaxation. Most of them were headed for a particular South American country to lay low for at least a couple of months, while two of the mercenaries were headed for Japan on another assignment after their vacation on the Japanese coastline.

As part of their work, once the bomb had been assembled and the device's detonator had shown it could be activated by a particular cell phone call, the physicist had left two such cell phones in an already purchased U.S. Mail postal box, # 723 in downtown Fairbanks. Silas, who had the other key for that box, planned to secure both phones on the late evening of July 3rd when he was supposed to be running home from the training grounds to have a late 8 p.m. dinner with his wife.

The Russian physicist had told Silas through a handwritten note, which accompanied the cell phones, that once activated, the countdown would take only five-minutes, giving the U.S. time to consider their actions in any foolish attempt to take control of the hostages and possibly capture the surviving AFBM members.

But, unknown to Silas, once the bomb had been activated, the count-down was actually only sixty-seconds, and it could not be aborted. The Russian mafia had been paid quite well for this bomb and the personnel, but they had decided that if Silas wanted to blow Eielson AFB up, the blast would then eliminate America's most northern fighter base, and these American terrorists would be blamed. In this event, if the new Russ-ian/Chinese Alliance decided to invade Alaska via the Bering Strait Ice Bridge, the U.S. response would be severely hampered with the removal of Eielson Air Force Base. At least two-fighter wings, and the pending arrival of a wing of B-52 bombers from Barksdale Air Force Base, and Eielson's air refueling capabilities by the KC-135 Tankers assigned there, would be then be rendered useless. As to the base, the land would also be rendered useless, unable to be reoccupied for a very long time due to a high degree of radiation. It was also believed some 100,000 or more Americans would be killed, and the Alaska Freedom Brigade Militia would also take the blame for this heinous crime and make things so much easier in the event an attack on Alaska was forthcoming by either China or Russia.

As to if Silas would actually arm the bomb and set the detonation process into play, that was still an unknown factor, and if he didn't activate it, the Russian Mob still had multi-millions in their coffers from what Silas had paid them for the nuclear device, along with the use of the physicist and six-mercenaries, plus their shipping costs.

No one outside of Silas and his private secretary knew about the expense and what it had cost him to bring this all about. All in hopes he could force this statehood vote and, if things went the way he hoped, to become Alaska's first president. With the exception of his wife, no one knew of the resentment he felt against his country for never offering him a general's star and forcing him into retirement. Because of this, he had felt this was a good way of getting back at the men who kept him from making the senior rank, which he had truly believed he fully deserved.

Had Clay known about the bomb, he would've immediately notified Agent Leslie File, and a N.E.S.T. nuclear task force would've been sent north to locate the device and taken Silas down as a traitor. But, as of yet, outside of those who already knew of the bomb's existence, Silas and only one other knew of the A-Bomb and where it was being moved to.

*JULY 3RD*

With tomorrow being the big event and with the attack planned for one p.m., two-hours before the Thunderbirds were due to fly, the senior staff had set afternoon and evening training sessions for all personnel. These were both classroom and physical training sessions to ensure all the troops knew exactly what their assignments were from the time they left the training area on the early afternoon of July 4th.

As a result of spending the night of the 3rd encamped, over a dozen large 12-man tents were in place to house the AFBM personnel for their last night. A full field kitchen was on hand to prepare the meals for the troops, and now the men and women on KP duty were busily working on an evening meal, which would include a large barbecue of moose, beef, and chicken for all to partake in. There would be no alcohol, but Silas had promised a gala event for all if they were able to carry off this mission. He had promised them that they would all be his guests at the luxurious Princess Hotel the Friday night following the election process, no matter how the voters decided. But Silas was pretty sure the vote would go the way he wanted, he knew that too many Alaskans were upset with how Alaska was being treated in Washington D.C., and he would make sure all the voters would know prior to the election the con-job the feds had done in the 1959 statehood election. With this information to support his cause, he truly believed the voters would vote for Alaskan sovereignty.

In the outside classrooms, the troops continued to go over what their individual and squad assignments were for tomorrow. All the weapons, supplies, and ammo were being loaded aboard the APC units, but it wouldn't be until 30-minutes before the attack order is issued that the APC would place their vehicle's automatic weapons into place and then load them. This was being done to prevent any casual observer walking by the training grounds on the access road, or across the large open fields, from seeing the new heavy armament the APCs now carried.

Silas only wished now that he had gotten ahold of four .50 caliber machine-guns instead of using the lighter weight M-60s, but he just couldn't swing the added costs. He was now pretty much broke and knew that unless they carried this plan off in getting the new election, he would not only be going to prison, but he would also have nothing left to leave to his family. All of his property, including his dealership, would be foreclosed on; whatever wasn't seized by the federal authorities would go to pay off his legal debts. He had been able to secure one-hundred thousand dollars in cash, and it was locked up in a savings box inside a Bank of America located in Seattle, Washington, under Colonel Silas's car dealership name. Only his wife, who was listed as the company's Vice President or Silas, could open that bank box, and she wouldn't even know about it until afterward. In the event it all failed, a lawyer and a good family friend, someone he had known most of his life, would hand her the letter that explained everything, along with the box key. The letter identified the box number and address for the bank. But even the lawyer didn't know what was in the box, only being told it was important family and corporation business documents his wife would need in the event anything happened to him.

Silas knew his wife kept a couple thousand dollars of mad money available in the event she needed to get away for a long weekend after one of their shouting matches, and this would cover her airfare and a couple nights in a nice hotel. There was also a second letter in the box, which was his written apology to her for the mess he had just made. Silas knew his wife would not be attending the Eielson Open House because she was visiting her sister in Anchorage over the fourth. In this way, he didn't have to worry about her being affected by the nuclear blast if the bomb was, in fact, used. His lawyer friend also worked and lived in Anchorage, so Silas knew he would also survive the bomb and could carry out his instructions.

As the mechanics and armorers continued working on their armored personnel carriers throughout much of the evening, others continued to fine-tune their skills in subduing their opponents. With tomorrow being the big day, it seemed as if no one wanted to sleep, especially among the many combat veterans. These troops knew how easily things could go topsy-turvy, and they could suddenly find themselves in a real shooting war with hundreds of women and children in their line of fire. For a few of the troops, who suffered PTSD from Nam, Iraq, and Afghanistan, it wouldn't bother them to shoot civilians or even American soldiers. But, Silas had worked hard to eliminate those *loose cannons* from his ranks. He truly didn't want a single shot fired tomorrow, if at all possible, nor did he desire to activate that nuclear bomb. But, he knew he would if it looked as if everything was going downhill, and he risked being put on trial for treason. There was something in his mental process that kept telling him he was in the right and even feeling of grandeur, that God had truly appointed him for this moment of historical note. He already planned to build his White House in Fairbanks, for he had never liked having the state capital in Juneau. There were no roads to it, and quite often during the winter months, one couldn't even fly there as the runway could become icy, and there was a risk factor in a passenger jet sliding right off. It had happened before when an Alaskan airliner had slid off the runway after landing.

Silas also had a bizarre fear of tsunamis and felt a really good sized wave might just take out the downtown capital someday. This fear was also helped along when he read a Christian fiction story entitled, *A Coming Storm* and also a couple other science-fiction books, where nuclear bombs had destroyed Seattle and elsewhere around the United States and had set off massive earthquakes, which in turn had sent towering tsunami waves up the Inland Passage. These 100-foot waves in that book had destroyed Prince Rupert, Ketchikan, Juneau and Haines, and also Skagway, along with smaller Alaskan Native Communities in the Alaskan Southeast. He did not want to be a victim of such a disaster and felt Alaska's heartland would be a perfect spot for Alaska's new federal capital.

If it happened and he was forced to activate the stolen A-Bomb, then none of it would really matter anyway. He would prefer going up in a bright flash rather than have to face the embarrassment of a drawn-out federal trial and possible death sentence.

Clay and Emy had a private meal together in the woods, taking their barbecue of mixed meats with them and fighting off the mosquitoes and flies that wanted their share. It finally got so bad they returned to the tent area and used an anti-bug screened-off shelter to finish their meal. Some of the people remained close to the barbecue pits as the heat of the fires seemed to keep the bugs at bay to some degree.

In the Command Tent, shared by Silas and of his two senior officers, Majors Alan Peterson and Norm Johnson, the three men consumed their delicious meal, drank iced up sodas, and talked over tomorrow's plans. It was during this talk Silas had made a decision, and he decided he needed to have at least one other trusted friend to know about the A-Bomb, in the event Silas became grievously wounded and could not activate the weapon in a last ditched effort to show the U.S. Forces his total resolve in this action they were taking. He just needed to figure out which of these two men could he confide in. He liked both men equally well, but that couldn't weigh into it. He needed someone loyal enough to stand firm by AFBM's commitment to this action. Both men had proved themselves over and over again, and it troubled him he couldn't decide the issue.

*Allen has been with me the longest; he is fiercely loyal... He also flew 27 missions in Operation Desert Storm as a C-130 pilot and the men like him. Norm Johnson is a retired Air National Guard Chief Master Sergeant and a former Marine who fought in Vietnam. In his case, the men hold him in awe, some of them even a bit afraid of his temper. But they all respect him for his duties in Nam and the medals he won over there. So, who would be best? A part of me thinks Clay might be the best man, but he is junior in rank to these two, and for a lot of his men, he's still an unknown factor; plus, there's that whole PTSD thing he is still being treated for. Though I haven't seen any outbursts of temper that could be PTSD caused, and Emy loves him dearly, so does her parents. But, it might offend these two if I place such a responsibility on a new man... Okay, I've decided.*

"Allen, could you leave Norm and I alone for a bit? I have something to discuss with him that needs to stay between the two of us. But don't you worry any, it doesn't concern you or any actions you've taken. Okay?"

"Sir, you're the Colonel, and if you want to talk with one man or a hundred, that is your privilege of rank. I'll just go back over to the kitchen and get some more of this moose...it's really great."

"Thanks, Allen," Silas said, and he added a big grin for effect.

Once they were alone and Silas knew no one was outside that could be eavesdropping, he began to tell Norm about his back-up plan. Norm remained totally silent, and for a brief moment, he could not believe what he was hearing. He had accepted the reasons behind the attack on Eielson and the need for a second vote of statehood, but this whole thing about a stolen Russian A-Bomb and Silas selling off or placing into hawk his home, cabin, and complete car dealership to fund this attack and also pay the price for the bomb, sounded to him as being really reckless.

Norm was having real difficulty in not just shooting his colonel between the eyes right then and there and crushing the nuclear weapon's special cell-phones that Silas had now showed him. Though Silas had decided to keep both phones in his hands, as he wasn't quite ready to hand one of them off to anyone until tomorrow.

Norm also knew that Silas had indeed made a serious mistake in selecting him over Allen, but Norm couldn't quite decide exactly what action he should take and when. But he had suddenly realized his AFBM Commander had a screw loose if he wanted to risk destroying Eielson AFB and in the process killing a possible fifty to one-hundred thousand people. Norm had only one ace up his sleeve, and he was going to have to use it now, though until he learned of this bomb, he had actually planned to wait to see if they had actually been able to seize Eielson. Now the whole bomb thing had changed all of his plans, and his time was quickly running out.

Later that evening, Clay had just entered a small four-man camping tent he shared with his wife, having just completed a check of all the night guards. Being early July and with Central and Northern Alaska experiencing the extra hours of daylight, it would remain light enough to walk about the camp without needing a flashlight during the night. But, before he got the screen part of his tent flap zipped up, he heard his name being called out in a loud whisper of a voice he recognized right off.

"Clay... Clay, you still awake?"

With a smile on his face, Clay glanced down at his wife and saw that she was in a deep sleep, evidence of this being her light snoring. Like most of the militia members, it had been a long tiring day, and the wake-up call was for 0600 hours. He'd been hoping to get a few hours of sleep, but that would have to wait another few moments as he saw to what Major Norm Johnson wanted.

Clay popped his head outside the tent screen opening and said, "Yeah, Major... I'm still awake. What's up, Sir?"

"We need to talk, and I mean right now. Let's go for a walk."

Clay could tell by the tone of urgency in Norm's voice it was something important, so he reached in and grabbed up his canteen belt that held his pistol. "Okay, I'm ready...where do you want to go...for this talk?" Clay asked. His combat antenna, which he had learned to rely on in the Middle East, had just popped up, and that put him on edge.

"Let's just walk, but keep moving and let's avoid the camp guards if possible... I don't want anyone overhearing us. So, keep it down to whispers....Okay?" Norm then led off, and Clay caught up and walked beside him. Clay could see that they were headed for the kitchen area, where they picked up some hot coffee in large Styrofoam cups. While training, both men took their coffee black, no cream or milk, and no sugar—basic military style. From the kitchen area, they then walked over to where one of the big Kenworth tractors was parked. All the APC units had been off-loaded, but the rigs would be left here for safekeeping when the AFBM launched their attack.

"Okay, Clay, I'm only going to ask this once, and I expect a truthful answer...Who the hell are you?" Norm held his cup to his mouth with his left hand, but his right hand was holding the butt of his pistol, though it was still holstered but unsnapped.

"What do you mean, Major? You know who I am...what's this about?" The two men were standing in front of the Kenworth Tractor and out of sight, as with most of the camp, except for a few guards and some troops carrying out last-minute details, were now fast asleep from a very busy day.

Norm then quickly drew out his pistol and pointed it right at Clay's midsection from 5-feet away. "I'll only ask you one more time, Clay...Oh, I know that's your real name, and I'm not going give you a list of my sources... However, I do know you're not retired Army. You were working Delta and had just finished an op with the CIA that went... well, a lot of people got killed, and you were sent home. I also know you just finished an FBI- op somewhere down in the South against some KKK people, and we're sent here to Alaska to infiltrate this group." Norm then gave Clay a hard look and then added, "Now, it's your turn, and please, don't try to jump me as I'd really hate to shoot you and possibly blow my own cover in the process. I've got something to share with you, a real butt-kicking plan neither of us knew about that Old Silas was keeping as a surprise. So, open up, or we can just shoot each other right here, and everyone loses, and very possibly thousands of people will die."

Clay briefly ran through his options, but the thing that kept him from disarming Norm and possibly breaking his neck was how the major had known about his most recent operations for the CIA and FBI and that Norm knew he was Delta.

"Okay," Clay said in a low whisper. "How you know about me better be explained real quick, or we do a Saturday night dance right here and now."

"When I left the corps, I was no longer a grunt, but I'd been working Intelligence. They offered a naval commission to Lt. Commander in the Navy Reserve and assigned me to the Seattle Navy Reserve Yard, but I continued to pose as a senior enlisted man working in Supply. They were after black marketers stealing equipment and weapons from the yard. Quite a while back, after making several busts, I was sent north to Anchorage and found myself assigned to the National Guard as a Senior

Master Sergeant, but my true rank had risen to a Full Commander...Not too bad for a former Gunny Sergeant....right?" He stopped, and both men briefly took a quick but thorough look around.

"The Navy, working in connection with both the Alaska Air and Army National Guard, was picking up stories of a possible splinter group beginning to form within the Alaska Defense Force up here in Fairbanks. Retired Colonel Wickersham was already under suspicion for possible involvement with this new faction, as he was the number two man in the ADF, and he also commanded the Fairbanks Post of the ADF.

"So, I was sent north, where I appeared on my false papers that I had retired from the Alaska Air Guard as a Chief Master Sergeant and a former Gunny Marine. My superiors felt my experiences, or at least what was listed on my records, might help Silas decide to take me on, and I sort of pushed things along with our friendship with me being his yes-man and feeding his over-inflated ego all the time. I'm surprised the man hasn't exploded with all the hot air in him, and I've had to keep my actual feelings well hidden. Basically, I was playing the dummy for him and Major Peterson. Because of my age and military experience, I eventually became one of Silas's majors, now third in command of the AFBM and the Fairbanks ADF.

"It's apparently worked out well enough because for some reason, he has just chosen me over Major Peterson... Tonight he revealed one of his dark secrets, and it scared me to death. I did some of my best acting, believe me...and that's why I've risked telling you who I am, so we both know about each other and can trust one another. Now, it's your turn, Clay."

"All right... you apparently know more about me than my own wife. But how? How did you learn about me? I'm working deep cover, and only my handlers know of who I am. You need to tell me who your source is."

"Okay...Okay. I first saw you at Basset Hospital. We didn't know each other then, and you had just finished your scheduled appointment with Doc Adams...a good man. But, Doc knew he wasn't feeling too great, and he thought it might be good for me to know about you, just in case I might be needed to pull your butt out of the fire. But, first, he needed to get the okay out of Washington, and that took a few weeks. Now we both see

Agent Leslie File...yeah, a bit of a straight-backed... Anyway, she's a former full-bird Army Colonel who worked intelligence for nearly 20-years with the Army Criminal Investigative Division.....CID. She's also really smart.

"Well, she briefed me on a few details, but not what your objective was. I was supposed to be made handy in the event your cover was blown and get you out safe before Silas, and his senior people could tie you to a chair and strap electrodes to your balls. A sure-fire way to get the truth out of anyone. The North Vietnamese and Russians used that technique with our Nam POWs. No one can take it too long without spilling the beans.

"So, I hadn't planned to reveal myself unless something came up that might force the issue. I only learned of what your two prior ops as a way of showing you who I am. But, I was given very few details, just items like the blown op with the CIA and the later op down South. I wasn't told who you were investigating in the SandBox because I didn't have a need to know. But I could use Doc Adams and Doctor File as evidence. Now it's your turn."

"Wow! I feel like I just learned who the other shooters were who killed President Kennedy...What about Santa Claus? Never mind, just needed a brief tension breaker. I almost took a chance at killing you a few minutes ago. But, as I've said, Emy doesn't know anything about me except what my official cover story is, and I'm really fed up with lying to someone I love so much and want to spend my life with. I'm afraid now I'll be responsible for sending her and her parents to prison, and she'll never forgive me."

"You might not have anything to worry about if Silas has his way... I have just learned tonight that he purchased a former Russian A-Bomb from the Russian Mob, who may have something going on with the Red Chinese. Both of those countries wouldn't have nightmares if Eielson went up in a big mushroom cloud. Now the bomb itself should've been delivered to the flight-line of Eielson Air Force Base earlier this evening. It's hidden inside a wheeled diesel-electric generator sitting on an unattached Air Force blue flatbed trailer, and it's probably now parked right up against the large hanger he wants to hold those hostages in."

"An atomic bomb...is he insane!?" Clay suddenly let go of his hot coffee cup, and it dropped right on his right foot and splattered the ground with its contents. He was shocked by such a plan and that Silas would be the one behind it. No one even suspected that a nuclear device had been snuck into Alaska. Though Clay had known that both the FBI and CIA had known of numerous nuclear devices having gone missing with the break-up of the Soviet Union. He had also learned that a lot of the missing devices had been removed from Soviet Missiles, but others were actual bombs taken from their nuclear storage supply. Clay had also heard of how such stories had been used for a handful of books and Hollywood movies, but this was the first word he had on such a device actually showing up here in Alaska. He just couldn't figure out what Silas hoped to gain from it, but then realized that with Silas's recent behavior, suicide might be considered a better action than going on trial before the country for treason if he could be taken prisoner.

"He hopes to use this as an escape option...right. To force the military into giving him a plane to leave Alaska if our plan of attack failed in getting the United Nations to promise this second election, as he has promised our people. I kept wondering how long he would want to hold these hostages as such an election could easily take a month or more to put together. I'm actually starting to realize just how many holes there are in his plans. Taking the hostages is one thing, but holding them and taking care of them for a whole month would prove nearly impossible, and that would give the authorities enough time to find and disarm that bomb.

"So, it's his plan to set the bomb off if things go south tomorrow, right?"

Clay knew the citizens of Alaska had been told there were no nuclear weapons in Alaska, and this would then prove to be yet another lie. But with the arrival of the newly assigned B-52s, Clay knew Eielson would soon see a nuclear depository on the base in order to keep these bombers armed in the event of war. He was sure that before too long, there would be protests outside the Main Gate, that some civilians would quit their jobs on the military installations. If those protests escalated, he knew it could also soon lead to the closure of Alaska's federal offices and courts.

Clay shook his head and then whispered, "He must have suspected from the beginning he might have to use this bomb..." He then hesitated and then also asked, "Does the device have a waiting period, a safety, just prior to its detonation... once the bomb is activated?" An additional wave of sweat was pouring off of him as he thought over the utter chaos that might occur when the AFBM troops learn of the bomb, knowing how many family members and friends that could perish in a nuclear blast.

"He told me the bomb had a five-minute period from arming to detonation, which isn't long enough to discover the bomb's exact location and get it deactivated. But knowing he was working with the Russians and possibly the Chinese, it might be even less. This bomb would be a good way to take out our northernmost fighter base, and now a new bomber base. Plus, now our militia force would then be blamed for everything. It just might give the Russians and their Chinese allies the opportunity they desire to invade during the winter months via the ice bridge up by the City of Wales." Both Norm and Clay knew that People used to walk across the ice pretty often just to say they did it. Going from Wales to Little Diomede Island, then crossing to Big Diomede Island, where they were usually arrested by Russian Border Guards.

"Silas is even crazier than I thought, but so was Napoleon and Hitler, and a handful of other lunatics," Clay said as he looked down at the ground and crushed the coffee cup with his right foot.

"So, Major, what is your plan?"

"One of us, most likely you, because you have the experience and training for it, has to sneak out of here and reach the federal and military authorities at Eielson and advise them of what Silas has planned. They have to locate that bomb, and I'll need to stay close in the event I need to shoot Silas in the head before he can activate that bomb. I say we let the attack come off as originally planned, except the base defenders will have to know what they are facing, including that damn bomb. We might lose some good people tomorrow, but we cannot let that bomb explode and possibly kill tens of thousands of innocent people, as well as losing Eielson."

"Oh, I can get out of here without much of a problem, but what about Silas and Emy...what are you going to tell them about where I am?"

"I'll have to come up with some plausible reason, especially for... no, it has to be good for both your wife and the colonel. I don't need Emy to be all suspicious-like. That might lead to Silas giving me a lot of heartaches. No, you'll have to be back before five a.m. if at all possible. Otherwise, Silas will suspect something and just might detonate the bomb right then. But, if I must shoot him to keep that bomb from being detonated, I wouldn't lose any sleep over it. I just didn't think he was this crazy. Oh, I saw the look in his eyes and could tell he was considering himself as Alaska's first president. But not this whole evil... Hitler-like dictator thing he's become. Had Hitler had such a device, I truly believe he would've used it on either Moscow or London and relished in it just before he ordered himself shot. He feared going on trial and being hung above all and took the coward's way out."

"Okay, enough about Adolf...I'm going to head out, pretend I'm checking on the guards and make my way onto Eielson. Hopefully, I can get to the Wing Commander before the base wakes up, and I can get back here before breakfast. But, do me a favor and try to keep my wife alive. She'll probably want to spit in my eye, but I guess with all the lies I've told her, she should be given the opportunity."

"I'll make sure she stays close to me, Clay... Now good luck and get moving!"

"Major, I'm glad you're on our side in this... May the Good Lord protect you tomorrow."

"Thanks, Clay, may the Lord watch over all of us. Now, remember, the bomb is hidden inside a mobile diesel generator... sitting on a flatbed trailer near the big hanger. I guess it's just a hollowed shell... but, it's got to be loaded aboard a big helicopter and possibly dropped in Harding Lake if they can't disarm it. It will still do a lot of damage, but the blast would be far enough away to save hundreds if not thousands of people... Good luck." Norm patted Clay on the shoulder, and then the two men quickly shook hands.

As Clay moved off towards the perimeter to check on the guards, Norm took a long extended route back to his tent. He still needed to do a bit of thinking before, hopefully catching a few hours of sleep. But Norm doubted if his mind would let him get any shut-eye. He felt as if his brain was about to explode, and right now, he wished he had a couple of beers tucked away in his pack to mellow him down a bit.

Clay still wasn't sure if he would need to disable the guards or just sneak by them. He had been well-trained in both skills, and he would make his decision once he got close to them and could see how alert they were. As to the two gate guards at the base, he knew he could get by them by simply staying in the thick woods to the west side of the gate shack. It would depend on where he spotted any patrols. If there were patrols, he would then have to decide on what he was going to tell the two SPs working the Eielson AFB Main Gate after crossing the Richardson Highway on foot.

# 14

# "GENERAL... I'M ABOUT TO RUIN YOUR DAY!"

*Main Gate*
*Eielson Air Force Base*
*11: 21 P.M. July 3rd*

C lay had very little problem in sneaking past the militia perimeter guards. In fact, he had contemplated giving the two-men a good tongue lashing after finding them sitting on their rear ends next to a couple of birch trees instead of staying on their feet and being mobile and vigilant. But, he knew his new assignment given to him by Major Norm Johnson far outweighed berating these two clowns. To bypass them, he only had to stay in the woods and occasionally low crawl through some thick brush to avoid being seen.

Now, the only problem he foresaw was exactly how he would approach the Main Gate and the two Air Force Security Policemen working there. Though the gate was open 24-hours a day, vehicles could not enter unless they displayed an Air Force or other military I.D. sticker, or a sticker from a federal agency on their front bumper, or the driver's side of the vehicle's windshield. Being that it was also after 2200 hours, or 10 p.m. in civilian time, he suspected the SPs were now asking to see the driver's military or federal I.D. cards. This inspection provided the SPs an opportunity to see if the driver might be coming home having shared in one too many alcoholic beverages or had possibly used illegal drugs. The SPs made a lot of DWI arrests at the Main Gate for subjects who had finished off far too much alcohol at one of the Fairbanks bars or having attended a private party at either the big city of Fairbanks or in North Pole. To the west of the base, there was a small hamlet known as Moose Creek, which also had one bar, known as Pete's Place, and often frequented by the military as they were well known for their weekend strip shows.

Clay had decided to unbuckle his canteen belt and was now carrying his canteen belt in his right hand. As he neared the gate after crossing the highway, he held this belt up in the air, not wanting to alarm one of the SPs. Especially after the SPs saw his military camouflage uniform shirt had the tag "ALASKA DEFENSE FORCE" sewed on, where normally it would be either U.S. ARMY" or "U.S. AIR FORCE." He wasn't all that sure how the SPs felt about militia members and just didn't want to take any chances with these two young men.

*This little meet and greet could make these two SPs nervous, and I hope to not get shot by an overzealous enlisted man. I'm also probably going to be put into handcuffs before they transport me to the SP Headquarters, but we're are running out of time, and that generator still has to be found and quickly. I just hope Emy will understand...I don't want to lose her over this, but the priority is finding that bomb. It's got to be!*

There was a single car at the gate waiting to make entry as one of the SPs checked out the driver's identification and gave the interior of the vehicle a once over. Meanwhile, the other SP was inside the gate but also observing the interaction. Clay also spotted a broken line of vehicles proceeding off the base, slowing down to the posted five miles per hour speed limit as they drove past the gate shack.

As he approached, there was still enough daylight out for him to see the gate shack across the highway as the sun had just reached the horizon. Clay knew the other SP inside the shack would have no trouble seeing him crossing the Richardson Highway, holding his canteen belt up high with his right hand to show he was peaceful. He wanted to make sure these young men knew he was not about to cause them any problems.

"Good Evening, Captain," The SP outside said, having seen the captain's bars on David's shirt and popped a quick salute, to which David returned. The SP had also taken notice of the pistol holster, with a weapon clearly visible. But then he saw the "Alaska Defense Force" tag over the shirt pocket; the SP began to wonder who this captain just might be, and why was he on foot?

"Gentlemen, I am a very peaceful man, and I'm holding my weapon up for you to see because I'm going to really need your help on an extremely important matter."

"Sir, are you with that militia force that's been training across the highway?" The Airman 1st Class SP asked. But Clay noticed how he kept his right hand close to the butt of his own Pistol. Clay also watched as the second man, a three striper, also known as a Senior Airman, stepped out to see what was going on.

"Yes, Airman, I'm with the Alaska Defense Force, but right now, an emergency has arisen, and I need to talk to one of your officers as soon as possible. It is extremely urgent, so would you please contact your Desk Sergeant and have an officer respond out here immediately? It is vital to National Security that I make contact with one of your superiors. If no one is available, at least provide me with transportation to your SP Headquarters… Or I can brief your on-duty Officer of Special Investigations (OSI), and you can hold on to my pistol to ensure you know I mean no threat to either of you."

The ranking airmen then stepped forward and took the canteen belt with the weapon from Clay's hand. "Why don't you step inside the gate shack and provide us with some I.D, Captain."

"I'll be glad to Airmen. Thank you for your courtesy." Clay walked into the gate and slowly removed his wallet from his right rear pocket. "All I have is my Alaska Driver's License and my Alaska Defense Force Militia officer's I.D. Card… Hope that will do….Oh, I forgot, I also have my U.S. Army I.D. showing I am retired on disability."

"Yes, Sir." Once the Senior Airman had all three I.D. cards and had given them a good once over, he then picked up the direct-line phone and made contact with his desk sergeant. Approximately four minutes later, an SP blue patrol car arrived at the gate, and Clay was then transported to SP Headquarters located in the Main Base area of Eielson. At the Desk Sergeant's order, his hands were handcuffed behind him for security.

Once the patrol car was headed for the main base with Clay in the back seat, the one ranking airman at the gate turned to the other and asked. "I wonder what the hell that was all about? He did say National Security... right?"

"You got me, Sam... and knowing how this military works, we'll probably never know. Nice enough guy, though, but he was sure acting a bit nervous-like."

"By his looks, he's one guy I wouldn't want to tangle with in a dark alley. Did you notice he wore an Army Combat Infantry Badge with a star on it to signify a second award? He's definitely seen some action. Oh, another car is coming in... back to work."

"Yeah, he really had something bothering him too. Wonder what's going on out there with those Militia boys... I think we'd better keep our eyes open in case there's any more of them out there wanting to visit. They'll have us relieved within the hour, and the next flight can then keep an eye on things. Now, I think I could use a beer before I hit the bunk... how about you."

"Naw, the wife is waiting for me. We have to talk about what we're going to be doing tomorrow morning with this Air Show thing. We have a lot to see before we show back up for work... There's going to be a lot of good food out there on the flight-line tomorrow. But by the time the Thunderbirds fly, we'll be inside going through guard mount and another inspection."

"Yeah, Rosy has a nice clean uniform for me to wear for tomorrow. Staff Sergeant Bradley ought to be real happy with me. Of course, I'd rather be walking the flight-line than humping this gate shack. Traffic is bound to be screwed up once the Thunderbirds finish their act, and we'll probably have forty to fifty-thousand cars trying to leave here all at once. One big giant traffic jam as the gate traffic tries to enter the highway, fighting it out with all those cars parked along the sides of the Richardson to watch the Thunderbirds."

"Well, it'll make the shift go by a lot faster."

SECURITY POLICE HEADQUARTERS

Ten minutes later, his belt and weapon now in the hands of the desk sergeant, Clay, was now waiting to see a second lieutenant. The swing-shift supervisor had called in the Officer, who was in charge of the SP Investigations Unit after Clay had somewhat demanded to see the on-duty OSI Officer. Clay didn't want to spend hours working his way up through the chain of command, but for the next hour, he was forced to sit through three interviews beginning with this 2nd Lieutenant, followed by the Operations captain who was also the SP Squadron's Executive Officer, and then a Lt. Colonel from Eielson's Base Command Center. Finally, when the clock was approaching 1 a.m., he was now being interrogated by the on-call agent for the Office of Special Investigations. Though the OSI rarely revealed their rank, Clay suspected this man was either a senior major or a new Light Colonel. Clay just felt this man had the bearing and style of a seasoned officer, but he had grown weary of having to repeat himself again.

"Okay, Captain, I am here... at your request. My name is Clark... Agent Clark of the OSI." He showed his OSI I.D. card to Clay. Though OSI Agents were allowed to wear civilian clothes, they were all active-duty military and either an NCO or an officer. By wearing civvies, military personnel and federal employees didn't know if they were speaking with an NCO or an officer, and agents had found that this helped them in dealing with military personnel.

"The other three officers seemed to believe you have vital information the OSI would find of great interest, though you refused to go into some of the details with them. I'm your last chance before you get shipped off to the Fairbanks Correctional Center as a guest of the Alaska State Troopers and charged with Trespassing on a Military Reservation. So, it's now on you to make me feel this has all been worth it, and be warned, I was awakened to come down here after only thirty-five minutes of sleep. It's been a very long day as we prepare for the Air Show."

"Believe me, Sir... you will soon understand why I'm here and how important this information is." Clay took in a deep breath and began. "I am

Captain Clay B. Jefferson, just as my driver's license, my Alaska Defense Force Militia I.D. and my U.S. Army I.D. states."

"Yes, we already have that confirmed by checking with the Army MPs at Fort Wainwright who provided a brief rundown on your military history... and that's the only reason I'm sitting here. Normally, I would've just waited until office hours to show-up here, but the urgency in your voice to see me has made us all... interested. So, keep going, and I'll make some notes." Agent Clark had a yellow legal-sized notepad in front of him on the tabletop and a black stick ink pen in his right hand.

"After we've been talking for a while, I would appreciate being provided with some water; my mouth is a bit dry."

"We'll see... now get talking, as I have a busy day scheduled and an Air Show to take my kids too."

"Agent, I doubt there will be any Air Show... not after you hear what I have to say," Clay said and then began speaking on who he really was. He provided Clark with his real background and the emergency phone number for Agent Leslie File and the emergency number for the Office of the FBI in Washington, D.C. When Clay was finished, and the agent's note pad had used up three whole pages, Agent Clark left the room and went to check on Clay's phone numbers, wanting to confirm these were, in fact, FBI telephone numbers that Clay had provided. Once Agent File was reached, and her identification was proven out, Agent Clark returned with a pitcher of ice water and two glasses and set them on the tabletop. He then stood by while Clay downed first one glass and then refilled it, to also finish that glass off. Almost immediately afterward, an SP Staff Sergeant entered the room with two ceramic cups of hot coffee, plus a handful of sugar and fake creamer packets.

Agent Leslie File had advised Clark she would be en route from Anchorage by special plane and that she would be landing at Eielson within the next hour or so. She also asked that the SP's meet her plane and transport her to SP Headquarters.

When Leslie and two other FBI agents arrived, which made it now just after three a.m., showing Clay that Leslie had made really good time in flying here, Clay suddenly stopped talking as he had not recognized the other two civilians with her. He had been briefing Clark on everything he'd been doing with the ADF and AFBM since he had arrived in Fairbanks. A moment later, the door opened again, and a one-star Brigadier General by the name of Joshua Hampstead walked in. He was wearing an Air Force's green flight-suit, which just happened to be the quickest thing he could get dressed in once he was awakened by Eielson's Command Post and briefed on the rising emergency.

Clay quickly jumped up and saluted the General, "Captain Jefferson... Sir!"

The General returned the salute and then brought his right hand up to shake Clay's hand. "Captain, normally, I'd say I am happy to meet you, but with what I've been briefed on so far, I'm not too sure that would be honest of me. Still, I feel you're a mighty brave man on a highly dangerous mission, and I thank you for getting this news to us." General Hampstead was then introduced to Agent Leslie File, but not the other two agents, who in Clay's opinion were clearly Leslie's security team from the way they kept an eye on everyone in the office.

"So, Captain, what else have you got for me other than your militia's attack with a force of some 123-troops... Oh, I already know about the automatic weapons and armored vehicles, but our SPs, assisted by the Army from Fort Wainwright, should be able to capture that force before it can leave your training area. I must admit, though, I was never in favor of having that training area so close to Eielson, and now I can show why it needs to be closed down. I've also been after the feds to get me a fence line built along the highway because, over the years, our SP's have stopped a lot of tourists who thought they could get a close-up of a F-22 taking off by walking closer to our runways. Some of my pilots have been highly judgmental of their commanders for not having our SPs shoot these people for trespassing. True, we've had a couple close calls over the years when our alert birds rush to take off.

"Oh, the sensors are great, but they just can't do the job when you're talking about nosey tourists. Now, what else can you tell me before I put a plan together to raid your encampment?"

Up until that very moment, when he had all three key people in the office with him, Clark, File, and now the General, Clay had withheld the vital information concerning the Russian A-Bomb. Now he decided was the time for him to drop the other foot, and he was glad to get it off his chest.

"General, I'm about to ruin your whole day... Sir." Clay then asked Leslie to ask her agents to stand outside. He didn't know them and would rather just speak to the three of them without any extras standing about. Leslie nodded her head and then told the two men to stand outside the closed door and make sure no one else tried to enter until General Hampstead or herself authorized it. Clay then began to provide these three people with the information concerning the Russian A-Bomb, how it was mounted and where it was supposed to be parked. He also provided everything he knew about how it was to be detonated.

"General, if you were to attack our camp right now, I am almost positive Colonel Silas Wickersham, in his present state of mind, would most likely detonate that weapon. He would rather commit suicide than face a lengthy sentence and the embracement of a federal trial for being a terrorist."

All three of the listeners remained silent, their mouths slightly hung open as their brains took in all that they were hearing and realizing the mess that Clay had just brought them. It was now 0346 hours. Clay knew he now had less than two hours to make it back to the camp, to pretend to wake up beside Emy and contemplate his next action to prevent that bomb from going off.

"Are you positive about this bomb being on base, Captain Jefferson? Everything... everything you have just told me about and now this identity of your Major Johnson? Well, I have to tell you this thing sounds like some apocalyptic science fiction novel," General Hampstead said in a voice filled with hesitation.

Agent File then spoke up, "General, I can confirm that Major Johnson is one of my people. He's been working undercover up here for nearly five years and is also a former Marine Gunny Sergeant with a lot of combat experience from Vietnam. He is also highly decorated with a Silver Star, a Bronze Star, and two Purple Hearts. Much as Captain Jefferson is also," Ms. File said to the men in the room.

She then continued, "If Norm says that Wickersham has gained possession of a Russian A-Bomb, I have to believe him. We all know that more than two-dozen nukes went missing from the Russian inventory, along with several Hydrogen Bombs we've never been able to locate and have lived in constant fear of them showing up one day in the hands of terrorists. We just didn't think our terrorist would turn out to be a retired U.S. Army Colonel with dreams of grandeur."

"My God!" General Hampstead replied.

Agent Clark looked down at his notes and realized these pages would eventually have to end up in the OSI burn bag. He doubted his supervisor would allow an actual file to be put together at his end; it would most likely become highly classified and go into the OSI's secret files in Washington, D.C. This also made him wonder if Colonel Wickersham, if captured alive, would be allowed to stand trial, or would he end up in one of those unmentionable highly top-secret jail cells for the rest of his life, along with any of the members of the AFBM taken into custody.

They also shared the same thought of what might happen if the news people ever learned of this information and all the crap that would be bound to follow.

"What about your wife...Emy, Clay. What do you think she'll do when she learns about the bomb...or do you plan to tell her?" Agent File asked.

"Right now, my whole direction was to get this information to you. As to Emy, I'll have to see how things are going down and make my decision then. Our priority has to be that we prevent Silas from blowing up the Interior of Alaska. Norm may or may not be given one of the two phones, but Silas will definitely have the other."

"Quite right, Captain. Once the notifications are made, we then need to get a search started right away to locate this generator trailer. We still have time, if we can find it quickly, for our experts to disarm it before this Colonel Wickersham launches his attack at 1300 hours... today.

"That means we have approximately nine-hours, and we only have one such large hanger that would be capable of even holding 500-hostages. That will make it a lot easier. But, we cannot limit it to just the flight-line... he could have also left it somewhere else... just about anywhere on the base and even in the housing area. Such a bomb would still destroy the flight-line... well, practically anywhere within ten to twelve miles. But depending on the size of the device, radiation could still spread out another ten-miles or more with a good breeze....maybe even further. North Pole and Salcha could also be in danger, so the Alaska State Troopers will also have to be notified, but I will leave that with Mr. Clark and Agent File to handle. My first priority is this base.

"We also can't let this rogue colonel suspect what we now know, nor can we launch our attack on the militia training field as I had just originally planned until we have assuredly disarmed that bomb. Even if you kill this Wickersham fellow, he still might have another back-up plan to detonate that weapon," General Hampstead said as he then slammed his fist upon the tabletop and exclaimed in a raised voice, "Damn!"

"What about you, Clay?" Ms. File asked. "If called upon, can you kill this Colonel before he awakens?" She had almost added Emy to that question but held that thought in place for the moment.

"Yes, but as I said, Norm told me the Colonel misspoke once and happened to mention there were those two phones. One for Silas and one for somebody else, and it might not be Norm who gets that second phone. It just might be someone no one would suspect. For the moment, I believe Norm was told about the phone in the event the Colonel was shot and couldn't push the digits to activate the phone detonation sequence. This might be why he provided Norm with the numbers, but someone else could also have those same numbers with that second phone. If I killed Silas... Well, the other man would most likely detonate the device, and he's probably someone like the camp cook or possibly an armorer, but someone extremely loyal to the Colonel that we'd probably not suspect."

"Could it be your wife?" Leslie asked, with a note of hesitation to her voice.

"No, I don't believe so. The one thing I know about my new wife is that she is a strong Christian lady... There's no way she would go along with such senseless butchery. She still hopes our surprise invasion can come off without anyone being seriously hurt... Emy believes that with so many civilians on the flight line, the Air Force wouldn't turn the base into a combat zone."

"Admirable, but she is still in effect a terrorist by any definition, Captain," General Hampstead said. "Your view of a strong Christian woman is a tad different than mine, but that's for another time."

"Yes, Sir, but I'd also remind you General that back in our colonial days, our patriot forefathers would have also been considered terrorists by the British... And not that I support this plan in any way, I am also deeply concerned with my new marriage surviving this mission of mine." Clay then pushed his chair back and slowly rose to his feet. He had been sitting for far too long and needed to stretch his legs.

"General, I'll have to be returning to the training field to keep Silas from suspecting anything and letting Norm know I've delivered the news to you all. He's prepared to shoot Silas in the head as soon as he sees a cell phone in the man's hands, and I'm his back-up. But as I've already expressed, I have a deep concern over that second phone and who might have it."

"Clay, what about your wife? What do you plan to do with her in the event there is an attack forthcoming on your unit?" Leslie asked.

Clay wasn't sure how to answer that question, but then he said, "Truthfully, I'm just not too sure how I'll handle her if she goes against me. She's loyal to the Colonel, but she is also my wife, and I know she knows nothing about the bomb. Still, she was prepared to commit treason in hopes of gaining Alaska its independence. If I have to... if I'm forced to, I'll probably have to gag her and hog tie Emy, plus sit on her to keep her from issuing any warnings to the others. She'll probably see me as a traitor, but I knew that could happen when I married her. Now, I can only hope she will one day forgive me... but for right now, I have to say she is not the first priority.... Finding that damn bomb is!"

"Captain, I will not accuse you of being a stupid man for marrying this woman, for I've learned that love can cause any one of us to do such idiotic things. But, I do hope it works out for you when all this is over... and good luck." General Hampstead walked up and shook hands with Clay, and so did Clark.

General Hampstead then looked into Clay's eyes and added, "You're an extremely brave man, Clay... I'm glad you were the one chosen for this extremely hazardous assignment." He then walked over to the door, opened it, and sent a runner to summon the SP Squadron Executive Officer, who was waiting back at the SP front desk.

When the Executive Officer arrived, the General took him to the side and in a whisper of a voice, "Listen carefully, Major… and this bit of information will remain highly classified… There is an Air Force flatbed trailer sitting somewhere on this base, most likely on the flight-line, and hopefully, this trailer is close by our largest hanger. There should also be a mobile generator trailer on this flatbed. If found, no one is to touch it! I repeat…. no one is to lay a hand on it! And advise your search parties not to use their radios anywhere near this device…EOD personnel will also be en route once the trailer is located.

"Now, if you do not find the trailer at the big hanger, then begin searching the entire flight-line and as quickly as possible. Use whatever manpower you may need.. and if you do not locate this trailer on the flight-line, initiate a search of the entire base proper to include the housing areas and schools. I shouldn't have to tell you, but if this device is detonated, then Eielson will become one very large and radioactive hole in the ground." Hampstead stopped briefly as he got his thoughts together and then continued.

" When you leave here, notify your commander that I want him to initiate a recall all of your squadron personnel, to also include your SP augmentees, with orders to report to your headquarters within 30-minutes. Less, if at all possible, but I know it is extremely early, and people will have to be awakened.

"Major, what we have here is basically a Defcon Three situation. So, I want at least two hundred men and women out there on foot and on patrol searching for this trailer. The FBI will handle, working with the local police, and State Troopers will handle everything off base. Now, do you understand your orders, Major?"

The Major looked at bit rattled by all this, but he understood the General's orders and replied, "Yes, General!"

"Then get moving, Major…we have so little time." General Hampstead released the Major and then turned back to Clay and added, "Too bad this Wickersham looney waited this long before he briefed your Norm fellow. A day earlier would have sure helped…But we'll work with what we have." Hampstead then ordered Agent Clark to get cracking from his end and then watched as Clark and Clay left the room.

Hampstead then walked over to the table, picked up the phone, and began dialing, so he could talk to the Eielson Command Center. The ECC was located up the third floor of Amber Hall, which also held Eielson's Wing and Base Headquarters.

"This is General Hampstead. Do you recognize my voice? Okay... today's codeword is Benjamin Franklyn... numbers seven-four-one-two... one-two... Okay? Are we clear now? Right... Now the first order of business... I want you to notify Colonel Ricker at Wing Headquarters...Yes, he's standing by. Advise him, I want him to immediately activate a full recall of all of his pilots and crewmembers. They are to be suited up for flying, with all their fighters fully armed and ready to go before 0500 hours this day. That's precisely sixty minutes from this contact time. I'll also want those newly assigned bomber crews and all tanker crews to be at their planes, ready for an immediate take-off upon command. You are writing all this down, right, Captain?"

"Yes, General... everything gets written down, Sir," the Captain replied.

"Okay... Now once the aircrews have been alerted, I want all on-base personnel to be recalled and for them to report to their squadrons, but no one off base is to be notified at this point. Make that very clear when you make your notifications. I also want my command staff recalled immediately to the briefing center... all of them! Got it? I want to brief them all at the same time. Also, you can tell them all of how upset I am. It might stir them into action quicker. The Base Commander can then handle his own briefing of his own senior staff members. But, let me repeat myself, so you completely understand what I'm saying here. I am putting this installation on a Defcon Three status, but the Main Gate will continue normal operations at this time. But I'll have someone's ass if I don't have all those crews with their planes by 0600 hours. This is not an exercise and certainly not a game... I want all of them on the flight-line preparing their planes to fly, but no one launches until I... I repeat, I give that order.

"You can also tell the Base Commander that I'll be at his office within ten-minutes to give him a complete briefing on why this is all happening. Also, I want all flight-line gates closed immediately...only on-duty personnel, including recall personnel, are to be on the flight-line until our SPs arrive in force. That means no civilians coming to set up a display for the Open House... any early arriving vendors will have to park on Flight-Line

Road, but all of them are to remain outside the flight-line gates, and that's to include all Army personnel from Fort Wainwright who might have arrived early to set up their static displays... They'll be arriving soon and expecting to get set-up for the Open House. But, for the moment, they are to remain with the vendors or tell them to visit the chow hall for some early breakfast... Also, call the chow halls and warn them of some early guests... A lot of them.

"Next item, I want all...all of the alert birds on full alert, pilots in their planes...right now! Yes, you heard me... All six of them to be readied for immediate launch. Next item, you're to get ahold of the Thunderbird's Team representative at Officer's Quarters... He's a Light Colonel, but I cannot recall his name... It should be in your contact listings. As of this moment, their show here at Eielson has been...postponed. They are to keep their F-16s at Elmendorf until they're directed elsewhere. Maybe they can entertain the Elmendorf crowd today or just return to the Lower 48 tomorrow... Not my problem right now... I also don't have time to answer his questions, but you can tell him he'll be briefed later this morning and to report to Wing Headquarters as soon as he passed on my orders to Elmendorf.

"Oh, I also want all squadron commanders, even the ones here on temporary duty, to be at my office by 0700 hours...Oh Hell, make sure they all initiate their squadron recalls as quietly as possible...with on-base personnel to show up for work within 30-minutes of being recalled. Then work with wing headquarters to schedule our reserve tanker crews... same recall, but they're to report to their squadron headquarters. But they should also be ready to fly... no shorts and Hawaiian shirts. They're to be in their flight-suits and with their flight bags ready. Their Squadron or flight Commanding Officers are to report to me within the hour at SP Headquarters and no excuses. All leaves are hereby canceled. Anyone who fails to show can expect to be facing charges, and you can advise them of that, too.

"Next item... am I going too fast for you, Captain?"

"No, General... and everything is automatically recorded... General."

"Good... Then notify Base Operations and the tower; this base is now closed to all air traffic... until further notice, but to also be prepared for an emergency order for all aircraft to be launched. As I said, we are now at Defcon Three… You understand that, Captain? Defcon Three. Anyone due to land here is of now to be diverted to Elmendorf Air Force Base or if they're low on fuel to land at Fairbanks International Airport or even Fort Wainwright. They will then stand-by their planes to await further orders. Also, no alert siren, everything is to be by radio, phone or by word of mouth…Oh, I also want all flight-line radio traffic to be ceased immediately, use only landlines and that's for all squadrons. You got that, Captain?"

"Yes, Sir!"

"Good! Now, without lights and sirens, or anyone acting stupidly, begin moving Eielson into Defcon 3 mode. As per emergency instructions, assigned personnel will be briefing the Fairbanks North Star Borough Mayor, North Pole Mayor, and Fairbanks City Mayor, as well as the Alaska State Troopers, as to what is going on here. You'll be briefed further when I arrive, so do not let your curiosity interfere with your carrying out their commands, but no, we are not at war. The rest will follow soon, Captain, I promise you.

"Now, before I hang up, my last order is for you to notify the Alaskan Air Command at Elmendorf and advise them that this is a possible Broken Arrow… Yes, a Broken Arrow and that I have moved us into Defense Condition Three. I'll be on the phone to them within thirty to forty minutes to give General Wiseman a full briefing, and I'll be with you real soon, so you'd better get the coffee on…Lots of real hot coffee and order up some Danish and breakfast sandwiches from the chow hall for the staff. I doubt if anyone in headquarters is going to have time to hit the chow hall any time soon." General Hampstead then hung-up the phone and then addressed Agent File.

"As per our operational plans in the effect of a Broken Arrow, which for you civilians means a nuclear incident is involved, I plan to close off the Richardson Highway at the western exit to the City of North Pole and then farther south at Mile 47, to prevent motorists from coming toward Eielson from either direction. I'll have some of the SPs on hand to assist the Alaska State Troopers at these roadblocks. There isn't time to call up the Alaska National Guard, and with this ADF involvement, it could prove too chancy as someone might get word by cell phone to one of those militia members out across the highway. That will then leave us with a couple thousand people to evacuate from their homes in Moose Creek and the Salcha area in the event the bomb is found, and we're unable to disarm it in time. But, as you know, I cannot risk the evacuation from occurring until we can confirm the presence of the bomb. It's an extremely touchy situation here as any sign of an evacuation might cause this Wickersham fellow to detonate the device. I only hope I am right in this; I do not want to be responsible for hundreds if not thousands of deaths, including my own and that of my family... God, I really hate car salesmen! Seems like some weird poetic justice that our mad bomber ends up being a car salesman!"

"General, what about all the dependents in base housing?" The General's aide, a young major asked. He had been outside the door, waiting for the General as the old man was inside talking with this Jefferson fellow. Learning what little he did, the young officer was now extremely concerned for his own wife and kid's safety, as they were home in bed, and he now wanted them on the highway to Fairbanks or even Anchorage. He wasn't all that sure twenty two-miles was far enough away to be safe.

"I thought about that, Major...but if this Colonel sees people fleeing the base in mass and no one on the flight-line for the show, he might just detonate the bomb out of fear his surprise has been found out. No, we'll have a Plan A and a Plan B... possibly a Plan C and D before we're done.

"As for Plan A, this will be for if we locate the bomb and have it disarmed, we will then attack the Militia's encampment with all the force we can muster to render them harmless. Or we don't find the bomb, and Plan B is implemented as we let the militia launch their attack, with our people ready for them, and Major Johnson or Captain Jefferson can take out this Colonel Wickersham before he can use the phone to detonate it. But there is still that other unknown man or woman, as Captain Jefferson explained. Somehow we have to learn his or her identity and silence them also or take them prisoner, if possible. But their life is not a priority; too many others are at risk here...And yes, if you're wondering, Plan A and Plan B can easily run into one another if we only find the bomb at the last moment. We'll just have to see what plays out."

The General knew that both this Norm fellow and Clay would be on hand and ready to put this man down. But, if possible, he would make sure his SP snipers will have photos of this Wickersham person if need be from his DMV records or his old Army records. He knew that OSI Agent Clark was already working on that issue. The General hoped that if this Norm or Clay failed, he could only pray one of the snipers will have the chance to make the kill shot.

"Not quite what we had planned for, is it, General?" Agent File asked as she approached the General.

"Ma'am, since wearing this uniform or one like it, I have yet to see everything go off as it was intended. But, we'll get it done, Agent File. The good guys almost always do."

Leslie had wished Clay good luck before he had headed out the door. Now she had her own work to do and emergency notifications to make. But then she remembered something and addressed the General, who was now walking in front of her as they headed down the long hallway. "General, what about notifying the Governor? I believe he landed in Fairbanks last night as he is one of the scheduled VIPs for the air show."

"Right, I forgot he was in the area, and if he wasn't, he'd have to be notified for the road closures we're making and the pending battle we may have to fight across the Richardson Highway. I'll get ahold of him before I give the mayors a call. But First, I need to brief Colonel Ricker, the SP Commander, as he probably thinks we just went to war against the Chinese or the Russians."

"Maybe we did," Leslie said just before she walked away. Then she stopped suddenly when the General addressed her. "Would you do me a favor? Have the FBI office in D.C. fax up Clay's photo...and that of Norm. I want all our people to know these two men are on our side and that they're not to be hurt. I'd really hate it if Norm or Clay were shot just seconds before we could take this Silas character down."

"Right away, General," Agent File replied, and then she darted off. She had a lot to do in very little time. She tried in vain to put out of her mind the picture she saw of a mushroom cloud suddenly rising up above Eielson Air Force Base, and it terrified her.

## 15

# "YOU'RE WHO? YOU'RE WHAT!?"

*Eielson Air Force Base*

The Main Gate to Eielson was under an early dawn morning, and it was just 3:14 a.m. when Clay was tactfully dropped off in the woods on the base side of the Richardson Highway. His pistol and canteen belt had been returned to him, and he was glad to see the gate traffic was still being allowed through; otherwise, it might have *sent* a bad signal on to Silas's people that something was wrong. Clay had also seen that the vendors and many of their vehicles, as well as Army personnel who were now starting to arrive in low numbers, were now being directed east via the Main Base Road. One of the SP's giving him a ride had informed Clay that all of the vendors and Army personnel were now being diverted to the high school parking lot. For those visitors who were expected to begin arriving all too soon, those people who had somehow gotten past the highway roadblocks would also be diverted to the base's elementary, middle school, and high school parking areas.

General Hempstead's other big concern was, in the event the bomb could not be located, and he ordered a mass exodus of all aircraft, could said action cause this man to detonate his device? Hampstead also had another concern for saving the aircraft, knowing that a nuclear detonation could trigger off a nuclear exchange between rival superpowers. But for the moment, he would not order the massive airlift unless the bomb could not be located, and then, he would have no choice but to launch all the ready aircraft and using both active runways. He also knew such an airlift would literally fill the skies with combat birds, and accidents happened. He just prayed that such catastrophic actions would not happen on his watch and headed for Wing Headquarters.

Clay wasn't made aware of it, but a regiment of Army Infantry and their two and a half-ton trucks and armed *Humvees* had now been activated and would soon be routed through the old dirt road that connected Eielson to Fort Wainwright on the backside of the military reservation. This would allow for the Army troops to arrive on Eielson without being seen by the Open House guests, nor the AFBM personnel still positioned in the ADF Training Field.

For the moment, these troops, nearly six-hundred-men, and women, all heavily armed, would be kept out of view from the highway while being placed inside and around the Ben Eielson High School buildings, including the school gym. Their vehicles would be parked north of the base housing area. Most of the troops thought it might be part of the Open House, a large scale drill to impress the citizens. For their senior commanders had decided not to brief them of the true story until after 1200 hours.

Still, the troops were all extremely curious about this movement, for at the Fort Wainwright armory, they had all been issued duty loads of live ammo, which also included ammo for their heavier automatic weapons. They had also been issued various types of grenades, and this really had confused them, along with the issuance of their B-40 bazooka-like weapons, which could shoot single projectiles of either explosive anti-tank rounds or anti-personnel rounds.

One enlisted man turned to his buddy in the back of one of the Army trucks and asked, "Did someone start a war or something?"

More than half of these troops were Afghanistan War veterans, and now that they found themselves on Eielson, many of them now wondering if the Air Force was expecting some sort of act of terrorism at Eielson's Open House. But as is the norm, the soldiers were not being told anything as of yet. When one of the young privates had asked his platoon sergeant for information, the NCO quietly and quickly advised him, "Just shut-up, quit asking questions, and check your gear again. When the Colonel is ready to share his plans with you, he'll let you know what you need to know. Until then, quit worrying. Got it?" The private wasn't at all satisfied with the answer, but he had been in this man's army long enough to know when to keep his mouth shut and not to bug his sergeant with any more questions.

After boarding the trucks and the convoy hitting the road, it had taken the mile-long convoy almost 40-minutes to make the 12-mile bumpy ride to Eielson via that back road. A lot of the troops had walked or driven over this road, but this was the first time with an issue of live ammo and grenades. For those veterans who suffered some degree of PTSD from their prior service in the sandbox, they began feeling the jitters that came with growing excitement. Most of the veterans had come to believe in the old line made so famous in the Army, "Hurry up and Wait!" So, they smoked their cigarettes, shot the bull, and gave their equipment another once over. Meanwhile, the new troops just stared at one another; their expressions showed all the many questions they wanted to ask but knew better than to do that right now.

Clay was able to sneak back through the lines without any problems, mainly because the two-man militia perimeter patrol to the west was now napping, right where he had spotted them earlier. He had to wonder what had happened to the non-commissioned officer supposedly in charge of these guards and soon learned that this man was also asleep inside one of the Kenworth-Tractors. Clay knew the NCO was an Afghanistan veteran, but he apparently hadn't learned anything from his duty over there, as a lot of veterans actually never served on an advance base or saw any combat. The urge to pull the young NCO up short for his dereliction was nearly overwhelming, but he let it slide as he continued to sneak towards his tent. He hoped to find Emy sound asleep, and he did, which allowed him to catch almost an hour of sleep before Major Norm Johnson appeared at his tent flap and woke him up.

"Let's get some coffee, Captain... I'd like to discuss a few things with you about today's planned events."

"Sure thing, Major," Clay replied and rolled his half-awake wife off his right shoulder.

"Bring me back some coffee too, honey... and a fried egg sandwich, please," Emy said with her eyes closed as she snuggled into her sleeping bag for another minute or two of sleep.

"What happened, Clay?" Norm asked as he caught up with him. His voice was showing how nervous he was feeling right then.

"Agent Leslie File says hi; she flew up immediately from Anchorage and arrived while I was in custody." Clay then advised Norm on what had transpired during his many interviews and wrapping things up with his discussion with General Hampstead. He could see in Norm's eyes his extreme concern over this whole operation and knew Norm was also probably wondering if he might survive it?

Norm then whispered, "I'm just surprised she's here so quickly... I just wasn't sure she had even planned to be here for today's big event."

"Well... she's here now and greased the way for my talks with General Hampstead... the Wing Commander. Never did see the Base Commander, but the General outranks him. I hated how long it took me to brief each of these officers before finally appearing before an OSI Agent by the name of Clark. Only then did I mention Leslie and my participation in this outrageous scheme to make our dear Silas President of Alaska."

Norm released a deep sigh and then said in a low voice, "Who else did you meet with?" They had paper cups of hot coffee in their hands and were slowly walking outside the tent area, talking in low whispers. Clay glanced over and spotted one of the tracked APC units, and though he knew the SPs had armored Humvees capable of carrying both .50 caliber and M-60 machine-guns, he wasn't all that sure they would be capable of stopping one of these old armored units, especially one that had been re-enforced with extra steel plating. So far, he had not seen any evidence of a 20mm or a 25mm cannon being mounted on any of the Air Force vehicles.

Of course, he knew the F-22's were reportedly armed with 25mm cannons, and some of the older F-16s were armed with 20mm Gatling Guns, and if need be, they could be used to destroy the AFBM vehicles if there was time to do so.

"The Wing Commander, General Hampstead... he's a really nice gentleman who took control right off, and he listened to every word I had to say. I informed him of who I actually was and everything I knew, and then Leslie showed up... She flew up pretty quickly from Anchorage in a Leer Jet when she heard I was in custody and needed her ASAP. She was able to back me up, and she explained how you were also an FBI undercover operative, like myself and retired military.

"Her information added a lot of juice to what I was warning them about. Then once General Hampstead had all the information, he started moving heaven and earth to prepare Eielson for a pending invasion. They also began their search for the bomb...Oh, Eielson has a pretty good team of Explosive Ordnance Disposal troops assigned there, and two of them are well-qualified in disarming a nuke. I expect they have already located the bomb by now and working to disarm it or get it the hell off Eielson if they can't. The fact that the bomb was encased in cement might be a serious problem for being able to disarm it.

Clay took in a deep breath and then continued, "They talked of carrying it off and dropping the whole generator into the deepest part of Harding Lake while evacuating the area at the same time. But, I suspect a lot of people are still liable to lose their lives if the bomb isn't disarmed, and we'd still have to deal with radiation contamination... Yet, Eielson, as an effective military base might actually survive if they can get it moved far enough away."

"But what about our attack?" Norm asked. He was feeling flustered, praying for tomorrow, so all of this would be over. "I mean, what am I supposed to do? Just let the attack go on, or do we terminate the Colonel and take our chances in locating that second phone?"

"From what they told me before I left, that if the bomb is disarmed, they'll allow the traffic to enter Eielson, but then divert all the cars back to behind the main housing area. They hope to use all the flight line buildings to conceal the vehicle traffic being re-routed to the other side of the base.

Once there, they'll be guarded by Army troops from Fort Wainwright. I imagine they're coming in on the backroad that still runs between the Wainwright and Eielson. It's all military reservation back there, mostly used for military exercises and hunting."

Norm glanced about and then said, "Which all means we'll all be walking right into a trap?"

"Well, they've canceled the air show, and the military on base is on alert. The Flight line will look busy enough, but once the militia starts coming across that first runway, Silas will soon realize he's been duped. He will either try to detonate the bomb, realizing his whole plan for the future has gone up in smoke, or he just might bring the unit to a halt and order everyone to surrender. But… well, look, Norm, there's so many things that can happen here… and all of a sudden. As long as Silas thinks he has that bomb, he just might think he can still use it as a threat and actually believe he might be able to escape, to hopefully flee into Canada through the deep woods above Tok. There's just no telling what he might be thinking when this all suddenly falls apart. He could just lose it and allow the militia to continue their attack, killing and wounding a lot of troops on both sides in the process.

"Well, as to escaping, we both know the US and Canadian border is just too long for the Canadians to patrol it, or for our side for that matter," Norm added.

"But listen Norm, both Leslie and this OSI Agent Clark don't believe the people were behind the purchase of that device originally and sold Silas this bomb, will give him the five minutes time they promised. If our guys locate the generator and find the bomb but are unable to disarm it, they truly believe the bomb will explode very shortly after Silas makes his call. Either still on the base or even at the bottom of the lake… But, will the signal even reach the device if it's dropped into a deep lake?"

"Hell if I know, but those signals reach up into outer space. So, it must be able to go cut through the water. They communicate with submarines… right? But I'm no tech junkie. So, this means you or I still have to kill him before he can activate it. But you're right. Neither the Russians nor the Chinese will have anything to lose because our unit will take the whole blame for this incident, and if the bomb blows, Central and

Northern Alaska will lose their primary defense of the northern and western Alaska shorelines. The Arctic will be open to them... for a short while, at least.

"Maybe they're planning on an invasion if this device goes off... just too many factors into this whole thing. It's all giving me a headache... I just wish now I would've been given the kill order on Silas long before this. They already knew he was a traitor... We had enough on him to curtail his operation a few weeks ago, especially with what you were picking up on. But because he's a big giver to different politician's campaigns, someone must've decided to hold off on bringing him in. It's come down to Politics...and I really hate that side of our society!"

Norm shook his head and had his hands on his hips as he considered his last statement and then added, "Apparently, there is a lot of secret messages going on between China, Russia, and this ASEAN group, that's an acronym for some ten South East Asian countries. Several of our intelligence services are concerned about this."

"Look, Norm, that's all great, but has no real bearing on what's going to happen today...here and now. Right?"

Norm glared back at Clay and then realized he was right. "Yeah, you're right. So, what do you want to do... right now... if we hope to survive this day?" Norm then took a sip of his coffee, made a face, and spit it out on the ground. "I've always hated GI coffee... We can walk on the moon, spend a fortune on our weapons and computers, but will the military ever find a way to make a decent cup of coffee?"

Clay shook his head in response to Norm's sudden complaint about his coffee. "We're about to be nuked, the world could be coming to an end, and you're standing here concerned about your coffee? Well, my friend, sometime this late afternoon or early evening, we'll either be glowing in the dark, standing in Heaven awaiting judgment or just maybe we will have defeated Silas's grand scheme without casualties. Then we can all go home in the satisfaction we've done our job at keeping the world safe for yet another day."

He then added, "It's too bad though, Silas and his people actually did show how that Washington D.C. bunch did pull off an illegal election back in 1959... which makes me wonder if we'll ever have a second one. I'm beginning to believe I'd vote for us to become a territory again... No federal income taxes... or maybe our own country. But being raised by my native family, I have grown weary of how our people have been mistreated for so long. It wasn't bad for me; I had the military and the schooling. Being an officer and only half-Athabaskan put me in a different category... Okay, back to reality... what now, Major?"

"Clay, it's still Norm when we're alone or off duty. But as to our next actions, we play it like were about to invade, and when one of us can take a kill shot as we come across the highway, I say we do it. We have to... besides, Silas is unstable, and I'd rather see the man dead than spending the rest of his life in a padded cell... or worse, executed following a lengthy trial that would embarrass so many other people. I owe him that much... and it's what I would prefer had it been me." Norm then shut up as Major Peterson walked up, carrying a paper plate of eggs and bacon in front of him in one hand and a cup of hot coffee in the other.

"Good morning, Gentlemen. Did you both have a restful sleep? You're sure going to need it before this day is done."

Clay presented his best morning smile, "With Emy beside me, I had a great night's sleep... Not sure about the Major, here."

Norm grinned and then took another sip of his coffee, then promptly spit it out again, "Don't know why I drink this crap! But yes, I miss my teddy bear and my pillows when I'm out on these overnighters." For a brief moment, Norman was somewhat concerned that Peterson might have heard something as he approached, but the man showed no evidence of that, and Norm relaxed a bit.

Tossing a blink Clay's way, he knew Peterson couldn't see, he asked his fellow major, "So, Allen, when this has all played out, and we win the right to another election... are you thinking about running for office if and when a new government is formed?"

"Not a chance, Norm. I plan to open a fishing lodge out near Denali. When the park is no longer a national park, I hope to buy up some land and spend my reclining years out there on one of those big lakes. Someone else can run our new government. What about you?"

"Oh, I'm going to live right here in Fairbanks and watch the world go around." Norm was about to ask Clay what his plans were when he saw Emy walking up, and she wasn't wearing her usual smile.

"Hey, Husband-dear, where's that coffee you promised me? And my sandwich? Did you see the line over there? I'll have to wait for a good twenty minutes now," Emy said as she came to greet her husband to let him know he wasn't off the hook.

"Sorry, Honey... I mean Sergeant Jefferson... I'll get you a cup right now... and your fried egg sandwich, too." Clay walked back to the kitchen and stood in line to get a plate load of eggs, sausages, and bacon for his lovely wife, and then a couple pieces of freshly made bread brought in last night from the North Pole Safeway Store's bakery. He was also carrying a cup of boiling hot coffee, which caused him to reinforce the cup with a second empty cup to keep his hand from being burned. *It may not be good coffee, but it's hot and a real eye-opener!*

When he returned to their tent, Emy was returning from washing up and had a white towel wrapped over her shoulders. "Looks like you need to shave, Captain. Can't have you looking so slovenly today, my darling. You'd look terrible for any photos taken of us by all the base visitors and news people. I'm so excited...or I should say nervous about today's action. I don't think I can eat this. Here, you eat it." Emy handed him back the plate load of vittles and began sipping the black fire the cooks had referred to as camp coffee. "Can't figure out why they make this stuff lava hot... could burn a lip off if one's not too careful."

"I learned early on it's how the cooks get back at us for making them pull KP Duty. I often wondered how many cooks were put before a firing squad for their poisoning or burning their commander's meals in past wars?"

Emy shook her head in response to his statement and then stood up on her tiptoes to kiss her husband lightly on the mouth, and then they both smiled at one another.

"Oh, I have news for you, Dear Wife... Today you are to stick at my side, to operate like a runner between Major Johnson and me. I was just briefed on that change, so you won't be inside that hot rod Rubber Ducky you hoped to be driving this afternoon. Sorry about it, Honey, but Major Johnson needed someone he could trust to ensure he gets the Colonel's orders down to us promptly and for my actions to get back to the major and the colonel toot-sweet. Are you okay with that, being a lowly runner?"

"Well, I'm a bit let down, dear husband, as I had hoped to run over a few of those city boy's hot rods with my APC. But being with you when we go to war is probably the smartest thing for us. Especially if we hope to have a family someday?"

Clay looked worried, "Are you pregnant, Emy?" Oh my god!?

"No, silly... We haven't been married long enough for me to even take a pregnancy test, and you, my dear husband, insisted on us waiting until we were married... remember? No, I'm just planning for the future... you know?"

Once breakfast was finished, the militia members spent the next two hours in outside classroom instruction. They were also issued their ammo, supplies and went through a final weapons inspection. Clay wasn't very happy to find over a dozen M-16s had not been cleaned after the last weapons training and gave each of those troops a good dressing down for the violations. Meanwhile, Emy continued working with her APC 706 crew to ensure they were all ready, and it didn't take her long to find a good man to replace her position as driver.

*11:35 A.M. AFBM TRAINING YARD AND FINAL INSPECTION*

For the last twenty-four minutes, Clay had the men and women of the AFBM lined up in four platoon-sized ranks, with the Headquarters Staff facing them, as Colonel Wickersham, assisted by both Majors Peterson and Johnson, who walked behind him. As Militia Training Officer, Clay walked behind the two majors and watched as Silas selected rifles at random from the troops and inspected them for condition and cleanness, as well as to ensure none of the chosen rifles had a round loaded in the rifle's chamber. They had all been ordered not to chamber a round until they prepared to leave the exercise area and head for the highway. No one wanted any accidents to occur, not at this stage of the operation. Silas had also inspected various sidearms and a few combat knives and bayonets from his various troops. This inspection also included Silas taking a few moments to have a brief chat with the various troops to help boost their morale. Once the troops were inspected, they were then allowed to return to their tents to finish up their scheduled duties.

Silas and his three senior officers then walked over to where the Armored Personnel Carriers were parked and did a brief inspection of each vehicle, and made sure all the automatic weapons were being readied to go. Silas hoped these heavier weapons would not be needed, but he wanted to be prepared in the event a pitched battle did occur. The APCs would provide covering fire if needed for the attack, capable of taking out any of the vehicles the SPs or the Army might have on hand. Belts of ammo were ready to go, but none of the weapons were locked and loaded as of yet. That order would be given when Silas issued the order to move out.

Though Silas had learned that the closest installation to Eielson that used actual tanks was at Fort Richardson, which is located outside of Anchorage, he still had to be concerned about the helicopter gunships the Army had at Fort Wainwright. Yet, he had hoped in putting this operation together that the Army wouldn't try to use them, not with so many civilians being around for the Open House, and then after seizing the flight line, the authorities would be concerned for those being held as hostages.

Clay had noticed that a dark brown six-passenger Chevrolet one-ton pick-up, with a cab-over camper mounted on the back, was parked by the kitchen tent. According to the plan of attack, he knew that very soon, there would be eight troops getting into this rig, with four troops sitting inside the truck and four men inside the camper. These men inside the camper would have with them an M-60 machine-gun, and it was their job to secure the Main Gate. Once this was accomplished, they would then position this weapon inside the Main Gate. Once the two SPs were taken prisoner, with the militia troops under orders not to shoot the SPs, they would be replaced by militia members, and the SP's would be handcuffed and gagged and thrown into the back of the camper. This maneuver to rapidly take over the gate shack had been practiced over and over, and Clay was satisfied it could be done in under ten-seconds or less.

With the exception of the two replacement gate guards, the rest of the AFBM was issued red berets this morning, mainly to help identify them to other militia members when and if the shooting started. The dark blue flash on the beret was that of the ADF symbol; two silver-colored crossed flintlocks. The red berets were just a safety thing that Clay had requested as Training Officer.

Besides their M-16s and the single M-60, the gate's 8-man detail would be armed with three M-79 grenade launchers and four Light Anti-Tank Weapons, also known as LAWS. Silas had tried to obtain a few Stinger Anti-Aircraft Missiles, which he had hoped to have in the event the U.S. Army did respond with armored Blackhawks and Cobra Gunships. But he had failed to do so. So, as part of their orders, the men at the Main Gate were to take hostages from out of the visiting vehicles in hopes of preventing any air assault on the Main Gate by Army or law enforcement personnel. With hostages inside the gate shack, Silas was pretty sure the Army would be prevented from opening fire on the Main Gate and need-lessly endanger these civilians. The terrain around the gate was flat and open for a good fifty or more yards, with the main tree-line some distance to the west of the gate. It was also felt that the highway would be blocked with lines of vehicles, all filled with visitors hoping to see the base. The men at the gate were to notify the SP Desk Sergeant by gate phone of just how many hostages were being held in the shack and how many good citi-zens were still out in their vehicles, not knowing why the traffic was all backed up around the gate shack. Silas wanted to ensure the Air Force would understand what might happen if they attempted to attack the gate.

*AFBM ORDER OF BATTLE*

The final plan was for the main AFBM force to assume position approximately one mile south of the Richardson Highway, remaining concealed by the thick woods. Once Silas received word the Main Gate was taken, and hostages were being taken from the vehicles trying to enter the base; he would then order the advance of his AFBM personnel. Once they reached the Richardson Highway, spread out in line formation and facing the base, the APC units, supported by infantry, would then launch their attack across the highway when Silas gave the order.

At exactly 1250 hours, the Main Gate was to be taken by the men in the civilian camper, hopefully catching the two gate SPs by surprise. Then at precisely 1255 hours, twenty-two men would then come out of the woods, across the highway from the Main Gate, and rush across the highway from the woods on foot to enter the base at the Main Gate. They would then seize some of the civilian vehicles from their owners, hopefully without causing any injuries to the owners, and to drive on to the base and head east down Flight-Line Road. They were to then park their hijacked vehicles behind the flight line buildings and then appear as if they were regular Army personnel, seemingly now assigned as extra flight line security for all the army static displays. Silas had learned that there would be at least two-Black Hawks Helicopters on display, one of the newer Cobra Gunships and even a single troop-carrying Chinook Helicopter. Yesterday, the Army had also delivered four M-119 105mm artillery pieces for display, along with personnel to answer the visitor's many questions concerning the equipment and life in the army in general.

But, as soon as the first shot began being fired into the air, as the main unit came across the highway, Clay's advance force of these twenty-two militia troops was to close in on the VIP Tent and to quickly take all the people there as hostages. Shots were only be fired in the event the SPs assigned to guard the VIP tent's occupants tried to fight back. But with total surprise, both Silas and Clay had hoped this could go down without any real serious harm being done. Once the VIPs were taken control of, Silas had high hopes the SPs would refrain from responding for fear of hurting a helpless civilian. But Clay knew all too well how men who had experienced combat might simply go into reaction mode, and they could easily have a blood bath on their hands.

Because of Clay's warnings, Silas had repeatedly advised his people the reason for the attack was to take live hostages, not to enter into a fire-fight that might endanger and hurt civilians. He had expressed to his people of how a lot of murders could assuredly put a damper on any plan for a new election. If this plan came off as hoped and no one was hurt, Silas actually hoped to get the people of Alaska behind him, but possibly also the other citizens living in the Lower 48 and Hawaii.

Once the AFBM had control of the flight line and all the civilians were under guard, Silas and his two majors would then begin selecting their five-hundred hostages. Silas only wanted healthy people between the ages of fourteen and fifty. He didn't want to have to deal with small children, nor did he wish to risk the lives of seniors, who might suddenly have a heart attack and die. He knew that this would lead to bad press stories and not help his cause.

When the hostages were chosen and searched for weapons and cell phones, they would be escorted under guard to the big hanger. Here their wallets and purses were to be taken, so the AFBM had identifications on everyone. This was especially important for the VIPs, who Silas would use in bargaining with the authorities. He knew he would have to release some of the people and would prefer using the VIPs for this while keeping the ordinary civilians as possible long-term hostages. He knew he had to allow for at least a month, and that was the real downside for this plan to work. Silas knew that just because they promised to hold an election, it didn't mean the government would honor their promise and hold such an election. But he also knew that a statewide election could be put together within thirty-days, and once the outcome was released, the government would be forced to honor it, especially if the United Nations had supported the election.

But during that 30-days Silas would still have to be concerned with some fool trying to bring about a rescue. He also had to keep his hostages fed, watered, bedding provided, and health personnel on hand to deal with any medical problems that could develop.

Once the APC units were all inspected, Silas allowed the men a twenty-minute period to grab up some cold roast beef, ham, and tuna sandwiches from the kitchen, along with iced-up cans of soda. There would be no alcoholic beverages allowed until they held their victory party, after the federal government held a second statehood election, to also be supervised by the United Nations to ensure validity. Silas just hoped the prisoners were smart enough not to take a chance in running off. He would then have to take an action he would rather not have to, by possibly wounding these civilians with gunfire directed at their legs. Any troublemakers would have to be removed from the hanger, and Major Peterson was given the task of dealing with them.

"Once they're removed from the hanger and out of view by the hostages, you can either set them free or lock 'em back up in another building. But, if you hold them, I want these unruly ones handcuffed to keep them out of trouble," Silas had ordered.

While standing there, smiling and chatting with his troops, Silas kept fingering his special cell phone now in his right front pants pocket. He kept wondering if he truly had the guts to activate this bomb if things turned sour for the AFBM. He kept thinking that he would rather go out in a single bright nuclear blast than face a trial, which he suspected would be broadcast around the world as newsmen attempted to show him as a traitor who attempted to blackmail the United States. Though only briefly, he did wonder if his troops would choose that same option themselves. But, he never asked, never informing them about his fail-safe option, for fear of having some of his troops turn away from him and quite possibly contact the authorities, or even take armed action against him. He just could not take that chance.

### OUTSIDE CLAY'S AND EMY'S TENT

"Emy, we need to have a talk... right now, but I want it outside the tent... Okay? Just some private business to take care of before the bugle call is sounded."

"Clay, we don't have any bugles, and why not inside the tent if you want it private?" She then grinned at him, thinking he might want to fool around one last time before the attack order is given.

"No, not inside the tent... it's too hot in there right now."

"Well, we can go behind the tent if you want some privacy or take a brief walk out into the woods... down by that little spring."

Clay liked the idea and agreed. "Okay, beautiful, but let me check your pistol real quick...I want to see something." Clay held out his hand, and without thinking about it, she handed her pistol to him, butt first.

Clay, now carrying her sidearm, led Emy behind the tent and out behind a thick stand of spruce and birch trees. The spruce were mostly only four to five footers, but some of the taller ones were shooting to up to over forty feet in height, while the Birch were now full of new leaves, with a light breeze blowing them about from the south. He knew once they were back by the spring that no one would be able to see them.

Once he thought he was far enough away from the main camp, he touched Emy's right elbow to tell her she could stop. But, it was right then that Emy suddenly noticed that Clay had tossed her gun aside and had now pulled his own pistol out. She also saw he was pointing it to the ground and the serious expression on his face concerned her. "What's up, Clay?"

"Just sit down on that log over there, Emy. We need to have a serious talk, and then it will be up to you for what we decide to do about my little problem with what's happening. Just remember, I am truly in love with you, and this is why I married you, and for no other reason. I just love you with all my heart and want to raise children with you... If we survive this day."

"Clay, what's going on here? You're really starting to frighten me."

"Keep your voice down and please don't yell out or scream... If you do, I might have to shoot someone, and I'd rather not do that. A lot of these people are my friends. But, I have to explain a few things to you before we begin this mission of ours. Major Johnson will be joining us in just a few moments, as he has a lot to say too."

"You're now really scaring me, Clay... What's this all about, and why the pistol... Why'd you toss mine away?"

"Honey, you know I fought with Special Forces in Afghanistan for six years... there and other less popular locations. I was a captain... Delete that... I now admit to you I am an active duty Captain in the U.S. Army, assigned to Delta Force and currently working for the Federal Bureau of Investigations... That's right, the FBI. My medals and wounds are real; I earned them, but a couple years ago, I was working with the CIA in a Middle East operation, and this operation became blown because one CIA Agent couldn't do his job. This blew the Op, and as a result, it ended up killing and wounding a lot of my men and quite a few civilians... All because that CIA agent couldn't do his job. He also died there, but after that, I refused to work with the CIA ever again. As a special operator, I have to volunteer for my assignments; I can't be ordered to work as a lone undercover operative.

With a shocked look on her face, she then glared back at her husband but held her tongue.

"Ok, that part wasn't easy, and it's only going to get more complicated, so please, Emy, withhold saying anything or slapping me until I am finished.... Anyway, the Army brought me home to heal up from my wounds, and I was soon assigned to work undercover against a violent KKK Faction in the hills of Tennessee. Once that mission was over, I was brought back home to Alaska to investigate the Alaska Defense Force. Word had reached the FBI that a violent faction inside the ADF was getting ready to take action up here in Alaska over some statehood issue. This, of course, ended up being the Alaska Freedom Brigade Militia, under our esteemed Colonel Silas Wickersham.

"Now, don't get all upset yet, because I have a lot more to tell you that may keep you from hating me, or at least wanting to cut out my liver." He noticed she wasn't smiling at that last remark and knew he could be in deep trouble with his wife.

"I had no mandate to meet you, to fall in love with you, or marry you. That just happened because I fell deeply in love with you, and I am now liable to spend a few years in prison for doing it. But, Major Norm Johnson, the man you know, is also working with me... I only found this out yesterday that he's is also an FBI operative, which has been verified. Now, as to why I am telling you all this is because I do love you and that Silas, who you love and respect, has gone out and purchased himself a nuclear bomb, probably from some Russian black marketeer. The bomb, reportedly one of the nuclear weapons reportedly missing from the Soviet Union break-up, was moved onto Eielson last night. Silas now plans to detonate this bomb if he feels this operation will not bring about the statehood election he so desires. This, in effect, would not only kill a possible 50,000 to 100,000 people at the Open House but so many others in the surrounding areas. It is also possible that clouds of radiation could reach the City of Fairbanks, killing everyone, and that includes your parents.

"His initial plan is to only use it as a threat in hopes of preventing the authorities from mounting a rescue attempt to free the hostages. He hopes, if needed, a threat of this magnitude will give him the time required to put together the new election over statehood. He strongly desires for Alaska to become a sovereign nation and for him to be the first Alaskan President."

Of course, Emy was struggling with what she was hearing. She had trouble believing what she was hearing from out of her husband's mouth. She tried to interrupt Clay, but he wanted to get everything said before he lost her full attention and didn't think now was the time for an argument or debate. Their time was extremely limited, but Clay really believed he needed to have Emy on his side before going into action.

"Wait a minute, please let me finish... okay? Now, as I said, the bomb is right now on the base, and if for any reason, Silas decides to detonate the bomb... out of fear, anger, or if he simply loses it, the AFBM and very possibly the entire Alaska Defense Force will receive all the blame. I sincerely believe that push comes to shove, Silas is quite capable of detonating the device. He put this plan together over two years ago and has borrowed or sold just about everything he owns in preparation for this plan to succeed. I also believe Silas would rather die than face the embarrassment of a criminal trial. Because if he is taken into custody, he will be facing charges for treason, conspiracy, and very possibly murder if anyone is killed in this attack, and then possibly be executed if found guilty.

"But, his actions could also remove Eielson Air Force Base from ever being used to help deter any enemy invasion from the north, and for the next thousand years, a good-sized portion of the Alaskan interior will be unlivable. I want Norm... Major Johnson, to brief you on some of the finer details, so you understand I'm not making this all up." Clay then took in a deep breath, exhaled, and then asked, "Now, do you have any questions?"

Emy looked at him with her eyes wide, partially filled with anger and also a mixture of disbelief and utter loathing for her new husband. Yet, there was also an inner voice speaking up, reminding her to trust this man she had fallen deeply in love with and was now married to.

But all she could reply with was, "You're Who!? You're What!? Is this some kind of big joke?"

Before Clay can reply, she tried to stand up, and Clay grabbed her by her canteen belt and forced her back down. At about the same time, Major Johnson showed up, and as he approached the couple and had overheard the last bits of the conversation. Norm now realized Clay had just risked everything by telling his young wife the facts of life and the real truth behind the so-called heroic Silas Wickersham.

"This couldn't have waited, Clay?" Nom asked in a stern tone. He also had pulled his pistol out and was glancing about the woods to ensure they were still alone.

"Norm, she's my wife, and we just might not survive this day. I didn't want this lie held up between us... I think too much of her... Dear God, I love her, and that's why I married her."

"Okay... okay. So, what have you told her so far?"

"Everything... well, almost everything. She doesn't know about my meeting last night or about the cell phones."

"What meeting... when?" Emy asked. She was now torn between beating both of them over the head with a small log and making her escape and hoping to find out more. But she was having a hard time believing Silas, who was like a kindly uncle to her, would be capable of such actions as to actually obtain and then consider detonating a nuclear bomb.

"I told her about Silas's plan, how he got control of the nuke from the Russian mob, and plans to detonate it if things start turning sour on the flight-line. She just doesn't want to believe that Silas is capable of such an evil thing."

Emy glanced back and forth between Clay and Norm. Though she had no reason to trust Norm, who she only knew through Silas and AFBM operations, she was having a hard time believing Clay would be making this all up. He wasn't a big jokester, and this went far beyond being humorous. Especially to pull something like this on the day of the attack.

"Emy, what your husband is telling you is the whole truth. Yesterday, Silas chose me over Major Peterson, for whatever reason, so he could inform another member of the senior staff of the existence of this nuke, and what he planned to do in the event it looked like we were about to lose everything. He spoke on how he would rather die... yes, die, rather than risk being put on trial for treason. He's fearful of possibly being hung by the federal government and the embarrassment it would cause his family.

In the event he is disabled in the attack, I'm supposed to activate the device in his place. But, both Clay and I now suspect a second man or woman... we don't know who at this point could be in possession of a second cell phone that would activate the arming device on that bomb. Supposedly, from the time of activation, there is supposed to be a five-minute delay in the event Silas changed his mind and wished to disarm the weapon. But, there is also a good chance the Russians, or even the Chinese, who might be involved in this, did not actually put into the device that five-minute delay.

"We know that if the bomb does go off, it would be Alaskan terrorists. Our AFBM and, most likely, the entire ADF would be blamed. The Russians and the Chinese would not be blamed, even though tests of the radiation, later on, would show it had been a Russian device. Of course, for us, none of that would matter. But for Russia and China, a strategic Air Force Base and all of its aircraft and personnel...Well, they just wouldn't exist anymore. Alaska and the United States would lose a key defense location, as well as thousands upon thousands of lives. It would prove to be to their benefit if Silas did actually detonate this weapon.

"Emy, we know now that the bomb was purchased and brought to Alaska. We now know Silas had it moved onto Eielson last night and supposedly placed beside the hanger where the hostages well be held. But, with a weapon of that size, anywhere on the base would do the same thing... Emy, he really wants to be the first Alaskan President and is willing to make a bargain with the devil to bring it about, which in this case meant foreign Black Marketeers."

Then Clay took over, "Intelligence has known for some time that dozens of Russian nukes went missing when the Soviet Union broke up. We conducted searches for them in the Middle East but were unable to find any. We do suspect Silas paid as high as twenty-million dollars to put this whole plan together, taking loans out on everything he owned and what he could borrow to arm the AFBM and purchase this old A-Bomb. He also had to pay for the personnel needed to smuggle the device over here, set it up, and deliver it onto the base."

Norm then interrupted and told Emy of how the bomb was brought to Alaska and onto Eielson. "Silas also advised me that he had confirmation that the bomb was delivered to Eielson late last night; he also showed me the special cell phone he had been provided with. But, and this is a big but, he also hinted at there being a second phone in the hands of someone he trusted, in the event Silas was taken out by a sniper or fell in the initial attack. If he had given me the second phone, we could've ended everything last night, and we would have had both phones in our hands. But for now, everyone in the know is deeply concerned about that second man or woman."

Clay looked deeply into Emy's eyes, hoping she could read his thoughts and knew he was telling the truth. "Honey, I know this is all a shock to you, and by my telling you this, I hope to show you just how much I truly love you... and trust you. Last night, after making sure you were asleep, I made my way onto the base and eventually met with General Hampstead, Eielson's Wing Commander. It took some talking, but he now believes what I was telling him was the truth. My FBI handler, Agent File, who also works with Norm, confirmed who I was, and she now believes Silas actually has that nuke and is prepared to use it. From his psyche profile, she was told by the experts that Silas was showing himself to be unstable and would most likely kill everyone than be arrested. Unless we can locate the weapon, disarm it, or move it elsewhere.

"The Air Show and Open House will not go off as planned... and the base's security force are at this moment now preparing to either attack us right here... if they've located and disarmed the bomb, or to meet us head-on when we attack the base. In either case, unless they get that bomb found and disarmed... or flown elsewhere to an unpopulated area, everyone dies this afternoon, and that includes all of us."

Clay holstered his pistol and placed his hands on Emy's shoulders, and looked deeply into her eyes, which still radiated with a mixture of bitterness and hostility. "Honey, I'm telling you all this because either the major here or myself may have to kill Silas before he can activate that nuke. I cannot hesitate and allow him the time to make that special phone call that would activate that device. But it's that second party that still concerns me... we just do not know who it might be."

"What if it's me? Would you kill me right here and now?" Emy asked.

Clay shook his head, "Emy, I would not be in love with a person who could be capable of such an inhumane act. I know you agree with this action of seizing the base and holding the hostages in hopes of a second statehood vote. But, you are not someone capable of killing thousands of men, women, and children in such a way. It would go against everything you believe in."

Norm glanced around again, keeping watch, and then he added, "He's completely honest with you, Emy, and this means your parents and your-self could be looking at spending a long time in federal custody for their involvement with the AFBM."

Clay then added, "There is also the stone-cold reality that those people that Silas dealt with have lied to him about that five-minute delay... That the bomb will most likely explode within sixty-seconds or less."

Emy was silent for a moment, and Clay watched as her anger began to drain from her eyes. He now hoped he had finally reached her. Otherwise, he was going to have to knock her out and leave her out in these woods, tied up and gagged. Then he and Norm would have to figure out how to take Silas down the quickest and easiest way. They both knew and had agreed they would have to kill him quickly if the military couldn't find or disarm the bomb and had decided to attack the training area. For then, Silas would know his long-term plans were evaporating right before his eyes, and he couldn't afford to be captured. Then they would have to seek out and identify the other man, which could prove nearly impossible. Putting their heads together, they had tried to guess at who it might be, but out of 123-AFBM members, any one of them could be the hidden man... or woman.

"Why didn't you tell me all this earlier, Clay?"

"As strange as it sounds, I wasn't sure I could completely trust you with this... knowing how deeply you felt about the Colonel and with your parents involved in some degree simply by their association with him. I just didn't know if your love was enough to keep you from turning me in... or if you would believe me. I had originally not planned to say anything... until this was all over. But then I learned of the nuke last night from Norm. I was trying to think of a way to take you into custody and getting you off base when the attack came off... You are my wife, I love you so very much, and I just don't want to see you in some federal detention facility, with me visiting you every Sunday afternoon. It's real hard to raise kids that way."

Clay had a smile to his eyes, and Emy couldn't help herself when she wrapped him in a big hug and whispered into his left ear, "I love you, too, my husband... but this is really going to be one hell of a stressful day."

"If you two have reached the point where you now believe one another, I think we'd better return to camp," Norm said and then added, "Someone is probably looking for us by now, and Silas will be getting suspicious if we don't turn up."

"Can I have my pistol back? Someone's liable to say something if they see me with an empty holster."

Clay didn't reply right away, but a gradual smile appeared on his face, and then he grabbed her by the hand and began guiding her toward their tent. Reaching their tent, he picked up her firearm and handed it to her butt first. "Your weapon, my lady. Try not to shoot your foot off... that might be hard to explain to our children."

Clay knew he could still be taking a chance, but he saw that Norm was prepared, for he had his right hand near the butt of his handgun in the event he needed to make a fast draw. Norm just wasn't all that sure about Emy and wanted to be ready in the event she aimed her weapon at her husband.

Norm also hoped he wouldn't have to kill Emy, for he was very fond of the young woman and of Clay also. He was pretty much convinced that Clay would never draw on his wife, even to defend his own life, and was relieved when Emy brushed the pistol off and holstered her weapon. She then drew the snap closure over the butt of the firearm and snapped it into place.

"So, dear husband, what do we do now?" Emy asked as they stood outside their tent.

"I guess we have to play it out... But one of us has to be by the Colonel at all times to keep him from making that call on his cell phone and then... Emy, it will have to be a kill shot to the head. We cannot take the chance of wounding him... he could still push those phone numbers and activate the device.

"What about his personal cell phone, Clay? He must be carrying two of them... one for the bomb and one for normal use. Can you make the kill shot if it's forced upon you, knowing he could be just talking to his wife?"

"Honey, I really doubt he'll be calling his wife as we launch this attack, or in the event we come under attack right here. In any case, if I see him bring a cell phone up, we'll have no other option but to kill him."

She hesitated briefly before replying, let out a sigh, and then said, "I have known the Colonel most of my life. But, to keep him from killing thousands of people... I guess I'd have to shoot and pray I was doing the right thing." Emy then walked past Norm and Clay and entered their tent to gather up her field pack and her rifle.

When she came out, with the rifle now slung over her right shoulder, Norm stepped up to be closer to Emy, and in a low voice, he whispered, "Emy, if you do see a phone in his hand, once we're committed, you have to kill him if Clay or I am unable to. We simply just cannot take the chance... He can't be allowed to activate that device, and you need to realize that this action might very well cost us our lives. The others will most likely turn on us with a vengeance once they see that it was one of us who shot him. We won't be given an opportunity to explain our actions, and we have to be prepared... Silas might just lose it when we attack the base and, in the heat of the battle, decide to just blow the place up. Anything is possible, and we have to be prepared for these possibilities."

"Yes, you're right,... and I'll be ready," Emy replied.

Clay then shook hands with Norm and said in a low voice, "Okay, we'd better look busy before Silas starts suspecting something, but keep thinking about who that other person might be."

Norm nodded his head in reply and then turned around and headed back to his part of the camp. He wanted to provide the two newlyweds with a moment of privacy before they headed back into the main encampment. Yet, in the back of his mind, he was still concerned with Emy's loyalty to her husband, questioning whether or not her allegiance toward Clay was stronger than her love for her parents and devotion to Silas and the AFBM? Though, at this moment, he was feeling pretty sure the whole nuclear bomb thing was a pretty good tool of persuasion to use to have her remain faithful to Clay. No one with a real brain on their shoulders would want to risk the deaths of thousands of civilians, especially kids, who were expected to be out at the base in mass to see the Open House and watch the Thunderbirds.

Clay then remembered something else he wanted to say to Emy, "Oh, I almost forgot... Once we start our attack or in the event the military opts to engage us here, make sure to let your blonde locks hang loose. I don't want some SP shooting you, thinking you were just another guy. I tend to doubt these men will be shooting the female members of the AFBM... hard to break our mother's training in how to treat our womenfolk... And if anyone asks, just tell them your hair clip broke. But I doubt they'll have time to berate you for wearing your hair out, not with bullets flying. Okay... will you do that for me?"

"Hey, if it keeps me from being shot by some adrenaline-pumping SP, I'm all for it. But, I'll wait until we've hit the front gate or if we come under attack right here... and I just might tell the other girls to do the same thing."

# THE LAST HURRAH

*The Alaska Freedom Brigade Militia Training Yard, July 4th*

A s of yet, there had been no attack on the training field, and now Major Peterson had sent two of his men to the highway, dressed in civilian attire, to check on the flow of vehicle traffic entering Eielson Air Force Base.

Colonel Silas Wickersham knew that if base security had learned anything about the AFBM operation, then the civilians would not be allowed on base, and the Main Gate would've been locked down. But the vehicle traffic was observed to be flowing quite well as dozens of vehicles, upon entry into Eielson, were then being directed to follow the commands of various SPs posted at major road intersections. Silas knew these SPs were simply advising these people on how to proceed through the base to find various parking areas set aside for this event.

Even though these two militiamen had binoculars, the thick woods and flight line buildings on-base prohibited them from seeing where the traffic was going after driving onto the base, with the exception of those vehicles being directed down Flight Line Road. The base officials had been using this strategy for the last half-dozen Open Houses to reduce traffic flow into congested areas and interfering with the base's routine affairs. But what the observers could not see was how behind those flight line structures, most of these vehicles were then being re-routed to make a left turn in front of Amber Hall and head for their newly assigned parking areas behind housing and out of harm's way.

General Hampstead knew he was gambling big, but he had directed the highway roadblocks that were now being readied, not to stop all traffic until precisely 12:30 hours. He did not wish to give this Colonel Wickersham any cause to suspect that his surprise attack had been compromised. According to what Clay had told the General, other than the two-teams being sent in to secure the VIPS and the Main Gate, they were no other personnel on the base. Though it had been discussed early on to have some observers on base, it was due to their limited numbers that Silas opted not to do that. He wanted to have the most people possible with him for when they launched their raid from across the highway.

Per General Hampstead's orders and in agreement with the Base Commander, those people currently arriving on base would be first directed to the new parking areas and then escorted by Security Policemen augmentees into Ben Eielson High School. If needed, both the elementary and junior-high-school would be used, and these schools provided these guests with restrooms and drinking fountains. These civilians were then only told of how Washington had sprung a surprise military exercise on Eielson, that was now underway and for them to please be patient. Vendors were also allowed to set up their outside stands in the schoolyards, where they then commenced to sell food and souvenirs to the hundreds of arriving guests.

General Hampstead also made sure the guests were made aware that the Thunderbirds' show would not start until the exercise was completed. For those people who decided they wished to now leave the base, they were then instructed that it was impossible at this time as all the traffic was currently flowing one-way to handle the influx of base visitors. They were then told they could depart the base at 2 p.m., which seemed to satisfy those people for the moment. Though there were some who then voiced their objections against the government for doing this on the Fourth of July.

A lot of people did take notice of how the schools and parts of the housing area were now surrounded by a large U.S. Army regimental force and began asking questions. But, they were then advised this was all part of the exercise and not to be concerned.

Through Clay's information, General Hampstead knew the AFBM would not initiate their attack on the base until 1300 hours, or 1 p.m. The General knew he was taking a real big gamble on risking so many lives, but he knew if the AFBM suspected anything was out of order, Colonel Wickersham might just set off that bomb. He would activate the road-blocks at the set time or when any shooting started. He had already figured it out that if he survived this day, he would most likely be retired, used as a scapegoat for the military, and he was actually okay with that if he was able to save lives. He knew that to set up the roadblocks any earlier would risk the AFBM being alerted to there being a problem. For the moment, the only thing going for him was that Captain Jefferson had said the AFBM only had 123-personnel, and they were all committed to the attack. Which would hopefully mean that there wouldn't be anyone avail-able to notify the AFBM of the stopped traffic. But it was still a big risk, though he had little choice with everything happening so fast.

Clay had also advised him of how various officers would be carrying brand new Motorola hand-held radios so they could receive their colonel's commands, and the General was working with his people to see if they could jam those signals once the AFBM was sighted coming out of the woods.

In dealing with the civilian leadership, General Hampstead had to threaten the immediate arrest of a very upset North Pole mayor, who had insisted on evacuating his town when he learned of the possible attack on Eielson.

"You can begin your evacuation of North Pole only after the road-blocks are in place and advise your people there will be orderly convoys taking all the evacuees onto Fort Wainwright until the all-clear is given. The man finally relented after being taken to task by his fellow politicians, who had agreed with the General. There would also be a civilian black-out on all communication via phones, cell phones, and CB radios. This surprised the politicians, who hadn't realized the military could take such strong steps in a national emergency.

General Hampstead talked to the various key city and borough government leaders, and this also included the Alaska State Governor on a joint-military phone line, set up quickly by the Army and Air Force working and the Tel-Alaska Phone Service, a civilian company. Thankfully, he was able to catch the ones who had planned to attend the Open House.

"Governor, ladies and gentlemen, I fully understand how you all must feel right now with all that is going on here in your Tanana Valley. You have cause to be frightened, concerned for both your citizens and your own family members and friends. But, if these terrorists start to feel like something is indeed wrong, they just might trigger that nuclear device before we are able to disarm it. If that was to happen, a whole lot of people would die. Not only that, but the Alaskan Air Command would then lose Eielson Air Force Base and its outlying areas. This, in turn, would greatly hamper our job to defend Alaska, in the event there is a grander plan at play here, one which could possibly lead to the invasion of this state by foreign armies, if and when such a horrific detonation was to occur.

"However, we are not sure at this point if such a plan is in play. I am only saying this because this is one of the principal reasons why our military installations are located in this fine state... to defend our nation from foreign invaders. But, as I said, this has not been confirmed as of yet, and these terrorists may just be acting on their own. But, we are looking at all possible scenarios.

"it's Eielson's Air Wing that protects Alaska's northern and northwestern coastlines, as well as our international border with Canada. Because of this, we simply cannot afford to lose Eielson's strategic location or, more importantly, all of the American citizens living here in our beautiful 49th state... Now, I'll talk with you all once we have the situation in hand. But, please, offer up your prayers that we are able to deter these people from doing any harm. But, if you should hear a very big explosion... well, God bless all of you." General Hampstead hung up.

The General was glad all normal telephone traffic was being turned off, leaving only the 911 lines open for use. He then got on the phone to Juneau, as he wanted to talk with the State's Emergency Command Center. He then briefed Alaska's U.S. Senator, who was outside the state for the moment.

General Hampstead had also advised the Governor not to place the Alaska National Guard on alert yet, as he explained the close tie the ADF had with the guardsmen. Though the senior commanders of both guard units were briefed earlier this morning and they were prepared to initiate a total recall of their personnel if the weapon was used, they were not to notify any other personnel for fear these people's close relationship to the ADF might create a problem, and the AFBM might be advised of what was happening on Eielson and the outlying areas.

Air National Guard alert birds stationed at Fairbanks International Airport were placed on standby at 1100 hours. Then at 1145 Hours, General Hampstead decided to launch his alert birds from both Eielson and Elmendorf Air Force Bases. Six fighters out of each base took off and headed west, with each of these F-22 flights now to be accompanied by a KC-135 tanker, which was also being flown out of Elmendorf Air Force Base.

On the advice from Washington, General Hampstead decided that if this was indeed a possible precursor to war, he wanted Alaskan's skies protected. He just hoped the AFBM outside of Eielson would simply consider it as part of the Open House, demonstrating to the public how quickly and nosily the Air Force could react, and it was an impressive sight as the first two primary fighters took off, kicking in their afterburners for a rapid climb into the skies and then followed a short time afterward by the four remaining alert birds.

Sure enough, the AFBM personnel had heard the launchings as the fighters took off, but as the General had hoped, the militia members did believe it was simply part of the show. Though it did cause a wave of excitement to surge through Silas, as he suddenly shoved his left hand into his pocket, wrapped it around his special cell phone, and squeezed it tightly.

General Hampstead, working with his senior officers, then prepared their plan for a massive launching of Eielson's aircraft. A mixed squadron of F-16s and F-22's once airborne would be sent towards the Bering Sea, but to stay within Alaskan skies. Meanwhile, a similar-sized flight of fighters would launch from Elmendorf Air Force Base and proceed south-west towards the Aleutian Chain, to stand ready in international or

Alaskan air space in the event the Chinese or Russian air forces might be moving on Alaska. US Satellites were also in play, observing the Chinese and Russian naval fleets to see if the ships were moving toward Alaskan waters.

This was all precautionary work that had been planned for years in advance. Each squadron would be supported by air refueling tankers. The remainder of Eielson aircraft, if launched, would then fly south to Elmendorf to standby until they could safely return to Eielson. If the need arose, additional tankers could be sent north from McCord Air Force Base in Washington State, who would then use Elmendorf as a temporary home base. General Hampstead was relieved to have such operations ready to be put into play if the need arose.

Even though the Bering Strait was ice-free at the moment because it was July, it didn't mean an enemy force might not be airdropped, or ships could be used to bring an amphibious force across the waters. But so far, Military Intelligence had not picked up even a whisper about a plan to invade Alaska, but the Joints Chiefs of Staff at the Pentagon didn't want to take any chances.

The President of the United States had also received a full briefing from his senior military advisors, and he was in contact with the Canadian Prime Minister. The President wanted the Canadian leader to be prepared in the event a nuclear device was set off in the Alaskan interior. For if it was to occur, the U.S. and Canadian authorities would immediately seal their borders closed as a precaution to keep radioactive infected victims from being able to flee into Canada and to prevent tourists on the Al-Can highway from approaching the contaminated area. People visiting Alaska who were already across the border could then be diverted to the southern route through Tok, to Glennallen, and eventually, the highway would take them to Valdez, Anchorage, or even the Kenai Peninsula.

As with everyone else who learned of this pending incident, the President also sincerely hoped that this bomb was found and disarmed. But this event had also made him wonder as to if there was any Russian and/or Chinese involvement and if this was, in fact, a prelude to war? As a result, early this morning, nearly every US military intelligence service, plus both the CIA and FBI, were now looking into this.

## *ALASKA FREEDOM BRIGADE MILITIA ENCAMPMENT*

With the exception of the guards walking the perimeter and those two troops posted at the entry to the training area, all of the AFBM personnel were now lined up in formation and standing at parade-rest. Colonel Wickersham, followed by Majors Peterson and Johnson, and then Clay, was walking the lines as Silas shook the hand of each man and woman in line. Once finished, he returned to stand in front of the group for his final address to his troops.

"Gentlemen and Ladies, members of the Alaska Freedom Brigade Militia, I wanted to take this moment to thank all of you for your loyalty to Alaska and to this organization...also your loyalty to myself and my officers and NCOs. This day might never have come about without such people as you and your dedication to this cause of ours. I will always be in debt to you and what you do here this day.

"Now, in all honesty, I know there is a good chance some of you might not survive this day, or you might become wounded, and there is even the possibility you might be taken prisoner. But, we, your senior staff, all hope our surprise attack will rule the day and with so many civilians... men, women, and children, on the flight line, that we can carry out this action without firing a harmful shot. Yes, this is my hope!

"Then, we will be able to force the U.S. Government, working in tandem with the United Nations, into holding the second statehood election... Though in fact, this would be the first legal vote concerning Alaskan statehood, as we all now know that the 1959 election was conducted illegally.

"But, unlike in 1959... this time, we will ensure all of the Alaskans will have their opportunity to have a legal vote in this election. That all the ballots will be printed out in English, as well as those areas of local native dialects, to also include the primary languages of the Middle East, Mexico, Germany, Japan, Russia, and China. Being that our Alaska now has so many new citizens from all over the world.

"As you've all been told when you joined the AFBM, the Washington D.C. Statehood Committee lied to us back in 1959 by first offering us a great deal of having to only pay 10% of the proceeds gained by the sales of our natural resources. This would then allow us to use the savings of 23% to set up our state government. But then they refused to honor their promise after the election and insisted on Alaska having to pay the 33%. As to why we didn't take them to court to put aside that election in 1959, I have no answer for you. We were treated much the same way as our Native Americans in the Lower 48 were, who suffered over 350-broken treaties in the last 200-years.

"No, only through another statehood election can we bring about change, and sadly, we will have to use force to carry out today's operation in order to force the U.S. into holding another election. We know from past experiences a U.S. Court can refuse to hear our argument or keep it tied up for twenty or more years. We cannot allow that to happen.

"Everyone of your names will be known by the Alaskans who witness this day, and the children to follow will hopefully see us as courageous men and women similar to the men of the Alamo and our other great patriots are known... Such men as Jim Bowie and David Crockett, Andrew Jackson and George Washington... and our other founding fathers and like them, I believe you will all be heroes for all Alaskans... And I wish for you to know just how proud I am to serve with you on this very historic day."

Major Peterson then stepped up and said in a loud voice, "We do this today for all Alaskans, for our families and those children who will come to grow up in a free Alaska!"

This statement produced a loud round of applause and shouts of praise until the Colonel waved his arms to quiet them down. Silas then continued on with his briefing, "Okay... okay. Now is the time for you to move into your forward positions. The advance crew who are to secure the Main Gate and led by Captain Jefferson, a highly decorated soldier who has seen a lot of combat in Afghanistan, will very soon move out from here in twenty-four minutes. Just as we've discussed over the last few days. We have secured two retired Deuce-and-a-half retired Army trucks, worked on by Wickersham mechanics, and now parked over by the APC units. These two trucks will carry Captain Jefferson's command to the gate, posing as Army infantry, who have been given the detail of coming onto the base to safeguard the various Army displays. But after leaving the gate, their target is, of course, the VIP tent and securing some very important hostages. Peacefully if at all possible. The dead make lousy hostages, as you well know." This remark brought forth a few chuckles as Silas had expected.

"The rest of you, once we've broken formation, should get some more water down you and make one last check of all your equipment. All three canteens you have are to be filled, as we won't be drinking their water for fear they may drug it to put us to sleep. But it won't be too long before our water buffalos have been pulled on base to refill our canteens. But, you should be prepared to only use your own water for at least 24-hours. I only requested you carry one canteen on your belt and two more in your pack because it was so warm. The current temperature is 87 degrees and will probably clear 90 degrees before this afternoon is over.

"You squad leaders, you are to make sure every troop has his full load of ammo, grenades, and each crew-served weapon to have its required load. Also, ensure your troops have made out their wills. They are to leave these wills with any last letters to wives, husbands, and family with Major Peterson. If you can't find him before we leave, just leave them in your packs, sealed in a plastic bag. But, I promise you I will do everything possible to ensure your last wishes are carried out.

"We will move forward to the departure line at exactly 12:40 p.m., staying at least 200-yards back from the highway, as not to be seen ahead of time. At this point, we will then lock and load, but unless told otherwise, your personal weapons are to remain on safe until we begin crossing the highway. Then only semi-automatic fire, as we needed healthy hostages and the fewest of casualties to press our cause forward."

Silas turned to Peterson, gave him and nod, and Peterson took over, "At precisely 1300 Hours when the Colonel gives the order, we will begin our advance on the Richardson Highway. Once we reach the highway, the Colonel will give the signal to advance further by raising his rifle and pumping it up and down several times. So, you squad leaders, and vehicle operators make sure you can see the Colonel. You will all then launch your attack and move forward at a double-time to secure the flight-line.

"As you've been told already, we will have to cross two double-lane runways and the grassy patch between them to reach the taxiway. There will be no shooting unless it is absolutely necessary, which means no shooting up in the air as we begin crossing the highway and the two runways. We continue to hope the civilians will believe this to be part of the show and that we can reach the flight line without firing a shot. This will make it difficult for the SPs and Army personnel to engage us. By then, we hope to have already secured the VIP Tent and have taken these important people hostage.

"A very short time ago, we all heard the alert fighters taking off from Eielson. This is either part of the big show to show the citizens their taxes are well paid, or some Russian or Chinese airliner has gotten lost over the arctic and is nearing our borders.

"Now, as you've been told in the past, you are to be gentle with these hostages; we do not want any troublemakers or problems with angry civilians. Nor do we want to have to deal with wounded hostages, so do your best to remain courteous at all times. These are your fellow Alaskans, and some of them may actually be your friends. Also, no one under 14 will be used as a hostage, and we prefer civilians over any military... and as you've been told before, no one over fifty years of age. We do not want to have to deal with possible health problems that many seniors are forced to handle.

"Okay, you all know where you're supposed to be, so get there fast when the whistle is blown, and the attack is launched. The platoon members expected to hold the hanger, and the growing number of hostages had better be there when we begin herding the hostage inside or have a real good excuse.

"Now, listen up! I know you're all anxious, but a few things have to be said... If a battle is waged, close in and secure the combatants in any way you have to. Again, no shooting of women and children, unless the female is in uniform, has a weapon in her hand, and you have no other choice. A lot of people will most likely try to run away, expect this. As you know, Third Platoon is under orders to provide a blocking wedge to prevent many of these people from escaping. Again, you've been shown the best way to assume a line formation, with rifles at the ready, to stop them from leaving the festivities.

"Lastly, Captain Jefferson, you are to make sure the VIP Tent is in our custody, for these civilians will end up being quite useful for when we start talking with the federal authorities. In the event Captain Jefferson is wounded or killed, that responsibility goes down to the next man in rank. Same for all the units.

"Now, be safe... all of you." Peterson then looked up and down the formation and then issued his final order to the whole formation. "Now move to your pre-attack positions... And be careful... no mistakes!"

Clay had to wonder if Silas had the nuke's special phone on him, or was it hidden somewhere still for him to grab before heading out to the camp perimeter? A part of him wanted to just shoot the colonel now, but he couldn't risk it, in the event Silas still had another back-up man or woman besides Norm. For whatever reason he had, Silas still had not trusted Norm with the second phone, but he sure wished he had. They could then have eliminated Silas during the night or even during the early stages of the attack, and the militia members would have hopefully suspected one of the SP snipers. But now, in the event Silas is killed, Clay was pretty sure a second man now had the responsibility to detonate the bomb.

"But who?" Clay whispered to himself.

*Lord, it would sure be a big help if you told me who I should be watching for... No help, huh? Okay, we'll do it the hard way.*

*AT THE MAIN GATE*

Eight AFBM members, using that one-ton Chevrolet six-pack truck with a large cab-over camper top, pulled up against Eielson's Main Gate. Dressed in Army green forest-like camouflage, the driver announced they were here to work on the flight-line and asked for a map of the base so they would know where to go and where to park. But, in very short order, the militia members had jumped out of the truck, with one of the troops from the back carrying a loaded M-60 machine-gun with a 100-round belt now in place.

In less than a minute, they had taken the two Air Force SPs prisoner, handcuffing and gagging them and then loading them aboard the back of the camper. Then, while the sixty-gunner and his loader held nearby traffic at bay, the other six AFBM members began taking numerous people out of their cars, while others watched, questioning themselves as to what was occurring, as the militia members returned these new hostages to the back of the gate shack. Here, these people were then handcuffed with zip ties and gagged, and then placed sitting on the floor. These were mostly adults, with a few teenagers tossed in. Adults with children were not bothered with, but the troops had quickly secured ten hostages.

As two of the men changed over to the SP's dark blue berets, they then assumed gate guard duty as the cars now emptied were quickly moved off to the side into a parking area by the others. Once this chore was completed, the bogus SPs began directing the traffic, with one man remaining in the gate shack to supervise the hostages. Both of these men had once served as Army MP's and new all about entry control and what to say to curious drivers as to what just had happened. "It's okay, Sir, it's all part of the show; hope you enjoy the Open House."

The two-man machine-gun crew had also remained at the gate in the event there were any problems. Meanwhile, the other four AFBM troops continued on base in their truck, with the captured SPs in the camper. Their next assignment was to secure the first flight line gate, which would then be manned by bogus SPs. No problems were expected, being that the gate had already been secured by Clay and his band of twenty-two AFBM volunteers. Once two of these bogus Security Policemen had taken over the flight line gate duty, Clay and his men proceeded onto the flight line with their target being the VIP tent.

While most of these men were somewhat surprised by how few civilians were on the flight line and a real lack of vendors, Clay did his best in acting as if this was nothing to worry about and proceeded to drive his truck toward the large VIP Tent, which had been set up near Base Operations. He really wasn't sure, but he expected the SPs to pop up any moment to surprise his force. Though Clay didn't think he would find anyone inside the tent, he did hope to find a trap, and hopefully, the SPs could use the element of surprise to take his force without firing a shot. Clay himself was ready to surrender at the opportune time.

At the appointed moment, one of the two bogus SPs called the SP Desk Sergeant over the landline and advised him, "Listen very carefully, this is to advise you that your main gate has been taken over by members of the

Alaska Freedom Brigade. We are now holding ten hostages, and any attempt to attack this gate will put these hostages at extreme risk. There are also dozens of cars stopped here that are filled with women and children, who would also be at risk in the event you attacked us. Now, do you understand what I've just told you?"

"Is this some kind of joke?" The Desk Sergeant asked.

"No... Now, do you need me to repeat what I just told you, or do I need to shoot one of my hostages to show you how serious I am?"

"No! Umm, I got you the first time."

The man at the gate then hung-up the phone, without another word, but smiled at his partner and the two-man gunner crew. He then stepped outside and began to inspect the stopped traffic. The plan was to cause a bottleneck at the Main Gate as people tried to enter the base from off the highway, hopefully causing a back-up of stalled traffic for several hundred yards from both the south and the north, or possibly even all the way back to the North Pole, or even the hamlet of Salcha to the south before long. That was another reason for the gun crew to remain in place; in the event anyone decided to object to this sudden action at the gate, the M-60 was there to dissuade them.

Within one minute of the call to the SP Desk, Silas issued the orders for his men to move forward and to cross the highway in line formation, with the APC units positioned amongst them.

Meanwhile, the SP Desk Sergeant had immediately notified his supervisor of what had just happened at the Main Gate. Already prepared for this because of Clay's warning, the Master Sergeant in charge of the on-duty Security Police flight ordered for the closest patrol vehicle to position itself at the intersection of Flight Line Road and the Main Base Road. This roadblock was to stop all traffic from approaching the Main Gate from inside the base. A second patrol vehicle was then dispatched to assist, in the event there were any problems, but both lanes were now blocked, and no one was being allowed to leave the base for the moment.

Within minutes of the militia members having left the gate to take up their next position, and less than a minute after the call was made from the gate to the SP Desk, a civilian driver stepped out of a white civilian step-van parked across the drive-thru lane and approached the gate. He acted as if he was coming to the gate to show his pass or to ask a question, and it caught the militia member by surprise. Right then, a second man stepped out of the Pass and I.D. Trailer placed near the gate, acting as if he had just obtained a visitor's map to the base. He, too, was casually walking up and attempted to begin a friendly conversation with the outside fake SP.

Meanwhile, from the backside of the step-van, the sliding door slowly and quietly opened to allow six additional real SPs to then take up a position on that side of the van. Once they were ready, the order was given, and the SPs rushed the gate shack. When this happened, the civilian who stepped out of the van, who was actually an SP lieutenant, quickly subdued the fake SP in front of him with a taser. While the second man from the Pass and I.D. Trailer, now aimed his pistol at the other three AFBM members. The additional SPs had been waiting for the order to move, having been sitting there across the roadway for the last thirty-minutes, nearly overheating from the heat in the van. They had retaken the gate without anyone being harmed, other than the one militia member who was unconscious from the taser.

The stunned machine-gun crew, who had been distracted by conversing with two attractive young women hostages, now felt the steel handcuffs being put in place as they looked down upon their brother-in-arms militia member, who now lay unconscious.

The Desk Sergeant was greatly relieved with how well the plan had been carried off, and within minutes all of the hostages were released from their zip-ties and allowed to stand-up and stretch their legs. Now disarmed and secured, the four prisoners were now on the floor in a sitting position at the back of the gate shack's interior. The change-over had come off without a single shot being fired or a fist thrown.

Two members of the SP reaction force returned to the step-van and returned carrying their own M-60 machine-guns, along with four-metal boxes of belted ammo. These weapons were then loaded and placed inside the gate shack, in the event the gate was again attacked and these men would be ready to defend it.

As the AFBM came pouring out of the woods on foot, escorted by the APCs, the men at the Main Gate started herding people out of the stopped cars and directing them toward a large ditch off the side of an access road that led to a small community known as Moose Creek. The SPs wanted all the civilians out of the line of fire in the event the militia members attempted to again attack the gate. But that was not part of Silas's plan. He had no idea at this point that the gate had been retaken by the Air Force, nor that he and his troops were now expected. This was also helped by where Silas had located his men to launch their attack. They were simply too far away to realize the Main Gate was back in federal hands.

*AT THE VIP TENT*

Clay, who had already led his force onto the base, posing as Army troops, was at this moment in the process of attacking the VIP Tent by surprise. Clay could now see that Silas and his main force were now moving across the first of two runways. One of the track APC 113s was being used to briefly stop any northbound traffic from running over the AFBM troops, while a Rubber Ducky APC 706 was to the north of the line formation to stop any southbound traffic from driving over the nearly seventy-five troops on foot. The rest of the militia were inside the APCs and would offload as soon as the APCs hit the flight-line tarmac, as they had been practicing for the last couple of weeks.

General Hampstead's briefing with Clay and what it entailed had quickly made its way down to the SP commander, so the men inside the tent and inside the Base Operations building were prepared for Clay's advance on the VIP Tent. Two M-60s inside Base Operations were ready if needed to disable the two stolen Army trucks if the militia members refused to cease their advance. With so many vehicles coming onto the base for the Open House, General Hampstead knew he was risking civilian lives, so he had ordered up the SP's best shots to be assigned to this detail. Except for three snipers, who had positioned themselves inside the base's control tower and were now a good 50-feet above ground. Their primary duty was to protect the VIPs, and any women or children seen to be in danger once the attack begins. The snipers were also ordered to wound and not take any kills shots, for General Hampstead knew a man manhandling a woman could just be the woman's husband wanting to get her out of harm's way. So leg shots were to be the order of the day if at all possible, and then shoulder shots, as this General knew these SP snipers were quite capable shooters.

General Hampstead also knew a lot of mistakes were liable to happen this afternoon, and innocent lives may very well be lost, but he was forced to deal with the big picture, and that meant not letting that nuclear device go off. Not that he would even notice as he and several thousand others would simply cease to be with the weapons initial blast. But he couldn't worry about that now.

## PRIOR TO THE MAIN ATTACK

Just after his last official call to the Pentagon, General Hampstead received word he'd been waiting for. The bomb had finally been located. Though the mercenaries had been told to put the trailer behind the big flight line hanger, they had ended up parking it beside a smaller hanger commonly used by the base's Civil Air Patrol, and it had taken time to find it. But the Explosives Ordinance People were now attempting to get into the device to disarm it. Yet, the concrete encasing was causing them some difficulty. This had then caused a lot of people on the base to start sweating, concerned they might not get it disarmed before the attack. The General ordered up a Black Hawk Helicopter, with a volunteer crew, to be standing by in the event the mobile generator needed to be airlifted off the base and hopefully and speedily delivered to either a remote location or Harding Lake. But there was an even chance the bomb if still live, might be detonated while being airlifted away. The General had no other option but to give his EOD personnel as much time as possible.

Then at precisely, 1230 hours, he ordered the highways to be blocked off in North Pole and in Salcha, which was actually not that easy of a thing to accomplish with so many vehicles now headed for Eielson from both the southeast and the northwest and traveling at an average speed of 55-miles per hour. This is why he chose to use the bridges just south of North Pole as one of the stopping points. Though these bridges didn't allow the front traffic an opportunity to turn around, it kept all the vehicle traffic from Fairbanks and North Pole areas from entering the danger zone.

The bridge in Salcha, going over the Salcha River, did the same thing for all the traffic coming north from the Delta Junction and Salcha areas. Volunteers were then quite busy notifying people in Moose Creek to begin immediate evacuations. Which the General knew would take far too long to save all of them in the event the bomb was detonated. He knew a lot of base personnel, both military and civilians, lived in Moose Creek, and now the General hoped and prayed at least some of them might be saved if they only had the time to get them out of the bomb's range of destruction.

Because of this emergency, the Army Base Commander at Fort Wainwright had volunteered a platoon of Army MPs to be stationed at the bridge roadblock to assist the Alaska State Troopers with the public. He had also notified the Fort Greeley Base Commander, who then also stationed a platoon of Army MPs at the Southeast Mile 47 road closure. Fort Greeley was originally built as the military's Cold Weather Training Facility but now played host to the Department of Defense for their defensive missile sites.

Posse Comitatus, the law that prevents the military from enforcing federal laws off of military reservations, was quickly and temporarily waved for this emergency to allow the MPs to assist the Alaska Troopers. There simply was not time to activate the National Guard, and there was still concern one of the guardsmen might have had a close friendship with an ADF/AFBM member and would pass this notice on to them. This waiver proved to be a good thing, as the road closure at 47-mile Richardson Highway and the roadblock east of North Pole was now experiencing civil problems. A lot of civilians were becoming mouthy with the Troopers over losing out on seeing the big show, but many of them settled down when the Army MP's arrived and were all armed with either M-16s or shotguns.

There was no way to get vehicles turned around on or near the bridges, so people had to remain with their vehicles and slowly stew under the Interior Alaskan July heatwave. Thankfully, someone had thought ahead, and a school bus was soon on hand to be used as a shuttle, offering people a ride back and forth from the roadblock to the North Pole Shopping

Mall. A second shuttle was being worked out using a Fort Greeley Army bus to run people back and forth to the town of Delta Junction, 43-miles east of the southbound roadblock. The shuttles were necessary as the vehicle traffic built up too fast for any of the vehicles upfront to be turned around and released to return home. Pretty soon, there were also two five-hundred-gallon mobile water tanks on hand to refill people's water bottles at both roadblocks. But there were certainly a lot of questions being asked for the reason and the explanation being given at this point was of how a federal exercise was currently underway.

General Hampstead had waited to the last moment, based on Clay's warning, on the exact time the attack was to begin. As it was, because of the fear a member of the AFBM might be notified by a friend of what was going on, over a hundred cell phones were temporarily seized by the troopers and their MP support. So far, it appeared no one was prepared to argue with troops or the State Troopers working together. Though in a matter of moments, several civilians and a few off-duty military personnel were placed under arrest for Disorderly Conduct by the troopers and would eventually be transported to the Fairbanks Correctional Facility from the northbound roadblock, while at the southbound roadblock, those arrested would then be taken back to Delta Junction for processing at the trooper substation. Eventually, all of those arrested would be transported to the Fairbanks Dentition Facility and given their chance to appear before a State Magistrate or post bail.

By 12:55 hours, the road closure just south of to North Pole had an estimated five-hundred vehicles backed up toward North Pole proper and on towards Fairbanks. While at the 47-mile closure, the on-scene commander, an Alaskan State Trooper lieutenant, estimated the vehicle count at just over 100-cars and trucks. Many of the vehicles from both roadblocks were now empty, while the passengers and drivers were transported to the North Pole Mall or the Town of Delta Junction until the emergency was over.

A lot of the soldiers, as well as the State Troopers, had their own questions about what was going on, for none of them had been told about the nuclear threat.

It was planned that by late evening and when and if the emergency was over, any vehicle not claimed at either roadblock would be towed away and placed in either a North Pole or Delta Junction school parking lots for the owners to claim them. The vehicles would be moved by both civilian and military tow trucks at no charge to the car owners.

## ON EIELSON AIR FORCE BASE

Prior to leaving the AFBM training area, Clay had appealed to Silas in asking that Emy be assigned to his group, and after a momentary thought on the matter, Silas had agreed. Now as Clay's unit of volunteers drove down the flight line to approach the VIP Tent in two Army cargo deuce-in-a-half trucks, Clay, who was riding shotgun, turned to his driver, Emy, and said, "Emy, before this thing cooks off, I think we need to pray together. There's a good chance before this day is over we'll next see each other in Heaven."

"Honestly, Clay, you can get so serious... But, I know how much you love me, and I hope to spend the rest of my life with you... Even if that might end up being only a few minutes from now. Still, you're right, my love, we do need to pray."

Not only were they concerned over the loss of life, but both of them loved Alaska and hated to think what kind of damage a bomb of such magnitude would do to their beautiful Tanana Valley. Knowing time was short, Clay prayed quickly, and they both finished with a quiet "Amen." He tightened his grasp around her hand and then added, "Well, it's all in His hands, just like it has always been. But, at least the Lord knows how we feel about it."

According to his orders, Clay used his team of troops to make it through the Main Gate, park his two trucks as close as possible to the Grandstand, and the VIP Tent. The men would then dismount the vehicle near Base operations and behave as if they were typical grunts, waiting to handle guard duty over some army equipment. Then, when the order was given, they were to unsling their rifles and make a mad dash for the VIP Tent.

Based upon the map Silas had provided Clay with of the flight line, his troops were looking at just roughly over a 50-yard dash to reach their objective. Clay's orders were then to secure the hostages and wait for the attack to begin, which according to the plan, should occur at roughly the same moment as when Clay hit the tent.

But, Clay and Emy knew there would be no VIPS in the tent and that he could probably expect a dozen or so SPs positioned behind a bunker of filled sandbags. Clay also knew that a second element of SP's would then come charging out of Base Operations, supported by the control tower snipers and M-60's. He only hoped he could get his troops to surrender before they got themselves killed or wounded.

Silas had hopes he would make it across the highway and both runways and would then be with the groups of VIPS within moments of making the highway crossing. Colonel Silas then planned to address the Base and Wing Commander and advise him of what his plans were while these men were under his men's guns.

Silas wasn't aware that the Alaskan Governor had planned to attend the Open House, which was to be a last-minute decision, but now the Governor was the guest of the Fort Wainwright Base Commander, both now anxiously waiting to hear how things transpired at Eielson.

With Clay knowing the VIP Tent would be empty, he was now only concerned with what sort of defense he'd be running into and how Silas might react when he discovered all of his plans had just gone out the window. Clay had to be mentally ready to deliver a fatal blow to end Silas's life and before this man could use that cell phone.

According to the new plan Silas had put together just the night before, Major Norm Johnson was to direct his people to attack Base Operations and then seize the control tower. But, by now, with the cancelation of the Open House, Clay was pretty sure Norm would end up facing a sizeable defense force, which would include snipers in this control tower. Clay reasoned that if he was running the defense of this flight line, knowing an attack was forthcoming, he would have at least four-snipers in that tower.

One at each corner window and a sizeable force inside Base Ops to keep it from falling into the hands of the AFBM. Clay also suspected another large force of SPs would be set-up in both of the nearby hangers, prepared to launch their own attacks when they saw the AFBM forces charging the flight line.

Clay still wasn't sure of exactly how many SPs the Air Force had assigned to Eielson Air Force Base, but he estimated about two-hundred and fifty Security Police personnel. He also believed General Hampstead would've sought assistance from the U.S. Army stationed at Fort Wainwright. So, if he was right, the good guys should outnumber the AFBM at better than four to one odds, and they already knew the AFBM attack would hit the base in force at 1300 hours. This left the advantage to the military troops, but Clay still didn't know whether the bomb had been found and handled by EOD.

The only thing in AFBM's favor was their armored APC units, now armed with automatic weapons. He knew those vehicles with such highly efficient weaponry could do a lot of serious harm before being disabled. This was just one of the reasons he removed Emy from being inside one of those APC vehicles. He suspected either the Army or the SPs would have B-40 anti-tank weapons, ready to be used when the AFBM arrived. Either one of those rounds would easily destroy either the APC 706 or APC 113.

Here at Eielson, Clay knew the SPs used the lightly armored Humvee vehicles, which could be torn up by either 20mm Gatling Gun or the 25mm cannon. He hoped after briefing General Hampstead on the AFBM armament, he would keep the Humvee vehicles behind sandbags or other cover until the AFBM APCs were taken out, or the occupants had surrendered.

As Clay moved into action, he knew that no matter how safe General Hampstead wanted this counter-attack to come off, there still remained a strong possibility a lot of civilians and troops could be killed or wounded in this action. But, if they could prevent Silas from setting the nuke off, Clay suspected Washington D.C. would see the number of casualties as being tragic but acceptable losses. This was a term he hated to see used by the military, and he had seen it far too often when innocent lives were lost. He was still haunted by all those dead and seriously wounded agents and the innocents who lost their lives when operations were blown, or battles were fought with just too many civilians in the line of fire. This was part of his PTSD nightmares, reliving that scenes over and over again and waking up teary-eyed and shaking from fear, his body covered in night sweats. He seldom feared the original operational plans, but the end results still sent shivers up his spine. It left him wondering what else he could've done differently to keep so many people from being killed or wounded.

Once he had become serious in his feeling toward Emy, Clay had wanted to share those bad memories with Emy, in part to prepare her for his nightmares and also hoping her love for him would help bring healing. But so far, he hadn't been able to. It would have exposed him to who he really was and just possibly blown this whole undercover assignment. But now, he knew when this was all over with, and both of them had survived, he would have a lot to share with his dear wife. He hoped with her love and the Lord's blessing, he could then start healing.

Now, as they proceeded toward the tent on foot, he also hoped the SPs had been supplied with photos of himself and of Norm. He didn't want him or Norm to be shot before they could take care of Silas and hopefully identify that second man or woman with the other phone.

Clay quickly glanced over at Emy and was glad she has unpinned her long blonde hair, and it was now letting it hang loosely over her shoulders. Had there been time, he would've asked Agent File to check her old military records and obtain an old photo of her to show the shooters. But that would've taken more time than they had. They were now simply out of time, and Clay was searching for Silas as he hustled forward toward the VIP Tent. He could only hope the shooters wouldn't shoot a confirmed female, and he knew she sure looked very female, even in fatigues. But he needed to get her undercover just to make sure and directed her toward the tent with a wave of his arm. "Follow me, Emy! We have to get undercover right now!"

He ran a couple more steps and then reached over to grab her free hand, "Drop your rifle! I'm hoping the SP's won't shoot someone not carrying a rifle." In response, she had a puzzled look on her face as she first glared at him, but then she understood and promptly tossed the rifle aside, but remembered to put the rifle's safety on first. A chambered M-16 bouncing off the hard pavement could easily fire a live round. Clay also hoped the others in his group would probably not notice her actions with everyone running at full tilt to breach the tent.

"You'll have to keep your pistol in the event you need to shoot Silas if I'm taken down or if we can identify the other subject in time." Clay wasn't sure with all the noise being created if she heard all he had to say, but he did see her drop the rifle. Now they were only seconds away from the tent, and he prayed there wouldn't be any shooting. As soon as he saw the SPs, he would order his troops to halt in hopes of stopping a firefight. But he also had to prepared to simply find an empty tent. In that case, he would order his people into a defensive position until he could understand exactly what the SP's were going to do. He was fully prepared to surrender his unit, but then he only had to be concerned with being shot in the back by one of his own troops.

Clay began wondering, *Who could it the second person be? Possibly First Sergeant Whitehead... maybe Chad Kenders? Rouse? Just too many possibilities... Could've been one of the cooks or even a medic... But it's bound to be an enlisted man. Someone Silas would think would be invisible and really loyal to the AFBM cause. Loyal enough to commit suicide, unless Silas failed to tell that man or woman what that cell phone would bring about. Maybe Silas only told him it was for a secondary explosive charge to be used in the event it looked like the AFBM was going to be captured. Silas could've told him it was a bomb made of Semtex or plain dynamite to cause a distraction to help cover them escape. Maybe just large enough to damage the big hanger. That's possible... I'm out of time!*

Clay's mind was racing as he suddenly burst into the tent and then suddenly froze, with Emy jerking to a sudden halt right beside him. Eyes now wide, Clay was now standing before some thirty SP's, all armed with M-16s and pointed right at them. "Surrender or die!" A young First Lieutenant SP ordered, his own rifle aimed right at Clay. The Lieutenant knew from his briefing who Clay was, but he had nearly two-dozen militia members now filling the tent, and it was looking like a Mexican stand-off.

"Everyone freeze! No shooting or we're all liable to die!" Clay yelled out. His troops had been charging in with their rifles in a carry position, while the SP's had their rifles up, prepared to shoot upon the Lieutenant's command. Clay also heard the noises outside between the tent and Base Operations and now knew additional SPs would be at their backs, preventing them from escape.

Clay glanced to Emy and then the others, and then he ordered, "Everyone just stand still, do not move... Lieutenant, we've apparently walked right into your trap. I have no choice but to offer you my surrender." He then looked over his right shoulder and ordered, "By my command, all of you lower your weapons to the ground. No sense in us all dying right here and now. They clearly knew we were coming... this is over, and I don't want any of you dying here for a lost cause. Now do it!"

There was some hesitation, but then the militia members knew their backs were also under the sights of other SP's. They had no chance if someone started shooting, and no one truly wanted to die this day. Clay then heard the sound of his men slowly and carefully lowering their rifles to the ground and breathed a sigh of relief. His men had been forced to acknowledge they had found themselves in a hopeless situation. But Clay also knew it would take only one hero amongst his bunch to set off a shooting war inside this tent and turned to face them. "No one says anything... we have been undone. Behave as prisoners of war and do not provide these men with cause to do anything that might lead to your being hurt ...or worse. You will be advised of your constitutional rights and—" Clay was stopped abruptly when the shooting suddenly erupted between the runway and the flight line. The battle had begun, but Clay's people were clearly now out of it.

"Listen, all of you, it appears they knew we were coming, and that means they'll have us outnumbered and outgunned. Our plan has failed to catch them by surprise, and this is why there are no VIPs here in this tent. That battle... the battle we had hoped to win is now lost." Clay hoped he wasn't hamming it up too much, but he didn't want one of his unit members to suspect him or Emy as being traitors. They were to be taken into custody along with the others until such time as he, Emy, and Norm could be separated from the group.

The SP Lieutenant then moved his people in to take charge of the prisoners, who were all handcuffed and led toward Base Operations, and taken inside. Clay was surprised he wasn't taken into custody, but he was relieved because he still needed to deal with Silas and that second suspect.

"Captain Jefferson?" The SP Lieutenant asked once they were alone, and the shooting outside had all stopped, but now people were screaming, and others were yelling for medics.

"Yes, Lieutenant, I'm Jefferson, and thank you for keeping your men under such control. You kept this from becoming a shooting gallery by your quick actions. What's happened about the bomb... was it located and disarmed?" Clay watched as Emy was led toward Base Operations and felt relieved.

"Yes, Sir... the device was located, and the EOD personnel have disarmed it, much to everyone relief, I might add."

" Lieutenant, I can only hope our investigation will reveal the identity of the person or persons who provided Colonel Wickersham with that accursed thing." From all his training concerning Weapons of Mass Destruction, or WMDs as they were also known, Clay and the SP lieutenant both knew the entire airbase would have been destroyed, and this included the Richardson Highway for easily ten-to-twelve miles in all directions. A Dozen or more civilian farms located across the highway would have been vaporized along with a good part of the Moose Creek Community. Then the winds caused by the detonation would launch dust clouds of radioactive contamination in all directions, very possibly taking in both the community of North Pole and parts of Fort Wainwright and also possibly parts of Salcha. Though 22-miles away, the City of Fairbanks could also fall victim to radioactive fallout if the winds were right. He knew that before midnight, an estimated 100,000 people could be dead or dying had the bomb been detonated, and he was now so relieved that the device had been rendered harmless.

Now he felt he could leave Silas and the other members of the AFBM in the hands of the Air Force and Army personnel. Clay now felt the battle for Eielson was over.

Having been inside the tent prevented Clay from seeing Silas's attack, but now Clay would soon learn that as Silas hit the second runway, his main force had suddenly come under heavy fire from a diving F-22 fighter, now strafing the AFBM and quickly disabling or destroying the charging APCs. This first fighter was then followed by a second and third F-22. Not only were all of the APCs blown up or just disabled, but the troops were also so stunned by these air attacks that most of them had dropped to the runway with their arms outspread. But the pilots were good at their job and had set their sights on the armored vehicles and not the infantry support. Still, most of the troops inside these APCs were either killed or seriously wounded by this concentrated fire. The advance was stopped cold before the AFBM could even reach the tarmac of the flight line.

Now standing outside and facing his former command, Clay knew Silas had been inside the lead Rubber Ducky, and by the looks of the destroyed vehicle, he suspected his former commander was now dead. General Hampstead had planned this air attack once the nuclear device was disarmed, not wanting to give this militia any chance of reaching the flight line.

Once the third fighter had completed its assault, it climbed into the sky, where the three jets remained in a covering formation. Meanwhile, SP's and Army personnel, some of them now coming from the units that had been guarding the civilians at the schools, moved in to take the surviving militia members into custody. Several ambulances were now appearing on the flight line, and Clay knew the medics would be extremely busy from the looks of things. As well as the Fire Department, who was now sending out trucks to douse the burning APCs. Though they couldn't get too close until all the live ammo had been cooked off. It would also be several hours before the active runways could be used again for the destruction of the APCs had made quite a mess, and troops would have to walk the length of the runways to ensure all the FOD (foreign object debris) was removed. Aircraft were now being diverted to either Fort Wainwright or Fairbanks International Airport. Within the hour, aircraft sent out to the Alaska coastlines were now returning to Elmendorf AFB or the other two airfields. Eielson would be closed until the runways were made safe, which was expected to be within the next 24-hours at best guess.

With the disarming of the device, General Hampstead did not have to order his wing of fighters, bombers, and tankers into the skies, and the old man was greatly relieved by how his plan had worked. Not a single soldier or Air Force person had been killed or even hurt badly, and the General knew he had Clay and this Norm to thank for that. But that would come later. Right now, notification was busily going out to civilian government agencies, law enforcement authorities, and military commands, to include the Pentagon. News reporters outside Alaska were centering their questions at Washington DC, but no one was ready yet to offer up any replies. Other than, "This matter is currently under investigation."

Clay knew that once the AFBM members had been processed and every one of them interviewed, only then could the major part of the investigation begin. But he wouldn't be involved in that, his role in the case was now over with, except for all the paperwork he would have to produce and this he dreaded. Still, Clay was extremely relieved that his beloved Emy was unhurt, as well as Norm, who was also taken into custody to avoid his cover from being blown. He would prove instrumental in the follow-up investigation by continuing to be looked upon as one of the prisoners. As for Major Peterson, he had also been killed, for he had decided to ride inside one of the APC 113's, believing the heavily armored vehicle would protect him during the initial charge. He was wrong.

Clay was loaded into an Air Force staff car and driven to Wing Headquarters at Amber Hall to be debriefed. He would later learn that Norm had survived and that a total of 78 prisoners had been taken into custody, some of them now in the hospital for their wounds. This meant that 45-AFBM personnel had been killed, either from riding inside the APCs or from being close-by during the attack. This had saddened Clay because he had come to know every member of the AFBM, and though he knew them to be traitors as far as America would look upon them, he could also see them as being true Alaskans. He knew the confusion of this would have its effect on him for some time.

He had also been told that Emy would remain with the other prisoners for now, until he could safely arrange for her release. While the other militia members might understand one of their officers having been taken away for interrogation, they might suspect something if Emy was also removed from the others. She was not the only woman, though, there were nearly a dozen female militia members who had survived, but nearly ten of them had died inside those APCs. Clay knew all of these ladies, and he also understood how they were all close friends to Emy. So, he was pretty sure his wife now had to deal with their loss, and this was a major concern for him.

Clay also thought of the other WMDs (weapons of mass destruction) his team had captured over the years while working as a Delta Force operative. But these were chemical or biological weapons the terrorists had in their possession or were still constructing. This was actually his first nuclear device, and he was greatly relieved this part of the operation was now over. His team had never had to deal with a nuclear device, though they were trained for it, and he had personnel on his team capable of disarming one if the need arose. Their Explosive Ordinance Disposal Team was extremely well trained, and they could render a nuke harmless in less than 90-seconds. Most of these devices would be 'recognized as dirty-bombs,' with a small nuclear pile and explosive range. They were not true atom-or hydrogen bombs, with the explosive capability this bomb Silas had obtained.

Clay actually felt that Silas had put together a pretty good plan of operation for the attack on the Open House, and it just might have succeeded had the authorities not grown concerned over rumors of rogue elements inside the Alaska Defense Force, possibly planning some sort of demonstration or operation to disrupt military operations within Alaska. This is what had led to Clay and Norm's involvement in the investigation. However, neither Clay nor Norm would ever learn exactly who had provided this initial information into said rumors. This was still highly classified and would never come out in the follow-up operation or in the follow-up criminal court cases. Clay and Norm, who would never be called upon to testify, nor anyone else in Alaska would learn that it was Silas's own wife who had been instrumental in providing this information. She had a secret boyfriend, a good looking young man she was seeing on the side, who just happened to work for a U.S. senator. Though she was not made aware of how in debt her husband had become in backing this whole operation, she only knew she would be well off once he ended up in jail, and she was able to sell all of his property off.

Of course, she would eventually learn of the bad news, finding out that outside that $100,000 in cash in that savings box, her darling husband was not only deceased but also dead broke.

She had grown weary of Silas, his heavy drinking since being forced to retire from the military, and all his big plans to become the Alaskan president. She not once felt he had any chance of being elected, and she had actually come to dislike Alaska and its freezing winters. No, she would never again return to Alaska and would go into hiding, now fearing of being found out and becoming the target of retribution by a member of the AFBM, or one of their family members, or friends.

*RETURNING THINGS TO NORMAL*

Gradually, Eielson Air Force Base returned to normal operations, though there was an increase in military air traffic over the Bering Strait and the Arctic Ocean. The Eielson Air Force Base Open House was canceled for this year, and the Thunderbirds departed Elmendorf Air Force Base for the Lower 48.

At first, General Hampstead had hoped the information about the nuclear bomb would not be made public, but within 24-hours, the world's news services knew all about it. Eventually, it would come out that a foreign power, rumored to be China, had some degree of fault in this weapon being first stolen from the Russian storage depot and then smuggled into Alaska. Both General Hampstead and the Base Commander knew that brand new fences were now being looked at, and extra security measures were being planned for the backcountry of both Eielson and Fort Wainwright. If it went as being planned, a lot of Alaskan hunters would now be prevented from using the military reservation for finding their game. But such was the price for added security.

Clay had also learned of how rumors had been being circulating that a large plane had crashed near Eielson and was carrying a classified cargo. This led to a newer rumor that the aircraft was a B-52, possibly carrying nuclear bombs. This led Clay to suspect someone in the command structure had actually started that rumor in an attempt to cover over what had actually happened at Eielson on July 4th. For with the new arrival of B-52s in Alaska, this event could have actually happened. Others began to hear of an actual battle having taken place, and the government realized there was simply no way to keep this event from becoming news and gave up trying, at least regarding the actual AFBM attack.

Sure enough, the news displayed the AFBM members as terrorists, which both Norm and Clay suspected would happen. But a few news affiliates had referred to them as communist sympathizers, supported by either Russian or Chinese communist regimes, which Clay knew these AFBM members were neither communists nor in league with any foreign countries. He knew these people were actually just attempting to bring about another statehood election, believing in what they had been told by Silas and his staff.

Clay had even investigated this while serving under Silas and had learned that certain Alaskan Native groups were actually in the process of bringing a civil suit against the federal government over the mishandling of the 1959 election and the so-called 90/10 offer being made. With all the news stories being produced, the people in Alaska and elsewhere would now start believing the stories of the Eielson attack. Soon, the forthcoming trials of those placed into custody would begin, and the news services would, of course, be reporting on them. Before long, Clay suspected that Silas would be remembered as just another Benedict Arnold, a traitor to America.

All of the AFBM members now in custody were being held without bail by the federal government and being held at Fort Greeley, pending these trials.

Knowing how the legal system worked, both Clay and Emy suspected that the federal authorities would probably be offering most of these people some sort of plea deal in hopes of preventing a series of long, drawn-out trials. They just were not sure how many of their friends would come to accept such a deal or would they desire to take their case to court.

As for Emy, the authorities had worked out a way to have her removed from the others now in confinement. It was released to the news that both Clay, Norm, and Emy had agreed to accept a plea bargain, though there were no actual charges pending against them. This was done in such a way that Emy could go be with her parents while Clay and Norm was off going through extensive debriefings and filling out lengthy depositions for the pending trials. Norm would eventually disappear, believed to be serving a lengthy sentence in a non-disclosed penal institution, when actually, after a two-month leave of absence and a bit of a change to his appearance, he was back working undercover for the federal authorities again.

Clay had later learned through courtroom documents as to why First Sergeant Whitehead, who held on the second bomb phone, had joined with the AFBM. Clay knew from Whitehead's history was that a man who had become disillusioned with America after his service as a Marine in Vietnam. He had moved to Alaska and had then later joined the Alaska Army National Guard. After six years with the National Guard, he had resigned and joined the Alaska Defense Force Militia and risen to the rank of First Sergeant. Clay had come to respect the man but was also concerned about the man's alcoholism. It was while writing out his many reports on the AFBM that Clay had come across one of Whitehead's interview transcriptions, which had explained his attitudes. He had lost all hope in America's government and hoped to have found a new democracy in Alaska. He was, in effect, a prime follower of Silas's scheme.

Once he finished reviewing Whitehead's interview transcription, Clay could only stare at the papers in his hand. He had come to know a lot of veterans who felt this way, from Vietnam to Afghanistan; even Clay had struggled with his own thoughts a time or two over the years. But, he knew what Silas had tried to bring about was simply the wrong alternative to the nation's problems. Burning down society was never the answer, for Clay believed change had to come from within, supported by good and fruitful ideas and plans. He now needed to reflect on his life and consider his future, especially now the Emy was now his wife and life partner.

Clay soon learned he was being promoted to Major for the great job he had done. But Clay would not accept the promotion; after discussing it with Emy and a lot of prayer, he had decided to leave the military. They would then return to Minto, where Clay and Emy planned to teach at a Christian school they planned on starting. He knew Minto now had a good-sized Christian population, and they both would also help out with the local church.

Also, in the making was their choice to legally change their names, assisted by the government, to avoid being hounded by news people and possible revenge seekers. So, Clay retired from active duty, and both of them resigned from the Alaska Defense Force.

Clay had also just learned that as a result of the in-depth investigation and his own written testimony, the Alaska Defense Force Militia would not be receiving any blame or tarnishing for what the AFBM had attempted to do. The ADF would maintain their certification as an Alaskan Militia Force. But, it would take almost a year for the Fairbanks Branch of the ADF to be built back up to its original strength, having lost nearly half of its force from this Eielson affair.

General Hampstead and the Eielson Judge Advocate Office also officially advised Clay and Emy during a closed-door meeting on how they would not be contacted by the federal prosecutor for any of the trials for the surviving AFBM Members. Both Clay and Emy had been earlier advised they would not be called to testify, but the prosecutors had tried to touch base with them regarding various topics surrounding the Eielson event. The only thing that Emy and Clay would provide was their unnamed written testimony as classified sources and their written reports.

The AFBM members were being charged with a multiple of unclassified felony charges, including Treason, Conspiracy against the United States of America, and numerous similar charges, as well as federal homicide and assault charges, all filed by the federal government and reviewed by a federal Grand Jury. Added on to this were the federal weapons violations, from the possession of automatic weapons and other illegal firearms, such as grenades and other explosives, and to include the smuggling of said weapons and ammo into the State of Alaska and the United States. Since only the Colonel and the First Sergeant knew about the Weapon of Mass Destruction, the AFBM troops would not be facing charges for that.

Before Clay retired, General Hampstead had pinned the Distinguished Service Cross on Clay's blazer, and Agent File was on hand to witness the ceremony. Though she was not supposed to say anything about FBI business, she did advise Clay and Emy that CIA operatives had identified the Russian mercenaries and the man who had tinkered with the bomb, and the CIA was now pursuing them outside the United States. Agent File also advised Clay that through back-channel messages, the CIA had notified the Russian Mob that such illegal activities would not be tolerated in the USA, and if Russia continued with such actions, they could face harsh retribution.

*AFTERMATH*

Prior to leaving Fairbanks and moving out to Minto, Clay and Emy spent two-weeks on Maui in the Hawaiian Islands, which proved to be a truly relaxing experience for both of them. They had only been home for less than ten minutes when their phone rang and expecting it to be Emy's parents, who had to go through an extensive investigation but were cleared of any wrongdoing, Clay was surprised to hear Leslie File's voice on the other end. Once the pleasantries were finished, she advised Clay that Silas's wife had been found murdered in an Oakland, California hotel. The local FBI suspected the Russian Mob and was investigating the incident alongside the Oakland Police Department.

"Well, Clay, you ready to go back to work?

"What, I was just retired from the Army."

"I'm not talking about the Army... Listen, Clay, your much too young to get out of this business... You'll grow bored with any other type of normal job, and your retirement pay isn't that great either, right?"

"Okay... what are you offering, Leslie?"

"No more undercover work. I want to make you a full FBI Agent, and you'll be assigned to the FBI Office right there in Fairbanks. Oh, you'll have to attend the FBI academy and additional studies concerning the Russian Mob... It seems the Russians are now sending their drugs out through various fishing fleets working in the Northern Pacific. You have the Native Alaskan charm to work with the sea-going native fleets out of Nome, Kotzebue, St. Lawrence Island, and Dillingham, plus some of the ports on the Aleutian Chain. We need to develop an army of informants who would be willing to notify us of when something is going on out there."

Emy was standing beside Clay, listening in on the conversation, shaking her head. "I'm sorry, Leslie... and please understand this is an exciting offer. But... Emy and I have plans for our future. We're now going to be doing the Lord's work in my old hometown of Minto. Visit us some time at... Goodbye, and thanks!" Clay then hung up the phone before she could reply, and Emy kissed him.

"Oh, before I forget about it, we have dinner over at Mom and Dad's tomorrow night, along with a few guests. Sort of a celebration."

"What sort of a celebration and for who?"

"Well, my darling husband... it's sort of for both of us."

"Why, what'd we do? What's to celebrate?"

"You and I passed the test this morning."

"Test, what test did we take this morning?" Clay was confused

"This test!" She then lifted up a pregnancy test. "I've taken three tests over the last six days because I wanted to make sure before I told you. But, buddy-boy, we're pregnant!"

Clay sat there, stunned, and then he reached over and wrapped his wife up in his arms, which led to a very lengthy kiss.

Later, as they cuddled on the couch, Clay said to Emy, "I know it might sound strange, but I just never thought we'd be parents... I had always suspected my prior jobs might have screwed me up physically from participating in this baby-making stuff. But now it seems the Lord has kept me safe. Wow! So, what do you want... a boy or a girl?"

"Oh no, Dear Husband, we're not going to play that game. I don't want to know until the kid makes its appearance. I, for one, happen to like surprises. But I have been thinking that if it were a boy, maybe one of the names we could consider is 'Norm,' that man did save our lives... Or possibly your favorite grandfather's first name."

"No, his native name is hard to pronounce, so most everyone just called him Stanley or Stan. But I don't want to name my son Stanley; that's a hard name to go with when you're young. Maybe we can use a name from out of the Bible... Like, Judah, John, or Matthew. But what if it's a girl?"

"No to any Judah Jefferson... As to a girl's name... Well, I've thought of over a dozen girl names so far, but now I think we still have plenty of time to figure out a name for our child. Maybe we'll wait until the child pops out and decide then after giving it... or him or her, a good look over and see what name will fit best. What do you think?" She asked.

"I think we'll be discussing names for the rest of your pregnancy, plus now we will have to add a new bedroom on to the old man's cabin out in Minto."

"I can't wait to move out there and start our new life. God is good... all the time!"

## THE END

*Thank you for reading Alaska Freedom Brigade. If you enjoyed this story, I would greatly appreciate it if you would leave a review.*
   William L. Casselman

# AUTHOR'S NOTES

The Alaska Defense Force is a lawful militia in the State of Alaska and supports the Alaskan National Guard in the event of an emergency. It has no relationship to the fictional rogue militia unit I have used in my story. Alaska Freedom Brigade is also a fictional unit. The Air Force Thunderbirds Demonstration Team is fictional in my story and has no basis in reality to the actual Thunderbirds Team.

The Air Force and Army Officers and enlisted men mentioned in this story, as with all my other characters in this story, are also fictional and have no relation in reality to the men and women stationed at Eielson Air Force Base or Fort Wainwright, both located here in Alaska, or other Alaskans.

The Alaska Independence Party, though a lawful political party in Alaska, has no relationship to the political party of the same name in my story.

My entire story is fictional but gives the reader a look at what could happen in the event the State of Alaska's law enforcement and U.S. military failed to keep a close eye on disgruntled civilians and the creation of a rogue militia force.

There are many people who live in our 49th state who feel the 1959 election for statehood was not conducted properly and feel a second vote should be conducted. There were many tribal members who did not speak English back then. Accordingly, based on United Nations laws, the ballots should contain (4) questions to be asked of each voter, but the Alaskan ballots only carried two questions. The Voter was supposed to be asked, do you want Alaska to become a member of the United States (Yes or No?). If not, does the voter wish to remain a United States Territory (Yes or No?).

The questions missing were believed to be, does the voter wish to become a sovereign nation? (Yes or No?), and does the voter wish to join with another country, (Yes or No?), and please name this country you wish to join. Some of the native Alaskans had relatives in Russia, and it was believed they might vote in favor of Russia if this question was allowed. Some felt Alaskans might wish to remain their own country, and this is why these questions may not have appeared on the ballot. In removing these two questions, the Ballot Committee made this election illegal.

Once the election was over, it was learned numerous villages never received ANY ballots, and the citizens were never allowed to vote. There were no interpreters sent out to the tribal communities to explain what the ballots were asking, as in 1959, numerous older members of the tribes were not able to understand the language spoken in the United States. For a lot of them, Russian or another native tongue was their language.

In 1959, the statehood election committee from Washington D.C. met with the Alaskan Statehood Committee and made them a fantastic offer. Washington understood that the Alaskans had a lack of funds to establish infrastructure as a State in the Union. So, the Alaskans were offered a financial break. Every state in the union pays 33% of the funds they make from their natural resources to the federal government. Alaska would pay only 10% of what they made, providing them with a needed break to build an infrastructure, which was necessary. But in reality, once the statehood vote was done and Alaska was now the 49th state, the 10% deal simply vanished, and Washington demanded 33%. Congress knew exactly how much wealth Alaska could produce through its gold and oil, and they wanted it.

As an added insult to this process, hundreds of military servicemen and women stationed in the state of Washington were airlifted from their bases and flown to bases in Anchorage and told how to vote. Technically, no election law was broken, as none existed for this territory. They were all Americans, though these troops were not citizens of Alaska.

# A PERSONAL NOTE

I wanted to add a dedication to an old friend of mine, whose name was Norman Johnson, an Alaskan Native from Dillingham, which is why his name was used for the heroic figure in this story. Norman is now deceased, but his family remains in Dillingham, Alaska.

He was a young man when I first met him, who suffered greatly from an early and aggressive physical disease. When I became a police officer in Dillingham, Norman was the Animal Control Officer. He spent a lot of time rounding up the dog's people had abandoned after finding out that dogsledding was not their sport and had left town.

When Norman heard my wife Mona and our four-year-old daughter, Elizabeth, was coming to Dillingham, where our daughter would meet me for the first time, Norman moved his family out of his house and offered his place to us so I could have some privacy with my family. At the time, I was living with three other police officers and sharing a room with one of them. For those few days, Norman and his family would live with his parents. This was an incredible offer I could not refuse, for I know it would have hurt his feelings, and it ended up being a joyful time for our family.

Later, during the violent fishing strike in Dillingham, Norman endangered himself by calling over the emergency line, which we could pick-up through our police car radios and radio scanners to advise us that myself and the officer riding with me were in extreme danger. An ambush had been set up at the north end of Wood River Road. At the time of his call, we were responding to an emergency call at a woman's shelter, which housed women who had been victims of abuse by either their families or their husbands. We immediately recognized Norman's voice as he reported that a group of men armed with rifles had set up the fake trouble call at the shelter to draw us into an ambush.

After our dispatcher confirmed there was no actual problem at the center, we then pulled off the roadway and parked on a small bluff that overlooked the access road. This single dirt driveway branched off the end of Wood River Road, then proceeded down to the woman's shelter located in a small valley. This entryway was mostly surrounded by heavy brush, but from our location, we could see several pick-up trucks parked behind these bushes. Using binoculars, we eventually saw eight-men, all armed with rifles, starting to climb out of this brush. We figured they had given us enough time and had probably thought we had been diverted away for another police call. During the fishing strike, our department was extremely busy, and this was one of the reasons the two of us were riding together, and working 12-hour shifts, 7-days a week.

Norman's message had clearly saved our lives. During the fishing strike, numerous boats and houses were set afire, and our patrol vehicles were shot at a couple times. I owe my life to Norman Johnson and reminded my son, John Leroy Casselman, of this when he also went to work for the Dillingham Police Department. By then, Norman had gone to be with the Lord, but John did contact the Johnson Family and again thanked them.

As a result, my beloved wife and I now have six children and seventeen grandchildren and great-grandchildren. Thank you, Norman.

# ABOUT THE AUTHOR

 William Casselman was raised in Southern California. He enlisted in the U.S. Air Force in 1971 to become a Law Enforcement Specialist/Military Working Dog Handler. He served the next ten years in the military and met his lovely wife, Mona Sue, at Eielson AFB, Alaska.

A Vietnam veteran, he left the service to become a police officer in Dillingham, Alaska, and spent the next twenty years in Alaskan police work. From patrolman to investigator, he has worked with four police departments and became Public Safety Director for the City of Whittier during the tragic Exxon Oil Spill in Prince William Sound in 1989.

William, a 40-year Christian, retired as Senior Investigator for the State of Alaska gaming program. With over 40-years in Alaska, six children and seventeen grandchildren, and great-grandchildren, William and his wife, Mona Sue now live in rural Alaska.

## OTHER TITLES FROM ALASKA DREAMS PUBLISHING

Please visit www.alaskadp.com to see these titles:

**By William Casselman:**

Apache Snow | In Search of Honor | A Coming Storm

Arizona Rangers Series – Blake's War | Legend of Silene

Rookie

**Titles by other ADP authors:**

Inspiring Special Needs Stories | My Life In The Wilderness

All Over The Road | Ghost Cave Mountain

Inside the Circle | The Silver Horn of Robin Hood

Alaskan Troll Eggs | Through My Eyes

The Professional Ghost Investigator | The Adventures of Jason and Bo

Seeds Of The Pirate Rebels

Please visit www.alaskadp.com and sign up for the ADP mailing list to be notified of future titles by Alaska Dreams Publishing.